## Advance praise for *Joe Nu*

"A moving tale of a life led differently
understanding, doesn't shy away from tragedy and violence."

—*Daily Mail*

"Prepare to have your cockles warmed by this adorable book about twenty-three-year-old Joe, who unexpectedly finds himself out of his comfort zone . . . His unique, charming voice makes this a joy to read."

—*Good Housekeeping*

"Sensitive, wise and funny, this beautiful book is filled with heart and delivered in a unique and incredibly endearing voice. I laughed, I cried, and I fell completely in love with the absolute treasure of Joe Nuthin'."

—Julietta Henderson, author of *The Funny Thing About Norman Foreman*

"A gorgeous, big-hearted story about friendship, resilience, and learning to value others for who they really are."

—Caroline Day, author of *Hope Nicely's Lessons for Life*

"An entertaining and life-affirming story with a charm all of its own. Told in a clear, authentic voice and woven with gems of wisdom, it pulls you in and has you rooting for the characters throughout. A real joy to read."

—Hazel Prior, author of *Away with the Penguins*

"Extraordinary. Melted my heart."

—Heidi Swain, bestselling author of *The Winter Garden*

"You can do anything with a little help from friends . . ."

—*Take a Break*

"The perfect wholesome read to snuggle up with a cup of tea and a plate of biscuits—you'll feel warm right through."

—*Chat*

"Fisher writes with a clarity that makes the empathy, compassion, and humor of this novel unputdownable."

—*My Weekly*

## Praise for *Faye, Faraway*

"A warm, witty, wholehearted glimpse inside a parallel universe. Genuine and touching, Fisher's narrative voice will appeal to fans of Kelly Harms, Lia Louis, and Julie Valerie. Exploring the power of believing in the impossible, *Faye, Faraway* is a delight."

—*Booklist*

"[An] enchanting debut . . . Fisher's achingly authentic characters leap off the page and capture readers' hearts. This addictive, emotionally heavy page-turner marks a delightful spin on the time travel genre."

—*Publishers Weekly*

"A lovely, deeply moving story of loss and love and memory made real. The sort of book that makes you feel the tenderness of joy restored, and the tearing pain of a choice between the two halves of your heart."

—Diana Gabaldon, #1 *New York Times* bestselling author of *Outlander*

"A magical combination of tenderness and grief starring an unforgettable protagonist . . . Fisher writes gorgeous, lyrical prose, and every scene is infused with magic and heart . . . Full of emotionally drawn scenes and careful ponderings about faith, spirituality and love, *Faye, Faraway* is riveting, surprising and deeply touching."

—*Bookreporter*

"Emotionally fraught, *Faye, Faraway* is an unputdownable debut from a writer to watch."

—*Bustle*

"Charming and powerful, *Faye, Faraway* captures the longing we all share to see once again those we have lost and to transcend time and space to answer the questions we wish we'd asked. The dual speed of time, the need to choose between past and present, and the importance of lightening the burden for those we encounter are explored with good humor, an acute sense of nostalgia, and compassion. An uplifting and healing read."

—Marjan Kamali, author of *The Stationery Shop*

"I really enjoyed *Faye, Faraway*. It's such an unusual, intriguing novel. The tenderness between Faye and her mother is very touching and I loved Faye and Eddie's marriage . . . It's a beautiful book and the first in ages that actually *interested* me."

—Marian Keyes, author of *Watermelon* and *Sushi for Beginners*

Also by Helen Fisher

Faye, Faraway

# Joe Nuthin's Guide to Life

## Helen Fisher

G

### Gallery Books

New York  London  Toronto  Sydney  New Delhi

# G

Gallery Books
An Imprint of Simon & Schuster, LLC
1230 Avenue of the Americas
New York, NY 10020

First Gallery Books trade paperback edition May 2024

GALLERY BOOKS and colophon are registered trademarks of Simon & Schuster, LLC

Simon & Schuster: Celebrating 100 Years of Publishing Since 1924

For information about special discounts for bulk purchases, please contact Simon & Schuster Special Sales at 1-866-506-1949 or business@simonandschuster.com.

The Simon & Schuster Speakers Bureau can bring authors to your live event. For more information or to book an event, contact the Simon & Schuster Speakers Bureau at 1-866-248-3049 or visit our website at www.simonspeakers.com.

Interior design by Alexis Minieri

Manufactured in the United States of America

10  9  8  7  6  5  4  3  2  1

Library of Congress Cataloging-in-Publication Data is available.

ISBN 978-1-9821-4270-4
ISBN 978-1-9821-4272-8 (ebook)

*This story is for my children, Cleo and Dylan,*
*who I only love when my heart beats, and also when it doesn't.*

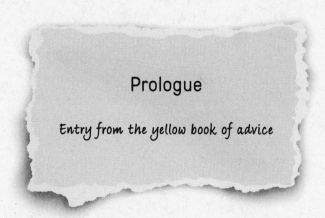

## Prologue

### Entry from the yellow book of advice

### FEAR

*It is so easy to let fear overwhelm you in this world. If you look at things in a particular way, it is always possible to see the fear or the danger in them. But what that really means is that if you look at those things in another particular way, it is possible to see the goodness and the possibilities in things instead. And not just in things, but people too.*

*Sometimes things frighten us, and we don't really know why. Like the way you're scared of red pasta sauces and ketchup, ever since your dad cut off the end of his finger when he showed you how to use the jigsaw in the workshop. You made a connection between the fear you felt when you saw your father in pain (and all that blood) and the pasta sauce you had for dinner that night. But you know that pasta sauce isn't the same thing, only* the same color, and yet it frightens you. What I'm trying to say is that while it's okay to be frightened sometimes—even if our reasons for it don't seem to make sense—don't let fear dictate or direct you.

Instead of fearing a thing, try to understand it.

Because understanding can change everything about the way that you feel.

# 1

## A man of no mean bones

J oe-Nathan's mum, Janet, always told him he didn't have a mean bone in his body, and he was thinking this as he wheeled a trolley of go-backs round the store: returning items that had been picked up by customers in one aisle and put down in another. He was certain that candles—for example—felt lost and lonely when they were abandoned among jars of peanut butter or the towels, certain that they were relieved to be reunited with their own candle-kind. Joe liked to think that if he were displaced, someone would do the same for him.

Joe worked hard to prove his mother right and to try to make other people feel the same way about him. To be considered a man of no mean bones was his *raison d'être*.

"There's a spill on aisle five," said Hugo, putting one hand on Joe's trolley and tilting his head as though he felt bad asking him to clean it up. "You okay to do it?"

Joe saluted. "Yes, sir, what color is it? Is it red?"

"It's just milk, and please don't call me sir. I may be old enough to be your father, but only just! If you call me 'sir,' you'll make me feel really old." He whispered the next sentence as though it were a secret. "I've always felt a little uncomfortable being the boss. Just call me Hugo."

"Hugo Boss," said Joe without humor (because none was intended) and saluted again. He tried not to look at Hugo's short fuzz of closely shaved hair, which covered his head from the apex to the nape of his neck. He always felt the urge to polish it clean so it was nice and shiny like his dad's head used to be.

Hugo smiled. "Okay, Joe. So, aisle five?"

"Sir!"

"No, don't call me 'sir,'" Hugo said again. "Remember, I'm old but not *that* old." And suddenly he was a whole aisle away, shaking his head and looking at his clipboard.

As soon as the milk had been mopped, Joe returned to his go-backs. He was a good mopper and cleaned the mop meticulously when he was finished. Hugo Boss was nice, and Joe knew he would never have asked him to clean up on aisle five if the spillage had been red.

Joe had worked at The Compass Store for five years. When he came for his interview (accompanied by his mum) he was overwhelmed by the variety of things for sale. The apparent chaos of the place made him sweat and he couldn't wait to get home. Hugo had said he was keen to have someone like Joe on board, and "not just because it looked good on the stats," but because he felt that Joe would be a positive influence and set a good example. He was offered the job, but wanted to turn it down, because—he told his mum—*the place just doesn't make sense*.

"He has OCD," Janet had said, when she explained on the phone why Joe wouldn't be taking the job.

"I understand," Hugo had said. "I really do. Would you come back in again and let me explain to Joe-Nathan how the store works? When he understands, it might just appeal to him."

"This place is called The Compass Store because the layout is designed around areas designated to north, south, east, and west, as well as northeast and east-northeast and so on," Hugo explained. He led Joe to the very center of the shop where a large mosaic of a compass was embedded in the floor and handed him a real compass (for sale on aisle three) and told him to go ahead and check: the mosaic was accurate.

"If you ever get lost, make your way to the mosaic, stand on the arrow pointing west, and walk straight ahead, you'll come to my office and I'll help you find your way. There's a lot of things in this store, Joe, and to the untrained eye they may not appear to make sense, but for most things, there is a link, a reason, and most *certainly* a place."

At that moment, a girl with bobbed black hair, red lips, and chewing gum walked by with a trolley that said "go-backs" on it. She winked at Joe and snapped her gum; the smell of smoke and Juicy Fruit was in her wake. Joe tried to wink back but did a long blink instead. She smiled at him with a perfect gap between her two front teeth. The manager explained what the go-backs were, and Joe suddenly found himself interested.

"Do you like puzzles?" Hugo asked.

Joe nodded. "Jigsaws."

"He can make his own jigsaws," said Janet. "His dad taught him how."

"Can he really?" Hugo had paused, put his hands on his hips, and looked at Joe with respect.

"Well, think of this place like a big jigsaw: every day, people move a few pieces around and we put them back where they belong. And we sell things too! Let's not forget that!"

"And you clean?" said Joe, watching an overweight, bespectacled man with a hearing aid push an enormous two-pronged broom casually down the center of the store.

"You like things clean and tidy?" said the manager. "Then this really is the place for you. We *need* you."

Joe turned slowly in the middle of the mosaic; his soft brown eyes scanned his surroundings. He liked the bright white background and the shiny white floors. He liked that customers moved around like slow-moving traffic, never bumping into each other. Where he could see that the bottles and cans and clothes and books were neatly stacked, he felt comfortable, but when he saw something out of place, on its side, or out of alignment, it snagged his senses like a rough fingernail.

There was the girl again: at southeast. He watched as she moved to east-southeast and put something on a shelf. Her black bobbed hair was a sharp contrast to the white store, and nothing about her looked out of place; she looked like she completely belonged. She was cool; Joe recognized that. She saw him watching and gave a little wave and another one of her gappy smiles.

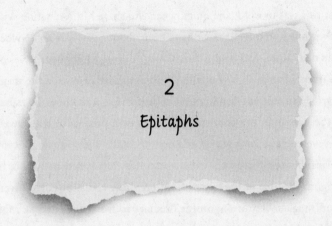

# 2
## Epitaphs

Making sure that her son had a secure job with a nice manager somewhere that was walking distance from home was one of the most important things on Janet's list to help Joe-Nathan prepare for independent life. There were plenty of things on Janet's list, and eventually she turned that list into a book—with a woven blue cover—handwritten in Janet's perfect cursive. Sometimes she sighed when she looked at her own handwriting and said to Joe, "They teach people how to write, but these days they don't teach anyone how to write *beautifully*."

She was a humble woman, but even she could not deny the beauty of her script. She took the greatest care over it and was proud to lay out her shopping lists and writing on the calendar with unhurried devotion.

Every Saturday, Janet and her son went for a long walk. Joe liked cemeteries best, and although there had been a time when Janet worried that this was morbid, she quickly came to share his fascination with gravestone epitaphs. It must have been about five years ago—when Joe's dad, Mike, had died—that he began to search for cemeteries on the internet and ask his mum to take him to them. He liked the small, gnarled cemeteries often found in villages. He got to know the names of the people in the ground there and saw a pattern in the flowers that were left at some graves and not others. He liked the larger cemeteries that felt more like towns with wide, lonely streets, where he recognized some of the names from previous visits, but many were like strangers, because he couldn't see and memorize all of them. Most of all, Joe loved the epitaphs.

One sunny day on one of their Saturday walks, Joe asked his mum an important question.

"Why are there words on the headstone? Why not just the name and the dates of the dead person?"

"Well, I suppose . . . ," said Janet, hesitating. "I suppose that at the end of a life, after all the lovely words have been said in the eulogy, people tend to whittle down the lives of others into a few words, maybe a sentence or two. They are words that tell the world how they should be remembered."

"Dad's says, 'Beloved husband and father.'"

"Yes, it does. It's how *he* would want to be remembered."

"But he was an accountant. Shouldn't he be remembered for what he did?"

Janet smiled and linked her arm a little more tightly into Joe's. She lowered her voice. "I don't think your dad would like it if strangers passed by his grave and thought that the only thing he was remembered for was money. In life, love is the important thing. At the end, if you have loved and been loved, then that's what you want to share with the world."

"But funny people want to be remembered for being funny," said Joe.

"Do they? I suppose they do."

"Yes. Spike Milligan's epitaph says, 'I told you I was ill.' So, if a funny person wants to always be remembered for being funny, why wouldn't Dad want people to know how good he was at woodworking and DIY and with balance sheets and financial statements?"

"Goodness, Joe, I worry what you'll put on *my* headstone!"

"I think it should say something about how lovely and clean you keep the house." Joe was earnest, unsmiling. Janet clung ever tighter to the arm of her honest, simple, kindhearted boy.

"Oh dear!" she said. "Anything about love?"

"Yes. Love, indeed. But also, your very nice packed lunches."

Janet stopped and turned so that she was face-to-face with her son. They stood among the trees, alive with whispering leaves and the sounds of birds they could not see. They both looked up, aware of the lack of everyday noise enabling them to hear these things. She reached up and stroked her thumb over his cheek and swept a strand of dark, windblown hair behind his ear.

"Would you like me to give you a shave later, and cut your hair?"

"Yes, please," said Joe.

"And I'll trim your nails and you can have a nice bath, and we'll get some fish and chips. And then we can watch *Friends* on TV."

"Thanks, Mum," said Joe, wondering why his mum's eyes were wet, when she had only described a really pleasant evening ahead and there was nothing to be sad about. Nothing to be sad about at all.

"Are you upset?" he asked, and when she said no, there was no reason not to believe her.

Joe crooked his arm like a gentleman. "My lady," he said, and his mum bowed slightly and hooked her arm through his again. Where the route divided into two, they took the left and wandered slowly along the sun-dappled pathway.

"It's just up here," said Joe. "My favorite."

Janet and Joe soon found themselves standing in front of a grave abundant with cut flowers, with little cards attached that Joe craned to read. They both stared at the words on the stone:

SHE ALWAYS SAID HER FEET WERE KILLING HER

BUT NOBODY BELIEVED HER

"It's funny," said Joe. "And clever. Which is why I like it so much."

"I know," said Janet.

"Who do you think brings all these flowers?"

"I couldn't tell you." Janet's brow creased. "I guess it's because this grave is anonymous, people overcompensate, feeling that this person—whoever she was—might not have anyone to come visit her."

"Is it attention-seeking?"

Janet opened her mouth and hesitated; attention-seeking was not something she associated with graves, but she could see where Joe was coming from. "In a way, I guess. Dad doesn't need anything on his headstone except that he was loved, by us. In the end, that's better than a joke and a lot of flowers from strangers, isn't it?"

"I guess," said Joe, thinking about Mean Charlie at work, who was always making Owen laugh with his jokes. "Can we go home now?"

# 3

## The rain could get to you

The front door of their house was for strangers. Joe-Nathan could not remember a time when the back door—on the right-hand side at the end of the short drive—was anything other than the only way in or out. A plastic corrugated awning was erected over the back door and it extended all the way to the garage. Joe liked the way the sun struggled to shine through the yellowing roof; lumps of dark moss were visible in places where it had fallen from the tiles on the house and the result was a homey, muffled, buttery light. As soon as he stepped under the awning, Joe felt safe and dry. His father had erected this covering himself so that if Janet came home in the rain, she could take her time finding her keys in her handbag and not worry about her perm or her shoes getting wet. It also meant that his wife and son could leave the house, get into the car, and reverse down the driveway without the rain touching them. That was the kind of person his dad had been, Joe thought, the kind who knew that the rain could get to you, but not once you arrived at your own back door, not if he could help it.

Janet held her handbag against her stomach and stood back so that Joe could access the door. For a moment he looked blankly at her, but she nodded encouragingly at the keyhole, until he said, "Oh." He pulled at the strap over his shoulder so that his satchel swung round to the front, and he unclipped it.

Janet had bought him the brown leather satchel for his birthday last year, and when he left for work in the mornings he took his satchel from the hook on the wall by the back door in the kitchen and—like a mantra—they would chant: *keys, wallet, phone; keys, wallet, phone.* But even at the weekends, whenever they went out (even when Janet had her keys), she made sure Joe took his satchel with him.

"It's like a game," said Janet to Joe as he traced a finger over the shiny buckle and lifted the bag to his face to sniff it. "If you aim to have those three things with you at all times, then even if you forget—or lose—one of them, you'll be okay. If you have your keys, you can always get back into the house. If you have your phone, you can always call someone for help. Your boss at work has a key for the house, you know, so if you ever need to, you can call Hugo and he'll help you. And it's always best to have your wallet in case you need a taxi, or money for food and drink, or any other emergency."

"Emergency?" said Joe, eyeing her over the top of his bag.

"Just in case, pet," Janet had said, but she couldn't help hoping that one day she would feel confident enough in Joe's ability to keep himself safe that she could maybe have a night away at a spa with a friend, like she used to when Mike was alive.

"Can I clean this with shoe polish?" Joe ran his hand across the smooth leather of the satchel.

"I don't see why not; it's made of the same thing as shoes." Janet rose from the table to get the polish and a cloth from the cupboard under the sink. She hesitated, and sat back down again. "You know where it is, don't you, love?"

Janet had tried to teach Joe the obvious practical things like how to tidy and clean; use the washing machine and dryer; how to hang things on the line; how to stack the dishwasher and when to top it up with salt and rinse aid. She had taught him how to have food like cereal in the house, so that he could eat even if he forgot to go shopping, and that it was a good idea to always keep a loaf of bread in the freezer. She encouraged him to sniff the milk before he poured it, and had taught him to cook five different meals: spaghetti carbonara; curry with microwave rice; sausage with mash and cabbage; minced beef and onions on a jacket potato; and chicken with vegetables. Janet also took Joe to the pub after work every Friday, because she felt that it was nice for a person to mark the beginning of the weekend with a few beers or a sherry, and it was one of her dearest hopes that he might one day take up the habit with some friends his own age.

Saturday night was a good night for a takeaway, Janet had told her son. She toyed with the idea of explaining that he didn't have to have one every Saturday and he shouldn't have one more than once a week. But with Joe it was better to keep things simple; having too many options stressed him. So, Saturday night was takeaway night: fish and chips or Chinese.

But inevitably Janet hadn't shown him how to do *everything*, and whenever she spotted a gap in his knowledge, she worked with him to form a pattern of useful behavior: how to unlock the door and lock it back up again (she had always done it herself because when they got home, they just wanted to get in, nice and quick). She had shown him how to check if the kettle felt heavy before he pressed the button, in case he burned out the element by boiling it dry; how *not* to put anything metal in the microwave; where to find things in the house, even if they weren't used very often, like the shoe polish or the sewing kit. However, it felt like there were a million things she hadn't prepared him for, and when she dreamed of a weekend away—just a little me-time—she felt the weight of these gaps.

Joe suspected that his mum was slowing down, because she had started asking him to do every little thing that she had always busied herself with. But in fact, Janet was speeding up—in a hurry to live more of life—taking steps to try to ensure that her son could cope on his own, and not just survive, but enjoy independence. She didn't want to think of him frustrated and crying, fruitlessly opening and closing all the cupboard doors in a hunt for the shoe polish to clean his leather satchel while she was elsewhere having her nails done before a nice massage and lunch. No, there was work to be done before Janet would feel any kind of ease at leaving Joe to fend for himself, even if it was for just one night.

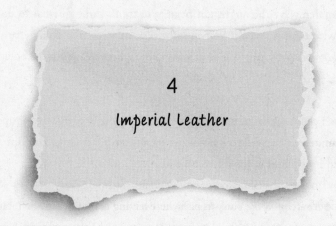

# 4
## Imperial Leather

All the things that Janet taught Joe-Nathan to do were written down clearly—and beautifully—in the pale-blue, faint-lined, hard-backed notebook and kept in a drawer in the kitchen along with things like guarantees for appliances, a small selection of takeaway menus, candles, some matches, and a telephone-and-address book, which included the numbers of trusted plumbers, electricians, their neighbors, Hazel and Angus, and Lucy, Joe's social worker.

The blue book was divided mainly into rooms in the house so that, for example, the section entitled "Living Room" included everything to do with the television as well as the furniture and how to clean it. The section labeled "Kitchen" was the thickest, because there were so many things to use in there, a lot of things that could go wrong, or break, and that were used frequently, but it didn't include cooking, which was under "Food"—another very long section of the book—complete with recipes and daily menu ideas.

Sometimes Janet and Joe would play a game where she would ask him a question and he would try to find the answer in the blue book, even if he already knew it. When he was tense, Joe couldn't think properly and so if—for example—something went wrong with the microwave, he might not be able to think through what to do, how to reset it, even if he had known what to do in a dummy run. The important thing was to at least know where to look in the book.

Janet put a white plastic bag, smelling deliciously of fish and chips wrapped in warm, vinegar-soaked paper, on the counter and put a couple of plates in the microwave.

"Joe, get the blue book and see what we should do."

He extracted the book from the drawer and sat at the kitchen table with it, smoothing his hand over the cover as he had seen people do in films just before they opened important books. He turned to the section labeled "Food," and searched for the subsection:

## TAKEAWAYS
### Fish and chips

*When you have collected the fish and chips bring it home and leave it on the kitchen counter in its bag. Wash your hands. The ketchup is in the fridge, the vinegar is in the low cupboard to the right of the oven, and the salt is on the table. Get out a plate and a knife and fork. Kitchen towels are next to the sink.*

"I need to wash my hands," said Joe, "and then I'll get all these things out." He left the book open and climbed the stairs to the bathroom. He filled the sink with water and held the bar of Imperial

Leather in the palm of his hand. The soap was almost finished and had that satisfying peak under the little label, which always took longer than the rest of the soap to wear away. He washed his hands, and let the water out, sluicing the bowl to get rid of the scum. He dried his hands and carefully laid the thin bar of soap on a towel. He returned to the bathroom cabinet above the sink and opened the mirrored door. He hummed gently to himself—the theme tune to *Friends*—as his eyes roamed the little cupboard for the tweezers. He found them, and when he shut the cupboard door—distracted as he was—he made himself jump when his face popped into view in the mirror.

"Oh! Hello!" he said without thinking, and then chuckled. "How do you do?" he said to the friendly man in the mirror.

"Very well, thank you," the man replied.

"And what are you doing with the tweezers?"

"Well, when the soap gets very thin, I take the sticker off the top, very carefully with the tweezers, so I don't rip it: it's red and gold and says 'Imperial Leather' on it, in curly writing. It's like a stamp, but for soap."

"How does the little sticker stay on the soap for so long, when it is always getting wet?"

"I have no idea; it is one of life's great mysteries."

"And *why* do you remove it?" asked the man in the mirror. But Joe wouldn't answer; he just stared back solemnly for a moment. Then he kneeled on the floor in front of the soap, his tongue between his lips—his face a couple of inches from the sticker—and carefully peeled it off. He walked with it to his bedroom and went straight to the stamp album in the middle of his large, well-organized desk. He had placed the album there earlier, open and ready, knowing it was time for the sticker to be taken off the soap. He put a spot of glue in the next space in the album and with great care he laid the sticker onto the glue, patting it gently into place with the flat side of the tweezers.

Without closing the album on the new—still wet—addition, Joe lifted the previous pages to have a look back through the book. There were sixty Imperial Leather stickers in the album now. Sixty soaps had been used since Joe's dad had died (about one whole soap each month for five whole years). It was a lot of stickers, a lot of soaps. A long time to miss a person.

Joe left the sticker to dry, returned the tweezers to the bathroom cabinet, and joined his mum in the kitchen for his dinner.

# 5

## A jigsaw is only ever one piece

Joe-Nathan was only ten years old when his dad built the work-shop at the end of the garden. Whenever his dad had a project—like building the awning over the back door, or erecting a new fence between their house and the neighbor's—Joe saw a lot more of his father's forearms, because Mike would say "Right" and fold up his shirtsleeves after work, like a man committed to getting a job done. Every weekday evening and every weekend for about six weeks, Mike worked on the building and gave Joe jobs (he was—his dad told him—*a great help*. Usually).

The workshop wasn't a rough affair; it was lovely. Mike had drawn plans with pictures to show where the workbench would be, and where the wood, the tools, and the paint would be kept. Joe sat on the steps of the workshop one day; his job was to color the plan in, and he added his own illustrations: colorful curtains up at the windows and the outside painted powder blue. On the day that it was finished, Mike and Janet had taken Joe to the end of the garden to show him that she had made the curtains just the way Joe had drawn them, and his dad had painted the outside in the exact same blue color that Joe had used in his picture. That had been fun. But nothing was as fun as being inside the workshop and making things.

At first Joe loved taking a rough piece of wood, cutting it to a satisfying square or rectangular shape, and sanding it down until it was as smooth as the heel of a baby's foot. When he was adept at that, Mike showed him how a lot of things could start in roughly that way: take a piece of wood, cut it into shape, smooth it down. And then more things could happen: drill holes in the wood, join pieces together with hinges, attach handles, paint it. The options were endless.

"Just think of something you would like to make, and break it down into components," his dad said. "Make a plan, and take on one task at a time, so that it's never overwhelming."

When Mike had first suggested making jigsaws, Joe had said, "But that is too many pieces to start with. I think we should do something simpler."

"But a jigsaw is only ever one piece, Joe. No matter how many parts you break it into, it is one simple shape, in the end. One simple image. It's like people: people are made up of lots of different parts, full of ideas and problems and idiosyncrasies. If we always had to look at people as all their different parts, we'd probably think it was too much hard work to get to know anyone at all. So, to start with, we just see the person as they are, as they present themselves, and start with learning something simple—like their name—and gradually get to know all the different things about them."

There had been a knock at the workshop door and Janet came in, looking sad.

"I just had a phone call from Hazel. Larry passed away last night."

Mike put down the block of wood he had been holding and leaned on the bench, breathing out slowly. "Poor Hazel," he said. "Poor Larry."

"She said it was a relief of sorts, but that doesn't stop it tearing you apart, does it?"

"Is she on her own? Should we go over?"

"Angus is with her right now. He knows how it feels. He's been there too."

"Angus has a habit of saying the wrong thing," said Mike.

"He has a heart of gold, and it's in the right place. He'll look after her. I said we'd go over this evening. We'll take a casserole and eat with her."

Mike nodded and Janet softly closed the door as she left.

"I do not like eating in other people's houses," said Joe.

"I know, but sometimes we just have to do things that make us feel a bit uncomfortable, if other people's needs are greater."

"Why are Hazel's needs greater?"

"Because Larry, her husband, died last night, and she is feeling very sad about it, and missing him."

"But she knew he would die," said Joe.

"Yes, sadly we all knew he would die. It's okay if you don't feel sad about it, Joe, but I'm telling you—and you can trust me on this—that Hazel feels sad, so even if you—or we—don't feel it in the same way, it is enough just to *understand* that she feels sad, and then ask yourself, 'How can we help?' We can keep her company. That's how we're going to help today."

"I could make her a jigsaw," said Joe. "Jigsaws cheer everyone up."

"I think that's an excellent idea," said Mike, and when he rolled his sleeves up, Joe rolled his own sleeves up too.

Joe spent most of that afternoon with his tongue between his teeth. He carefully drew the design of a cat on a piece of paper. (Hazel loved her cat, although she said you can't always tell if a cat loves you back.) He was pleased with the image, which showed a smaller cat fitted into a larger cat, and he drew the lovely jigsaw shapes—with their curves and their boxy straight lines—and then stuck the piece of paper to a piece of wood (Joe loved the spray glue). Then the most exciting part happened: Joe's dad stood behind him while he used the jigsaw machine to follow the outlines he had drawn, and when each piece had been cut, Joe pressed it out of the shape and cut the next, until all the jigsaw pieces lay in front of him on the workbench. The next part was exciting too (in fact, there was almost nothing that wasn't exciting about making a jigsaw): Joe flicked the switch on the electric sander and used it to sand away the paper design that had been stuck to the piece of wood. He loved the velvety softness of wood after it had been sanded, and liked to pat the little mounds of fine sawdust that lay on the bench.

After the edges had been smoothed, Joe took his favorite tool—the heat gun—to decorate the cats with eyes and whiskers, and to write the letters J.N. on the back of one of the pieces. Then Mike found a shoebox, which they filled with shredded paper, and Joe laid the jigsaw gently in the box and closed the lid.

Ten-year-old Joe could not wait to go to Hazel's house that evening, to show her what he'd made, but when she opened the door, he wondered if her husband had died longer ago than he had been told, because she looked as though she had been crying for a week. He handed her the shoebox.

"What's this?" she said.

"It's something to make you feel better about your dead husband," he said.

Janet opened her mouth to say something, and Mike laid a hand over his eyes. But Hazel placed one hand on her chest and clutched her damp tissue tightly in the other. "I can't wait to see what it is," she said, and they followed her through to the living room.

# 6

## I thought you would be next

Hazel's lounge was large and bright and well-ordered, and Joe-Nathan liked it. The most untidy thing in the room was Angus, a scruffy, thin, red-haired man who was wearing a frown and a badly buttoned-up shirt. When he smiled at Joe, the frown lines were still there, so it was obvious that frowning was something he did a lot. He stood and held out his hand to shake Joe's, and then Mike's and Janet's. Joe liked that he shook his hand first, but didn't like the fact that he had shaken everyone's hand except Hazel's. The thought that Hazel's hand had been left out made a fragmented pattern in Joe's head: something unfinished that his mind strived to complete. After a short, intense period of discomfort, Joe took Hazel's hand and shook it, and then Angus's and then his mum's and dad's. Then he felt better.

"Your buttons are wrong," said Joe to Angus as he held his hand out to him.

"A lot of things are wrong with me, lad, my buttons are the least of my worries. You're lucky I'm even wearing a shirt," he said. But nevertheless, Angus rebuttoned his shirt.

Now that the hand-shaking and buttons were sorted, the switch in Joe's mind that flicked up to say "something is wrong" settled down again and he leaned back in a chair. His arms lay on the wooden armrests and his feet dangled several inches from the floor. On the table to the right of the chair was a magazine about fishing, a small pair of glasses, and a bottle of pills. This must have been Larry's chair, thought Joe, which was good, because that meant he wasn't taking up a seat that anyone else needed now.

Hazel placed her hands on top of the box and looked at Joe. "Thank you for this," she said.

"You do not know what it is yet," said Joe.

"It doesn't matter," she said. She opened the box and lifted the puzzle out, placing it back on top of the box.

"Oh, Joe, it's absolutely lovely," she said, and dabbed at her eyes with the damp tissue. Janet crossed the room with a box of fresh dry ones. "I really like the way you've done their whiskers, they're so friendly."

"I used a heat gun," said Joe, and he sat up straight in pride.

"Did you really?" Hazel asked.

"Yes. And an electric sander to get the paper off and a jigsaw to cut, which is the name of the saw and where the name of the puzzle comes from."

Hazel blew her nose and nodded.

"Does it make you feel better about Larry being dead?" Joe asked, and he glanced at Angus, who made a snorting sound.

Hazel gave a short, sweet, tired little laugh. "Yes, it does, Joe, dear. Thank you so much."

"No one made a jigsaw for me when Allison died," said Angus.

"Who is Allison?" Joe asked.

"My wife. She died four years ago."

"I was only six then. I did not know how to make jigsaws," said Joe.

"I wasn't here. I didn't know you anyway," said Angus. "I moved down from Scotland after she died."

"I will make you a jigsaw soon," said Joe. "It might cheer you up."

"It would have to be one hell of a jigsaw, mate. I'm a miserable bloody git," Angus said.

Joe, Mike, Janet, Hazel, and Angus sat down for stew. Angus had not been planning to stay, but when he pointed out that no one had made him a stew (let alone a jigsaw) when Allison died, he had been invited.

"You need a good woman to look after you and feed you properly," said Hazel.

"What would a good woman want with me?" Angus said.

"Well, Allison wanted to be with you, and she was a good woman," said Janet. "I *assume*?" she hastily added.

"Aye, she was the best. I was a better man when she was around. She was my one, and now she's gone, I've accepted that."

"But you're still young enough to have a second chance," said Janet. Angus snorted again.

Joe looked at Hazel and then at Angus. He did a little bit of math in his head. "Allison must have been a lot younger when she died than Larry was when he did," he said.

"Aye, she was. A *lot* younger."

"But I thought the oldest people died first."

"Sadly, it's not as simple as that, Joe," said Hazel, taking a sip of tea and smiling at Janet and Mike.

"I thought *you* would be next," said Joe, looking at Hazel, and Mike put his head in his hands and half laughed. Which Joe remembered later, because in fact, it was his dad, Mike, who was next.

# 7

## Dinner and dessert

Joe-Nathan walked to work avoiding all cracks in the pavement, but didn't everybody do that? He also saluted white cars and mirrored the trees along his route that sent him hand signals. The top of one tree in the distance looked like a hand waving with all the fingers close together and the thumb sticking out; the top of another gave him a rock-star gesture that he'd seen on music posters, with the little finger and the first finger protruding arrogantly and the middle two tucked in; the third, closest to The Compass Store, was Joe's favorite: the top of the tree must have been brutally pruned at some stage, leaving two stumps above the trunk confidently giving the peace sign. It gave Joe a sense of well-being to reflect the peace sign back; he felt that the tree appreciated it. After the peace sign, there were just four strides over some uneven paving, before going through the sliding doors of the shop.

Eyes down, Joe headed due north, hit the mosaic, and turned sharply on his heel—military-style—to face northwest, which led more or less directly to the staff-room. He never said a word until his satchel was in his locker, his green tabard was on, and his lunch box was safely refrigerated.

The staff-room contained six round tables, a coffee machine, a kettle, a large fridge, and a vending machine, which Joe had never used. As soon as he had fastened the Velcro on the sides of his tabard, and placed his lunch box on the top shelf of the fridge (so nothing could drip down onto it), he surveyed the room. Mean Charlie was at the furthest table, talking quietly with Owen. Charlie glanced at Joe and, while his eyes were still on him, Owen said something that Joe couldn't hear. The two young men laughed in Joe's direction. It was nice to see people laughing, but Owen's laughter (he laughed a lot, especially when he was around Mean Charlie) and Charlie's (in particular) felt like it had nothing to do with happiness or joy.

"Hey, Joe," shouted Owen. "I hear you're scared of spaghetti sauce." Owen laughed again, and Charlie elbowed him, but in a friendly-looking way.

"Yes," said Joe.

"I had a terrifying night with a jar of mayonnaise once," said Owen, his expression serious.

"Did you?" Joe said.

But Owen didn't answer, just giggled hard and leaned into Charlie, who smiled and pushed him away.

There was one other person in the room sitting at another table, a woman he had never seen before. She looked older than Joe, maybe forty, her hair was in a tight blonde ponytail, and she was holding a cup of coffee as if she were scared to let go.

"Hello," said Joe.

"Hi," she said, smiling gratefully. Her eyes were big and her mascara was magnified behind her glasses. She looked just like his auntie, thought Joe, if he *had* a very happy, smiley auntie.

"What is your name?" Joe asked, trying to remember what his mum had taught him about meeting people for the first time. He suddenly remembered he should have said his own name first.

"My name is Joe-Nathan," he blurted out, just as she was replying. She repeated her name.

"I'm Phillipa," she said. "Jonathan?"

"Joe-*Nathan*," said Joe slowly. "I like to keep the two parts of my name separate, like dinner and dessert."

"That's a nice idea," she said. "Maybe I should call myself Phil-*Ippa*."

Joe said, "If you like." He held out his arm and she stood, making a friendly pantomime of formally shaking his hand, just as the manager had done when Joe had accepted the job.

"Nice to meet you, Joe-*Nathan*. Actually, you can call me Pip. Everyone does. Only my mother calls me Phillipa."

Joe was uncomfortable: his hand was at a loose end and he felt a nagging urge to shake the hand of everyone in the room, as he always had. Normally he would go ahead and do it, but he *could not* shake Mean Charlie's or Owen's hands and so Joe was left with a jittery sense of unfinished business, like an itch in his brain that he couldn't scratch. He shifted from foot to foot until Pip asked him to sit down. He liked the way Pip sounded like his mum and thought how—like Hugo was technically old enough to be his dad—Pip was old enough to be his mum, but only just. Joe shook his head. His shift was about to start so he left the staff-room and went to get one of the large metal trolleys full of soup cans from the warehouse, ready to stack in aisle eight. He was still left with the feeling that something was wrong or unfinished, and the feeling might easily last until lunchtime. He tried to distract himself by repeating the name *Pip* in his head.

As Joe pushed the heavy cart through the double doors of the storeroom, he saw Mean Charlie waiting to come the other way. Joe paused and tried to make room for him to pass, but Charlie came too close and barged into Joe's shoulder. He loomed over so that their heads were nearly touching and whispered in Joe's ear. His breath was damp.

"Dinner and dessert? My arse. Joe-*Nathan*? More like Joe-*Nuthin*. A man with *nothing* to offer." Then he disappeared into the warehouse. Joe made his way southwest and tried to rub Charlie's breath from his ear. He sang very softly to himself the lyrics to the theme tune from *Friends* and after a little while, he started to feel better.

The store was quite busy even though it was early. Joe liked the way that busy places were described as "hives of activity" and liked to think of customers as bees flying up and down the aisles, going about their business, never bumping into one another. Meanwhile, Joe lost himself within the rhythm of checkout bleeps, loudspeaker announcements, and the footsteps and voices of people around him.

On the back of the staff tabards were the words "I'm a director! Let me help you find what you're looking for." Owen walked toward Joe with a glass jar of marinara sauce in his hands and threw it into the air, catching it low, but keeping eye contact with Joe the whole time.

"Uh-oh, watch out, spaghetti sauce," Owen said, pretending to fumble.

Joe clutched his chest and stood very still, but Owen placed the jar on a shelf of towels and said no more; Joe's heartbeat eventually returned to normal and peace resumed.

Joe put a can of Campbell's soup on the shelf at the end of the aisle. The label was red and white and the curving text was pleasant to his eye. It was satisfying to set the can on the shelf—measure it by sight alone to be perfectly level with the next one—and then turn it until exactly the same amount of label could be seen on the front of every can.

"Excuse me?" someone said.

"Can I help direct you?" said Joe as he turned around. In front of him was a large man with a scrappy ginger beard, looking down at an equally scrappy piece of paper with horrible handwriting on it.

"I'm . . . uh, looking for . . ." The man glanced up and stopped when he saw Joe. He frowned and let his gaze slide from Joe's face to his shoes, and back again. Joe followed his gaze and looked down at his tabard, his clean light-gray jogging bottoms, and his shiny shoes. *Oh*, thought Joe, *I wore the wrong shoes again*. Janet had explained that he should always wear trainers with sportswear, but it was a rule that just wouldn't stick, because Joe defaulted to smart shoes as a good clothing choice.

"Never mind," said the man, and he walked away.

Joe watched the man head slowly eastward, weaving in between other customers. The man's head tipped from side to side until he saw another green tabard (Joe could tell, even from behind, that it was Owen, who—by the way—hated helping customers). The man tapped Owen on the shoulder. Joe watched. He admired the way Owen seemed to have been expecting the tap on his shoulder, the way he casually turned, when the tap would have made Joe jump. Owen didn't say anything to the man or smile; he did not say, "Can I help direct you?" as he was supposed to do, as Joe had done; Owen's lips did not move, except to adjust slightly to an expression that suggested that he did not like the man at all. Joe continued to watch, expecting the customer to walk away when he saw Owen's cold reception, perhaps even return to Joe for a better customer experience. But that didn't happen. The man asked Owen a question Joe couldn't hear, and Owen jerked his thumb southeast and turned away. The customer didn't seem offended or disappointed or confused, but simply looked back down at his little piece of paper and wandered in the direction that Owen had pointed.

And Joe felt something; he wasn't very offended or disappointed or confused, but he felt *something* that he couldn't find a word for, something that was a diluted mix of those three things.

# 8

## The last man on earth

Joe-Nathan turned back to the soup cans and hummed along to the piped music that could—if he chose to focus on it—distract him from the other noises in the store. They were playing one of the happy songs, so happy that Joe could stop thinking about any bad feelings when he heard it.

Stacking cans was a soothing and utterly engrossing exercise, interrupted only once in a while by customers asking for help (and half the time they too told him not to bother, before he had a chance to find out what they were looking for), and by customers trying to take one of the cans that he was stacking (which Joe did not mind— people were here to shop after all, and he could always fill the space with another can).

"Hey, loser, what are you doing?"

Joe snapped out of his stacking-trance and looked toward the voice. It was Chloe: cool, black clothes, black boots, dark bobbed hair, red lips, gap in teeth. She strolled toward him, her green tabard looking like a mistake, her hands thrust into her pockets.

Joe stumbled to start talking. "I've nearly finished stacking the soup," he said.

"Not you," said Chloe, her expression softening as her eyes shifted slightly, so that she was looking straight at him. Joe realized now that when she first spoke, she hadn't been looking at him. "You're not a loser, Joe." Her eyes shifted again, looking past him.

"I'm talking to *you*, fucker. What are *you* doing?"

Joe turned 180 degrees to see who she was talking to, only to be surprised at how close Mean Charlie was. While Chloe waited for Charlie to answer, Joe's peripheral vision was alerted to an anomaly in his soup cans: some had been poked in toward the back of the shelf, so that they were out of line, while others had been turned so that their labels were higgledy-piggledy.

"Oh," said Joe, suddenly feeling as though he were spinning. "What's that doing there?" He was staring at a tin of Heinz baked beans among the Campbell's soups.

"What's your problem?" Chloe demanded, and again, for a moment, Joe thought she was addressing him.

Charlie lowered his voice conspiratorially and tilted his chin toward Joe. "I don't think I'm the one with the problem here, know what I mean?"

"I absolutely don't know what you mean, Charlie. Now fuck off."

Chloe glared at Charlie until he took his hand from the shelf and moved away. She patted Joe on the arm and headed back to where she'd come from. But Charlie changed his mind and casually walked back again, calling out, "Hey, Chloe, I've noticed something." Chloe turned back like she was tired. She pushed her sleeves up her arms

(Joe saw a mark—the tip of a tattoo) and came to stand beside Joe again. Charlie talked to her as if Joe were invisible. "I've noticed you always get really fiery when you're around me. It's like this undirected passion. So, I'm going to make this easy for you."

Chloe folded her arms and Charlie went on. "I can tell you find me hard to resist. I'm betting a psychologist would say that you like to scold me because you find it tough to start a normal conversation with me. So, let me let you off the hook. I'd like to take you out for a drink."

Joe knew from watching a lot of *Friends* that Charlie was asking Chloe out on a date and that a date (especially a first date) was an exciting thing, full of prospect. He smiled at Chloe, waiting to hear what she would say.

She squinted hard. "You know what, Charlie? The hardest part of working with someone like you is that I have to be polite in front of customers, when what I really want to do is punch you in the face. I'm not sure what gave you the idea that I would *ever* want to go for a drink with you, but I'm going to guess that you've mistaken me for someone else. So let me be clear: if you were the last man on earth, I wouldn't join you for a drink."

Charlie scoffed. "'S'okay, I can wait. I catch your drift: you're hard to get. I like that. And I know for a fact that if this dude *here* was the last man on earth . . ." Charlie flipped his thumb at Joe. "Then you wouldn't join him for a drink either. So, your insult is a little lame. Maybe you should work on it." He winked.

Chloe turned to Joe. "Do you drink?" she asked, with the breeziest smile.

Joe wavered. Conversation was like traffic, and he needed more time to change lanes. Charlie was doing one of his quiet laughs and Joe was prompted into action.

"My mum takes me to the pub every Friday night at six o'clock."

"That sounds wonderful!" said Chloe. "I'd love to join you!"

She flicked a sneer at Charlie, grinned at Joe, and shot off westward. Joe looked at Charlie, who grunted, elbowed the Campbell's cans so that now every single one of them was out of kilter, and headed in the opposite direction.

Joe looked east at Charlie and west at Chloe. It would probably be best if he went to the toilet for a few minutes, so that nobody could speak to him while he tried to work out what had just happened, or until he had at least come to terms with not understanding. He told the cans he would be back shortly and went to the mosaic, to get a better sense of where he was in the world. He followed the arrow to the southern toilets and took time out. His mum and his manager had both advised him to do this when he was stressed or confused, and he was definitely confused. His mum would be able to explain things when he got home, and in the sure knowledge that she would enlighten him, he carefully washed his hands and steadied his thoughts. Then he returned to the soup display and started over again, helping the cans to be the best that they could be.

# 9

## Alive in the corner of his eye

Joe-Nathan knocked at the back door and waited under the plastic awning for his mum to open it. It was quiet; only the rustle of trees and the filtered hum of the main road could be heard. Joe tipped his head back and looked up at the moss, then closed his eyes and let himself sway. Coming home was a lovely moment, a gentle, calming feeling unlike any other. Joe waited and knocked again. He pressed his face against the small window in the door. The glass was textured, patterned like flowers so that it felt like you could see through, but you couldn't, you could only see bouncing shapes and colors in roughly the right places. Joe made his eyes work harder. He thought he could see the blue of his mum's dress, but she wasn't moving.

"Mum, let me in," he said, knocking again as he spoke.

"Have you got your key?" said the blurred face above the blurred blue dress. "Let yourself in."

Joe had observed more frequently that his mum was tired: she was *right* there, why didn't she open the door like she used to? Suddenly Joe had an idea of how he could help. He swung his satchel round and got out his keys, fumbled a little, but made his way in. There was Janet, in her blue dress, and now she stood and came to kiss him on the cheek.

"Hello, my love, have you had a good day?"

"I have had a very good day, thank you. Have you had a good day?"

"Yes, I have, thank you."

"I would like to make dinner for you tonight," said Joe, so pleased with himself for this idea that his smile reached his ears.

Janet put her hands on Joe's cheeks and she had that mixed-up expression he kept noticing lately: the one that was happy and sad at the same time.

"I would love that, Joe, thank you. What a nice thing to do. May I ask why you want to do that?"

"You keep asking me to do everything, and I suppose you're tired and getting very old, so to help, I would like to cook. I'll use the blue book and lay the table and everything."

When Joe's dad died, Janet and Joe ended up pushing their rectangular dining table into a corner of the kitchen, so that two sides of it were against the wall, and two were not. Joe had the idea of putting a framed photograph of his father's face on the wall above one end of the table at roughly the level he would be if he were sitting with them. It was important that the photograph be a happy one, but not too smiley. "Dad would never have smiled all the way through dinner," Joe had said. Janet liked the idea of the picture, but had refused to let Joe lay out cutlery and crockery underneath Mike's photograph.

"It's enough that the image of him is here with us. The tableware is a step too far," she said, and Joe had nodded.

Now and then, while he was eating at the table, Joe could pretend his dad was there, alive in the corner of his eye. Janet sometimes did the same. It was a lovely picture: a closed-mouth smile; a shaved cheek (which Joe knew had felt rough in reality, and had smelled of Imperial Leather soap); a little brown hair visible above his ears; a friendly, shiny dome of a head; a smart but comfortable-looking brown suit jacket; and a tie that Joe had given his dad one birthday, with its purple-and-pink paisley pattern.

The downside of having the table in the corner was that neither Joe nor Janet could look out at the garden while they ate. But they couldn't hang the photo frame in thin air, and there was no competition between the garden and the face of his father. If the weather was warm enough, then after their meal Janet and Joe would take a cup of tea and a biscuit to the bench against the back of the house and sit—usually in comfortable silence—and enjoy the early evening outside.

The footprint of the garden was larger than that of the house and divided into three squares, which lay in a row going up and away from the house. The first square was a tidy lawn with a small, old tree on the left. The next square had been a vegetable patch, but as time went on, it had converted more into flower beds and shrubbery, which demanded less care (though Janet still grew onions, as they were such a useful vegetable). The furthest square was at a higher level and was taken up by the workshop. Joe remembered helping his dad to build it, and had never forgotten the day that his dad had got frustrated after hitting his thumb with a hammer and shouted at his son, "Sometimes help is *no help at all*." Joe hadn't understood what that meant, but he remembered his dad had hugged him a lot after that, and said sorry a *lot*.

The workshop still had its original curtains in the windows. They would never be allowed to become like those dirty gray-sepia kind that a lot of neglected sheds had, but brightly checked ones, with tiebacks, which Janet washed every now and again. The workshop was as important as any other part of the house, and Mike had spent a lot of time in there; he liked to fix things around the house and make things and loved passing on his skills to Joe. Joe loved it when he and his dad sat on the outside step of the workshop and had a bottle of beer each. It hadn't happened very often, but Joe's dad had been correct: "A bottle of beer tastes best after a good day's work."

As promised, Joe cooked for Janet that night and the carbonara turned out well, although there was probably enough to keep them in leftovers for two more days. Janet made a pot of tea and they took their cups out to the bench. She felt drowsy after all the food, and closed her eyes, her cup balanced carefully on her lap. When Joe spoke, she realized she had drifted to that place very close to sleep and had to ask him to repeat what he just said.

"Chloe is coming to the pub with us on Friday."

Janet tried to picture her. *Oh yes, Chloe.* Joe had told Janet enough stories about her to guess that she might be a bit wild and almost certainly one of the good ones.

"That will make a nice change," said Janet.

"Change," said Joe. The word made his palms sweat.

"Did you invite her?" asked Janet. She doubted that he had,

but also doubted that this girl would have invited herself. Then again, Joe *had* cooked dinner. Maybe his independence was taking on momentum.

Joe tried to answer, but faltered. "I cannot remember if I asked her, or if she asked me," he said eventually.

# 10
## Assumptions

Janet had mixed feelings about assumptions; she was subjected to them frequently, and was not immune to making her own from time to time. She and Mike were told that they couldn't have children and the medical profession had been so certain of this that they didn't use contraception and ended up having Joe-Nathan when Janet was forty-two. She hadn't known she was pregnant and by the time they found out, she was too far along to "do anything about it" (as someone very insensitive had pointed out) and she was pleased. If she and Mike had known sooner, then there would have been a lot of awkward conversations with doctors about the wisdom of having a baby at her advanced years, all those conversations about how Mike would be too old to kick a football around with their son, as if that really mattered. The delay in their knowledge took the decision-making out of their hands, and that suited Janet just fine, because this was a dreamed-about baby, a baby they thought could never be. They had been prepared for difficult news when he was born, but everything was fine, and they scolded themselves with relief, for worrying about something that hadn't happened.

But people looked at Joe and made assumptions, and people looked at Janet too—at how old she was—and blamed her. *Is it any wonder?* she imagined people saying; in fact, she had once heard those exact words through the back of someone's hand.

It was only when he was four years old that the differences in his learning and behavior became something they were conscious of; and maybe Joe was who he was because of Janet's age, and maybe he wasn't. Either way, she would never undo him, wouldn't change him, would never take away any of the things that made him exactly the person he was, even if there had been a choice in the matter. Joe was wonderful. People didn't understand the joy he had brought them both, and the joy he brought others. Not until they experienced it for themselves.

If she *could* undo one thing, it would be her fear for him in the future. If she'd had a son who wasn't so vulnerable, then she would still worry about life hurting him, but she would be more confident that he could meet the world head-on and have a fighting chance when it threw its punches.

Janet knew that assumptions were lazy: a simple way of filling in the blanks when there wasn't enough information. Assumptions were a way of connecting the dots to give you a picture that worked, but not necessarily the right picture. Not necessarily the truth.

Janet had tried to teach Joe about making assumptions, because of course they could be useful sometimes; *sometimes* there is no choice but to fill in the blanks, and the point is to do it sensibly, sensitively, and accept that we may be wrong. But she worried that Joe might assume that a smile and a laugh was friendly, and this—Janet knew—was certainly not always the case.

Janet was only human; she couldn't help making assumptions herself now and then. When she had first met Chloe, she refused to speculate in any of the boring ways that people might, on the basis of her heavy eyeliner, her heavy boots, her *don't-care* stare, and so on. In fact, on the rare occasions that she had spoken to Chloe at The Compass Store, she had found her to be very nice, and that was enough for Janet. And yet she couldn't help but assume that Chloe must have somewhere better to be on a Friday night than the Ink and Feather with an old woman and her son.

As she always did on a Friday at 5:30 p.m., Janet went to meet Joe at work, so they could walk to the pub together. This time, Chloe was waiting with Joe at the entrance to the store; she was saying something to Joe and he nodded. When they saw Janet, Chloe hooked her thumbs through the straps of her little rucksack, as if she was all ready to go.

"Thanks for letting me join you," said Chloe. "I hope I'm not intruding or anything?"

"Of course not!" said Janet. "The more the merrier."

Joe looked concerned. "Just the three of us is enough," he said, as though he was worried that his mum and Chloe might start inviting passersby to come with them.

It took half an hour to walk to the pub. They didn't take the quickest route; they took the scenic one, with the most trees. Joe loved trees and Janet liked to tell people that when he was a little boy he had said, "If more people were more like trees, then people would be happier."

Chloe seemed at ease and talked about the people at work, always bringing the conversation back to Joe with an anecdote that high-lighted his best qualities: his kindness, his humor, his charming per-fectionism (which Janet thought was the nicest way she'd ever heard OCD described).

As they walked, Janet asked Chloe where she lived and whether she shared with friends or lived with family, but somehow Chloe managed to divert the conversation away from herself and back to Joe, so that after a few minutes Janet realized that Chloe hadn't really answered any of her questions at all.

The pub was busy—even this early—because it was used by tradespeople who had come straight from work to dampen the dust in their throats, and as a result there was typically a strong mix of regulars and newcomers. It was a mildly rowdy bar in a welcoming way that Janet liked; she could not abide a very quiet pub.

The Ink and Feather was a wood-paneled place with a long bar six paces directly in front of you as you walked through the door. No music played, but there was always enough chat in progress to enable everyone to speak without their conversation being overheard. Janet led the way and ordered a large sherry and half a lager, then asked Chloe, over her shoulder, what she would like.

"Um, vodka and tonic, thanks." Chloe turned to speak to Joe and frowned when she saw that he'd wandered off. She watched as he approached a table at which three young men in high-vis jackets were sitting; watched as Joe held out his hand, and one of the men shook it. The next man hesitated and then did the same; the third—catching on slowly—put his pint down, wiped his hands on his jeans, and stood very slightly as he too shook Joe's hand. Joe left the table and the men went back to their drinks. Chloe turned on the spot gradu-ally, watching in fascination as Joe went to every person in turn and shook their hand. Janet handed Chloe her drink and she took a sip, keeping her eyes on Joe.

"What's he doing?" Chloe asked.

"He always does this," said Janet. "He sometimes does it in other places too, but always here; shakes everyone's hand. Wants everyone to feel welcome."

Joe made his way round the room and Chloe could see who the regulars were: the ones who were familiar with Joe and his hand-shaking routine. Some would stand up enthusiastically and give him a fulsome handshake, clasping Joe's hand between both of theirs and asking him how he was. Others who were new here were more likely to waver, unsure what to do, unaccustomed to a friendly stranger; but polite amusement seemed to be the general reaction. Chloe smiled and clinked her glass with Janet's; they both continued to watch. Chloe saw the quizzical expression on the faces of two middle-aged men as Joe interrupted them with his hand held out. One said something and Chloe saw Joe's face crumple slightly. The other man said something too, and then they both laughed. Joe looked from one man to the other, his hand suspended above their table, ignored and embarrassed. Joe didn't move. One of the men said something else and the other one roared with laughter so loudly that the pub plunged into silence; all eyes were on them. Chloe knocked back her drink in a flash and handed her glass to Janet. Before Janet could blink twice, Chloe was standing beside Joe.

"Shake his hand, you fucking arsehole," said Chloe, loud enough for everyone to hear. One of the men said something inaudible and she banged her hands so hard on their table that a pint fell over and spilled into his lap. He stood up, cursing, and spat on the floor near Chloe's feet.

"Let's go," said the other one, scowling at Chloe and Joe. "I know a place where we can drink without being hassled by retards."

Chloe pulled a fist and hit the man square in the jaw, instantly doubling over and clutching her hand in agony.

The man looked over toward the bar, one hand held to his face, the other raised in the air, as if to ask whether anyone was going to do anything about this. The landlady was on her way, a tea towel slung over her shoulder.

"You're barred," she said to the men as she laid the tea towel over the beer to blot it. "And you, young lady"—she looked at Chloe—"there's ice at the bar for your hand, and a double vodka on the house."

Janet stared in stunned silence with her hand over her mouth as Chloe and Joe returned to her, and was still lost for words when they sat at a table with their drinks in front of them, Chloe's hand resting with a freezer bag full of ice over her knuckles. The first person to speak was Joe, who knew that his mum was not a fan of violence.

"Chloe, you cannot punch someone every time they call me a retard," he said.

Chloe looked at Joe, shaking her head. "Yes, I can," she said. "I can, and I fucking will."

# 11

## Strange and rather lovely

Janet had told Joe-Nathan that he didn't need to apologize for Chloe's swearing. "On occasions it can suit a person. I think Chloe is one of those people who suits swearing. And I don't say that very often!" she said, smiling at Chloe in exactly the same way as she had been smiling at Joe lately: definitely happy and sort of sad. It worried Joe, that confusing smile; he wasn't quite sure what it meant.

Joe had four half-pints of beer, and Janet kept up with Chloe, having one more sherry than normal, to calm her nerves after the excitement.

"I'd be too scared to punch a great big man like that," said Janet.

"Bullies really push my buttons," said Chloe. "I didn't have time to think about being scared. I punched him before that signal reached my brain."

"Do you get into a lot of fights?"

"Not physical, Janet. But I can get quite verbal." She winked at the older woman. "I expect that surprises you."

"Indeed, it does," said Janet, winking back.

"Please do not talk in codes with the winks and things you do not mean. It is hard work trying to follow the conversation."

"Sorry, Joe," said Janet. She turned to Chloe and started to explain what Joe meant.

But Chloe raised her good hand to stop her. "No need. I get it," she said. "Sorry, Joe."

When Janet invited Chloe back to their house for something to eat after the pub, she noticed Joe startle slightly. Chloe hesitated but said, "I'd love to." Which made Joe startle again.

Janet suggested that the two of them sit in the lounge and watch some TV while she prepared dinner. Chloe rubbed her fingers over the corduroy covering on her chair; it was comforting. The room smelled of Shake n' Vac and when Janet—wearing a brightly flowered apron—brought Joe a large glass of orange soda and asked Chloe what she would like ("Something stronger if you want?"), Chloe felt like she and Joe were two kids pretending to live in an old-people's home.

"Can I have some too, please?" Chloe said.

While Janet went to get Chloe's drink, Joe pointed the remote control at the television, his face creased in concentration. He turned to Chloe as the screen came to life.

"Season nine, episode two," he said.

"Season nine, episode two of what?" she said.

"Of *Friends*. It's called 'The One Where Emma Cries.' I thought this would be a good one to watch because of what happened in the pub."

"Why?"

Joe looked at Chloe as if this were a trick question. "You do not know?" he said.

"I really do not."

Joe turned more fully in his chair. "In this episode Ross is angry at Joey and Joey invites Ross to punch him. Ross does not want to punch him, but in the end, he does. Joey ducks without really meaning to, and Ross hits the metal post that is behind him. The way Ross reacts when he hurts his hand is like you in the pub after you hit that man. It was not funny when it happened to you. But it is funny when it happens to Ross, you will see."

"Okay, cool," said Chloe, and Joe hit play on the remote.

The sound of their laughter filtered through to the kitchen and in to Janet, who took her time grating cheese and cutting tomatoes. When the sandwiches were made and bowls of crisps and cucumber and a small coffee-and-walnut cake were laid out on the table, Janet quietly made her way back to the living room as the episode was ending, and she hovered outside for a moment.

Her hand was just touching the door handle when she heard Joe say, "Am I your boyfriend?"

Janet held her breath. She knew the answer and she guessed that Chloe could probably handle the question quite well, but she wasn't sure how Joe would feel. Rejection is always painful.

"No," said Chloe. "We're friends."

"Good friends."

"Yeah, good friends, Joe, like them on the TV show."

"On the TV show some of the friends are girlfriend and boyfriend."

"I know. But not Phoebe and Joey. They are *just* friends. You're Joey, and I'm Phoebe. You do look a bit like Joey, y'know," Janet heard Chloe say.

"You do not look anything like Phoebe," said Joe.

"I don't look anything like anybody," said Chloe.

"No," Joe agreed.

And Janet breathed again, because it wasn't a rejection: Joe wasn't hoping that Chloe would be his girlfriend, he was simply after clarity. And what could be better than having a bit of clarity about who your friends are? All evening, Chloe had made it abundantly clear what a good friend she could be. Janet opened the door and invited them both to come through to the kitchen.

"This is nice. Feels like a tea party," said Chloe, sitting where Janet indicated she should. "Is that your dad?" She pointed at Mike's framed photograph.

"Yes," said Joe.

"He looks like a really nice person," said Chloe. "Oh, Janet, I'm so sorry, will you think I'm rude if I take the tomatoes out of my sandwiches?"

"I'd think you were ruder if you tried to eat them when you really don't want to."

"It's funny, I like ketchup, but I can't do a real tomato." Chloe carefully pulled the thin slices out and laid them on the side of her plate.

"I am the opposite," said Joe. "I am scared of red liquids. They make me think of . . . you know . . . all the bad things. Blood. My dad . . ." Joe swallowed hard. "He cut his finger off once and . . ."

Chloe and Janet waited for him to finish the sentence, but he never did.

"What about baked beans?" Chloe asked.

"They are fine. They are within the orange range. In addition, I can eat a real tomato. Texture is important."

Chloe nodded. "I get it," she said. "But one of the reasons I don't like real tomatoes is the texture: that blobby wet bit, there." She touched the part she meant, on the side of her plate with her cake fork, and grimaced. "I can't stand the snotty bit on an egg either." Chloe made a soft gagging sound. "Eggs in general make me think of eyes." She shrugged. "People are strange, though, aren't they?"

"Yes, they are," said Janet. "Strange and rather lovely."

## 12

### Adventures waiting

When Joe-Nathan was at work, Janet busied herself with chores and visits. For a long while she had convinced herself that this was enough life for her; she was happy with her role, felt useful and content. But Janet read a lot of books and had seen people like herself between the pages, convincing themselves that they too were happy and content when—in fact—they were in denial about what they were missing out on, filling their time up as if they were coloring within the lines of a picture. This is what Janet had been doing in the years since Mike had died, and now she yearned to color outside the edges. The more she thought about what life might have to offer, the more her emotions began to clash together like contestants in a game. Guilt had been the strongest contender since she had begun to think like this, but resentment was starting to show signs of strength. Not resentment of any one person, and certainly not resentment of Joe, whom she could not love more than she did, but resentment that she had become a servant to her own existence.

Janet had disqualified resentment when she realized that it was the wrong emotion; it implied a feeling that things were not fair, or that she was annoyed or angry with her situation, and none of those things were true. Janet simply wanted more.

She knocked on Hazel's door and took two steps back. Waited, and knocked again. She strolled around the side of the house and found Hazel and Angus in the back garden sitting on wooden chairs under a big shady tree. When Angus saw Janet, he got up quickly and brought another chair from the shed, unfolding it as he returned.

"It's just getting warm enough again to sit outside, isn't it?" said Hazel.

Janet said nothing, and sat in the chair, nodding her thanks to Angus.

"Is something wrong?" Hazel said.

"No, why?" said Janet.

"Because something is clearly wrong," Angus said, as though she were a very bad actor.

Janet tutted (at herself, not Angus). "Look at us, all widowed and drifting through life."

"I'm not drifting," said Hazel lazily.

"I think you are," said Janet. "I think we all are."

"Widowed and waiting," said Angus. "Or am I 'widow*ered*'?"

"Exactly," said Janet, slapping the back of one hand into the palm of the other. "Drifting, waiting, I feel like I'm biding my time until I die. I feel as if Joe is almost independent, as though he could cope without me, if he really had to, and so now, *what about me?* Am I just waiting to die?"

"Janet!"

"I'm serious, Hazel. I'm in a hurry to get living."

"I was like that for a while," Angus said, staring unblinkingly at the grass just beyond his feet. "Felt like time was running out, and I was standing on a platform, waiting for a train to come."

"What happened?"

Angus sighed. "I waited, and hoped, and looked down the tracks for a bit, and then I sat on the platform and accepted that the train would never come. I stopped waiting, stopped letting it bother me."

"But you're talking about meeting someone, I think, aren't you?" Janet said.

"Well, what are you talking about?"

"I'm talking," said Janet, "about climbing down onto the tracks and walking along them to see if there are any adventures waiting for me to find them."

"You're talking about a spa weekend, I think," said Hazel, who leaned back, shut her eyes, and tilted her head to the sky.

Janet laughed. "Well, that would be a start," she said.

"I don't do spas," said Angus.

"What about a walking weekend?" said Hazel, eyes still closed.

Angus grunted.

"We could book into a really nice pub, walk during the day, and then just eat and drink in the pub in the evening," said Hazel.

"Hmm," said Angus, in a more positive tone at the mention of the word *pub*.

"It sounds like a nice idea," said Janet.

"It might be a good way to ease you into your adventures, start with something manageable."

"What about Joe?" said Angus.

"Well, it might be a good way to ease him into a little bit of independence. I admit I would be more comfortable if one of you were around, while I was away."

"I could stay back, if you like," said Angus.

"Oh, no! You must come," said Janet. "I think Joe's got a friend who might be willing to keep an eye on him, and if we don't go too far . . . it might have to be just one night away, to start with," said Janet.

"That's settled, then," said Hazel, rising up from her chair.

"Where are you going?" said Janet, suddenly worried.

"To get my diary," said Hazel, calling back over her shoulder.

"Oh, goodness," said Janet, looking sharply at Angus. "It's really going to happen."

The widowers chose a weekend a month away, to give the weather time to improve and allow Janet enough time to put a plan in place for Joe. She could talk to Lucy, Joe's social worker, about what needed to happen. Then Janet had to leave, and Hazel asked Angus if he would mind putting the chairs back in the shed before he left too.

"The forecast tonight is rain," said Hazel.

But Angus took longer than expected, and when he emerged, he was holding something black in his arms.

"I'm so sorry, Hazel," said Angus. "It's your cat, poor Banjo. I thought she was asleep, but she's dead."

That evening, after Janet told Joe about the cat (but not the walking weekend), Joe had rolled up his sleeves and gone to the workshop. He cut a piece of wood to the size and shape of a novel, with a pointed stake at the bottom. He sanded it down, plugged in the heat gun, and carefully inscribed the headstone. Then he varnished it with wood protector and clamped it into a vise to allow it to air and dry overnight. The inscription read:

HERE LIES BANJO,
WHO PROBABLY LOVED HAZEL

# 13

## The world can be a messed-up place

"Hey, Joe-*Nuthin*, I heard that Chloe and another girl had a fight over you in the pub at the weekend." Mean Charlie accosted Joe-Nathan at his locker before he'd had a chance to close it, turn the key, Velcro his tabard, and get his lunch box in the fridge. Joe would not say a word before those things had been done, and he was uncomfortable even looking at anything other than what he would normally look at before those tasks were complete.

Joe was prepared for some variety in the day: the weather changed, people changed, and the jobs he was expected to do at work changed. But all these things changed within roughly confined parameters. For example, he rarely experienced weather he hadn't seen before, and when new people were around at work they only tended to do roughly what other people did. Hugo Boss would stick a list of jobs for him on the pinboard and he had never been asked to do a job he was unfamiliar with. If things changed—within certain boundaries—Joe could cope, as long as he had completed the basics. These basics set him up for the day, just like having a shower and breakfast might for many people. The main difference was that there were a lot more things on Joe's "basics" list: he greeted the trees with a wave, a rock-star gesture, and the peace sign, he went straight to the mosaic compass and turned northwest, he put his satchel in his locker, pulled his tabard over his head, and then all he had to do was close his locker, fasten his tabard, and deposit his lunch box. After that he could engage in a bit of eye contact, a bit of conversation, and a variety of tasks and people (within boundaries). If he couldn't complete the basic morning tasks without being interrupted, then it was like stepping out of the shower without rinsing the shampoo out of his hair, or leaving the house with no shoes on. *He wasn't ready*.

Mean Charlie swerved his head like Kaa the snake in *The Jungle Book*, trying to force Joe to look into his eyes by getting his face in front of Joe's, even though Joe looked at the floor, then the ceiling. Joe tried to remember that while Kaa the snake is frightening in the book, he's calculating and strategic rather than evil, and that he cared for Mowgli on account of him being Kaa's equal because of his intelligence. His mum had explained this to Joe when she'd read him the story.

Pamela came to the lockers; she had worked at The Compass Store forever and had a motherly air about her. She reminded Joe of a hen, with her breast feathers all puffed up and looking as though she had chicks to defend. Mean Charlie bowed his head slightly and took a step back, while Pamela retrieved a bottle of Impulse from her locker and sprayed herself with it. She locked eyes with Charlie but did not smile, and looked at Joe intently when she asked, "Are you okay?"

Joe nodded. Pamela slowly closed her locker and walked away.

Charlie waited a heartbeat or two before stepping too close to Joe again. "So, is it true, did she fight for you?"

Joe wouldn't speak. He could smell Mean Charlie's coffee on his breath and hated the thought of it now being in his own lungs. He held his breath so that no more could get in. He stared hard at the polystyrene tiles up above and gave a sharp nod in reply to the question, in the hope that Mean Charlie would go away.

It worked. Mean Charlie let go of Joe's locker and stepped backward. Joe seized the moment and swiftly closed the door, turned the key, Velcroed his top, and trotted quickly over to the refrigerator, the fastest he'd ever done it.

"Well, well, well, who would have thought the ladies would love you?" Mean Charlie looked over his shoulder to smirk at anyone in the room. An older man ignored the scene entirely, scanning a leaflet about life insurance; a young woman tapped her mobile phone. Owen was the only other person in the room and he scoffed, repeating Charlie's words, "Yeah, who'd've thunk it?"

And Mean Charlie said, "Right?"

The store was white and shiny bright. Joe could almost imagine that the place smelled minty, so clean and fresh it felt on that Monday morning. He breathed in and out hard, filling his lungs with the clean store air, expelling Mean Charlie's bitter breath with every exhale.

While Joe was in the middle of exhaling Charlie's breath from his lungs, he felt something knock into his knees and it unbalanced him for a moment. Joe looked down and looking up at him was a small child—sucking his thumb—with a thin blanket trailing from his mouth to the ground and a little beyond, like an unhygienic blue muslin veil.

Joe didn't say anything, because he was concentrating on clearing his lungs.

The child spoke around his thumb. "I need the toilet."

Joe paused and changed lanes in his head. He needed to stop thinking about Charlie and switch to helping a customer find the toilets. The child waited and didn't appear to blink.

"I can direct you," said Joe. The child didn't say anything and still didn't blink (unless he was blinking at the same time as Joe). "You need to go to the mosaic and then, to get to the southern toilets, you need to head south."

There was a long pause during which Joe's words seemed to travel slowly from his face down toward the child, who looked up at him from a long way away. When the words reached the child, he finally blinked.

"I don't know what that means," said the little boy, thumb still in mouth.

"Would you like me to show you?"

"Yes, please," said the child, and Joe walked off toward the mosaic. The child reached up and took Joe's hand; it was horribly damp and warm and sticky, and Joe grimaced. He looked down at the child, who smiled at him wetly.

Joe said, "This is my job." It was the only way he could cope with the small dirty hand that he wouldn't normally touch.

"Okay," said the child.

He could wash his hand soon, Joe thought, and Charlie's breath must almost be gone by now. He would be back to normal shortly.

Before they reached the mosaic in the center of the store, a woman blustered toward them half running, hand clutching her chest as though she were holding her heart in place.

"Where were you?" she yelled at the child. "You frightened me!"

The small boy looked up at Joe calmly, as if he didn't know how to answer the question but maybe Joe did. Before Joe could speak, the woman yanked the child away from him and clasped him against herself. She was angry and relieved and upset, but those feelings were so smashed together that Joe couldn't work them out; she was like a storm. He had seen customers like this before, when their children wandered off.

The woman walked away, talking to her boy in short, inaudible bursts.

"I need the toilet," the boy said again. Then they disappeared.

Joe looked down at his hand. He couldn't see the stickiness, but he could feel it. He spread the fingers of his hand, then closed them into a fist and opened it wide again. Yes, it was sticky all over.

"I'm sorry," said a voice.

Joe looked up from his hand, and there was the woman again. She looked different to the way she had looked a few seconds ago, as if she had a friendly identical twin. She pushed her hair out her face, and wiped a hand across her cheek, where a tear had been drying on its own.

"I should have said thank you." She paused. "For looking after him." She smiled weakly and the little boy held his blanket to his cheek and leaned into her neck.

"You are welcome," said Joe. "But you should probably wash his hands."

The woman nodded and walked away.

Joe wheeled a trolley of go-backs to the mosaic and then—item by item—returned things to their rightful homes. A happy tune started playing and Joe was in a good place, doing a good job. As usual he became lost in his activities and it was just like being woken up gently when he felt a hand on his arm.

"Huh?" he said.

"Only me," said Chloe. "How was the rest of your weekend?"

"Um, I watched some *Friends* and I made some things and I went on a walk with my mum in a graveyard."

"Huh, nice. Which episodes did you watch?"

"Well, I watched season one, episode one on Saturday morning. Sometimes I like to go back to the beginning and see how it all started."

"And then you went to the graveyard because you like to see how it all ends?"

"No. I went to read the epitaphs," said Joe.

"Really?" Chloe shrugged and then grinned. She adopted an American accent. "*Your tombstone can say whatever you want it to say, mine's going to say, 'Phoebe Buffay, Buried Alive.'*"

Joe smiled and nodded. This was such a good day! "Season six, episode two!" he said. "'The One Where Ross Hugs Rachel.' But you are paraphrasing," he added with an earnest expression.

Chloe laughed loudly at that, and just then Charlie walked by. He scowled at them and started singing, "*Love is in the air, everywhere I look around.*"

Once he was out of earshot, Chloe said, "Charlie's telling people I got into a fight with a girl over you. Just ignore him, okay?"

"Chloe, I . . ."

"What?"

"He asked me if that happened and I nodded."

"I don't care, it's fine, ignore him. He's a troublemaker."

"I do not think he likes me," said Joe.

"Seriously? What gave you that idea?" Chloe raised her left eyebrow so high it nearly came off the top of her head.

"It is just the way he looks at me and talks to me, the things he does to me, and the way he laughs. He smiles at me and it is not a real smile."

"But that's all?"

"Yes, that is all."

"Well, Sherlock, my friend, let me tell you, *I agree*. I don't think the guy likes you. But that's okay, y'know? Why would you want him to like you? He's an arsehole."

"But I do not have a mean bone in my body."

"Huh?"

"I do not have a mean bone in my body, so why would he not like me? If a person has no mean bones, then how can someone not like that person?"

"Listen, the world can be a messed-up place. Some people don't like nice people precisely *because* they're nice, because it makes them look bad. Put a guy like Charlie next to you and he looks ten times worse than he does next to anyone else."

"What can I do to make him like me?" said Joe.

"*Nothing*. You need to realize that you don't need to make Charlie—or anyone at all—like you. You're perfectly likeable just the way you are. It's not *your* problem, it's his. Don't do anything. Just ignore him." She smiled. "I gotta go. Work to do."

But as Joe wheeled his trolley to the household section (east-northeast) to return a lightbulb to the lightbulb family, he knew that there was usually a way to make a person feel happy, and so there must be a way to make Mean Charlie feel happy when he was around Joe. He just had to work out what to do, and then do it.

## 14
## Lucy

Joe-Nathan knocked at the back door, but his mum didn't answer it, and Joe didn't call out, but swung his satchel round and got out his keys. Tongue between his teeth, he put the key in the lock, trying to get it in smoothly and in one go, but before he turned it, he heard voices—conversation—and he froze. The words were coming from the kitchen and he withdrew his key, pressing his face against the little window. There were more colors—taking up more space than usual—but he couldn't make them out; it was like looking into a kaleidoscope and trying to see people there. He pressed his ear to the glass and the voices stopped briefly.

"I can see you, Joe-Nathan!" his mum called out. "Come on in, Lucy's here."

Joe had forgotten that Social Worker Lucy was visiting, and he never forgot anything, so he wondered if his mum had forgotten to tell him. This added to his growing uneasiness about her; Joe never forgot when Lucy was coming because Janet never, *ever* forgot to tell him when they were having a visitor.

Joe closed his eyes, breathed deeply, put the key back in the lock, and entered the kitchen. He hung his satchel on the hook inside the door and faced his mum.

"Hello, my love," she said, getting up and kissing him on the cheek. "Have you had a good day?"

"I have had a very good day, thank you. Have you had a good day?"

"Yes, I have, thank you."

Joe turned to Lucy. "Have you had a good day?"

"Yes, thank you for asking."

Joe held out his hand for Lucy to shake and then he shook his mum's hand too.

"I was just telling Lucy that you make a very nice cup of tea, so we thought we would wait for you to make it for us. Is that okay?"

"Yes," said Joe, but he stood silently for a moment, before raising a finger and saying, "Blue book." He retrieved it from the drawer and Janet and Lucy refrained from speaking while he found the page. He read aloud:

"Kitchen. Kettle. Making tea: Put water into the kettle and press the button to boil it. Get a cup for each person and put a teabag in each cup. Milk in the fridge, sugar and sweetener in the cupboard above the kettle. Teaspoon in the cutlery drawer. You need to ask each person if they take milk, sugar, or sweeteners, and how many."

"The famous blue book," said Lucy. "I think we could all do with one of those, Janet."

"He's also got his portfolio case, if you remember?" Janet said. "The one in his bedroom?"

"Ah yes, another thing I could do with in my life! Joe, can you remind me what's in it?"

Joe turned away from his tea-making task. "It is full of spaces for papers ordered alphabetically for life things, like my birth certificate. Some of the spaces are empty, but labeled ready for documents and certificates when I get them, so that I don't lose them. If I learn to drive, my driving license will go under C, for car."

"Would you like to learn to drive?" Lucy asked, leaning back as Joe put a cup in front of her.

"I do not need to drive. I walk to work and I walk to the pub and I walk to the shops and Mum drives us to the cemetery or we can catch the train. Walking is healthy and driving is dangerous. So, I do not think so."

"Sounds sensible to me!" Lucy said, ticking something in her notepad. "How's work?"

"Work is good, satisfying. I am doing a good job. The boss is nice, Chloe is nice. People are nice."

"Good. And you still go to the pub every Friday, you two?"

"Yes, and last Friday Chloe came too and there was a fight."

"A fight!" Lucy pulled a dramatic *tell-me-more* face at Janet.

"Joe-Nathan didn't fight," Janet said. "Chloe—his friend from work—hit a man who was being unkind to him."

"Did she?" Lucy looked at Joe. "How did that make you feel?"

"It made me feel that she did not like it when someone called me a name and instead of using her words to explain it, she explained it with her fist."

"Wow," said Lucy, looking at Janet as though she was—frankly—impressed. Janet nodded as if to say that she too was—frankly—impressed.

"And how did you feel when that man called you a name?"

Joe hesitated. "It made me feel disappointed. I wanted him to know that I liked him; that is why I wanted to shake his hand. I wanted him to like me. But he did not."

"I think we all want to be liked, don't we?" Lucy said. "But it doesn't always happen and that's okay."

"That is what Chloe says."

"I'm liking the sound of Chloe," said Lucy, writing something else down. "Do you have other friends?"

Joe felt the urge to tell Lucy that he had six special friends that he saw on the TV every day: Chandler, Joey, Ross, Rachel, Monica, and Phoebe. But he didn't. He cleared his throat and tried to remember the question. Oh yes. "I have some good neighbors. They are in the blue book. I can trust them and they will help me and I can help them. There is Hazel, and she is a window."

"You mean a *widow*," said Janet.

"Yes. And when she is sad, I make her jigsaws. Then when her cat died, I made her a wooden plaque to put in her garden for when she buried her. I wrote the epitaph on it with a wood-burning pen." Joe stood up straighter.

"That's so lovely," said Lucy. "Any other neighbors?"

Joe sagged slightly because Lucy hadn't asked about the epitaph and the wood-burning pen.

"Yes. There is also Angus. He is short and angry at the world. Sometimes he talks fast and I find it hard to understand him. I have also made him jigsaws, but once it made him cry."

"He has a heart of gold," said Janet.

"Oh, yes, that was the important bit, sorry," said Joe. "Angus. Heart of gold."

"And how do you think you would feel if you were on your own in the house one night and needed help? Who would you ask for help?" Lucy put her pen down and smiled at Joe.

"Pardon?" said Joe.

"It's just that your mum was talking to me before you got home . . . ," Lucy started to say.

"I said no such thing!" Janet quickly said. Lucy looked at her and frowned.

Janet cleared her throat. "Biscuit?" she said, and shot up from the table; she took a purple tin from a cupboard and put it on the table.

Janet made a fuss of opening the tin and handing it round. She flushed at the thought of her conversation with Lucy earlier, the sharing of a desire to want time to herself, the suggestion of a whole day and night away. The guilt warmed her neck, even though she knew she had nothing to feel guilty about. She reddened further as she recalled Lucy's encouragement and the words *Maybe one day you'll even meet somebody. You're still young, Janet.*

"I'm sixty-five!" Janet had said, glancing at Mike's photo.

"That's still young these days," Lucy had replied.

Later, after Lucy had put her notepad in her bag and said goodbye, Joe asked Janet why she hadn't told him about Lucy's visit.

"Didn't I mention it, love? Oh dear! I'm sorry. Lucy visits quarterly. So, let's make sure all the visits are marked on the calendar." The kitten calendar came down from its place on the wall, and they went through it together with Janet's diary, writing the word "Lucy" every three months. While she wrote the name on the calendar, Joe stared at the side of his mum's face.

"Are you okay?" he asked.

"Yes!" she said, as though it were a silly question.

# 15

## New things were not impossible

t was a gray day and Joe-Nathan quickened his pace to get to work
before it rained. He was not a fan of umbrellas, hats, or wet hair,
and breathed a sigh of relief as he stepped through the sliding doors
and headed for the mosaic, still nice and dry. There was comfort under
the safety of the Compass Store roof where he could spend a whole
day unaware of the weather (unless he paid attention to the effects it
had on the customers that came and went). The Compass Store was
like a spaceship: self-sufficient and detached from the outside world.
Joe had worked out that if there was a disaster that resulted in him
and his colleagues being locked inside the store, then the food and
drink in here—divided among the thirty members of staff that were
on shift at any one time—would last . . . well it would last a very
long time. Joe tried to work it out exactly, but he couldn't do it in
his head, and he kept being distracted by the work: the go-backs,

the shelf stacking, other tasks and additional things in his routine. He would have to take some time at home with pencil and paper to work it out properly.

He closed his locker and fastened the Velcro on the sides of his tabard, put his lunch box in the fridge, and went to the noticeboard to get his list of jobs just as Pip hurried into the staff-room, her cheeks pink, her hair wet and stuck to her face, her sweatshirt soaked through. She slipped slightly on the linoleum floor in high-heeled shoes, and said "Oof" as she recovered her balance.

"Ugh!" she said, pulling her top away from her skin as it clung to her. "It just started coming down out there. It's biblical! I was only in it for thirty seconds! Oh, my hair!" Pip opened one of the drawers under the sink and pulled out a clean tea towel. "Do you think anyone would mind if I . . . ?" She rubbed the tea towel over her hair before Joe could tell her not to.

"You're wearing the wrong shoes," said Joe. "I do that some-times."

Pip looked down at her bright pink stilettoes and grinned.

"Sometimes you have to make an effort to look nice," she said, and winked.

Joe removed the slip of paper from the noticeboard, which Hugo Boss pinned there for him every day. That was when he saw the large handmade notice, above his list of tasks:

THE COMPASS STORE STAFF
QUIZ NIGHT
Saturday, May 18

*Teams of four to six,*
*£8 a ticket, fish and chips included, all profits to charity*
*BYOB*

Joe stared at the sign. *BYOB?* He quietly said the word out loud, *byob, byob, byob*; and wondered if it was a spelling mistake. What did it mean? What other word was like BYOB? BOB? YOB? BOY? But why would any of those words be on a quiz-night poster? Joe was lost, staring at the poster, and didn't notice Pip standing beside him, absentmindedly drying the ends of her hair.

"Are you going?" she asked.

"Pardon?"

"To the quiz. Do you want to get a team together?"

"I do not know. No. Mum and me have a takeaway on a Saturday night."

Pip hesitated and looked at Joe sideways, as if she were trying to work out how tall he was. "I wonder if they'd let your mum come along too? I reckon Hugo would be okay with that. He's so nice."

"Hugo Boss is very nice," said Joe.

"Yes," said Pip. "Very, *very* nice. If you know what I mean." Joe thought he did know what she meant.

Pamela tottered over to the poster. She too was wearing higher heels than usual and Joe wondered why so many people were wearing the wrong shoes on the same day.

"Are *you* going to the quiz, Pamela?" Pip asked, smiling warmly.

"I am indeed," Pamela replied, straight-faced. "Hugo has asked me to sit with him and be the scorekeeper and to help organize the event. I am an excellent organizer," she said.

"Are you?" said Pip, her face suddenly devoid of smiles. Joe noticed that Pip did not sound happy at all about Pamela's organizational skills, although it was difficult for Joe to imagine not being happy about those.

Pamela walked away and Pip tutted.

Joe stared at the poster again and held his breath. Saturday night fish and chips, but *not* at home. His palms felt damp and it was a bit hard to swallow. But he *did* enjoy questions and quiz shows. Maybe it would be okay, if his mum could come too.

"I could ask Chloe to join our team," Pip said. "Then we'd already have a team of four if your mum comes along. It might be fun?"

"It might be fun," Joe repeated.

"Okay, then. Let me arrange it. I'll speak to Hugo about your mum, but I have a funny feeling he'll be fine." She winked at Joe *again*. Maybe it was a habit, thought Joe; well, he had plenty of those himself.

"It might be fun," Joe said again, as if convincing himself. "It might be fun."

"Don't worry about it or anything. Just save the date," said Pip.

Joe's morning was spent with the go-backs and folding towels. Hugo Boss had stopped by while Joe carefully placed a glass vase in aisle ten. Hugo waited until the vase was safely on the shelf and then asked Joe if he'd like to start his checkout training next week. Joe said yes. He liked the idea of the checkout tills, pressing the buttons, scanning things, but he was comfortable with shelf stacking and all the other things he was used to doing. New things were not impossible, but they took some adjustment. One new thing at a time was good, and when the new thing became old, it was good to have a long period where nothing new appeared in his life. In this way Joe knew that gradually his life would become full of things that he felt comfortable with. As his mum liked to say, *slowly, slowly, catchy monkey*. Joe smiled inside: first he thought about the checkout, and then he thought about sneaking up behind the monkey and catching it.

"Oh, I almost forgot!" Hugo bounded back toward Joe's trolley and held both hands up as if he were about to sing in a musical. "Pip asked if it was okay for your mum to join your quiz team, and the answer is, of course, *yes*! This is going to be the best quiz night ever. I need to make my mark." Then he sprang off, taking a pencil from behind his ear and writing something on his clipboard.

Joe paused. Checkout training *and* a quiz night. These were two quite big new things in his life at the same time. He made his way to the mosaic, turned south, and took some time out in the toilets. He washed his hands in cold water and breathed in through his nose and out through his mouth. When he got home he would talk to his mum about this: she would make him feel better about all the changes.

In the afternoon, Joe noticed that there were more customers than had been in the store earlier and they all had dry hair and clothes, which meant the rain must have stopped. Joe often observed the streams of customers; he liked the way they moved around each other like cars in the street: the etiquette and laws of space between them; the predictable apologies when one invaded the invisible area beyond which no two strangers should enter. Sometimes—like cars—customers collided, and sometimes they were nice about it and sometimes they weren't, but nobody ever died or got injured or had to call the insurance company, so it was always better than actual traffic. Joe didn't typically feel comfortable around lots of people, but at The Compass Store it was different, because here he wore a green tabard and somehow this separated him from them, more like a visitor at a zoo, keeping a safe distance.

He glanced around; the store lights were so bright he imagined that it was a sunny day outside, but now and then he glanced at the entrance—which was all glass—and could see that the sky was still dark and stormy.

Joe needed to concentrate; he had a dangerous stacking job: pasta sauces. He started with the safe ones: carbonara, then béchamel. After that it was puttanesca, Neapolitan, and marinara: all the red ones. He was comfortable enough with the sauce when it was inside the jars and there was no problem while the lids were on. But the thought of dropping a jar of the stuff focused his mind intently so that the rest of the store and the people around him vanished as he carefully took each jar in two hands one-by-careful-one: a palm underneath the jar, the other tightly gripping the sides.

Joe was absorbed in the slow determined rhythm of placing each red jar on the shelf and he grew in confidence as the jars on the shelf began to outnumber the jars still in the trolley. He was holding another tightly when he was gently touched on the shoulder. He turned and retained his grip with commitment as he faced the sadly reluctant face of Hugo Boss. The sounds of the store rushed at Joe as though the volume had suddenly been turned up on everything: the music, the checkout beeps, the footsteps and voices of strangers. Hugo was waiting for Joe to reply—or so it seemed—but Joe hadn't heard what he said.

"Are you alright?" said Hugo.

"Yes," said Joe.

"Come with me, Joe. I need to tell you something."

"What is it?" asked Joe, hoping it wasn't yet another new thing. Hugo smiled the smallest smile Joe had ever seen. Sometimes he didn't understand the meanings of smiles, but a sharp fear struck like lightning. He looked at the red sauce in the jar and felt his throat tighten. Why he was frightened, he didn't understand, but the fear was real anyway.

He looked east and happened to see Chloe in the distance near aisle five; she raised a hand to wave, and then he saw her expression crease. Her waving arm came down and the other went up, she seemed to take an enormous leaping step toward him, but it took an age for her foot to hit the floor; he felt sure he heard the second hand of a clock boom three times before her boot even struck the ground. He saw her mouth open slowly as if she were yawning—or slowly shouting—but no sound came out. Joe looked down at his hands and saw they were empty, the jar of spaghetti sauce hung in the air between his fingers and the floor. The hands of the clock abruptly spun forward—catching up the moments that had just been suspended—and the glass smashed into the bright white tiles at his feet, sending up a spray of sieved tomatoes toward him. He didn't feel a thing as his face met the floor seconds later.

# 16

## In the sauce

Joe-Nathan did not want to open his eyes. He could smell pasta sauce and feel something damp easing through the material at the back of his tabard and his *Friends* T-shirt. He guessed that he was covered in red and lying in red.

"I've turned him onto his back, but he's conscious, so I haven't put him in the recovery position," Hugo was saying. "I think he's just squeezing his eyes shut."

"Joe?" It was Chloe talking and Joe turned his head slightly in the direction of her voice, but did not open his eyes.

"Chloe?"

"I've got some wet wipes, Joe, is it okay if I wipe your face and neck? You've got some—stuff—on you."

He nodded vigorously, pursing his lips tightly now that it was confirmed he had red sauce on his face. If it got inside him it would be terrible. The wet wipe touched his forehead and it smelled nice and clean but was cold and unpleasant. The wet wipe touched his cheek and it hurt. He flinched.

"Yeah, buddy, you're going to get a shiner, for sure," said Hugo.

"What are we going to do about his clothes?" said Chloe.

"I have a lot of lost property—you wouldn't believe what gets left in the changing rooms and staff-room—but as it's Joe I think I'd better get something new off the shelves." Hugo called out loudly, "Pip! There's glass here, and we need a couple hazard signs."

Joe heard Pip's high heels *clip-clop* quickly in his direction.

"Oh goodness, what's happened? Is he okay?" she said breathlessly.

"I think so," said Hugo.

"Are you okay?" Pip asked very softly, and Joe didn't know who she was talking to, until Hugo cleared his throat and said, *"Yes, of course."*

"Tell me how I can help," said Pip.

"If you can get this all cleaned up, that would be brilliant."

"Anything for you," said Pip, and Joe heard her shoes *clip-clop* away.

"You're in there, boss," said Chloe.

Hugo tutted. His voice dropped. "Help me get him to my office, will you? Somewhere private."

"Course," said Chloe.

Hearing Hugo and Chloe talk about him, so close, while his eyes were shut, made Joe feel like he was dead, and it wasn't so bad. It was very relaxing to not look at anyone or talk to anyone. He had never lain down on the shop floor, and apart from knowing that he was in the sauce, it was oddly restful.

With a lot of apologies and reassurances, a lot of arm gripping, and a perplexing hand on his waist (he didn't know if it was Hugo's or Chloe's), Joe was guided from the spot where he'd fainted, to Hugo's office. Somehow, he was helped to change into clean clothes and seated on a sofa having seen nothing but the inside of his eyelids. He began to dread the moment of opening them.

"How's the cheek, Joe?" said Hugo, and Joe touched it.

"It hurts."

"It's going to," said Chloe.

"But hey, you should see the other guy!" Hugo said.

"What other guy?" said Joe.

"Joe, open your eyes." It was Chloe and her voice was low and kind.

"No, thank you. What did you want to tell me?" Joe turned to face where he thought Hugo might be standing. He felt the sofa move as Chloe sat down next to him. "Please do not tell me it is another new thing."

"Uh . . . this isn't easy, but . . ." Hugo hesitated.

"Is it about the quiz?"

"No."

"Checkout training?"

"No."

"Oh no," said Joe. "It *is* another new thing."

Joe felt something touch his hand; he pulled it away and rested it in his lap, realizing a moment later that it was probably Chloe's fingers accidentally touching his. He shuffled to the right, to give her more space.

"Joe, please, look at me."

Reluctantly, Joe opened his eyes. He had liked it in the dark, more than he would have expected, and the light seemed harsh, there were too many colors, too many things in the room. He focused on his lap: now just his hands and his trousers were in his line of sight and, in the background—blurred—the carpet and the tips of Hugo's shoes. Hugo crouched down and now there was the whole of Hugo too. Joe breathed in through his nose and out through his mouth.

"Joe, your mum has . . . gone to a better place."

"Where?" Joe tried to think of a place that his mum liked better than home, but couldn't think of anywhere. "The pub? The cemetery?"

"No, Joe, sorry, she's . . . gone to sleep."

"How do you know?" Joe said.

"Hugo!" said Chloe. "You need to be *more* honest and direct, not less."

"I'm not very good at this," said Hugo.

"No shit," said Chloe. She tutted. Hugo stood and took a step away, turned his back to them, and seemed to put his hand up to his mouth. Joe turned to Chloe. She squeezed her eyes together and gave a little nod, as if to ask, *Ready?* and although she didn't say that word out loud, Joe gave a little nod back, as if to reply, *Yes, ready*.

She took a deep breath and said, "Your mum has died."

Joe had seen enough television and heard enough stories to know that here were words that signified not just *something* new, not just a change, but *everything* new; *everything* changed. And Joe was familiar with the way he felt about change and new things. He turned his hands over and looked at his palms but they did not sweat. He felt around his eyes, but there were no tears. He waited for the rush of something awful, like standing on a platform waiting for a fast train to speed through the station, vibrating in his veins and making him feel like he would be pulled under. But nothing came. It was quiet in the room; he would never have predicted that. There should be crying and wailing; where was it? The words were monumental, he knew that. But they were just words; they had been spoken into the room quietly and melted into the air like steam.

"What did you say?" said Joe, to see if it would happen again.

"Your mum has died."

Yes, it happened again: the words came and dissipated; Joe followed with his eyes where he thought the words had gone in the room and imagined them dissolving slowly, pressing—as they went—against the closed window, trying to get out of the room and float into the sky, disappear among the whispering of the trees.

"Can you open the window?" Joe said.

And Hugo said, "Sure thing, buddy." He flicked the latch, pushed it wide, and let the words out of the room.

## 17
### Understanding the now; understanding the next

The three of them were silent. Hugo got a chair and brought it over to the sofa; sat in front of Chloe and Joe-Nathan, his legs crossed, his arms crossed, his head bowed. The silence was lovely, peaceful, and Joe began to worry about what it would be like when the silence ended, in the same way that he'd worried about breaking the spell of having his eyes closed. He thought back to that time, just a few minutes ago, when things were dark and easy. That was when he thought his mum was still alive. And now he knew she wasn't.

Chloe cleared her throat and Hugo looked at her, but she didn't speak.

"Do you want some water or anything?" Hugo asked.

Joe didn't want any water, and he wasn't sure if Hugo was talking to him or not, so he didn't say anything. Still, the silence had been broken, and it was okay.

"What do I do now?" Joe asked.

"Well, I guess you can go home," said Hugo. "Take some time off, compassionate leave."

"It is only four seventeen," said Joe, looking at the massive clock on the wall.

"Not long till leaving time," Chloe said.

"It is Friday," said Joe. "Mum meets me at five thirty and we go to the pub."

Chloe and Hugo stared at each other. Hugo blew out through his lips and sounded like a tire slowly losing air.

"Do you want to stay at work like normal and then walk with me to the pub?" Chloe said.

"Yes."

"Do you want to stay in my office for a little while?" Hugo added.

"No."

Hugo Boss lowered his voice and spoke to Chloe. "Will you stay with him?"

Chloe nodded.

"If he wants to go, will you go with him?"

Chloe nodded again.

"I'd better talk to HR," Hugo said, almost to himself.

Chloe and Joe folded curtains together and slid them onto big hangers and then onto the rails that enabled customers to look through them easily. They worked slowly because time didn't matter right now and there was no hurry for curtains. Everything Joe did was just a way to get from one moment to the next; that was the way Chloe saw it, anyway.

"I liked your mum. She was nice," she said.

"Yes, she was nice," said Joe. He paused and listened in his head to the words they'd just spoken—*was*—the use of the past tense.

"Was, was, was," he said, and then shook his head to make the words go away. They didn't sound good, or satisfying when he repeated them; they made him feel queasy. He tried replacing them with something else. "Pip, pip, pip, byob, byob, byob." He nodded and continued to murmur these words under his breath.

"We could leave a bit earlier than usual, if you like," said Chloe.

"Why?" said Joe.

"Get to the pub a bit earlier. Hugo will let us do what we want."

"But why go early?"

"Because it's better than being at work."

"I do not understand what you mean."

Chloe put down her end of the curtains and leaned on them, her head tilted to one side.

"There are things I do because I like doing them, and there are things I do because I *have* to do them," Chloe said. "When I'm doing something I have to do—like work—I'm always thinking about getting it over with, so I can go and do the things I want to do."

"You spend forty hours a week at work," said Joe.

"Forty-two."

"You spend forty-two hours a week wishing you were doing something else?"

"Uh-huh. Everyone does."

"Not me. When I am here, I know what to do and when to do it. It is soothing."

"But the pub is better."

"But that is later. It is after work on Fridays. When the time comes, I will know what to do. If we go now, I will be in the wrong place, at the wrong time."

They resumed the curtain folding and did it in silence for a while.
"Are you okay, Joe?"

"Yes."

"About your mum?"

"I will not know what to do when I leave the store at five thirty.
It is okay while I am here because this is always where I am at"—he
looked at his wristwatch—"at four fifty-nine on a Friday. But what
will happen at five thirty?" Joe didn't often look ahead. If he was
comfortable in what he was doing in the moment, and knew what
came next, then life felt like a series of stepping stones: good steady
ones, not the kind that were slippery or too small or too far apart.
Joe was at ease with the comfort of his known world: understanding
the now, understanding the next. Sometimes he would think ahead
a little, maybe to the evening, but there was no real point; it would
come when it came and he knew what it would involve when he got
there. But as he dared to imagine five thirty today (when his mum
would normally be next, but now she would be never), he heard his
heart thumping and his breath coming fast.

"What will happen?" he said again.

Chloe looked very sad and Joe was sorry to see it. She had stopped
folding again. "I don't know," said Chloe. "But I'll be there with you."

# 18
## The only part that's easy

The storm that Joe-Nathan felt would rage down on him when he exited the store at five thirty did not happen. As the doors slid shut behind him and Chloe, he ducked and held his hands over his head, but as his arms slowly returned to his sides, he could see that nothing really looked any different. He suspected there was turmoil, a churning of air, a tornado brewing somewhere, but wherever it was, it was not outside the store waiting for him.

Chloe hooked her thumbs through her rucksack straps. "Ready?" she said.

Joe nodded once.

"We're going to get to the pub one step at a time," she said. And they walked.

"How do you think she died?" Joe said after several minutes.

"Oh," said Chloe. "Well, that's the first thing people normally ask, and it never came up."

"Are we supposed to guess?" Joe asked.

"No, of course not," said Chloe, realizing she should ring Hugo and ask him some questions.

"Where do you think she is?"

"I don't know that either, I'm sorry, Joe," she said. "When we get to the pub, I'll call Hugo and find out who we should speak to." They walked in silence again.

"I should cry but I cannot feel the tears coming," said Joe, touching below his eyes as he and Chloe walked under the trees.

"How do you feel?" Chloe asked, unsure what to say or do.

"I am thinking about the way her shoes would normally be clipping the pavement."

"Hmm," said Chloe. "It's been such a shock. It was so unexpected."

"Death is not unexpected."

"Well, no. I . . ." Chloe glanced at Joe. "I mean, what you're saying is we can all expect death at some point. But she wasn't ill."

"No, but she was old. And when old is over, then there is death."

"Well, she wasn't *that* old. And even if it's expected, death is still a horrible surprise when it happens, right?" Chloe wasn't actually sure what *was* "right" anymore. She thought she was saying the right thing until Joe spoke, and then what he said seemed right, even if it was counterintuitive.

"There is nothing I can do about it, is there." Joe stated the fact as he saw it.

"No. That's what makes it so hard," Chloe said.

"No." Joe stopped briefly and stared at her. "That is the only part that is easy." He started walking again and Chloe took a beat or two to restart and catch him up.

✦

The Ink and Feather was starting to get its first after-work customers, mostly wearing high-vis vests. On the surface, it appeared that this Friday was the same as usual for everyone else; meanwhile, for Joe, this was the first ever Friday in his whole life without his mum. As he and Chloe walked through the door, a hassled-looking woman with a briefcase stepped down from a stool at the bar. She held her hand to her chest, closed her eyes, and blew out a lungful of air.

"Oh, Joe, I'm so pleased to see you," said the lady. She looked at Chloe and said, "I'm Lucy, Joe-Nathan's social worker." (She didn't shake hands, in case it sent Joe off on a mission to shake everyone's hand in the pub that instant.) Lucy was pink and flustered; sympathy drew her eyebrows together so that they almost met in the middle, and Chloe wondered if the woman was going to cry.

"I'm so sorry, the wires got crossed. Your boss received the phone call about your mum, but I wanted to be there to tell you what had happened. He told me you'd be here. I'm so sorry I let you down."

"Chloe told me," said Joe.

"Thank you, Chloe." Lucy smiled. "I've heard about you."

"All bad I hope."

"Nothing bad at all, as a matter of fact," she said in earnest.

Lucy returned her full attention to Joe. "I'm sure you have lots of questions about your lovely mum. Shall I buy us all a drink and then we can sit and talk? What will you have?"

"Beer," said Joe.

"I'll have a vodka and tonic please, lots of ice," said Chloe.

"Ice for your hand?" Joe said.

"Just in the glass, thanks, Lucy. Joe drinks halves."

While Lucy was at the bar, Chloe watched Joe do the rounds,

shaking hands. The sun cut through the windows in that determined way that it does after rain. *God help any fucker who isn't nice to him today*, she thought, flexing her hand (her knuckles still hurt a bit from last week).

The hand-shaking passed without incident and the three took up seats at the same table as last time. Lucy sat where Janet had sat and took out her notepad and pen, laid them in front of her, straightened them up, and looked at Joe with tenderness.

"Your mum was a very special person, Joe. What have you been told?"

"She died today."

"Have you been told anything else?"

"No."

"We realized as we were walking here that we don't know how she died, or where she is now," said Chloe.

"Your mum's heart stopped working," said Lucy, pausing after this piece of information as if she were feeding a child and making sure that the last mouthful had been swallowed before she continued. "It's a called a heart attack." Pause. "She died straightaway." Pause. "She didn't feel any pain." Pause. "Right now, her body is in a special room at the hospital, and I can take you to see her tomorrow, if you want to do that."

These words felt different to the ones in Hugo's office. These words didn't float away and try to find the door, the window, the outside world. These words lay on the table in front of Joe, like sheets of paper being placed on top of one another, one at a time.

"Did she fall over?" Joe asked, picturing a man on television he had seen clutching his chest and crashing to the floor.

"I think so. She was in the supermarket and it was sudden, so I don't think she had a chance to sit down."

"Where?"

"In the supermarket."

"I mean, where in the supermarket?"

"Oh. She'd gone through the checkout and was carrying her shopping bag toward the exit."

"Where is it?"

"The supermarket?"

"No. The bag."

"Oh. Sorry. It's in the boot of my car."

"Can I see?"

"Yes, of course. It's yours. I'll go and get it." Lucy rummaged for her car keys. "I'll be back in a minute."

"You okay?" Chloe spoke quietly and wedged her hands in her armpits to stop herself from reaching out for Joe's hand.

Joe stared at the table where he imagined the words that Lucy had used were placed. He had heard the words and understood them. But they were a safe distance away. There, on the table: words he could revisit and replay, but not feel. It was *information* and he understood it, but it hadn't touched him yet.

Lucy returned and carefully placed the carrier bag on the seat beside Joe. He glanced at it and then leaned closer, peering into the space between the handles.

"Would you like to see what's in there?" Lucy asked, and Joe nodded. "Shall I get the things out for you?" He nodded again.

There wasn't much in the bag. Janet would have done her big shop on Tuesday. She always did something simple for a Friday night tea after the pub and then there would be a takeaway on Saturday, a roast on Sunday, leftovers Monday, so she wouldn't have needed much. Lucy carefully placed two pints of semi-skimmed milk, a pack of four croissants, and a jar of lime marmalade in front of Joe.

He delicately lined them up and turned the jar so that the label was square on.

"This was her favorite," he said, and he sensed a noise in the distance: the train coming, the one that would rush through the station and roar in his ears.

"Oh. Hang on. One more thing in the bottom of the bag," said Lucy, but Joe stared at the pale green marmalade and didn't blink. Lucy slowly placed the last item next to the others, and carefully adjusted it so that it was in line, label facing forward, as Joe himself would have done.

Joe stopped staring at the marmalade in order to look at the final item Lucy had set on the table. In an instant, the roar that he had heard in the distance rushed at him and filled his head. From somewhere, wherever they had been hiding, Chloe's words from earlier—the words that had dissolved and floated away in Hugo's office—abruptly regrouped into something small and solid—like a bullet—and shot at him hard and fast, striking him in the middle of his chest: *YOUR MUM HAS DIED*. Joe put his hands over his ears.

He touched his face once more; still no tears. He looked at Chloe— *there* they were: the tears were on *her* face, and her arms were tightly crossed as if she were stopping her hands from getting away and her mouth was downturned: sad.

He lifted the last piece of shopping to his nose and breathed in. "Imperial Leather," he said.

# 19

## The perfect fucking Friday night

ris, the landlady of the Ink and Feather, was intrigued by the three-some seated at the table in her pub: Joe-Nathan was there, but not Janet—unusual; the girl who had thumped one of her patrons the previous week; and another lady who managed to look both professional and yet too pink and blustery to be anything truly official. When she saw the items lined up on the table, the relative quiet of the pub and her own curiosity drove her to come and speak to them.

"Hallo, Joe, love. Where's your mum?"

"Dead," said Joe.

Iris froze.

"What?" she said, and looked from face to face to face.

"She is *dead*," said Joe, more clearly this time.

Iris slowly slumped into the seat next to Chloe and shook her head. "This is *terrible*," she said. "Terrible! What happened?"

Lucy looked at Joe to give him the chance to speak, but he took a sip of beer and looked to Lucy. "Well, I was just explaining to Joe and Chloe that Janet had a heart attack today and . . ." She paused, sighed.

"Died," Joe said, helping Lucy with the end of the sentence when she didn't seem to be able to think of the right word.

They all sat there for a few minutes, the women shaking their heads and saying *well, well* and *what a shock*. Then Iris stood, took a discarded tumbler from the next table along, and extracted a teaspoon from her apron pocket, which she proceeded to rattle inside the empty glass until everyone in the pub was looking her way and waiting for her to say something.

Iris cleared her throat and wiped her eye. "Today a very good woman died, and I want everyone to take a moment." There were only about fifteen people congregated at this early evening hour, and they listened to Iris speak. Some nodded, others leaned back with their arms folded, patiently listening to her description of Joe's mum.

"Janet understood the importance of—well, the importance of a lot of things—but she understood the importance of the pub, of marking the end of the week, the beginning of the weekend, with a drink. It was nothing to do with drinking, and everything to do with the fact that when you walk through that door . . ." Iris's voice cracked; she stopped, swallowed back a sob, raised her chin, and breathed hard through her nose, gathering strength. She pointed at the door to the pub, and her voice raised in an attempt to control it. "When you walk through that door, everyone in here is equal."

A few subdued voices murmured, "*Hear, hear.*"

She looked around the pub with shining eyes. "And anyone who doesn't agree with that can get out." Iris said sorry and blew her nose, before continuing. "Every Friday evening, Janet brought her boy here, and she told me that. *She* told me that in here it doesn't matter who you are, where you're from, or how clever you are." Iris threw her hands up as if she was exasperated. "I can't believe she's gone," she said, staring into the middle distance. The pub remained quiet, waiting. "I don't care how intelligent you are, or what job you do," Iris said. "First time you come in here, I'll learn your name; second time you come in here, I'll *remember* your name. People like Janet understood the importance of that and she made sure her son knew the importance of that too." Iris glanced at Joe and nodded, then she shouted to the barman, "Bring me two bottles of Harveys and twenty shot glasses."

Customers murmured respectfully in their seats as she quickly filled the glasses and put one in front of every person present.

"Before we toast the fine lady, Janet, with her favorite drink, I wonder if her son would like to say a few words?"

Both Chloe and Lucy sat up straighter. Chloe started shaking her head. "You don't have to," she said to Joe, but he was already asking Lucy to move out of his way, and he stood next to Iris, who handed him a shot of sherry.

"Go on then, lad," said Iris.

Joe spoke slowly, and loudly. "My mum's heart stopped working today. But before it did, it worked very, very hard." He looked at Lucy, to check that was right, and Lucy nodded firmly, then downed her sherry in one go. Joe took a dainty sip, grimaced hard, and said, "Yuck."

The attending crowd said "To Janet" as one, before downing their own shots. And the pub gradually resumed its normal state.

When Joe sat down again, his barely touched sherry still in his hand, Chloe took it from him and downed it.

"Here," said Iris, putting the bottle of Harveys on the table. "It's yours." She returned to the bar, shaking her head every step of the way, muttering, "Oh, Janet, Janet, Janet" under her breath, as if Janet had disappointed her.

Neither Chloe nor Lucy had been drunk on sherry before, but when Lucy fell from her seat on her way to the toilets, she left her car in the car park and got a taxi home. She asked if Chloe and Joe wanted to share the ride, but Joe wanted to walk as he usually would, and Chloe promised she'd see him home safely. Joe refused a fifth half-pint and waited while Chloe grimaced her way through every shot and when she said a sentence that was more than fifty percent swearing, he said, "Can we leave now?"

Joe carried the plastic carrier bag with his mother's last shopping in it and Chloe walked him home, tripping and giggling, then saying sorry, all the way. They came to the back door and stopped while Joe got his keys out of his satchel. It was peaceful except for the soft hiccupping that came from Chloe, who swayed gently next to him. Then, nice and easy, Chloe leaned over and threw up near the back door.

"Ugh, sorry," she said, looking down at it and wiping her mouth with the back of her hand. "Sherry is a bloody horrible thing; no wonder people drink it in such small glasses."

As Joe went into the kitchen and wondered what to do about clearing up the vomit, Chloe walked into the house behind him and drank straight from the kitchen tap.

"What are you doing?" said Joe.

"I gotta crash on your couch, I can't walk home like this."

Joe reached out for the normality in his present situation and struggled to find it. There was vomit on the doorstep and an inebriated woman in the kitchen who wanted to sleep on the sofa. He was home much later than normal and hadn't eaten his tea yet; his mum wasn't here and would not be here tomorrow to take him to the cemetery. And she wouldn't be here ever again. He closed his eyes and tried to focus on his sweating palms; there was at least familiarity in that. He wished it was Monday morning so he could go to work and feel completely comfortable knowing how he fitted into the world. He was doing what Chloe did, wishing his time away, and in that moment—for one moment—he really understood her.

"I am going to get a bucket and wash your sick away, then I am going to eat some cereal and go to bed," he announced.

Chloe winked one eye, and held on to the back of a kitchen chair. "Sounds like a perfect fucking Friday night to me!" she said.

# 20
## The box

The next morning, Chloe ate a croissant with her hangover and said she had to go. Joe-Nathan wore his pajamas at breakfast and poured himself a bowl of cereal.

"I have only eaten cereal since my mum died," he said.

"Maybe you should do some shopping," said Chloe. She swirled the dregs of some tea in the bottom of her cup and cleared her throat a few times. "I'm sorry about being sick and sleeping in your living room. And I feel like I should stay with you but I *really* have to go." Chloe winced at her own words; she could stay, if she made a few phone calls, but she didn't want to, and it was as simple and selfish as that. *Shit*, she thought, *who died and made me the babysitter?* She thought of Janet and felt really, really guilty.

"It is okay, I want you to go," said Joe.

"Oh!" Chloe laughed.

"It is not normal, you being here, and I want normal things."

"Yeah, course. That's great. You want me to call you later and check how you get on this afternoon with Lucy, at the hospital?"

"No. That is not normal," said Joe.

"I'll give you my number, just in case," said Chloe. Joe fetched the address book from the kitchen drawer; she wrote her number, drew a small picture of a smiley face next to it, and left.

Joe watched three Cheerios floating in the milk at the bottom of his bowl and decided not to eat them. He suddenly thought of them as a family and didn't want to separate or destroy them, but ultimately, something awful was going to happen, whether they were eaten or thrown in the bin. At least they were together. He washed them down the sink and wondered why anyone would name a cereal after another word for *goodbye*.

He was just running the tap to flush the milk away when there was a knock at the front door. He stopped the tap and turned, facing the front of the house. He held his breath, waited. The knock came again. A knock at the *front door*. He was frightened. Whoever was there was not someone he knew well because only strangers came to the front door, and his mum had usually answered it to people selling religion or expensive kitchen cleaners and somebody once who was looking for a lost cat. Joe stood very still, waiting for whoever it was to go away. No one would stay at the front door if no one answered it.

He had just begun to breathe once more and turn back to the sink when the knock came again. He jumped and the bowl nearly slipped out of his hands. He placed it very quietly on the draining board and crept toward the hallway, peering around the corner from the kitchen and tiptoeing closer to the door. He had only taken a few steps when the letter box snapped open and a pair of eyes caught him.

"He's in!" said an abrupt voice, and the letter box snapped closed.

It opened again moments later and a second pair of eyes found him hovering in the hallway.

"Ah, Joe," said a softer lady's voice. "It's me, Hazel. Angus is here too. Will you let us in?"

Joe didn't move. He knew that Hazel and Angus were safe people, but he had never opened the front door and invited a visitor into the house without his mum present. He wanted them to go away. He couldn't deal with visitors on his own. He closed his eyes.

The letter box snapped shut again and he could hear their voices on the other side of the door. First there was the soft voice of Hazel, her words were like butter, melting away before he could work them out; then the second voice, Angus. His voice was like the knife in the butter and each word cut through, so that he heard one half of their conversation:

"*Mmm mmm hmm,*" was all Joe could hear of Hazel's voice.

"Tell him, then," said Angus.

"*Hmm mm hmm,*" she said. Joe could still not make out her softly spoken words.

"Just tell him that she sent us." Angus sounded a little cross now.

Then there was a moment's silence before the letter box opened again. "Joe, darling, we heard about what happened to your mum and so we have come to see you. Janet sent us."

*Mum sent them?* Joe thought. *How?*

"Come to the back door," he managed to say, and he heard them walking round the side of the house.

Hazel and Angus were illuminated by the golden light under the awning at the back door. Hazel smiled sadly and Angus stood bracingly: legs apart, lips pursed in a way that made him seem busy and efficient. He was holding a box, the lid held closed by a wide, light-blue ribbon, like a present for a newborn boy.

"Can we come in?"

"Yes," said Joe.

"Where shall I put this?" Angus asked.

"What is it?"

"It's quite clearly a box, is what it is, Joe. I would think that was obvious."

"Perhaps you could take it through to the lounge, and then we can all sit in there comfortably," said Hazel, laying a patient hand on Angus's shoulder.

Joe led the way and sat in his usual chair. Hazel straightened the cushions—which were all bunched up at one end of the sofa following Chloe's sleepover—and opened the window a crack.

"I'm going to make a lovely big pot of tea. You boys chat, and I'll put a brew on."

Angus and Joe were left alone together. The box sat on the coffee table and Joe stared at it. Angus sighed heavily a few times and finally spoke.

"Why is it that the chattiest person always leaves the idiots who can't make conversation alone together? *I* should be making the bloody tea."

Joe just looked at Angus.

"Not you, Joe, you're not an idiot. I'm talking about me."

"We do not have to make conversation," said Joe.

Angus gave Joe a rare smile. "How you doing, mate? Bad news about your mum. She was a good person."

"I do not know how I am doing," said Joe. "I am just waiting for things to happen. When the clock gets to a certain place, I know to do things. In between those times, I just wait. But there has not been much in-between time yet."

Angus nodded gently and continuously and said "Aye" several times in a meaningful way in response to nothing obvious, until Hazel returned with the tray of tea things, then he shot up and took the tray from her. Hazel picked up the box from the table, so he had room to put it down, and then she sat with the box in her lap.

"Shall I be mother, then?" Angus said, leaning forward and lifting the pot.

"Angus!" said Hazel.

"Oh Jesus, sorry about that, Joe," said Angus. "Just a turn of phrase."

"Dear Joe," said Hazel, and Joe liked the way it sounded as though she were reading a letter to him. "I'm so, so sorry about your mum. She was very much loved and we'll miss her." Now her face crumpled like an old apple. "But no one will miss her as much as you. You were her life, you know."

"Yes, I know," said Joe.

"And she always worried that if—when—she died, things would be difficult for you. She tried to prepare you, as best she knew how. Oh damn it," she said, and fetched a tissue from her cardigan sleeve, wiping away tears as though they were an inconvenience. She sniffed and sat up straighter. "Anyway, she gave me—us—this box. She gave it to me to start with, but I'm even older than your mum, so, just in case, we brought Angus on board, to be a guardian of the box too."

"An afterthought," said Angus, raising his eyebrows at Joe. Joe frowned.

"Not at all, not an afterthought; more like backup, a safety net," said Hazel. "Are you with me?"

"What?" said Joe.

"Do you understand?"

"Understand what?"

"This box is from your mum," she said, patting the top of it. "To be given to you in the event of her death."

# 21

## In the event of my death

Hazel handed the box to Joe-Nathan and now he sat with it in his lap. He pulled the end of the ribbon gently and the bow slipped away from the top and the sides. He lifted the lid and felt a smile on his face. Then he closed his eyes because it was too hard to look for a moment. He opened them and looked again. He heard a sound like a sob and looked at Hazel, but she was still and quiet, as was Angus. The sob had come from inside himself, he realized, and gone again, *through that open window*, he thought.

In the top of the box was the face of Joe's mum: Janet's photograph, framed. She was smiling a gentle kind of smile. You could see her teeth, slightly crooked; her peach-colored cheeks, softly powdered. She was wearing her blue dress—the one Joe liked best—and a pair of pearl earrings. Attached to the glass was a Post-it note, which said, in her beautiful handwriting, *Hang this on the wall above the kitchen table, next to your dad.*

Joe laid the frame carefully on the arm of his chair and looked into the box to see what was underneath. Next was a book with a plain yellow cover. He lifted it out but didn't open it.

"Your mum said you already have a blue book," said Hazel, quietly. "She told me it has all sorts of helpful everyday things in there. This book, the yellow one, is for things she felt might be helpful but that don't belong in the blue book. Now and then when she'd pop over for a cup of tea, she'd get that yellow book out and jot something down."

Joe smoothed his hand over the yellow cover and opened it to the first page.

*My dearest Joe-Nathan. I wish I could always be there to help and advise you. But as I am not, herein find some words of guidance that might be useful one day in your life. I am not an expert in any of these areas, but if you had asked me about any of these things today, then this is what I would have said.*

"It's an advice book," he said.

There was a list of contents and Joe scanned them, things like Presents; Clothes; Love; Friends; Fighting; Travel; Swearing; Accidents and Injuries; and Funerals.

"It is not alphabetical," he said.

"No," said Hazel. "Your mum said that would bother you. It's because she added things as she thought of them, and her thoughts didn't come alphabetically."

Joe turned to a random page in the book and looked at the title at the top of the page: "Love," it said. He didn't read any further but looked up at Hazel. "I don't understand."

"What don't you understand?"

"Mum said that she is not an expert in any of the areas in the book, but here is a section on love, and she *is* an expert in love. Was. Is. *Is is is.* She loved me every day of my life."

Angus cleared his throat. "I don't know what your mum has written about in there, but I expect she's talking about *relationships*. Wouldn't you say so, Hazel?"

"Yes, I imagine your mum anticipated that one day you'll meet someone who is more than just a friend, and whatever you might have asked her about that, she has probably tried to answer."

"Oh," said Joe, carefully closing the book and laying it on top of the photo frame.

"But she did love you very well, you're right about that," Hazel added. "Anything else in there?"

"A letter," said Joe, extracting an envelope from the bottom of the box. It was a thick cream envelope with the words "To be given to my son in the event of my death" on the front. "Should I open it now?"

"I would," said Hazel, taking a sip from her cup.

Joe looked at Angus. "Aye, I would too."

Joe-Nathan carefully undid the envelope and took out the letter and began to read aloud.

*Dear Joe-Nathan,*

*If you are reading this letter for the first time, then that means that I have recently died and Hazel or Angus, or both, have come to see you with the box tied up with the blue ribbon. You will know what to do with the photo frame: put a nail in the* wall and hang it at the same height as Dad's photo, so that you can see both our faces when you eat your dinner.

Remember to use the blue book for all the usual things.

The yellow book is my way of trying to answer the questions that you might not yet have asked me. It's only advice, and you don't have to follow it. There are no hard and fast rules for the topics in that book, but there are some suggestions that might make some situations easier to navigate. I hope so.

Don't be afraid to ask others for help. Try to understand who your friends are. Friends will always allow you to lean on them. Sometimes you need to let them help you. And remember to help them too.

When the Imperial Leather soap gets thin, I know, of course, that you take the sticker off and put it in your album, as a way to gauge how long it has been since Dad died. And I suppose you will do something similar for me. I have often thought about it and wondered. If you ask me, I suppose it makes sense to simply continue with the soap stickers. Funny, though, that less soap will be used, and so the stickers will come less quickly now that we are both gone. I'm not sure it matters and I thought I would let you know that, because I imagine it will worry you.

Lucy has said that when the time comes, she will take you to see my body if you want to. This is entirely your choice; please don't think you have to. For some people it is helpful to see the body of their loved one, it helps them to grieve and move on. Other people really don't like the idea of it. It shouldn't be scary, it's just me, just my body. I like to think my soul will be with your dad.

I imagine that you must be feeling rather strange and that

*perhaps you have expectations about how you should feel. When someone dies, lots of people expect you to act a certain way; they can expect you to cry a lot, for example. But people feel and experience grief in many different ways, so don't feel that you have to cry. You might feel angry, or you might not. You might feel really sad, but you might not. Whatever you are feeling is alright, there is no right or wrong. If something makes you happy during sad times, that's good, be happy.*

*I have spoken to the funeral director: Hazel or Angus, or both, can take you to see him, and I have explained that you must choose my epitaph. Please do that for me, Joe.*

*We've always had each other until now, and I hope that I have given you enough to enable you to be independent. It is my hope that you will live well and happy. Allow your routines and habits to act like scaffolding, to hold you up and keep you strong, but remember that scaffolding is the support for something you are trying to build, it is not the building itself.*

*Try not to be too afraid of change, because it is inevitable.*

*Remember always that I love you and nothing can change that, not even death. And remember always that I believe you do not have a mean bone in your body.*

*Goodbye, my beautiful boy.*
*Love from Mum XxX*

*PS. I have written instructions for you to make your own packed lunch, in the blue book under Kitchen/Food/Packed lunch.*

Joe stopped reading and looked up to see that Hazel was still dabbing a damp tissue under one eye, then the other, then back to the first again. Angus sat with his head bowed, staring at his lap with both hands over his face, as though he might be bored.

Hazel whispered, "Beautiful." But Angus just sniffed and asked if there were any biscuits.

"Yes."

"Where?" said Angus from behind his hands, still looking at his lap.

"In the cupboard above the kettle," said Joe, and Angus stood up and turned away so quickly that Joe couldn't even see his face. Joe had noticed the time on the clock on the mantelpiece; it was 10:17 a.m. Angus took seven whole minutes to bring the biscuits back.

# 22

## Not as stupid as you look

Monday morning came as a relief. Joe-Nathan felt at ease as he left the house and headed for the relative certainty and normality of a working day at The Compass Store. His mind was focused as he gave the peace sign to the tree just before he entered the shop; that particular habit, that fraction of routine, calmed him and connected him to his day. He felt even more at ease as he turned northwest—staff-room, locker, tabard, lunch box.

Joe had worried about his packed lunch on Sunday evening; he'd never made it before. He set his alarm thirty minutes earlier than usual, to prepare for this new challenge, but Janet's instructions in the blue book were clear and he had found it easy; he was proud.

He took Hugo's note from the pinboard to see what his jobs for the day were, and collected the big double-pronged broom from the storeroom. He had to sweep each aisle from the north, all the way around to north-northwest, sixteen aisles in total. All his jobs on the list today were his favorites: jobs that took a long time to complete and were free from the possibility of spillages or breakages. Jobs that allowed him to tune in to the music and tune out of everything else. All the customers seemed peaceful, wandering the aisles as if they were visiting a gallery or strolling through a park with nowhere in particular to hurry to. People smiled at him and there was warmth and kindness. A gentleman asked him if he knew where the batteries were, and he directed him to the right place. His workday brought him blessed purpose, predictability, and belonging. Joe—at this moment—was absolutely in the right place.

"Hey, Joe," said Hugo, just before he started sweeping. "Why don't you put this on?" He started to undo a small package while Joe waited.

"What is it?"

"A present. A pedometer," said Hugo. "I thought you might like to tell me how many steps it takes to go completely up and down each aisle around the compass points. Would you do that for me?"

Joe saluted. "Yes, sir."

"Don't call me sir," said Hugo. His voice was stern but his smile was real.

"Hugo Boss," said Joe.

Hugo tutted in a friendly way. "How are you feeling?"

"Okay."

"You let me know if you need anything or feel unhappy, or need to go home. Anything, okay?"

"If I am lost, I stand on the mosaic and head west to come to your office, and you will help me find my way," Joe said.

"You got it," said Hugo. "Here, clip this to your belt loop." He stood with his hands on his hips and watched Joe take a few steps, then look at the pedometer, then take a few steps more and look again; then he continued on his way methodically.

Joe was all the way to east-southeast before Chloe jogged up to him, slightly breathless. She stopped and leaned forward, hands on thighs, while she caught her breath. "I'm late in," she said. "I don't normally start so early on a Monday, but I asked them to swap my hours to match yours. And I've fucked up on the first day." She blew out hard. Joe could smell minted smoke. "How are you doing today?"

"I am okay today," said Joe. "Better than yesterday."

"Yeah, you sounded sad on the phone last night."

"You have spoken to me every night since Mum died."

"It's only been three nights. Do you want me to keep doing it?"

"No, thank you." A new routine was a big decision, and Joe wasn't ready for a new addition to the routine.

"Okay, then. Find me if you need me." Chloe moved a sweaty strand of hair from her forehead and tucked it behind her ear.

People in the store seemed more gentle today. Colleagues who normally said nothing nodded wisely at him with furrowed brows; Pamela touched his arm as she passed and when Joe flinched she said, "Sorry," and then "Sorry" again, and Joe wondered why she had touched him when most people knew not to. But apart from that, nobody spoke to Joe again until he reached southwest, when he saw a pair of feet planted in the V of his broom. He looked up for the first time in ages and saw Mean Charlie standing there with his arms crossed.

"I heard about your mum," he said.

"Who told you?"

"Hugo. He told me to be kind to you."

"That was good of him," said Joe.

Charlie made a sound that was caught somewhere between a laugh and a sigh, which Joe could not interpret.

"Yeah, well. I'm sorry your mum died."

"Thank you."

"Was she nice?" said Charlie, tucking his arms even tighter under his own armpits.

"Yes. She did nice things, she loved me, and took me to the pub on a Friday."

"Just you and her, was it?"

"Yes. I am alone now."

"Dad run off a long time ago, did he?"

"He died."

"I expect he was a tosser though, right?"

"He was nice too. He taught me to make stuff and we would share a beer after we worked together in the workshop."

"Well, aren't you the lucky one."

"They are both dead," Joe said, thinking that Charlie must have misunderstood; how could he be described as lucky?

Charlie did a big sigh. "Well, everything changes now, doesn't it, Joe? And change is something you're not cool with, right?"

"I do not like change and new things because of survival instinct. This is a very big change, a very big new thing, but—in a reversal of my usual system—this time I have to adjust to it, or I will not survive."

"Wow, that's the longest sentence I've ever heard you say," said Mean Charlie. "And you're not quite as stupid as you look."

"Thank you," said Joe.

They both looked northeast toward the sound of determined footsteps coming their way, and saw Chloe. Charlie walked away, hands in pockets now, and was around the end of an aisle by the time Chloe got to Joe. "What did he want?" She jerked her head in Charlie's general direction. "Was he an arsehole?"

"No," said Joe. "Hugo told him to be kind to me, so Charlie was doing that. He said he was sorry about my mum; said I was lucky and told me I am not as stupid as I look."

"Oh, that's great," said Chloe, snapping her gum and looking in the direction that Charlie had disappeared. "That's really, seriously kind of him."

# 23
## So perfectly like herself

The thing that was hardest to get used to at first was the difference in the quality of quiet in the house. Joe-Nathan and Janet had not been noisy co-dwellers. Janet was the loudest: she would shout Joe's name up the stairs, or from another room, while Joe only spoke when he could see his mother's face.

Joe watched TV or looked at his encyclopedias or his other books as he usually did, but oddly, these activities lacked purpose now that there was no one in the house while he was doing them. Joe realized that a life is lived differently when there is someone there to witness it. And that made him wonder about his habits and rituals. He concluded that some things he did were important even if he was the only witness of his own activities.

When Joe got to his back door after work that Monday, he closed his eyes, tilted his head up, and imagined that the sunlight warmed his eyelids. He had always felt that coming home was a lovely moment, a gentle, calming feeling unlike any other. He had linked that feeling with simply *coming home*, but it didn't feel the same now and he concluded that it must have been coming home to his *mum* that had brought that feeling; this in turn made him wonder if coming home would ever feel that special again.

He swung his satchel round to his front to get his key, and went into the kitchen. He hung his bag on the wall and retrieved the blue book to help him decide what to eat for dinner.

In the end, Joe had to look at the section entitled "Kitchen/Food/Possible options when there isn't much food in the house," and made himself beans on toast. He set the table neatly for his dinner and as he took up his knife and fork, he looked from the photo of his father to the photo of his mother.

"Have you had a good day?" he said. But saying the words aloud lacked any satisfaction that they might possibly have held. In fact, the silence that echoed following his question seemed brash and unpleasant. He cut his toast carefully, and while he chewed, or drank his water, he gazed at his mother's face.

He thought of the letter in the box that Hazel and Angus had brought, and what his mum had said about visiting her in hospital after she had died: *It shouldn't be scary, it's just me, just my body.* Lucy had come to collect Joe on Saturday afternoon and it had felt very strange to be in her car, which smelled different to his mum's car and had an empty crisp packet in the footwell. It had felt strange to walk into the hospital where—again—the smells were new and people walked in seemingly haphazard streams, like ants. He quite liked the long white corridors, which made him think of work and long for Monday, when he would know what to do and everything would be where it belonged, including himself.

Lucy spent ages explaining what things would be like when he saw his mum's body, and how it wasn't too late to change his mind. But her words started out as information and then became a buzz, which he tried to ignore. When she stopped talking, he said, "My mum said it should not be scary and she is usually right."

And Janet *was* right. The only surprising thing about seeing her was that she looked so alive, simply asleep. Joe had imagined that a dead body would be completely different to a live body. But in his mother's case, at least, that wasn't true; she was very much the same. Lucy had gasped and held her hand to her chest. "Sorry, Joe, it's just that she looks so perfectly like herself, doesn't she?"

Joe had reached out and touched his mum's hand. It was freezing cold. He would never forget that.

When the beans and toast were all eaten, Joe tidied away and made a cup of tea, which he took outside to drink while he sat on the bench that leaned against the back of the house, and looked out over the garden. The old tree was whispering and the grass moved gently. The clouds stirred slowly and changed almost imperceptibly and he watched as one big cloud that looked like a fish swallowed another cloud and then transformed so that even though you couldn't see the moment it had changed, the cloud was no longer a fish, but something amorphous that might soon become very definitely a hippo, or a castle, or a teapot. Clouds were good: they change completely without jarring the senses, unlike life, which changes completely with no warning and no delicacy at all.

"Mean Charlie spoke to me today," he said to his mum on the bench next to him. He waited for her to say something like, *Oh yes? And what did Charlie have to say?* But there was silence and he looked to his left and remembered, once more, that she was gone.

## 24
### Clear

The days continued to move along, one into the next, punctuated by enough markers to keep Joe-Nathan moving almost as predictably as the days. He felt like a man he saw in a film once, who found his way through an underwater tunnel by pulling himself along a rope that had evenly spaced knots along its length. The weekdays were the knots and Joe focused on one knot at a time. Tuesday was as it should be, and so was Wednesday; nothing new, nothing eventful, nothing to consult the yellow book about.

On Thursday morning he had three full trolleys of go-backs to keep him busy and he carefully returned vases and packs of crayons and myriad other items to their own kind.

"Hey, Joe-Nathan," said a voice.

He turned from the shelves to see Pip, with an upside-down smile.

"I heard about your mum; I was really sorry to hear it."

"Thank you."

"I had been looking forward to meeting her at the quiz night," said Pip.

"You will never meet her now, at anything."

"That's true," said Pip. "But hey, you should still plan on coming. When my uncle died, my auntie said that being around other people and doing normal things was the best thing."

"But quiz night is not normal."

"Oh, yes. I see," said Pip, pausing to consider the truth of his statement. "But you'll be with me and Chloe. We can all dress up nice and it might be fun. So . . ."

"Yes, it might be fun."

"Well, good, that's settled, then," said Pip, and her smile turned the right way up.

+

At the end of the work day, Hugo rushed up to him, breathless.

"Joe, there's a spillage on aisle fifteen. Can you get a mop? And be careful, please, I'll send someone to help you."

"What color is it?" Joe asked as Hugo dashed away.

"It's clear," Hugo called back over his shoulder.

"Clear?" Did that mean it would be clear what color it was when Joe saw it, or clear as in transparent? Hugo would never, ever send Joe to clean up a red spillage, but he couldn't recall what they sold in aisle fifteen. Joe fetched the mop, as instructed, but on his way he took a detour via the spillage, so that he could see what it was first. He left his go-back trolley and went to the mosaic, turned northwest, and headed down aisle fifteen. He couldn't see any spillage at all. He walked more quickly and was suddenly hit by an overwhelming aroma of the swimming pool.

"Huh?" he managed to say, just before his legs went from under him and he slipped onto the floor, something wet and slimy and transparent underneath him.

"Bleach," he said to no one; the store was quiet and no customers were in the aisle. He put his hand to the floor and tried to push himself up. His hand slid away so that now he was lying on his side in it. He lay there for a moment, thinking that he would have to get onto his knees in order to get up, but all his clothes would be ruined as a result.

"You idiot."

Joe turned and saw Mean Charlie's shoes. He craned his neck and saw that Charlie was smiling down at him, shaking his head. In one hand he held a mop, and in the other, two bright-yellow slip-hazard signs featuring a stickman image that looked exactly as Joe must have looked in the moment before he fell down.

Charlie placed the hazard signs at either end of the spill and then pulled on a plastic glove. He held his hand out to Joe, offering to help him up.

Joe had shaken a lot of hands but he had never touched Charlie. He looked at Charlie's hand and hesitated.

"Come on, grab hold," said Charlie.

He really didn't want to, but he couldn't get up by himself.

Joe reached up with a hand covered in bleach. He was glad that Charlie was wearing a glove, partly so he would be protected from the chemical, but also so they wouldn't have any skin-to-skin contact. Joe braced himself to hold on tight; he wanted to get up in one go, so that it was over with quickly. The two men held hands and Charlie pulled hard, at the same time as Joe. Presumably it was because gravity was in Joe's favor—what with him being on the ground pulling downward—but whatever the reason, Mean Charlie overbalanced, and Joe pictured a different stickman in another awkward position, as Mean Charlie fell on top of him.

Joe inhaled sharply and squeezed his eyes tight shut. He started panting. Never ever in his life had anyone been on top of him.

"You total fuckwit," said Charlie, who quickly lifted his weight off Joe and got onto his hands and knees in a crouching position above him.

Joe opened his eyes briefly but the smell of bleach and the bright lights framing Charlie's angry face were too much to take and he shut them again.

"Pip-pip-pip-byob-byob-byob-pip-pip-pip-byob-byob-byob," he repeated over and over.

"What the fuck?" said Charlie. He stood, but gingerly, and his feet were not in real contact with the ground, so that he looked like Bambi on ice for a moment before he went over sideways and landed with a grunt on the floor again, face-to-face this time with Joe. Joe locked eyes with Charlie and in the same way that he was normally compelled to look away, he found his gaze trapped; he stared into Charlie's eyes in a way he had never done with anyone before, so *why*—no, *how*—could it be that he saw something familiar there? The answer came from nowhere and it came as a picture: it was the same look he had given himself in the bathroom mirror when his reflection had asked why he removed the little stickers from the Imperial Leather soaps. Mean Charlie was solemn; Mean Charlie was sad.

But Charlie broke eye contact, said "Fuck sake," and crawled away from Joe. Charlie sat in the bleach that he had now smeared across the floor while he took his shoes off and then planted his feet (just in socks) on a dry patch and stood.

"You do the same," he said to Joe. "Just scooch over here and take your shoes off."

It was nice—this sentence—thought Joe; it was a helpful sentence without a single swear word in it. Joe did as he was told and soon he and Charlie stood side by side in their socks, their clothes and hands covered in bleach.

"Oh, boys, *boys*," said Hugo, hurrying up the aisle. "*PAMELA!*" he shouted, and she bustled into view looking pink and pleased to be of help, in her green tabard. "Get more hazard signs and close this aisle off." Pamela nodded and disappeared. Hugo fumbled at a bunch of keys on his belt, muttering, "Where is it? Where *is* it?" and gestured for Joe and Charlie to follow him. "No, leave your shoes. Quick, quick, we need to get you both into the shower."

# 25

## Like a peach

The shower room at The Compass Store was made available to anyone who wanted to cycle into work and wash before their shift started. It was rarely used. There were two large cubicles and a brown tiled floor, rough enough to prevent slippages. There was a big mirrored wall above two sinks, a hand dryer, and a hair dryer that was attached to the wall, like in a sports center.

Hugo walked briskly south-southwest, to the right of the toilets where Joe-Nathan liked to clear his head. As he walked he talked fast, emphasizing words by making a chopping motion with his hand. Charlie kept up with the boss, but Joe had to do a little jog now and then to stay with them.

"You boys must strip down as fast as you can, put all your clothes in a corner of the shower room, and get under the water immediately. Don't wait for it to warm up; get under, get that bleach off your skin quickly." Hugo grabbed a couple of bottles of shower gel in aisle five without even stopping and passed them to Joe and Charlie as they walked, pausing briefly—irritably—as Joe struggled to simultaneously walk and take the bottle from him. "Get this soap all over you. Tip your heads back as you wash your hair; don't get anything in your eyes. Understand? *Hurry up, hurry up, hurry up*," he said, as though by saying it, they might all get there faster. "And don't just wash once, wash twice, wash everything, make sure you get all that bleach off." They arrived at the showers and Hugo had the key ready, got them into the room in one swift movement. "I'll get someone to bring you towels and clothes to wear. Don't touch your bleachy clothes after you've put them down. Come to my office together when you're finished." With that, he let the door click shut, leaving Mean Charlie alone with Joe.

For a moment they stood motionless. However, Joe had been given clear instructions, and so he undid his tabard and took it to the corner of the room, laying it down carefully. As he did so, Mean Charlie's clothes flew past him, landing on top of Joe's tabard and piling up quickly. Joe glanced over his shoulder and winced as a pair of balled-up socks sailed close to his face. "You heard Hugo, hurry up," Charlie said.

Charlie's cubicle door slammed and was followed immediately by running water and an expletive as he stood under what must be very cold water. Now that Charlie couldn't see him, Joe removed his clothes, folding them and laying them down neatly. The shower was different from the one he used at home, but with relief he noted that there were only two words on it: *on* and *off*. The temperature was set for safety, no adjustment possible; the lack of choice was reassuring. Joe lathered up and rinsed, remembering Hugo's instructions to wash twice, wash everything, and not get anything in his eyes. There was the sound of a knock and the door to the shower room cautiously clicked open, followed by Chloe's voice calling out, "I'm not looking. I've brought towels and clothes for you both. I'm going to leave them by the sinks." Then the door clicked shut once more.

Joe began to worry; Mean Charlie would probably finish showering quicker than him, and be wrapped up in a towel, or even partially dressed by the time Joe was done. Next thing, Joe would have to leave his cubicle naked and Charlie would see his body. Mean Charlie was bound to say something horrible.

It was happening already: the flow of water in Charlie's shower stopped and Joe heard Charlie take two wet steps, then the cubicle door opened. Joe turned off his own water and wanted to cry. He stayed where he was and his skin was covered suddenly in a cool wave of goose bumps.

"Here," said Charlie, and half a towel appeared over the top of Joe's cubicle door. Joe pulled it down and dried himself, tying the towel under his armpits with relief. Slowly he slid back the latch on his door and made his way to the pile of clean clothes at the sink, which Charlie was sifting through. Charlie wore his towel around his waist; he didn't look at Joe.

"It's just sweatpants, T-shirts, and hoodies, all the same size," said Charlie, separating the things up. "Here." He kept some for himself and pushed the remaining things closer to Joe.

In front of the two young men was a large mirror, which filled the wall across both of the sinks. Joe didn't want to look at Charlie, and he didn't want Charlie to look at him, but the general proximity and the existence of the mirror made it very difficult indeed. Joe noticed that Charlie's body had muscles on the front. Not big muscles, but you could see where each one was. Joe knew his own torso was soft and pale in comparison. Joe looked again, as briefly as he could. Charlie had a lot of yellow bruising around his ribs on both sides and there was another bruise—a green one—further up, under his clavicle. Charlie turned away from Joe—shaking out a folded T-shirt—and in the mirror, Joe saw that Charlie also had muscles in his back. Joe would like to have muscles in his back too. But Charlie had more bruises there as well—on top of all the muscles—and one of them was really, *really* big and black, right near the bottom, where Joe knew a kidney would be.

Joe stood still and Charlie fixed him with an accusing look in the mirror. "What are you staring at?"

"Your muscles," said Joe.

"Stop being a perve and get dressed," Charlie said.

"And your bruises," said Joe.

Joe looked down at his own skin: there wasn't a single bruise on his body and yet he had fallen harder than Charlie, straight onto the floor into the bleach. Charlie had fallen on top of him, and then fallen once again onto his side. It was quite a hard fall, but Joe was surprised to see that already Charlie had bruises all over him.

"You are like Ross," said Joe as Charlie briskly pulled on a T-shirt and some underpants on under his towel.

"Who's Ross?"

"Ross Geller, from *Friends*. Season nine, episode five, 'The One with Phoebe's Birthday Dinner.' It is mentioned twice in the episode. The first time, Rachel asks Ross to knock a door down and he says, 'I would, but I bruise like a peach.' And later in the same episode Joey reminds himself that he cannot hit Ross because he bruises like a peach."

*"What?"*

"So, you are like Ross, because we both just fell, but I did not get any bruises and you got lots."

Charlie stood motionless and stared at Joe until Joe was forced to look up and away at the ceiling tiles. Joe thought back to his ency-clopedias and recited: "Bruises occur when capillaries in the skin are broken and blood leaks out of the vessels and makes a mark beneath the skin. Eventually the blood will be reabsorbed back into your body and disappear," Joe said to the ceiling. Charlie said nothing, and Joe continued. "But if you bruise easily and often you should see a doctor, because you might have a vitamin deficiency." Joe felt pleased to be helping Charlie. Charlie would be relieved, he thought (he probably didn't know about the vitamin deficiency).

Charlie spoke, but he didn't *sound* relieved. "Mind your own business, get dressed, and stop looking at me, you fucking deviant. Christ, you'll be asking me out on a date in a minute."

"No, I will not," said Joe. But he did get dressed.

## 26
### Accidents and injuries

Chloe was sitting on the floor outside the shower room wearing a pair of rubber gloves and holding a screwed-up black bin liner. When Joe-Nathan and Charlie emerged, she jumped up.

"You okay?" she said to Joe.

"Yes," said Joe. But Chloe looked at Charlie like she wanted to hit him.

"What have *I* done?" said Charlie.

"I just don't trust you to behave like a decent human being is all."

"Charlie handed me a towel," said Joe. "And he is hurt."

"No, I'm not," said Charlie, scowling. "Anyway, we have to go see Hugo. Come on, Joe, hurry up."

Chloe watched as the two of them walked away toward the mosaic at the store center. From behind, wearing the same clothes—apart from Joe's hair looking so long and disheveled—there was very little difference between them.

"Oh, my goodness, you look like twins!" said Hugo as Joe and Charlie sat down in his office.

Charlie tutted.

"We look nothing like each other," said Joe. "We are simply wearing the same clothes. Also, Charlie has muscles, and I do not."

Charlie closed his eyes.

"Well, I've just checked with Health and Safety and I need to ask you a few questions. Very important that you answer honestly." He looked at his computer screen. "Okay, do either of you feel itchy? Nauseous? Dizzy or faint?" He looked back over at them and they shook their heads. Hugo checked the screen again. "Any marks or welts on you? Any burning sensations?" Again, they said "no" in unison. But Joe turned to stare at the side of Charlie's face.

Hugo noticed. "What is it, Joe?" he asked.

"It's just that Charlie does have marks on him."

"No! I don't!" Charlie said, turning to stare back at Joe. "Honestly, Hugo, I don't."

Joe put a hand to his own ribs, remembering where all Charlie's bruises were.

"Are you sure?" Hugo said to Charlie, concern lining his face.

"When he fell . . . ," Joe started to say.

"No!" Charlie interrupted. "I've got a birthmark and Joe was fucking staring at me in the shower." He glared at Joe.

"Okay, Charlie, that's enough," said Hugo. "No need for the language. I'm sure Joe was just trying to help." He exhaled and there was disappointment in the sound of it. But he patted the desk in an efficient way and said brightly, "Okay, good. The three main things are that you quickly washed the bleach off, took off your contaminated clothing, and now I need you to watch for any reactions. Just let me know as soon as possible if your skin feels uncomfortable, or you feel unwell. As for your clothes, let me know how much they cost to replace and The Compass will cover the expense."

"Cool," said Charlie, "my trainers were getting old."

"Every cloud," said Hugo, raising an eyebrow at him.

Joe was surprised that Charlie didn't immediately walk off in a different direction when they left Hugo's office, but as soon as they reached an empty aisle, Charlie rounded on him, all but pinning him against the shelves of printer paper in aisle seven.

"I don't want you talking to anyone about me," said Charlie.

"But your bruises look really bad," said Joe.

"Shut up!" said Charlie in a loud whisper.

"Hugo Boss is right: I am only trying to help you."

"I don't want your help," said Charlie. All his words came out as hisses and he looked sideways, as if he was worried about being seen. "Why can't you understand, you *total* idiot?"

"I do understand," said Joe. "A person's body is a private thing. But Hugo said it was important to be honest about whether we were hurt or not. And you are hurt."

"I'm *not* hurt."

"The bruises . . ."

"Are none of your business. Don't tell anyone about them. Do you understand? Like *you* said: it's private."

"But I am trying to help you," said Joe.

"Trust me," said Charlie, getting very close to Joe's face. "You are the last person on the face of the fucking earth who can help me."

The yellow book lay on the kitchen table and Joe stared at its cover while he ate his dinner that night. He had consulted the book regarding funerals and he had an appointment with the funeral director on Saturday, which Hazel and Angus were taking him to. Janet had left such clear instructions that Joe had concluded that a funeral was a very straightforward event with nothing to do except turn up in certain places at certain times. And he was nothing if not a good timekeeper. So the only thing that he needed to work on was the epitaph for his mother's headstone, and he wanted it to be just right. It was hard to say everything that needed to be said in so few words.

But tonight, as Joe finished his sausages with microwave mash, cabbage, and gravy, he planned to consult the yellow book on another matter, which he hoped would be listed under "Accidents and Injuries."

"I plan to prove Mean Charlie wrong," said Joe to the framed photos of his mum and dad. "I want to prove to him that I *can* help him. And then he will understand that I do not have a mean bone in my body, and *then* maybe he will like me."

## 27

## Arnica

Joe-Nathan sat on the bench in the back garden with a cup of tea in his hand and the yellow book beside him where his mum would have sat. The sun was warm and the clouds moved quite quickly across the sky; he could see partial reflections of them on the windows of the workshop at the end of the garden, which almost made it look as though something were moving about inside. It had been a long time since Joe had made something in there. He thought about sitting on the steps of the workshop with his dad and sitting on this bench with his mum, and how all changes seemed to have a diminishing effect in terms of the number of people in a person's life. He used to sit there, on those steps, with his dad, and now, if he ever had a beer there again, he would be alone; he used to sit here on the bench with his mum, and now he was alone here too. Joe realized that his world would get smaller or emptier, with the people in it picked off one by one, until he was gone too, and then it wouldn't matter. In the meantime, he thought, it would be very nice to make something again; perhaps another jigsaw for Hazel; perhaps something useful for Angus; or maybe something for Chloe: a box to collect money every time she said a bad word; she would be rich by the end of the year.

Joe put his empty cup on the arm of the bench and picked up the yellow book, smoothing his hand over the cover before opening it up. He checked the contents page and turned to "Accidents and Injuries/Injuries/Bruises." Underneath, Janet had written the following (something about her handwriting made Joe feel like he could hear her voice when it read it):

*Don't worry too much about bruises. If you have bumped into something or been hit by something, then a bruise is normal. If you start getting bruises for no apparent reason, then go to the doctor. Bruises will go through a range of colors before they disappear and you can't do much about them, but you could try rubbing arnica cream on them. It helps the body heal itself more quickly, can make bruises go away faster, and could reduce pain and swelling. We have some in the cupboard under the sink in the bathroom.*

Well, thought Joe, if arnica can help bruises, then arnica it will be. He said, "Thank you," closed the yellow book, returned it to the drawer with the blue book, and found the arnica cream in the bathroom. He brought it downstairs and put it in his satchel so that he wouldn't forget to take it into work for Mean Charlie the following day.

## 28
### Am I helping you?

"What are you doing after work?" Chloe asked the next morning, breezing over to Joe-Nathan and leaning over the end of his trolley.

"Is that a trick question?" said Joe.

"Okay, so it's Friday, you're heading to the pub at five thirty. Want company?"

"I will go whether I have company or not," said Joe.

"Okay, Prince Charming! What I'm trying to say is can I join you? And Pip's been hassling me about quiz night, so she wants to come along too and talk strategy. You okay with that?"

"Yes. That might be fun. I like strategy: the skill of making or carrying out plans to achieve a goal," said Joe.

"Yeah, exactly what I was going to say. I'm glad you're on my team, Einstein."

"Why?"

"Because you're clever."

"I have a very narrow range of knowledge, and I am slow, which is not ideal for quizzes. I pause TV quiz shows so I have time to answer before the contestant does. I do not know much."

"Between us we'll be fine. See you later."

It was a soothingly uneventful morning at work: no surprises, spillages, or breakages, and Joe's mind wandered to the tube of arnica cream in his satchel. He was full of anticipation at the thought of giving it to Mean Charlie and imagined a scenario where he gave the cream to Charlie and Charlie smiled: a real smile. He might even pat him on the side of the arm, as men tended to do when they were thankful or grateful or pleased in some other way. Charlie might say thank you, or he might just nod a *silent* thank-you, like they do in American movies, the kind of nod where everyone understands everything without words. Then Joe imagined asking him on Monday if the arnica had helped, and in his mind, Charlie said yes. This, Joe thought, would be a new beginning for them both.

At lunchtime, in the staff-room, Joe sat at his usual table and placed his lunch box and a glass of water neatly in front of him. His packed lunch followed Janet's instructions from the blue book:

### KITCHEN
*Food*

*Packed lunch: a sandwich or a wrap with cheese, ham, or peanut butter (this is so you get carbohydrate and protein)—wrap it in foil or cling film before you put it in your lunch box; a piece of fruit like an apple or a banana (they don't need wrapping or a separate container); a salad item: carrot sticks or cucumber; a prewrapped chocolate biscuit like a KitKat or a caramel wafer. Take water instead of fizzy drinks because water won't stain things or make them sticky if it leaks in your bag.*

Janet had been careful to never include a boiled egg or tuna in his packed lunch, as these were smellier food items that could (and, at school, often did) invite insults and ridicule. They were things that Joe enjoyed, but only ever ate at home.

Joe laid out his packed lunch neatly on the table in front of him from left to right in the order that he was going to eat it: peanut butter sandwich (it was the easiest and tastiest sandwich to make); carrot sticks; KitKat; then the banana came last. Fruit was always eaten last because if he left chocolate to the end, then Joe found himself wanting to eat chocolate all afternoon. He drank a whole glass of water before he started; this was Janet's suggestion; she said it would help fill him up and stop him eating his food too fast.

Joe didn't mind if someone joined him at the table while he ate, but he didn't like to talk or listen to them; he just wanted to concentrate on his food, so he was often at the table by himself, unless Chloe happened to have the same lunch break (which was rare) or Pip (both of whom had become used to talking and getting no response from Joe and were quite relaxed about that arrangement).

Mean Charlie came into the staff-room, put money into the vending machine, pressed some buttons, and thumped the machine unnecessarily as a Lion bar dropped into the tray at the bottom. He stooped to retrieve it, ate it swiftly while he stood at the coffee machine and made himself a drink.

Joe felt his palms sweat. He had never initiated conversation with Charlie, and his habit was avoidance. Joe quickly made his way through his lined-up lunch items, reluctant to let Charlie leave before he'd given him the arnica. He ate his banana uncomfortably fast and wondered if it would ever go away, so determined it seemed to adhere to the roof of his mouth. Finally, he swallowed it down and washed it away with more water. He cleared his rubbish and took his lunch box to his locker. He opened his satchel, put his lunch box in, and took the arnica cream out. While he did all this, he peered at Mean Charlie over the top of his locker door. Charlie caught him looking and tutted, then turned his attention to a magazine that was left on the table. Something caught his curiosity so that he didn't notice Joe approaching until his shadow fell across the thing he was reading. Charlie looked up, and when neither of them spoke, Charlie shrugged and said, "Can I help you, young lady?"

"It is me, Joe-Nathan," said Joe, pointing at his own chest.

"Oh, yes, of course, I didn't recognize you with your clothes on."

"I have . . ." Joe hesitated; he was distracted by the unexpected dialogue, which was nothing like he had imagined.

"Yes?"

"I have brought you something to help with your bruises," said Joe, focusing again, and he tried to smile. But he must've done it wrong because Charlie did not smile back; he looked horrified. Or maybe scared. Joe wished he had his expressions chart with him (the one he had used a lot when he was at school) to try to match Charlie's expression with some emotion that made sense.

"What's that?" said Charlie, looking at the tube that Joe was holding out, but not moving to touch or take it.

"It is arnica cream, for bruises."

Charlie just stared at Joe.

"You rub it on and it can make them better quicker," Joe went on.

The door to the staff-room opened and a small group of people entered the room, including Owen, who glanced over at Charlie and Joe with questioning eyes. Charlie snatched the tube from Joe and shoved it between his legs.

"Use it as soon as you can," said Joe.

"Thanks," Charlie whispered hurriedly.

"Am I helping you?" said Joe, feeling that progress was being made.

"What? *Yes!*" Charlie was looking beyond Joe at Owen. "*Go away.*"

"Okay," said Joe, and he made his way back into the store, even though his lunch break wasn't over yet.

But before the door closed behind him, he heard Charlie say to Owen, "Big dope."

# 29

## Simple rules

Joe-Nathan laid out some ground rules as he, Chloe, and Pip walked to the pub after work that day. "No sleepovers and no vomiting near my house," he said.

"I have no problem with those rules," said Pip. "Wow, you youngsters are wild! Mind you, when I was your age, I hadn't had a good night unless I threw up or got a shag. Which one of you was sick last time?"

"Chloe. And the week before that there was a fight, which was better than the vomit," said Joe.

"That fight actually happened?" Pip looked at Chloe. "I thought it was just a rumor."

"It wasn't really a fight; I punched a guy in the face and that was the end of it." Chloe shrugged and popped her gum.

"Sounds like a rough pub," said Pip, grinning.

"Rough?" said Chloe. "Joe and his mum have been coming here every week for years. How rough could it be?"

When they neared the Ink and Feather, Joe said he would get the drinks. "I have been looking in the yellow book," he said, "and there is quite a lot under the section 'Pubs.'"

"What's the yellow book?" Pip asked.

"It is like the blue book, but with advice that is concerned with social life experiences, rather than practical life experiences."

"Uh, okay, well, what's the blue book? Did you buy it?"

"The blue book is where my mum wrote down everything she thought I would need to know to be independent in the house. But she wrote another book too, a yellow one, which I received in the event of her death. The yellow book is mostly to do with feelings and what to do in environments outside of the house. It has been very useful so far." Joe thought back to the section on "Accidents and Injuries" and how it had led to his conversation with Charlie today.

"*Am I helping you?*" Joe had asked. "*Yes,*" Charlie had replied. The memory of it made Joe smile inside.

"I think the yellow book is going to be useful in getting Charlie to like me," said Joe, just before they entered the pub.

"What?" said Chloe, stopping dead. "I told you, you don't have to do that."

"What's all this about?" said Pip.

Chloe suddenly looked mad and sounded it. "Charlie at work—he's an arsehole—he's mean to Joe and Joe thinks it's important that he changes Charlie's mind about him, and gets him to like him. I told Joe he shouldn't bother; Charlie's not worth it."

Joe opened the door and Chloe tutted and stamped inside. The three of them stood at the bar. They stopped talking while Joe concentrated on buying drinks. He had read the page in the yellow book several times to familiarize himself with it:

## PUB
### *Buying drinks*

*I have always bought the drinks when we go to the pub, but when you go with friends you should each take it in turns to pay. It might be easiest if you go first. Ask everyone what they want, order the drinks at the bar, and pay for them. Whoever you are with will buy the next drinks in turn. Don't remind them to buy drinks. When everyone has bought a drink—if you are staying for more—then it is your turn to buy again. You don't need to buy drinks for other people in the pub, only the friends that you are with.*

When all the hand-shaking was done and they were seated at Joe's usual table, Pip said, "I agree with Chloe. If people are mean to you, you shouldn't waste your time trying to be nice to them."

"Why not?" Joe asked.

"Well, look at it this way," she said, tying her hair back like she was about to get serious. "We used to have a cat and we loved it, and then this other cat started coming to the back door, begging for food, and we fed it—but only outside—and our cat seemed to like this other cat and we thought of it as his friend. Then one day, I put food outside and this cat was eating it, and our cat went outside and the other cat pounced on him, attacked him. Well, I stopped feeding the other cat, because he was bullying *our* cat. And I said to my little

140

sister, 'If a kid at school was bullying you and came to our house, I wouldn't feed them, I wouldn't invite them in for dinner!' Know what I mean?"

"Totally," said Chloe, and they all sipped on their drinks.

"So . . ." Joe looked confused. "So . . . if you had a bully and he was hungry, if he was starving and begged you for food, you wouldn't give him any? Because he's mean?"

Nobody said anything for a moment. Joe wondered if he'd spoken unclearly so he re-phrased it. "If someone is mean, and they beg you for food, should you feed them, or not feed them? Even if they are just a schoolkid—like your little sister was—are you saying you should not feed them?"

"I . . ." Pip faltered, looked from Joe to Chloe in desperation. "No, I . . . gosh, Joe."

"He does this," said Chloe with a shrug. "He makes you think. It's very fucking annoying."

"When you put it like that," said Pip.

Chloe was shaking her head.

"Is that what you mean?" Joe asked again, expecting an answer. "You would not feed a bully even if they were starving."

"Well, maybe. I guess I might, come to think of it," said Pip, sinking back in her seat.

"So, what was the point of your cat story?" he asked.

"You kind of ruined the point of her cat story," said Chloe.

"Oh."

"But I still say *fuck* Charlie, you don't need him, and I don't have a cat or a dog story to back up my point," said Chloe. "Just instinct. Simple rules. If someone wants to fight you, hit back as hard as you can; if someone doesn't like you, walk away."

Joe nodded. He liked these words, because they did indeed sound like simple rules that were easy to follow. He'd been tempted to tell Chloe about Charlie and his bruises and how his plan with the arnica cream was working, but between Mean Charlie's demands to not talk about his body, and Chloe's insistence that he *not* try to get Charlie to like him, Joe made a firm decision to say nothing.

"Changing the subject," said Pip, getting a pen and pad out of her bag. "Let's discuss quiz night. What are your specialist topics?"

# 30

## Closure

Friday evening at the pub had passed without any sleepovers, vomiting, or fighting and Joe-Nathan returned home after four half-pints, made himself cheese on toast, watched four episodes of *Friends*, and went to bed. It was the quality of stillness in the house that troubled him more than anything since his mum had gone. Angus had said that the funeral would bring him closure and things might be easier after that. But Joe hadn't really understood the meaning of closure and had turned to *Friends*, season two, episode seven ("The One Where Ross Finds Out"), and played and replayed the part where Rachel leaves a voice mail for her ex-boyfriend, telling him that she's over him and she describes *that* as "closure." He lay in bed wondering whether—after the funeral—he, like Rachel, would be "over" his mum. And he knew that to be over someone meant to start to forget them and be happy again, without them. If he forgot his mum, there would still be the photograph at the kitchen table and the blue and yellow books to remind him of her, but if he got over her completely, would those things be enough? He'd been to his dad's funeral and he hadn't forgotten *him*. He wouldn't let this funeral make him forget his mum, he would make sure he remembered her every day. But if he could just get used to the silence in the house when she wasn't there, if only it felt the same as the silence in the house when she *had* been there, he would feel more at ease.

Joe woke at 4 a.m. and lay in bed ruminating over these things. This was new, as Joe had never had any problem sleeping, except when the weather got very hot or when he'd been ill, but his thoughts alone had never kept him awake. It was sleeping time, and he should be in bed, so he was reluctant to get up, even when he had been awake for forty-six minutes.

But when he had been awake for exactly sixty-one minutes, he threw his duvet cover back and got up. He flicked on his desk light and pulled a photograph album down from the shelf, folding the cover back to expose its first empty page. Leaving it open, he padded to the bathroom and pulled the light switch, blinking against the assault of light. He put the plug in the sink and while it filled with water, he looked at his reflection. He didn't see anything in his face to suggest he was a man who had lost a few hours of sleep, or who missed the quiet presence of his mum.

When the sink was full, he took the Imperial Leather and washed his hands over and over again, and then over and over again, again. Until the soap was worn away and he deemed it thin enough. He retrieved the tweezers from the bathroom cabinet and laid them—and the soap—on a towel. He left them there while he scrubbed at the scummy basin until it shone. Then he carefully removed the sticker from the top of the soap and took it to his brand-new album, dabbing a little glue and placing it reverently in the top left corner of the first page. The stickers in this album would represent the number of soaps used since Joe had lost both his mum and his dad.

"I will never forget you," he vowed.

Joe's alarm was set for 8 a.m. on Saturday, an hour later than on a weekday. But after he had put the sticker in the album, he'd gone back to bed and could not get back to sleep, and he regretted that extra restless hour he had to stay there, waiting for the alarm. More and more he felt like Chloe: wanting to be away from the now, and into the next, long before its moment had come. It was not a good feeling.

Hazel and Angus had arranged to collect Joe at 10:30 a.m. and take him to see the funeral director. Hazel had explained that Janet was there now, in the chapel of rest, and the funeral director wanted to talk to Joe about the arrangements and what would be expected of him, which—as far as he understood it—was very little. His main job was to come up with an epitaph for her headstone, and there was no hurry for that, as it didn't actually need to be ready for the funeral. But still, it was a job that needed doing. After breakfast, and once he was dressed, Joe had two hours left before Hazel and Angus arrived, and he spent them in the workshop at the end of the garden. The workshop's wholesome old-fashioned smell of sawdust made Joe think of Sundays, sunny days, and his dad. In the back, there was a cupboard, and inside it, shelves for small pots of paint and brushes and other tools, all clean and neatly displayed. But it was also where Joe stored his epitaph etchings and now and then he liked to look through them. Each one was a small wooden plaque, A4 size; the edges were rubbed smooth with care and engraved using Joe's favorite tool: the wood-burning pen. There were six so far, which he had copied from the headstones he had seen or heard about in the last five years, all of which had impressed him in one way or another:

HERE LIES GOOD OLD FRED,

A GREAT BIG ROCK FELL ON HIS HEAD.

I TOLD YOU MY FEET WERE KILLING ME.

ANOTHER ONE BITES THE DUST.

DIED FROM NOT FORWARDING THAT TEXT

MESSAGE TO TEN PEOPLE.

PHOEBE BUFFAY, BURIED ALIVE.

IT'S DARK DOWN HERE.

But although each of these epitaphs had pleased Joe (he found them all funny), they did not inspire him with what to put on his mother's gravestone. She had said she wanted him to choose, but how could so few words do her justice? All the things she had done for him, all the ways she had looked after him and cared for him; there was no room on a headstone for all the ways he wanted to remember her. But all those things she'd done, and the things she had left behind—her books, her legacy of care and devotion—they came from love, and that had not gone away; she had said as much in her letter, even death couldn't take that from him. Joe's mum had died, but her love hadn't. Quite simply, her heart had stopped, but her love survived. He heated his wood-burning pen up and practiced writing words onto a clean, sanded A4 plaque, just to see how they looked.

# 31

## Bodies in bins

The funeral director was nice, but Joe-Nathan was desperate to leave. The room was gloomy and too quiet, muffled like a snowy morning. Gentle music played somewhere a long way away, but it wasn't happy enough, and Joe longed for Monday morning and the clean white Compass Store, smiling customers, unsmiling customers, lockers, trolleys, and happy music. But that was forty-six hours away.

Hazel sat upright to one side of Joe, and Angus slumped on Joe's other side, arms firmly crossed. The funeral director looked the saddest of them all, with his mouth picture-perfectly downturned just like on Joe's old expression cards.

"I was very sad to hear about the passing of your mother," he said. "I met with her when your father passed and I've met with her twice since then, and while I try to make it a habit to remember everyone who comes through these doors, I do see a *lot* of people."

If it were possible, the funeral director's mouth turned down even more. "However, I do clearly remember your mother."

"Why did she come to see you?" asked Joe.

"Why? To plan her funeral, of course. She didn't want to burden you with the process. It can be a lot for people to handle while they're grieving, so it's not uncommon. But your mother was keen to make this as easy as possible for you. Our meeting today is to discuss the plans she made, and outline the choices that she would like *you* to make. I assure you, you have nothing to worry about, and the finances have also been dealt with."

"What finances?"

"I mean it's paid for."

"I did not know you had to pay to be buried," said Joe.

"Oh yes!" said the funeral director. "And it can be very expensive." He looked at Hazel. "Although we do have some excellent lower-cost options, and a variety of payment plans."

Joe saw Hazel clutch her handbag tightly, and Angus said "Christ" under his breath.

The director turned his attention to an open file on the desk in front of him. "Janet has a list of requests that cover everything, including an invitation list." He handed a piece paper to Joe and he glanced down at the list of names and numbers. "She has provided a description of what she would like to wear, including shoes. If you could arrange for those to be brought in as soon as possible, I'd be obliged. She has a music list, but she would like you to choose one song, Joe, to be played last; anything you like. She has a list of readings, but again, she would like you to choose a poem, or a short reading, or write a speech. If you don't want to speak on the day, she asks that Hazel or Angus, or another friend, read it on your behalf. Also, you are to come up with her epitaph. No hurry for that, though, whenever you're ready." Now the director smiled at the three of them. "All pretty straightforward, as I say. We just need a date. How long do you need to prepare? I have a cancellation on Friday, otherwise it'll be the week after. We're pillar-to-post at the weekends."

"How can you have a cancellation?" Angus asked, with a touch of disgust.

The director glanced briefly at Angus and ignored him.

"Any preference?"

"I work Friday, and then go to the pub at five thirty," said Joe.

"Ah, yes." The director turned to another sheet in the file. "The wake is to be at the Ink and Feather. I have a check here, and some instructions for the landlady."

"I work on Fridays," Joe repeated.

"Most people in your position take a day off for a funeral," said the funeral director.

"Aye, they do," said Angus, and Hazel nodded at Joe.

Joe felt queasy at the thought of missing a day of work, but he nodded and the director said, "That's settled, then, Friday it is."

There were a few more formalities before they left, then Angus led them out, walking swiftly and three steps ahead.

"Wait up," said Hazel.

Angus turned and stopped, hands on hips. "Sorry, I can't stand places like that." He shuddered theatrically and then looked deliberately at Joe. "When I die, put me in the wheelie bin—the black one, not the recyclables—bag me up first, they collect on a Tuesday."

"Oh, Angus, that's grotesque!" said Hazel. "Don't listen to him, Joe, he doesn't mean it."

Angus pointed at Joe. "I do mean it. Here . . ." He stood with his arms in the air. "See if you can lift me up. I want to be sure you can get me in the bin."

Joe hesitated. He didn't normally touch people, but he put his arms round Angus and lifted. Angus was short and wiry, and though it wasn't easy, he managed to lift him right off the ground.

"Right, you're the man for the job—you can put me down now. And look, if you can't lift me on the day, lay the wheelie bin on the ground and slide me in, it might be easier."

"Angus!" Hazel hit him on the arm with her handbag. "Stop it!"

"Better that than a bloody reasonable prepayment plan. He was measuring you up for a coffin with his eyes," said Angus.

"Yes, I did notice that," said Hazel. "I will consider the wheelie bin option."

"Although," said Angus, with his hand on his chin, "our friend Joe here might get in trouble if he gets caught putting bodies in bins. On second thought, mate, don't bother."

Joe was relieved at not having to get involved in anybody's funeral but his mum's.

"Okay," he said.

## 32

### A sofa that is outdoors

On Sunday morning, Joe-Nathan made a list of jobs—including starting the swear box for Chloe—and set his alarm to go off twelve times throughout the day. This gave him one hour per task—although he allocated two hours to the woodworking—and took him all the way to seven o'clock in the evening, when he would make dinner, watch *Friends*, and go to bed.

Structure brought purpose and certainty and provided those stepping stones that got him from one end of the day to the other. He even made an adjustment to his Monday morning alarm, planning to get in to work earlier than normal, partly to make up for needing a day off for the funeral on Friday, but also because he could not wait to get to The Compass Store.

✦

Monday morning, when Joe gave the peace sign to the tree near the store entrance, he felt all the breath leave his body in one big sigh, as though he had been holding it in since Friday afternoon. He watched his feet as he stepped carefully over the uneven paving slabs and felt their familiarity soak into him through the soles of his shoes. The doors slid back and Joe walked slowly through them. Everything was about the *now*—the only thing that mattered, the present moment, within which all was well—as Joe headed north to the mosaic and faced northwest (as if he were heading home from a foreign country) and made his way to the staff-room.

The staff-room was empty and very tidy, as if the last person to be in this room had been the cleaner. Joe put his satchel in his locker and pulled his green tabard over his head, neatly Velcroing the tabs so that they were perfectly aligned. He put his lunch box in the empty fridge (which smelled slightly of Dettol) and sat down at one of the tables. He did everything slowly, feeling the value in it all. He closed his eyes and listened to the tiny sounds and non-sounds in the room. The fridge made a complaining noise and he opened his eyes, scanning the tables, appreciating the chairs neatly tucked under, the spotless surfaces, the items in the corner of the counter that people had left behind, which the cleaner had piled all in one place. His gaze moved along to the sink, the cloth that had been folded carefully and draped to dry over the shiny, curved tap. But something had tweaked his attention in the pile of things left in the corner. Among the other things—a red shirt, a book, a small umbrella—there was a white tube with purple writing on it, slightly squeezed at one end, but otherwise looking brand-new. Joe rose from his chair and tentatively approached it. It was—as he had feared—the tube of arnica cream.

Joe picked it up and wondered if it could possibly be a different tube he was holding, but no, this looked exactly the same, bent over slightly at the end just as the one he had given Charlie had been. The calming feeling that Joe had experienced since arriving in the staff-room started to recede as his thoughts intruded, trying to decide what had happened. Could Charlie have used it and then left it behind? This didn't seem likely: Charlie probably wouldn't have put it on his bruises at work; he was very secretive about them and would have waited until he got home. He must have simply left it here by mistake. As Joe's mum would have said, *Sometimes the simplest explanation is the right one*. Joe read the writing on the side of the tube: "Tradition-ally used for the relief of bruises." Joe took the tube to his locker and put it in his satchel, determined that when he saw Charlie, he would make sure he gave it to him and that Charlie put it in his pocket or his bag and not just on his chair between his legs, where it could be forgotten. And Joe would do it very privately so that Mean Charlie wouldn't be angry with him and would understand that Joe still only wanted to help.

Joe was on soup-can duty again. Setting up the cans was one of his favorite tasks, as it absorbed him fully. Still living in each moment as he did it—not thinking about the previous can and not thinking about the next—he quite surprised himself when he stood back and saw the huge and immaculate arrangement he'd produced. He was also quite surprised to see numerous customers, who were moving smoothly about like shoals of fish. One came close and reached out for a can among Joe's stack. Joe made a noise and stepped forward, holding up his hand. There was a strange moment in which the customer slowly continued to reach for a tin, without breaking eye contact with Joe, who looked back as if to plead with them not to touch. The tin of soup was carefully deposited in the customer's trolley as if it might explode and the customer walked away backward, eyeing Joe as if he were a poorly caged animal.

Joe sighed.

"Hey, looks good," said Chloe. "How you doing?"

"I'm okay," said Joe. "You are invited to my mum's funeral on Friday. Apparently, it is not proper invitations, like for a birthday party, I just need to tell you about it and you can come, but you do not have to."

"Of course I'll come. What time?"

"Three o'clock and you are invited to the wake, which is like a party, afterward, at the pub. You will get two free drinks."

"Thanks, Joe."

"And no fighting or vomiting," he said.

"Don't you know there's always a fight at a funeral?"

"Is there?" said Joe.

"I'm kidding, I'm really kidding. Don't worry, and hey, I only hit one guy and I only threw up once. It's not something I do all the time."

Chloe patted the trolley. Joe looked at his watch. It was twelve twenty-two. "Have you seen Charlie today?" he asked.

"Nope, haven't had that pleasure yet." Chloe winked and walked away.

The soup cans were all done, and Joe returned the trolley to the warehouse before heading back to the mosaic and then west, for Hugo Boss's office. The door was open, and Hugo was leaning on his elbows, staring at his screen. Joe stood there for a minute, not wanting to interrupt.

"Hi, Joe, how you feeling?" Hugo sat up straight when he saw Joe.

"I am okay."

"Can I help you? Come in, come in."

Joe took a tentative step into the office and looked at the carpet.

"What is it, Joe?"

"Is Charlie in today?"

"No, he's off."

"Is he sick?"

"It's a sick day, but nothing to worry about, nothing to do with the bleach. Are you okay, by the way? Any aftereffects from the chemical?"

"No."

"Good," said Hugo, and then he waited for Joe, who looked like he had something else to say.

"I have something for Charlie. Can you tell me where he lives?"

Hugo leaned forward sympathetically. "I'm sorry, Joe, I'm not allowed to give out personal information. He'll probably be back tomorrow, or Wednesday. Can it wait till then?"

"No," said Joe.

"I'm really sorry, but it might have to. I can't tell you where he lives. It's the rules."

"Oh. The rules."

"Can I help you with anything else?"

"You are invited to my mum's funeral on Friday. It is not proper invitations, like for a birthday party, I just need to tell you about it and you can come, but you do not have to."

"Gosh, Joe," said Hugo, standing up and making to move around his desk. "I didn't know your mum very well."

"No, but you were on her invitation list. She wrote next to your name that she greatly appreciated the way you look out for me, and your kindness."

Hugo's forehead crumpled and he put his hand to his chest. "It would be a privilege to attend. Thank you."

Joe left Hugo's office. His next task was broom duty and he

returned to the warehouse via the mosaic to collect the big two-pronged sweeper. It was satisfying to push it along and collect the dust, even more satisfying when there was something more substantial, like a bottle lid or screwed-up receipt that jostled along in the crook of the broom.

"Hey, Joe." It was Chloe again. Joe paused the sweeping. "I was thinking, on Friday, do you want me to come to your house before the funeral, you know, make sure your tie is straight and shit?"

Joe thought of the swear box he was making, which he hoped to have finished by the end of the week; Chloe really could be quite rich by the end of the year. "Yes. I am wearing a tie. Hazel said she would help but she might not do it right."

"I'm sure she'll do it just fine, but I'll come early anyway. Are you thinking about a haircut?"

Joe put his hand on his head. "No."

"I just thought if you're going to get it cut, you might want to do it before the funeral. And maybe your nails too."

Joe held his hands in front of him, balancing the arm of the broom against his stomach.

"Charlie's off sick," he said.

"So?"

"I wonder where he lives."

"Why? You going to take him a bunch of grapes or something?"

"No." Joe thought once more about explaining how he wanted to take him the arnica cream, but he knew she'd disapprove.

Chloe shrugged. "I think he lives down near the gasworks, just past that little row of shops and takeaways. Pip said she heard he has a sofa on the front lawn. What a fucking stereotype." Someone said, "Excuse me," and Chloe turned toward an old woman who was with an even older woman, words were whispered about *women's issues,* and Chloe led them away to aisle eight.

Joe smiled inwardly, picturing the opening credits of *Friends* where his favorite six characters happily rearrange themselves around a sofa that is outdoors in front of a fountain and next to a standard lamp.

Could it be true that Charlie lived in a house with a real sofa outside? Joe could barely think of anything more wonderful.

# 33

## A good price

Before he went out that night to find Charlie's house, Joe-Nathan finished his dinner, cleared his dishes, drank his tea on the bench in the garden, and consulted the yellow book. He wanted to see if his mum could give him any advice on going somewhere you have never been before and knocking on a door you have never been through.

The nearest thing to relevant advice he could find at first was under "Travel."

### WALKING

*When planning a walk make sure that you leave early enough to get home at the time you want to. Don't walk on your own in the dark. Take your satchel and make sure you have your phone*

*(charged) and enough cash to get home in a taxi if you need to.*
*Take water and a snack and wear comfortable walking shoes.*

Joe could do all these things, but they didn't particularly help ease his mind about going to Charlie's. He looked through the list of contents again and was interested in "Visiting," which he thought might help him further.

## VISITING
### *Short visit*
(not overnight—see section below if you sleep over
at someone's house)

*Arrive on time if you can. Don't be more than fifteen minutes*
*early. Try not to be late. Knock or ring the bell at the front of*
*the house, unless you have been asked to do otherwise. Take two*
*steps back from the door after you have rung the bell or knocked.*
*When they open the door, smile and say hello or introduce*
*yourself in the normal way, and wait for them to invite you in.*
*Ask if they would like you to take your shoes off (remember to*
*wear socks with no holes in, just in case!). Wait to be invited*
*to sit down, people will usually indicate where you should sit.*
*Don't put your feet on the furniture (not that you would!). Don't*
*ask for a drink unless you are very, very thirsty and in that case*
*ask for water. Always wait to be offered and don't ask for food.*
*Always ask before touching people's things or looking at their*
*bookshelves. Don't look in the fridge or inside any cupboards.*
*Don't tidy people's things for them, or rearrange their stuff. If*
*you need the toilet, ask them where it is and make sure to leave*
*the towel and sink and bathroom as you found it.*

*More difficult is knowing when to leave. If you are only*
*staying for a cup of tea and a chat, then a good rule of thumb is*
*about one hour. But don't leave suddenly if you are in the middle*
*of a conversation. If you want to leave but don't know how, say*
*something like "I really must be going," and stand up. Make*
*sure to thank them for their hospitality.*

*Depending on how you feel, you can suggest that they visit*
*you next time, but you don't have to do that.*

Joe read through these instructions and the ones on travel/walk-
ing a few times. They didn't quite answer his questions about visiting Mean Charlie. After all, he didn't know exactly where he was
going, and he hadn't been invited. He packed his satchel with what he
needed, making sure that he had the arnica. He squeezed his eyes tight
shut and his mouth moved slightly as he prayed that when Charlie
indicated where he should sit, it would be the sofa on his front lawn.

He knew where the gasworks were. The little parade of shops and
takeaway places that Chloe mentioned was where he and his mum had
got their Chinese takeaway. It was a little further away than the chip
shop, which was why they always had Chinese delivered, but still,
the top of the gasworks were visible when he'd walked down a few
streets in the right direction, and he followed that building until he
was in roughly the right area.

Joe walked under familiar trees, and then the trees became less and
less abundant and more and more unfamiliar, until there were none
at all he recognized. Everything became brick and broken pavement
and weeds pushing up between paving slabs. Some of the little front
gardens had a bit of grass, but mostly it was shingle or more paving.

The tidiest places had lots of red geraniums in lots of pots and a variety of garden gnomes and gray stone animals. There weren't many people about and he wished there were, until he saw some teenage boys and girls sitting on a wall swinging their legs, and then he wished there weren't.

He stared at his feet as he continued to walk in the direction of the gasworks, hoping that the boys and girls wouldn't speak to him. They said nothing at first, but he felt their eyes looking, and when he glanced up, one of them blew smoke in his direction.

"Stacey will give you a blow job for a fiver," one of the boys in a hoodie shouted. But a girl elbowed the hooded boy and said, "Oi, shut up." The others just laughed and Joe continued on his way with no other comment from them. He wondered what a blow job was. He'd been offered one before and said no. He should have asked his mum and was curious as to whether five pounds was a good price. Perhaps it was something she had written about in the yellow book; he'd look when he got home.

It took Joe twenty-seven minutes to get to the Chinese takeaway and he assumed Charlie's house was nearby, which meant he would need to leave by 7:45 p.m. to make sure he was home before sunset. That gave him one hour (assuming he found Charlie's house quickly), which—by his mum's guidance—was just the perfect amount of time for a cup of tea and a chat, and—of course—handing over the arnica cream.

## 34

### The words were good

Only one house in the street between the precinct and the gas-works had a couch in the front yard, but it didn't look like the one from the opening credits of *Friends*. There was something about the house and garden that made Joe-Nathan feel lonely, like he sometimes did when he looked at the things in the go-backs trolley and worried that they might feel discarded, lost, displaced. The sofa at the beginning of *Friends* was big and orange and old-fashioned; it looked well-made and regal. More than that: it was familiar and the friends looked like they were having fun around it. It was crazy because it was *outside*, but crazy in an amusing way; Joe had always dreamed about running around that sofa, sitting on the arm, sitting on the seat, standing behind it, just like Chandler or Joey or any of them.

However, the sofa in the front garden of *this* house wasn't crazy in an amusing way; Joe didn't even want to touch it. It was small and green and one of the seats was completely sunken in, as if it were the only side anyone had ever sat on; the other seat had a deep brown stain on it, which might account for no one sitting there, and one of the arms had wiry white stuffing and a spring coming out of it. Crumpled beer cans lay all around.

The grass of the lawn was unhealthy-looking with brown patches and dandelions. There was more green sprouting up through the cracks in the path leading to the house than there was in the garden itself and Joe stepped on it as he approached the door. He thought back to the yellow book, knew he had to knock and then stand back two paces, so that's what he did. He knocked, he waited, and no one came, but Joe knew that he had knocked very lightly—because the sofa had unnerved him—and it had taken him a long time to get here, so he thought it was worth another try. He knocked louder and took two steps back again.

From somewhere on the other side of the door, Joe thought he heard a slam and then grumbling. The grumbling got louder—but no more distinct—along with a shuffling sound, then a latch clicked, keys jangled, and the door opened.

In front of Joe stood a man in a vest and shorts. The vest used to be white and the man inside it was either muscly or fat (or both); Joe couldn't decide. He had a can of beer and a bored-slash-irritated expression.

"My name is Joe-Nathan," said Joe, remembering his manners. "What is your name?"

The man's expression didn't change but he held the can to his lips and tipped it back as though he were draining the last few drops, except he wasn't, he was draining a full can. When he was done, he wiped his mouth with the back of his hand and belched softly.

"Who wants to know?"

"Me. Joe-Nathan."

Although the man almost filled the frame of the door, Joe saw Charlie appear in the hallway through the space between the vested man's neck and shoulder. Charlie looked confused.

"Joe? What're you doing here?"

"Hi, Charlie, how are you feeling? Hugo Boss said you were sick today."

"Bloody lazy, not sick," said the man. "Who is this weirdo, Charlie, friend of yours from work?"

"Yeah, we work together."

"Well, invite him in," said the man. "Pour him a drink, let's get to know each other, Joe-*Nathan*. Charlie never invites his friends over."

"No, Dad," said Charlie, shaking his head quickly and looking pointedly at Joe. "What are you *doing* here?"

Joe pulled his satchel round to his front and undid the buckle, extracted the arnica cream, and held it out at arm's length. "You left this at work by accident," said Joe.

Charlie leaned past his dad to grab it from Joe, but his dad snatched it first and squinted at the side of the tube, moving his lips as he read the words, swaying slightly. "What the fuck is this?" said Charlie's dad.

"It's for Charlie's bruises," said Joe. "I saw them the other day after the bleach incident. He bruises like a peach, but I suppose you already know that, being Charlie's dad."

"Oh, you know about Charlie's bruises, do you? Think you're Florence Nightingale, eh? Well, why don't you come on in so we can all inspect them properly?" Charlie's dad stood to one side, and Joe did not want to push past him, but took a tentative step closer to the door; his politeness at accepting the invitation was held at bay by the smell of Charlie's dad (who smelled like a beer towel) and the look in his eye, which seemed partly excited and partly angry. Joe had seen the look before, possibly in a movie.

Mean Charlie pushed past his dad, came outside, and planted two hands flat on the top of Joe's chest, pushing him backward. Joe stumbled slightly on the paving but stayed on his feet. He clutched his satchel to himself, for comfort, and closed his eyes.

Mean Charlie leaned right up close to Joe's face, so that their cheeks brushed against each other, and he hissed in Joe's ear, "*Please, for God's sake go home, and don't come back here, don't come in.*" Then he pushed Joe backward again, a little less hard, and shouted, "Fuck off, you moron, you're not invited."

Charlie's dad said, in a much softer voice, "That's not very polite, Charlie. If your *friend* has come to help you with your bruises, then the least you can do is get him a drink and show him a little hospitality. Come on in, Joe-*Nathan*."

Joe stared at Charlie's dad. He understood the words, and the words were good; but his stomach told him that they were not.

"He's not my friend," said Charlie. "Go *away*."

Joe stared at Mean Charlie. He understood these words too, and these words were bad; but his stomach told him they were not. He was confused, but Joe knew Charlie better than he knew Charlie's dad and—not knowing whether to trust the words, his stomach, or the person he knew better out of the two people giving him instructions—he decided to listen to Charlie; he stepped away. He turned and adjusted his satchel so it sat comfortably on his bottom and glanced over his shoulder, feeling the sudden sting of tears behind his eyes. Charlie was already at his front door, his father growling something inaudible at his son, while Charlie squeezed awkwardly between his dad and the door and pulled it shut.

Joe thought of the yellow book. This visit, this encounter, was nothing like his mum had described. He took one more look at the sofa in the yard, and was about to turn away when he noticed the little tube of arnica cream, white and purple, lying on the ground by the doorstep.

# 35

## No negotiation required

The thought of approaching the house again made Joe-Nathan feel the same way he did when he watched people on the TV go into the cellar. But he knew that he wouldn't be able to sleep or stop thinking about that tube of arnica if he left it there on the ground. It was the same discomfort that motivated the care and pleasure he took in returning items to their rightful place in The Compass Store. He would have felt no less uncomfortable leaving a kitten or a crying child there all night.

The door to Charlie's house was closed and he didn't think it would open again; curtains were messily drawn against the front window and Joe hoped that he wouldn't be seen as he stepped onto the weedy, broken path and warily made his way toward the house and the tube of arnica once more. He bent down to retrieve it and pulled his satchel around, so he could put it inside. The instant he lifted the flap of his satchel he heard a yell, almost as if it had come from the inside of his bag. He stopped: frozen with the arnica still in his hand. As he dropped it into his satchel there was another yell, and it came not from the bag but from the house, and Joe felt the hair rise up on the back of his neck, wondered for a moment if someone was shouting at him.

The door didn't open and the shouting continued from behind it. Joe took a step back. He had to get home. Charlie had told him to after all. This place was not nice. He thought about the things that he loved at home: the awning, lovingly erected by his dad over his own back door, the calendar in the kitchen with the cats on it, and the photographs of his mum and dad at the dining table. He thought about his stamp albums and longed to wash his hands again and again so he could put another soap sticker inside, but most of all he wanted to be in his chair, in his living room, watching *Friends* on TV. He loved every episode, but he would watch "The One Where Everybody Finds Out." It was his favorite, and most comforting because it was such a relief when all the secrets were uncovered and the lies could stop and suddenly everything made sense to everyone.

He took another step backward, but then he heard his name. Not clearly, but quite loudly. He heard a gruff voice saying the exact words he had used: "*My name is Joe-Nathan. What is your name?*" and then a laugh, which turned into a brief, wet cough and then into shouting again. By now, Joe nearly had his ear pressed against the wood of the door (he didn't want his skin to actually touch it), but he still couldn't hear much; it was like the conversation he had overheard with Angus and Hazel, where he could only hear what Angus was saying, and Hazel's voice was muffled.

"*WHAT IS HE, SOME SORT OF WANNABE SOCIAL WORKER?*" Charlie's dad yelled.

"*He's hmm mm a hmm,*" was all that Joe could hear of Charlie's reply.

"*INVITING PEOPLE ROUND HERE TO POKE ABOUT IN OUR BUSINESS.*"

"*I mm hmm mmhmm.*" Charlie's words came as if shouted from under a pillow.

"*WELL, HOW DID HE KNOW WHERE WE LIVE, THEN?*"

Again, Charlie's reply was inaudible. And then the actual words stopped and Joe heard a crash and an almighty *oof*. Then there was the clatter of feet on stairs and a thump and another *oof* as if someone had been kicked and the air had left them all in one go.

Joe took several steps backward and stumbled, not quite falling, then he turned and walked away quickly, watching his feet, only looking up now and then to check where he was and cross the road.

He saw the teenagers, still on the wall, and he watched their gaze follow him as he marched along the other side of the road.

"In a hurry?" one of them shouted.

"Stacey says you can have that blow job for free now, if you're still interested." Then he heard the clatter of their laughter.

How could the blow job have dropped from five pounds to free in such a short time frame? Why was the price so variable from the same source? Joe knew that the cost of a thing could vary wildly depending on who was selling it; he knew that much from working at The Compass Store. But from five pounds to free from the same seller, with no negotiation required! That was unusual.

The journey home was four minutes faster than the journey out to Charlie's place and Joe was sweating. He took off all his clothes and put them in the laundry basket, then showered and put on clean, pressed pajamas and his slippers. Whenever he shut his eyes he saw that poor sofa in Charlie's front garden, but what he couldn't stop hearing was what sounded like someone being pushed down the stairs and being kicked when they got to the bottom. Poor Charlie, poor Charlie, poor Charlie. To think of all the bruises he would have now, on top of the ones he already had from the bleach incident. Joe wasn't even sure that arnica would be any help now.

If this had happened to Joe, then his mum would have taken him to the hospital. Joe hoped for a moment that Charlie's dad would do the same. But he knew—Joe knew—that he wouldn't. Joe knew it wasn't an accident. He *knew*, and it worried him like nothing else ever had—that Charlie and his dad were fighting. Joe remembered what Chloe had said about fighting, because it had been such a simple rule: if someone wants to fight you, you hit back. Was Charlie hitting back? He was very strong (he had good muscles). Who had fallen? Who had said *oof*?

Joe recalled a section in the yellow book under the heading "Fighting," so he got it out to take a look and see what his mum had to say about it. And while he was there, he would look and see if she had written anything about blow jobs.

# 36
## Fighting, according to Janet

**FIGHTING**

*Physical and verbal fights*

Physical (for verbal fights, see the next section)

*In an ideal world, nobody should be fighting with anyone. But this is not always an ideal world. I hope you never find yourself in a physical fight, but I am writing this just in case you do. I'm not sure how to advise you, because situations vary so much, all I can do is tell you what I think. If someone attacks you, try to remove yourself from the situation.*

*Rules of thumb: walk away from a fight, it takes courage. Avoid violence, that's wise. If you are attacked, try to shield yourself.*

*It takes courage to walk away when someone tries to fight you, because it makes them feel like they have won and they may say things to try and make you stay and fight back, especially if they think they can beat you or they want to hurt you. Don't listen to them, walk away, that is the wise thing to do. If you <u>can't</u> get away, then protect yourself: shield your face and eyes and shield your body. If you can call for help, do that. Call 999. If you can't shield yourself and you cannot get away, then you need to hit back. And if you have to hit back, then do it as hard as you can.*

*PS. (I add this several months after I wrote the rest.) When Chloe punched the man in the pub, she did it to defend you. I do not think you should ever hit anyone in the same way, but I do admire anyone who tries to protect someone who is being bullied or attacked. That doesn't mean that you need to fight or hit anyone in order to defend those who need help, but it does mean that when you know someone is being hurt, you should help in some way and not just ignore it. That man in the pub spoke badly to you (verbal) and Chloe hit him (physical) and while I don't condone or encourage violence, I do recognize when defense comes from the heart, and there is a lot to be said for that.*

Fighting, according to Janet, was quite different to Chloe's advice. Chloe missed out all the bits about walking away, avoidance, and shielding and had jumped straight to the part where you hit back as hard as you can. Joe wondered whether he should mention this to Chloe, in order to keep her safe in future fight-related situations.

He thought about Charlie and his dad fighting in their house. It would have been difficult to walk away because they both lived there and even if one of them *did* walk away, they'd have to go back for their dinner and to sleep. So, did that mean they had to resort to just hitting each other as hard as they could? Joe reread his mother's words and wondered what Charlie would have to say about them.

He found nothing in her books about blow jobs.

## 37

### Always more likely to be wrong than right

The next morning at work, Pip, who was wearing very high heels, tottered over to Joe-Nathan as he folded T-shirts using the magic shirt folder.

"Hugo says I can start my checkout training in a couple of weeks. We're doing it at the same time. We could have started sooner, but Hugo says you've got too many things in your life to adjust to at the moment, so he's delayed it a bit."

"Hugo told me." Chloe had told Joe to watch Pip when she talked, told him to notice how pink her face went whenever she talked about Hugo and to notice how she mentioned Hugo as often as she could.

"Aren't you excited for it, though?" she asked breathlessly. "I like the buttons and things on the till. Does that make me weird?"

"I like the buttons too."

"Well, if we're both weird, then between us it's normal, right?"

"I do not know."

"Anyway, I don't care." Pip waved her hand as if she was wasting her time with this conversation and had more important things to think about. From behind her back, she pulled a piece of paper. "Now, in the pub we talked about our specialist subjects, for quiz night? You're good on *Friends* and woodworking, Chloe knows about stuff from the eighties and literature, and I'm okay with pop music, TV, and fashion. So, I've drawn up a study list, because I think there's gaps in our general knowledge."

"I have never heard a woodworking question on a quiz show," said Joe, in agreement.

"Exactly, but still, if there's a woodworking question in *this* quiz, you might be the only one who knows the answer. So, it could be an advantage. Anyway, I have a plan. I know a man on the inside." Pip winked hard.

"A man on the inside of what?" Joe asked. Pip went very pink indeed.

"Never mind," she said.

She turned the paper so that Joe could see it. "I've listed some things that might help us. I thought if we all study the same sheet, then at least one of us will remember something. I've got capital cities, kings and queens of England in the right order, first lines of famous books, and things like how far the moon is from Earth."

"384,400 kilometers," said Joe.

"Oh, yes, that's right!" said Pip, checking out what she had typed on the page. "You didn't mention that on Friday!"

"The distance between the moon and Earth isn't a specialist subject. It is just a fact," said Joe.

"But knowing facts is very useful," Pip said, with a serious expression. "I've also listed the planets in order . . ."

"I know them too," said Joe.

"And flags," said Pip. "Any good with flags?"

"No."

"Me neither. I don't have a color printer, so I've drawn them—here, look—and colored them in by hand and labeled them by country."

Joe nodded.

"I'm going to slot this into the side of your locker, okay? Don't forget to take it home to study!" Pip wagged her finger and adopted something like a stern teacher's voice and expression. Joe watched her trot away in an impractical flurry of skirt and shoes. "See ya later, Joe-Joe," she called out down the aisle. A mother passed by with her child strapped into the front of a trolley and the toddler banged the handle with a plastic giraffe and shouted, *Joe, Joe, Joe, Joe.*

Joe returned to folding T-shirts and lost himself in the perfect pile he was creating. He folded them in order according to color and the result was a beautiful rainbow of gradually darker greens that turned into blues, then purples and pinks, then oranges, then yellows. He stacked them neatly on the T-shirt table and stood beside them. A woman with a young son stood beside him and smiled; he assumed that they too were admiring the satisfying color order and neat edges in front of them. The boy reached out and pulled a pink T-shirt from the middle of the stack, dragging the other T-shirts along with it, and some fell onto the floor.

"Oh, don't do that," said the lady kindly to her son, and she smiled at Joe as if something nice had just happened, when in fact something horrible had. She stooped to pick up what had fallen and folded a pink T-shirt haphazardly, placing it on top of the others; she patted it, then walked casually away, holding the boy's hand.

"Not your tidiest work," said Chloe, coming up beside him and looking at the disarray.

"I did not do this," said Joe.

"I know, I saw the whole thing."

"The customer is always right," said Joe sadly.

"Yes, but the customer is not *always* right in the head, and they're not *always* fucking respectful." Chloe gathered up the T-shirts in her arms. "Come on, I'll help you fold these again, but once they're on the table, walk away fast before you see anyone mess it up."

Chloe handed the shirts to Joe one at a time and he placed them in the magic folder and flipped the sides until he had another beautiful pile. They worked in silence until Chloe said, "Anything on your mind?"

"Have you seen Charlie today? Is he off sick again?" Joe reached out for the next T-shirt, but Chloe paused and crossed her arms, still clutching the garment.

"You're very concerned with Charlie's health lately. Don't worry about it. He's probably taking a couple of sickies and—well—doing whatever it is he does when he's not here. I don't really understand why you're so hung up about him. He's *mean*, he's not your friend, and he wouldn't put you out if he found you on fire."

"But what if you are wrong?"

"About what?" Chloe handed Joe the T-shirt.

"About Charlie. What if he is not as bad as you think? What if he has got reasons to be mean? What if he is not happy?"

"Happy? Who's fucking happy? Being unhappy is not a reason for being mean to other people, it's no excuse."

"What if he needs help?"

"Help with what? I mean, yeah, the guy could use some work on his social skills. But *whatever* is going on with Charlie, it's got nothing to do with you; it's not your job. Let someone else help him. Let him help his fucking self. *You*, my friend, are not the man to help him."

"But what if you are wrong?"

"You think *you* can help him?" Chloe scoffed.

"He said I could not." Joe shrugged.

"You *asked* him?" Her face creased.

"And you are also saying that I cannot help him."

"Look, whatever help that idiot needs, it's not the kind of help you can give him."

"But what if you are *wrong*?" Joe asked yet again.

"Listen, no offense, but between the two of us—in interpreting someone like Charlie?—you are always more likely to be wrong than me, always more likely to be wrong than right."

"Why?"

But Chloe didn't answer his question. She looked angry and started to walk away. But before she was out of earshot, she shouted, "Cut your nails and get in touch with your hairdresser. You need a haircut."

And Joe thought to himself how impossible that was, because his mum had always cut his hair for him.

## 38

### The trees didn't worry

The next morning, Joe-Nathan felt the presence of his mum's funeral rolling toward him from the end of the week and knew that he—and it—would collide soon. Today was Wednesday. No funeral today, no funeral tomorrow, but there would be a funeral the day after that. Joe swallowed; there was something stuck in his throat. He swallowed again to try to get rid of it, but it wouldn't go away. What if the thing stuck in his throat got bigger and he couldn't breathe? His breath came quicker and he worried that he would die here on the path on the way to work and the cars would drive past and not stop.

He looked up into the trees and focused on the smaller branches at the top, the ones that moved in a breeze he couldn't feel down on the ground. He listened as intently as he could and imagined that he could hear the trees breathing—calmly, slowly (the trees didn't worry about the end of the week; the trees didn't think about funerals)—and he tried to replicate that imagined rhythm. Soon he saw the tree that looked like it was waving and he waved back. Then the tree that gave him the cool rock-star sign appeared and he gave the rock-star sign back. And finally—mercifully—the tree that communicated peace rose into view and Joe gave the peace sign and was at ease again. He took a couple of long strides and entered The Compass Store.

Two colleagues that Joe rarely worked with or spoke to were on the shop floor, polishing the shiny, white cosmetics counter. As he walked past, they paused in what they were doing, stopped talking, and looked him up and down. The bigger one shook his head and the smaller one laughed nervously. Joe wondered why. He didn't stop to ask; he never spoke to anyone before he'd reached the staff-room and done everything he needed to do in there. But he looked down at his footwear and saw that he had unthinkingly worn his funeral shoes on the wrong day with the wrong trousers: pastel pedal pushers (which were a little on the tight side). His shoes were black and so shiny they looked wet, and they seemed too big against his white legs. He recalled very distinctly his mum's advice on fashion and knew that he should never have paired formal footwear with something summery. He also checked his top in case he had spilled food on himself at breakfast: porridge stains on a black T-shirt were very unpleasant. But no, there was nothing obviously wrong above his waist.

He almost bumped into Pamela as he was going through the staff-room door and she was coming out, but he managed to take a large step back before she had a chance to make contact. She gasped when she saw him, and Joe wondered if she was as relieved as he was that they had not touched. She opened her mouth as if to say something, but he quickly entered the staff-room and walked straight to his locker. He'd only been in the room a few seconds when a cruel hoot of ridicule pierced the quiet from the other end of the room.

"The fucking state of you, man!" Owen was with two other young men that Joe didn't recognize and they all stared and laughed at him. Owen stood up instantly and came toward Joe, holding his phone out in front of him. It made the shutter sound of a camera at first and Owen tried not to laugh as he clicked it repeatedly.

"Wait a minute." He was laugh-talking. "Let me get this on video. What the hell? Did a blind person give you a makeover?" He turned and walked away from Joe, stopping to look at the footage he'd just taken. "Wait till Charlie sees this, oh man," he said to the others. "He's gonna piss himself."

## 39

### Under his skin

Charlie was late to work but he hadn't been in for two days, so turning up at all was probably a bonus. He yawned and looked at his watch; the time did nothing to motivate him. In his back pocket his phone pinged repeatedly and he smirked when he noticed a flurry of photos from Owen because it would be something rude or stupid. Owen would do anything to get Charlie to like him, and that was slightly nauseating, but that didn't mean that the photos and videos he sent wouldn't make him laugh, because they usually did. As the pictures and a clip opened on his phone, he stopped to flick through them. Below them was a message from Owen:

Look at this muppet, think he's trying to reinvent himself. Get your arse into work, maybe have some fun with him today!!!!!!!?

Charlie put his phone in his back pocket and the pictures did what the clock had failed to do: quickened his pace. Joe brought out a frustration in him that Charlie couldn't contain or explain. Every time he spoke to the man he wanted to lash out. He had a face he wanted to punch; he couldn't comprehend how a person could have so many obvious problems and get away with seeming so happy. He was like a fucking baby in a grown man's body, and he was stupid, stupid, *stupid*. So why, *why*, did the guy get under his skin?

Charlie entered The Compass Store like a man on a mission, walking down the aisles toward the staff-room with the focused determination of an assassin. He passed Pip in aisle fifteen. She was reorganizing the cards; people did like to pick up the cards and then return them to the wrong section, and who wanted to accidentally pick up a *"sorry you're leaving"* card when what they wanted was a *"get well soon"* card?

"Hey, Charlie, you feeling better? Hugo says you've been away for . . ." Pip's voice faded as she realized he had no intention of stopping.

He was a few paces from the staff-room when he crashed into Joe, who was pushing a go-backs trolley in the opposite direction.

"Charlie!" was all Joe managed before Charlie grabbed him by his arm and shoved his trolley to one side. He pulled Joe along the short empty corridor that linked the staff-room and the storeroom to the public part of the shop, gripping him tightly.

"Charlie, what? You're hurting me . . . ," said Joe, too shocked to be able to fully register being touched by him. Charlie looked over his shoulder, back toward the staff-room. He let go of Joe's arm and pushed him ahead. Joe took a few stumbling steps, almost tripping over his glistening shoes, which seemed so much longer than his casual shoes, and then broke into a short-paced jog, so that Charlie wouldn't push him or grab him again; he held on to his sore arm where Charlie had squeezed it so tightly.

"What the absolute fuck were you thinking?" Charlie hissed, looking over his shoulder yet again.

"I'm sorry," said Joe. "I did not mean to upset you, I just wanted you to have the arnica. I should not have come to your house."

"Not *that*," said Charlie. "I'm talking about your fucking fashion sense. You look like you've come to a fancy dress party dressed as three different people."

Joe said nothing. Charlie was really angry, and maybe it was that that stopped Joe asking which three people he meant.

Joe continued to trot slightly ahead of Charlie in short steps as if his ankles were tied together; Charlie walked fiercely behind him. They proceeded back down aisle fifteen and Pip turned to them both, a stack of misplaced cards in her hands. She smiled instinctively when she saw the two boys, but her smile slipped like the sentiments of the cards she was rearranging: from a sunny, bright, "*happy birthday*" type smile to "*deepest sympathy*," in a flash.

"Are you okay?" she said to Joe, but she turned almost 180 degrees as they whizzed past her wordlessly. When they got to the end of the aisle, Charlie paused, reached up, and grabbed a box from a shelf, and then they both disappeared around the corner. Pip tucked the cards under her arm and fished in her jeans pocket for her phone. Her finger hovered over Hugo's phone number, but much as her instinct told her to message him, a stronger instinct diverted her elsewhere. She looked up Chloe's number and texted:

Are you in today? Just seen Charlie and Joe. Don't know what's happening but Joe looks really upset and Charlie looks furious. You should see Joe, he looks awful. Pip x

# 40
## The only one smiling

Chloe's shift had technically started half an hour ago, but if she walked into the store with enough confidence and didn't bump into Hugo, then she could probably get away with it. And *if* she could get away with it, she thought, then maybe she should do it every day, and accept the rap if she got caught now and then. Her dad always parked without paying for a ticket and said he got a fine on average every two years, which was still cheaper than paying every time he parked. Same principle, Chloe thought, and if it worked for him, why shouldn't she?

She looked at her watch and showed the world how little she cared by slowing her step and stretching her arms high above her head.

In her back pocket, her phone pinged. She stopped walking altogether, because she *really* didn't care how late she was and this study in casual nonchalance amused her. She swiped the screen and read

Pip's text. *"Fuck!"* she said, like the night watchman who had fallen asleep while the burglars broke in. Chloe instantly broke into a run, her feet barely touching the ground, trying to slide her phone back into her pocket as she did so.

By the time she arrived at work, four minutes later, Chloe was sweating and she leaned forward, hands on her knees, trying to breathe. She had never run so fast in her life, except that time she and some friends had stolen beer from the corner shop and got chased by the owner. But she hadn't felt like this. Back then, she and her friends had hidden inside the old coal bunker, trying not laugh and watching Mr. Singer turning in circles, *literally* scratching his head, trying to work out where they'd gone.

Chloe got her phone out of her back pocket again and texted Pip: Where are you?

Pip replied immediately: aisle 15, N-W.

Chloe trotted toward the mosaic, pulling her crumpled green tabard from her bag and yanking it quickly over her head. When she got to Pip, Pip was wide-eyed and serious.

"Where did they go?" Chloe asked, looking up and down the aisle.

"That direction." Pip pointed. "But I don't know where they went after that. Charlie was like a prison guard, frog-marching Joe, and Joe looked terrified. He looked *terrible*. He looked like a prisoner of war! Charlie took something off the shelf, not sure what it was. Whatever was going on, Joe didn't like it, and I remembered what you said about Charlie being really mean to him. And in the staff-room I heard Owen and all that laughing about Joe, taking the mickey out of him."

"Why didn't you follow them?" Chloe said.

"I didn't think of it." Pip faltered at the irritation in Chloe's expression. "I was going to go see Hugo . . ."

"Jesus," Chloe tutted.

"What?" said Pip. But Chloe just shook her head.

"But I didn't tell Hugo—I messaged *you* because you look out for Joe and I thought you might be around. I mean, I don't think Charlie would really hurt Joe." Pip's forehead creased. "He wouldn't, would he?"

Chloe was already walking in the direction the boys had gone and Pip watched her go. Pip stood completely still, holding the cards for a full minute before returning to her task, preoccupied briefly by guilt about Joe and the way she seemed to have upset Chloe. And then she was preoccupied by thoughts of Hugo.

Chloe walked fast, assuming that she wouldn't find Charlie and Joe out in the open, but hidden somewhere, in the shower room or the men's loos. What was Charlie thinking? What was he planning? She'd long been aware of his gibes and nasty comments toward Joe, but they'd always been subtle insomuch as other members of staff weren't always conscious of it. She assumed that Hugo knew something was going on, but he was too soft to call it bullying and projected his well-meaning nature onto others. Hugo seemed to find it hard to see nastiness as a real problem, perhaps because he couldn't imagine inflicting it himself. Whatever the reason, Chloe thought he was too quick to give the benefit of the doubt.

She walked with purpose and no interest in helping the customers who held items toward her, their mouths opening to ask a question and shutting again before the words came out when she passed them without acknowledgment.

As she neared the vicinity of the toilets and shower room, Chloe heard urgent banter; the words were indistinct, but clearly someone was trying to insist on something, and someone else was resisting. She shoved the door of the shower room, but it was locked. She pressed her ear against it, but heard nothing from inside. She pushed open the men's toilet door, only to see a shocked customer holding out the waistband of his trousers and peering down the front of them.

"Hey!" he said, and Chloe let the door fall shut.

Suddenly the voices she had heard were back, and now they were raised.

"No, Charlie! Stop! No more. I do not understand why you are doing this to me." Joe sounded close to tears, or already crying.

"And if you tell anyone who did this to you, my god, I will make you wish you hadn't." Mean Charlie's voice was cruelly pointed; if his words had been written and not spoken, then the nib of the pencil would have snapped off against the page.

Chloe followed her ears to a storeroom door that stocked the hazard signs and seasonal promotional items that were displayed around the store at holidays: Halloween, Easter, Christmas, Valentine's Day, and so on. She reached out for the handle, but the door slammed open before she touched it and a brisk, angry-looking Charlie emerged, red in the face and brushing his hands together. He and Chloe were unexpectedly almost nose-to-nose, and Charlie veered sideways.

"What the fuck have you done?" Chloe said, following his swerve and meeting him practically nose-to-nose again.

"None of your fucking business, you nosy slut. Get out of my way." Charlie shoved past her and stormed off. Chloe opened the store-cupboard door and took in the sight before her in one flash: Joe stood in the middle of the floor between the stacks (a laughing leprechaun was in the background, promoting St. Patrick's Day offers). Around his feet and on his shoulders, drifting down his front, were clumps of his dark hair, and his face was red and wet with tears. Discarded on the floor in front of him was an electric shaver and Joe's head was completely bald except for a dark shadow of stubble. Chloe froze for a moment, then let the door swing shut, leaving Joe alone while she flew after Charlie. She ran at him and jumped on his back, yelling out as she did so, and Charlie grunted in surprise.

"Get off me, you mad cow," he said, and he swung round to try to throw her off, but when that didn't work, he prized her arms off and backed away with a face that might be mistaken for someone with a wasp in his mouth.

Chloe was as persistent as a fly at a garden party and came at him, her right arm outstretched. She slapped him using the leverage of her whole body, throwing her weight behind it so that it was more like a punch to his face; Charlie's head snapped to one side. She launched herself at him, thumping his chest, and Charlie grabbed her round the waist, ducking his head down beside his arms so that she couldn't get to him, but she pounded on his back and when it felt like she wasn't hurting him enough, she started pinching his skin under his T-shirt, as hard as she could.

Charlie screamed and brought her down to the floor, landing on top of her. He rolled off immediately, but before he could get up, Chloe jumped on him, straddled him, and thumped at any part of him she could reach. Customers gathered round and some filmed the fight on their phones. One lady pleaded ineffectually for the fighting to stop.

Hugo appeared and didn't hesitate to grab Chloe's hands as Charlie shielded his face with his arms.

"Kids, kids, what's going on here?" Hugo's voice was more suited to scolding children arguing over an ice cream, but nevertheless, Chloe's flailing stopped and she allowed Hugo to heft her to her feet. Her face was red and strands of her hair stuck wildly to her face. Her hands left Charlie, but her eyes never did and they pierced him with hatred. Charlie uncrossed his arms and likewise met her gaze with vitriol. He winced as he put a hand on the ground and pushed himself up to standing.

Joe stood in the open doorway of the storeroom, tearstained and sniffing.

Pip appeared and stood beside Hugo, concern etched around her eyes.

"Can someone please explain what's going on?" Hugo looked from Charlie to Chloe and back again.

"What's the point?" said Chloe, her eyes still boring into Charlie's. "It's not like you'll actually do anything about it."

"I beg your pardon? What's that supposed to mean, young lady?" Hugo still sounded as though he was chastising his own children.

"Charlie's a bastard, and you're soft as shit," said Chloe.

"Chloe!" said Pip, putting a hand on Hugo's shoulder.

"Oh, fuck off, Pip," Chloe spat, but reddened in an instant. She looked at Hugo. "It doesn't necessarily make you a bad person, except it means you might let bad things happen and not do anything about them."

Charlie's cheeks puffed up and he blew out hard, shaking his head.

"Charlie?" Hugo said. He patted Pip's hand; she withdrew it and walked over toward the storeroom.

Charlie broke his gaze with Chloe and looked at the customers that were still mingling about; Hugo seemed suddenly aware of them too. "Show's over, folks, move along please. Sorry about this." Hugo laughed, uncomfortably. "Lovers' quarrel probably."

"What the *fuck*? I wouldn't touch him with a barge pole." Chloe voice was two octaves higher than usual. "And also, Hugo, totally inappropriate."

"Oh my gosh, you're right, I'm sorry, Chloe. Listen, what *is* going on here?"

Chloe looked over at the storeroom and pointed at Joe, who wiped his sleeve across his nose; Pip took a tissue from her sleeve and handed it to him. Chloe wiped her arm across her eyes where tears of frustration felt like they were diluting her utter loathing of bullying in general and Charlie in particular.

"I think the three of you had better come to my office so we can talk in private," said Hugo. "Pip, be a love and bring us a pot of tea, so we can discuss this like adults."

Pip puffed up at the word *love*. She was the only one smiling.

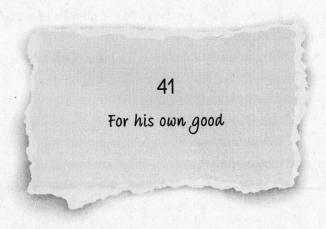

# 41

## For his own good

"I guess I'm old-fashioned, but I don't think boys should be fighting with girls," said Hugo.

All was quiet for a few moments, and then Joe-Nathan said, "Nobody should be fighting with anyone, that's what my mum said."

Hugo nodded with his mouth downturned and his eyebrows raised. "Yes, Joe, and actually I think she was just right about that." He sighed sadly and looked at the three young people sitting in his office. "Who wants to start? Who can tell me what this is all about?"

Hugo's question was met with silence.

"If you don't talk to me, I'm going to have to get HR involved, and I don't want to do that."

Chloe exhaled long and loudly, then she locked eyes with Hugo. "Charlie's bullying Joe," she said.

Charlie threw his hands in the air and brought them down with a slap on his thighs. "Bullying? What the hell? No, I'm not!"

"Don't worry, Charlie," Chloe said in a kindly tone. "Hugo won't do anything about it. Maybe he'll give you a slap on the wrist, maybe he'll send you to bed without any tea, but there won't be any proper punishment."

"Uh, thank you, Chloe, that's quite enough," Hugo said. She crossed her arms and looked at him challengingly.

"Bullying is a really serious accusation," said Hugo.

"I know," said Chloe.

Charlie continued to shake his head, his lips pursed tight.

Hugo looked at Joe, who stared at his hands in his lap. "Is Charlie bullying you, Joe?"

"I . . ." Joe looked at Chloe and then he looked at Charlie. "I do not know."

Hugo grimaced slightly. He addressed Chloe. "And what makes you feel that Joe is being bullied?" he said.

"Well, for starters, Charlie just shaved all the hair off Joe's head in the store cupboard."

"Did you?" Hugo sat bolt upright and stared in disbelief at Charlie. Charlie cleared his throat. "Yes."

"Did you *want* him to shave your head, Joe?"

"Um." Joe turned to look at Charlie and once more—like on the day of the bleach accident—he momentarily had a sensation that he was looking at his own eyes in the mirror. Charlie broke eye contact first and held his head in his hands. "Well," said Joe, looking at Hugo now. "No, I did not want him to shave my head. I asked him to stop."

"Charlie!" said Hugo. "What on earth . . . ?"

"He needed it." Charlie breathed the words into his hands.

"Pardon?"

Charlie looked up, dry-eyed, stubborn. "I said *he needed it.*"

"Un-fucking-believable," Chloe said.

"Chloe . . . ," said Hugo, in response to her language.

"He needed a bloody haircut, what can I say?" said Charlie, rounding on her.

"*Agreed*," said Chloe, "but not by you in a dark room against his will."

"I can't believe this," said Hugo. "If a person doesn't want you to cut their hair, you can't just forcibly cut it off. Please don't tell me you think that's okay."

"Was for his own good," Charlie mumbled.

"I'm sorry, but you're going to have to speak up," said Hugo.

"*I SAID IT WAS FOR HIS OWN FUCKING GOOD!*" Charlie shouted so loudly that Hugo appeared to be thrown into the back of his chair by the blast.

"Charlie, this is no good, no good at all." Hugo put his hand to his forehead and moved some papers on his desk. He opened a desk drawer as if he hoped to find something helpful in there, but, finding nothing, he shut it again.

"So," said Chloe, her mouth twisted. "What are you going to do, Hugo? Tell Charlie he's been a naughty boy and not let him have any dessert after his dinner?"

"Well, I wouldn't call it bullying exactly," said Hugo.

"Fuck sake," said Chloe, closing her eyes.

Hugo ignored Chloe and stared sadly at Charlie. It was almost possible to hear the cliché in Hugo's expression: *You've let me down, but worse than that, you've let yourself down.*

"I think it's assault, Charlie. I'm sorry, but you've left me with no choice. I'll be speaking to you privately in a moment."

Charlie got to his feet and tucked his shirt in where Chloe had pulled it loose during their fight. "Don't bother, I know what's coming."

"I need to speak to you formally," Hugo continued.

But Charlie had already turned the handle of the office door and was gone before Hugo could say another word.

As the door swung shut, Hugo's office fell into the sort of silence that presses on your eardrums and makes you feel as though you've been pushed up against a wall. It was the kind of silence a person might try to keep if they were hiding from someone who wanted to hurt them, Joe thought. Although he needed to take a deep breath, he was too scared, in case he made a noise and something bad happened. Something *else* that was bad.

This day had not gone well at all, what with the thing that seemed to be stuck in his throat on the way to work; the way Owen had laughed and photographed him; Charlie grabbing his arm so hard and taking him to that cupboard that was too, too dark, until Charlie found the light switch; the way it felt to have a person other than his mum touch his head. Horrible. *Horrible.* The buzz of the shaver and the way it vibrated on his skull (which frightened him in the same way he was frightened for the eggs in the supermarket trolley when it rolled over rough ground); the way his hair fell from his head and landed in soft clumps all over him (how would he clean himself up at work afterward? Would he have to get in the shower again and wear strange clothes?); the way Chloe had looked at him when she opened the storeroom door: a look that didn't match any of the pictures on his expressions chart, a look he didn't think he'd ever seen before, what did it mean? And then the fight. Poor Chloe, being called a slut; that was a bad word. Poor Charlie, being hit all over again; now there would be bruises upon bruises upon bruises. And now Charlie had left and Joe wasn't completely sure why.

But Chloe was smiling at him, so that was one good thing.

Hugo stared at his office door and Joe noticed that he hadn't blinked in a long time.

Joe ran his hand over his head. He had wondered what Hugo's head must feel like with that short fuzz all over, and he hadn't imagined it being very nice. But Joe's head felt really nice: slightly rougher than velvet and just as addictive to the touch.

Joe began to get used to the heavy silence in the room, even though it had only been going a minute.

"Wow," Chloe said.

The word seemed to break Hugo's fixation on the door, and he blinked. He opened his mouth as if to speak but his tongue just clicked against the roof of his mouth.

There was a knock at the door and Pip came in with a pot of tea and five cups and milk and little packets of sweetener on a tray.

"Sorry it took so long," she said, smiling at Hugo with newly applied lipstick.

"Fine, fine, just set it down here," Hugo said, pushing papers and a folder to one side, making room.

Pip smiled at Joe as she put the things on the table and said, "I like your new haircut."

# 42

## Too simple

Hugo suggested that Joe-Nathan go home to wash the bits of hair off himself and change his clothes, and Chloe agreed to go with him. Knowing that Joe would be keen to get back to work and return to normal, Hugo asked them to come back as soon as Joe had washed and changed and not to delay or do anything else. Joe was reluctant to leave work—it was yet another thing that threw this Wednesday out of kilter—but the bits of hair were itching like crazy, so he was pleased at the prospect of washing it off.

While Joe was in the shower, Chloe looked round his bedroom.

"Don't touch," he had said, just before he left the room to go to the bathroom, when he saw her reach out to pick up a large paperweight with a dandelion clock head inside it. "*Anything,*" he clarified.

"I won't!" Chloe held her hands in the air—as if to demonstrate her innocence to the police—and then stuffed them into the tight pockets of her jeans to remove the temptation to touch. She wandered from shelf to shelf and item to item as if she were looking at artifacts in a museum. Joe's books were organized according to color in an undulating rainbow effect as the black and dark blues turned to light blue and then into turquoise and green, then to light green, yellow, and white, much the same as he organized the T-shirts at The Compass. She read the words on the book spines (none of which were broken) and saw none that she had read.

Chloe withdrew a hand from a pocket and opened Joe's wardrobe door, pausing (as she realized that she was going against his wishes) to make sure she could still hear water running in the shower. His clothes were pressed and carefully hung with gaps between each item. She quietly closed the wardrobe door and turned, looked at his chest of drawers, and had no doubt that the clothes inside would be as tidy and organized as everything else she could see. She wandered over to his desk and admired his pen pot, with one of each color pen; an in tray and an out tray with just a few papers in each; a notebook carefully squared away in the far corner; and two large, identical photo albums sat side by side at the front of his desk. She wondered if there were baby photos inside and glanced toward the bedroom door, listening again for running water. She carefully lifted the cover and then a few of the pages, noting row upon row of Imperial Leather soap stickers.

"What the . . . ?" she mumbled to herself. She closed the first album and opened the next one, saw the single Imperial Leather soap sticker in the top left corner and frowned.

Chloe heard the bathroom door open and quickly closed the album and leapt across the room to the bed. She jumped on it and sat cross-legged, trying to give the impression that she'd been there the whole time.

Joe stood in the doorway of his bedroom with a huge pink towel wrapped round him, under his arms and falling almost to his ankles. "I told you not to touch anything," he said.

"I . . ." Chloe faltered, wondering what she had left out of place; how could he tell?

"You are touching my bed, you are crinkling the cover," he said.

"Oh, right!" Chloe got off the bed and started to straighten it out.

"I will do it. You will do it wrong," said Joe, without a hint of criticism. "And please do not look while I get dressed."

"Course," said Chloe, and she went and sat on the landing at the top step of the stairs, looking at her fingernails.

A few minutes later, Joe appeared, dressed and slightly pink-faced from the shower.

"You know what?" said Chloe, standing up. "Pip's right, that haircut does actually suit you. Not everyone can pull off a buzz cut." She reached out to touch the side of Joe's head, but he ducked out of the way with a squeal. "Sorry," she said, "it's just very, very short just there on the side. How did he get so close to your head? I can see your scalp." She tutted.

"Why did Charlie just walk out?" said Joe.

"He's been fired," said Chloe, frowning. "You were there."

"But fired for how long?"

"For like, forever, I guess," she said.

Joe didn't speak but looked at Chloe with his mouth ajar.

Chloe's eyes widened and she shook her head slightly. "Hello! I think the words you're looking for are *thank you*."

"Thank you for what?" Joe asked.

Chloe sighed and crossed her arms. "For getting rid of your bully for you. For making work easier for you because Charlie won't be there giving you a hard time."

"Do you think he bullied me?"

"*Yes*," said Chloe. "I couldn't believe that, when you said it in Hugo's office, that you 'didn't know' if Charlie was bullying you or not. How could you not know? Isn't it obvious? And Hugo said it was assault, him cutting your hair, so you know. You get it, right?"

"No."

"Even before cutting your hair against your will, he belittled you and said things to make you feel bad."

"Did he do that to you too?"

"No."

"He called you a slut and he said other horrible things sometimes. He called you a mad cow."

"But he didn't bully *me*."

"I don't understand the difference."

Chloe opened her mouth to speak. Charlie had been bullying Joe for ages, she was in no doubt of that, but Joe was once again blurring the edges on something she had thought of as completely clear and in focus.

"It's different for me, because I'm not . . ." Chloe stopped.

Joe waited for a while before prompting her, "Not what?"

"Because you're . . . different . . . Joe, he picks on you because of that and that makes it bullying."

"You're different," said Joe.

"But you're disabled," said Chloe, wincing after the words had left her mouth. "He says things like 'You're not as stupid as you look,'" she added, feeling very uncomfortable.

"That is a compliment," said Joe, "because I do look really stupid."

"And he also said once that if you were the last man on the face of the earth, then I wouldn't go out for a drink with you, which was mean."

"Yes, but you had said that to him first. You told *him* you would not go out with him if he was the last man on earth. But that was worse, because you did go out for a drink with me and not him."

"It's different when I say it to Charlie."

"Why?"

Chloe didn't answer.

"Are you bullying Charlie?" Joe asked.

"God, *no*. For fuck's sake, Joe, you're making this conversation impossible."

Neither spoke for a minute.

"Sorry," Joe said eventually.

"Look, I know what I'm talking about," said Chloe, looking very definitely as if she wasn't quite sure what she was talking about at all. "And I'll tell you for absolute certain, Charlie was bullying you— *assaulting you*—when he cut your hair."

"You said it looks nice."

"Not the point," said Chloe, and she placed her thumbnail in the gap between her front teeth. "He cut your hair off without your permission. He *physically* got hold of you and shaved your head. I mean"—she gave a short humorless laugh—"who *does* that?"

"He said sorry," said Joe.

"When?"

"When he started shaving, when I started crying."

"But you didn't want him to do it, and you told him to stop?"

"Yes."

Chloe shrugged. "It's too simple; case closed."

## 43

### The tiniest air punch in the world

When they returned to work after Joe-Nathan's shower, the rest of Wednesday was as normal as a day can be after a very abnormal start. It couldn't be completely normal, in the same way that when a person has been in a car crash, the rest of their day is impacted by the accident. Even a bad dream can seep into a day and make it strange, so there was no way that the second half of Joe's Wednesday could be normal, after being dragged along a corridor, hidden in a room, having his head shaved, watching his friends fight, and seeing one of them fired. And to top it all, a shower at 10:06 a.m. was something Joe had never done before in his life.

Luckily, when he returned to work, Hugo distracted Joe by taking him to the main warehouse and introducing him to the largest consignment of paper napkins that had ever come into the store (an ordering error, apparently). Not all the napkins could be brought onto the shop floor, but more than usual had to be transferred inside. So, there was some rearrangement of shelves to make room for them, and Joe and Pip were in charge of arranging the napkins in the space provided.

"Oh, this is so exciting!" said Pip, and she clapped her hands.

"Yes," said Joe, thinking of the uniform shape of a pack of napkins, and how satisfying they would be to stack (unless Pip was a sloppy stacker, in which case this would be a frustrating task). The packs were softish, which caused a dilemma: he would need to make sure that there were the same number of packs in each pile, otherwise they might get squashed down unevenly and result in an irregular appearance.

"Look!" said Pip, peering down into the open box of napkins. "Look at the colors! Red, white, blue, gold, and black!" She whispered to Joe, "Those five colors, in varying combinations, are the colors of *so* many flags on the review list I made up. We can review while we're doing this, and people will just think we're talking about napkins."

"Why does it matter if people think we are talking about flags?"

"Because flags come up in quizzes, and napkins never do."

"In the sixteenth century, in Flanders, they made napkins the size of an ell and a half. What is the length of an ell?" said Joe.

"Pardon?" said Pip.

"It is a napkin question that I heard on a quiz show once."

"Oh. I don't know."

"It is the length from the elbow to the end of the middle finger."

"Is it?"

"Yes. Who invented the napkin?"

"Joe . . ."

"No," Joe said. "It was the Romans."

"Good grief," said Pip. Joe's breadth of knowledge surprised her.

"Which author of a famous diary paid someone forty shillings to teach his wife to fold napkins?"

"I don't know," said Pip.

"Samuel Pips."

"Pepys."

"What?" said Joe.

"It's Samuel 'Peeps,' not 'Pips,'" said Pip. "Oh my *god*, Joe." She was still whispering. "You're a napkin expert!"

"Yes, I suppose I am," said Joe. "I read about them in the N section in an encyclopedia."

"But we'll practice flags as well, okay? I'll ask the questions, and see if you can answer them."

"Yes. You hand me the napkins and ask questions; I'll stack the napkins and answer."

"Cool," said Pip, and relief swept over Joe now that he knew the stacking and pattern formation would be all his own work.

"We're going to be such a great quiz team," said Pip. "Although it's a shame there's only three of us now."

Joe looked at Pip and thought how much his mum would have liked to sit at a table with Pip and Chloe and him, eating fish and chips and answering questions.

Joe said, "You are invited to my mum's funeral on Friday. Apparently, it is not proper invitations, like for a birthday party, I just need to tell you about it and you can come, but you do not have to."

Pip was holding three packs of napkins: black, gold, and red, and now she clutched them to her chest. "Oh, Joe, that's really kind of you. I'd like to come, thank you for inviting me."

Joe nodded and pictured the quiz night: a square table with just the three of them around it, a gaping space where his mum should be.

"Should we get a fourth member for the team?" said Joe.

"Who are you thinking? It would be wonderful if Hugo could join us, but he's the question master." She sighed sadly.

Joe said nothing and shifted from foot to foot.

"I think everyone who works here—who's coming—already has a team sorted," said Pip.

"What if we ask someone who does not work here?" Joe asked.

"I don't know if that's allowed," said Pip.

"My mum did not work here."

"No, but Hugo made an exception."

"Why?"

"Because she was so important to you," said Pip, with a face that looked like it wanted to cry.

"So, I just need to find someone else who is important to me?" Joe said.

Pip shrugged. "Give it a go," she said. "You know what Hugo's like, I'll twist his arm. And Chloe won't mind who you invite."

"She might," said Joe.

"She won't," said Pip. "Go for it!"

"Okay," said Joe.

"Right," Pip said, with a shifty glance east and west. "Back to business." She held the three packs of napkins against her cleavage. "What country has black, gold, and red vertical stripes?"

"Belgium," said Joe.

"Yes!" whispered Pip, and did the tiniest air punch in the world.

# 44

## Not divisible by five

Thursday, the day before his mum's funeral, Joe-Nathan was solemn. He gave the day the notice it deserved. It would be understandable to anyone that a person would give reverence to the day they buried a parent; it was undoubtedly a singular day. Only one day in a person's life could be referred to as "the day my mum died" or "the day of my mum's funeral." But likewise, Joe was aware that there was also only one day that could ever be "the day before my mum's funeral"; Joe wanted to pay attention to that too. For the same reason, he also liked to pay attention to exact times on the clock. Clock times such as 2:45 and 5:15 were given far too much attention; people were always rounding up or rounding down to the nearest five. Joe felt sorry for the 4:44s and the 9:03s, and was true to them whenever he could be. He simply could not understand why the times between the other times were any less significant than those divisible by five.

Work that day (the day before Janet's funeral) at The Compass was quiet and straightforward: no confusing conversations, no fights or questions, and no laughing that sounded like it came from an unhappy place. There was stacking and go-backs and some mopping of spilled lemonade, then lunch and other jobs that Joe felt completely at ease with. He was at the satisfying stage of making a pyramid display out of cans, when one of them dropped. He picked it up and turned it, observing the new dent, and he was reminded of the crumpled beer cans next to the sofa in Charlie's front yard. Then Charlie came sharply to his mind. Joe looked at the store clock: 3:37 p.m. Charlie would normally be here, and he wasn't; he was at home. Or perhaps he was somewhere else. But he *was not here*, and he *should be here*. Joe's palms began to sweat; he wiped them on his jogging bottoms. Once again, he found it hard to swallow. He pictured himself pushing a go-back trolley with Charlie inside it; he imagined pushing it from Charlie's house to The Compass Store, where Charlie belonged—right now—at this time between times not divisible by five. Joe felt uncomfortable, something like when the arnica cream was left by Charlie's front door and Joe felt compelled to rescue it; he felt the same way about Charlie, only it was worse. Much worse. Maybe because Charlie was bigger. *No*, that couldn't be right, Joe thought. It wasn't because Charlie was bigger than the tube of arnica. It was because he cared more about Charlie. Joe remembered the section on friends that he'd read in his mum's yellow book, and realized that even if Charlie did not think of Joe as a friend, Joe thought of Charlie as his.

## FRIENDS

*Friends are so important in our lives, and as with so many things that involve people, there are not always hard-and-fast rules. Friends are people, and people are all different, which means friends come in all shapes and sizes, and ages and personalities. You may think of some friends as more important than others. Some people have a best friend, but not everyone does. Friends can fall out or argue, but that doesn't necessarily mean that the friendship is over. Sometimes after a fight you simply need to say, "I regret that we fell out." Sometimes, it's more complicated than that. Much of the time, things may seem very easy with friends; other times, you may feel you need them more than usual. If you need help from a friend, ask them for help. Sometimes friends will need to lean on you more than usual. Friends will sometimes ask you for help (always help them) and sometimes they will only give you clues that they need help. Now and then you may just get a feeling that something is wrong with a friend, and when that happens, in my opinion, you should investigate—ask them more than once if they're okay, if they need help. Sometimes you just have to leave friends alone because maybe they don't want to be helped, and I don't know why that is, but it happens now and then.*

*It may be that occasionally you're not sure whether you can trust that someone is your friend. A lot of this you can work out by looking at how they behave toward you, the way they speak to you, and the way that they look out for you. But it isn't always simple.*

So, as I say, there are no hard-and-fast rules, but I am quite old and I've had a few friends in my life. I have even lost a few. In my experience, the following is usually true about friends:

Friends love you for who you are. They appreciate your differences, even if they don't understand them.

Friends will be there for you when you are in trouble, or upset.

Friends will support you in your dreams and ambitions.

Friends will tell you the truth, even if it hurts to hear it, because it is better to hear the truth from a friend than someone else.

Friends have your back. They are always on your side.

Friends keep your secrets. And you should keep your friends' secrets. However, I believe there are some circumstances when a friend's secret is dangerous and requires you to find help for them and you might have to tell someone in order to get that help. I'm afraid you will just have to work out for yourself when that is the case. But as a general rule of thumb, friends keep your secrets safe.

Friends make time for you.

Friends are always there for a shoulder to cry on.

Friends make you feel better about yourself.

Friends sometimes make mistakes (and sometimes you will). Sometimes you may need to forgive your friends (and one day, you may need them to forgive you).

Joe wasn't sure how the rules of friends worked if only one person out of the two wanted to be friends. But his mum had said there were no hard-and-fast rules. And out of the ten general rules of thumb, Joe could say he was a friend to Mean Charlie on five points, and Mean Charlie was a friend to him on two. So, there was work to do, but by the end of the day known as "the day before his mum's funeral," Joe was determined to be a friend to Charlie on six points of the friends' rules of thumb, and not just five.

# 45

## A friend like me

It had started raining before Joe-Nathan got home from work, and he run-trotted up his driveway to get under his dad's yellow awning before he got any wetter. His head felt different with rain on it now that his hair was shorn so short (much colder) and it was nice—in that he did not have wet hair—and bad—in that raindrops now trickled from his head down his neck into his collar. He swung his satchel round to his front and took out his key. The kitchen was gradually beginning to feel normal even without his mum in it. Only now and then did he start to speak to her before realizing she wasn't there, and when that happened, he would say, "Oh," and sigh. Sometimes, he would sit and talk to her photo in the frame over the dining table as a poor alternative (but nonetheless an alternative) and wished that he could tell her about Charlie and ask her what he should do. Yes, there was the yellow book, but the yellow book did not help with specific and complex situations like this one.

Joe cooked spaghetti with little cubes of ham that he fried in a pan and added a jar of carbonara sauce. He laid the table and faced his mum and dad. He looked slightly to the side and didn't blink for a long time, so that they became blurry and he could imagine that they were really there.

"Charlie got fired because he cut my hair at work," said Joe. He imagined what his mum might say, something like, *"How do you feel about that, Joe?"*

"I feel sad about it," he replied, and imagined his mum saying, *"Why do you feel sad about it?"*

"Because I want Charlie to understand that I do not have a mean bone in my body."

*"And why do you want him to understand that?"*

"If he knew I did not have a mean bone in my body, he would like me, and we could be friends."

*"But you have friends. Why do you need Charlie to be your friend?"*

Joe paused. He didn't know the answer to this question.

"I think Charlie needs me to be his friend. I think Charlie needs a friend like me."

*"And do you need him?"*

"I want to help him. I do not know why."

*"But hasn't he been mean to you?"*

"He made a mistake. I forgive him, but he does not know that. And sometimes . . ."

*"Sometimes what?"*

"Sometimes I think he likes me, even though other people think he does not. And sometimes when I have looked at his eyes I feel like I understand something about him."

"*And?*"

"And?"

"*Why do you think he needs you?*"

"I think he is in trouble, and friends should be there for you when you are in trouble. And I do not think there is anyone there for him."

"*When are you going to help him?*"

"As soon as I have cleaned my dishes and put some dry clothes on."

Joe wore a hoodie. It wasn't his usual choice of clothing, but because he wouldn't wear a hat or use an umbrella, a hoodie was a concession in wet weather. He looked at the time—6:22 p.m.—and calculated that although the sky was overcast because of the rain, it wouldn't be twilight for hours, so he had plenty of time to get to Charlie's and back home again well before nightfall. He knew the route, having taken it once before, and was prepared this time for the trees running out and the pavement becoming more ragged and the weeds pushing their way up through the snags in the concrete. It was too wet for teenagers to sit on the wall and call out to him, and three people passed in the opposite direction but they had their heads down and walked quickly, paying no attention to him at all.

Two things surprised Joe as he headed for the gasworks and Charlie's place. The first surprise was when he crossed over the road to the precinct of shops and glanced up. He was intimidated by a figure walking toward him: shoulders hunched high and hunched over, hands in pockets, face hidden by a dark hood and coming straight at him with no obvious intention to step to the side. Only when Joe swerved sideways to avoid him—and the dark figure mirrored him— did he realize that he was walking toward his own reflection in the glass window of a key cutter's shop.

The second thing that surprised him was also a man, but this time it definitely wasn't his reflection. He heard voices coming out of the Chinese takeaway and recognized one of them. The voices were accompanied by two men who came out of the takeaway, each with a white paper bag transparent with oily food. Charlie's dad bit into a large spring roll; strands of carrot and cabbage hung over his chin, making it shiny with grease. The other man was an equally sloppy eater.

All Joe could make of their conversation was mumbled laughter and swear words and he thought once more of the box he had made for Chloe; he would give it to her tomorrow, on the day of his mum's funeral.

When he saw Charlie's dad, Joe froze and hunched his shoulders even higher. He stood completely still on the pathway and squeezed his eyes shut, waiting to be recognized, chastised, or embarrassed in some way. The two men navigated around him, and when Joe opened his eyes, he saw they had walked on, leaving him with nothing more lasting than the word "weirdo" in their wake, uttered by one of them as they passed. They were walking in the opposite direction to Joe, which meant Charlie's dad wouldn't open the door when he reached Charlie's house, and with that knowledge, Joe found himself able to breathe more deeply.

He paused at Charlie's broken gate to look at the sad sofa getting damp in the front garden. The empty cans were slightly different and in different positions, which meant that someone had at least cleared the old ones away. There was a tinny *ping-ping* sound as raindrops hit the newer crumpled beer cans, and a more sullen *pat-pat* as rain fell into a puddle that was forming in the sunken seat on one side of the couch.

The house looked gloomy and unoccupied, but Joe knocked, and then knocked louder, until behind the glass, a light came on from somewhere further inside.

# 46

## Five years old

Joe-Nathan took two steps back from the front door, as per his mum's instructions in the yellow book. When Charlie opened the door, he was wearing jeans and a Ramones T-shirt, nothing on his feet and a stick of Peperami in his hand. He stopped—mid-chew—when he saw Joe.

"What are you doing here?" he asked.

"I have come to see you," said Joe. He looked at the ground and said, "As a friend."

Charlie snorted, then leaned forward out of the door, looking both ways. "I guess you better come in." Charlie turned and walked into the house, leaving Joe to close the front door and follow him along a narrow passageway to a kitchen.

"Would you like me to take my shoes off?" Joe asked, looking at Charlie's bare feet and remembering his mum's advice.

"What for?" Charlie asked.

"I don't know," said Joe.

Charlie leaned against the countertop and folded his arms. Joe noticed a calendar on the wall. It had a picture of a big American car in front of a diner. The calendar was wonky and showing the month of January. Joe felt as though his eyes were getting bigger in his head as he stared at the white car with the red leather seats. The temptation to turn it to the correct month and make it hang straight was almost unbearable; he could feel his blood vibrating.

*Don't tidy people's things for them, or rearrange their stuff.*

*Why not?* thought Joe. *Wouldn't it be helpful to straighten it and change it to the correct page?*

"What's up?" Charlie asked.

"Your calendar," said Joe. "It . . . it is wrong."

Charlie looked over at the wall to where Joe was looking. "I meant, why are you here?" he asked.

Joe continued to stare at the calendar. He decided he couldn't speak until it was squared up and turned correctly to April.

"Joe? *Hello?*"

Joe stared unblinking and nodded slowly at the calendar.

"Fuck sake," Charlie muttered, and he pulled the calendar up and off its nail, roughly turning the pages over until they showed a shiny chrome truck driving at night in April. Then he lined up the little hole in the calendar again and returned to the kitchen counter while it swung to a stop. Joe observed that it still wasn't hanging straight and beads of sweat formed on his forehead.

"Better?" Charlie raised his eyebrows.

"It's wonky," Joe whispered, tucking his chin into his collar, expecting Charlie to shout at him. But Charlie just sighed and went over to the calendar, carefully adjusting it until it was right.

"Want a drink?" Charlie said.

"Yes, please."

Charlie opened the fridge and bent down, grabbing two bottles. "Beer okay?" he said, holding one by the neck and holding it out to Joe.

"No, thank you."

"What do you want, then?"

"Have you got any milk?"

"What are you? Five?"

"Twenty-three," said Joe.

Charlie put the beers back in the fridge and leaned in, searching.

"I can't remember the last time anyone drank milk in this house. Hang on, what's this?" Charlie crouched down and reached right into the back, pulling out a dented carton of milk. Charlie opened the carton, and sniffed it. He shrugged and got out two glasses, pouring carelessly so the milk splashed and smeared the sides; he handed a glass to Joe, who reached out for it very slowly.

"Take it, then, what's wrong with you?"

"You do things differently. It makes me uncomfortable."

"Christ, you need to man up. You lost me my job; you don't hear me whining about it."

Charlie led Joe away from the kitchen and into the living room. The curtains were drawn roughly across the window in a way that suggested they were never opened. The overhead light was on, something Joe did not like in a living room. He preferred lamplight in any room except a kitchen, bathroom, or hallway, and the furniture in here cried out to Joe that it wanted to be rescued: removed from this room with its too-harsh lighting; it wanted to be cleaned and cared for. The room smelled of old smoke and Joe noticed an ashtray on the coffee table: the stubs of skinny cigarettes nose-down in a dense pool of ash, like a strange garden of tiny, white, wrinkled tree trunks dying in dark gray soil.

Charlie perched on the edge of an armchair and put his glass of milk on the floor between his feet. Joe breathed in deeply through his nostrils, trying to calm the nerves that alerted him to the full glass just waiting to be kicked over.

"Can I see your bedroom?" Joe said.

"Jesus, you really are five years old. Do you want to play with my toys?"

"No, I really am twenty-three. What toys do you have?"

"Fuck sake," said Charlie again, shaking his head. But he smiled slightly and pushed against his knees, stood, and grabbed his glass. Some of the milk slopped over the edge. Joe gasped and looked away.

There was nothing on the walls—no pictures—as they mounted the stairs, although Joe noticed that where the sheets of wallpaper met, the paper rose away from the wall slightly. He could see where someone had put their finger into the gap between the sheets and pulled the paper so that it had ripped in an increasingly narrow strip along the wall, like one of those pointy triangular flags. In Joe's house, the stair wall featured evenly spaced framed photographs of Joe at various ages, and a framed certificate from when he had taken part in a spelling competition at school. In Joe's house the wallpaper was perfectly aligned, but Charlie's wallpaper was completely out of kilter. Joe looked away, but he was running out of places to look in Charlie's house. There was a tiny landing at the top of the stairs, framed by three closed doors, and Charlie opened the middle one.

"Welcome to my room," he said, walking over to the window, which overlooked a playing field, rusty play equipment, and what looked like a primary school in the distance. Charlie leaned against the windowsill, took a sip of his milk, grimaced, and put it down on the bedside table. Joe breathed a little more easily and placed his glass next to Charlie's.

"Sit down. This place isn't really big enough for two grown men to stand up in."

The only place to sit was a single bed, which took up almost half the room. The sky-blue duvet cover was wrinkled and didn't contain the duvet properly (it looked as though a small child had tried to hide in the bottom of it) and Joe was desperate to shake it out. He stood uncertainly, shifting his weight from foot to foot.

"Sit," said Charlie.

Joe closed his eyes and sat down so slowly that his thighs burned before his buttocks reached the bed. He kept his eyes closed and Charlie laughed softly and muttered something under his breath. Then Charlie took a sharp intake of breath and Joe opened his eyes. Charlie stared at his bedroom door, frozen, his mouth slightly agape. Joe heard it too: the sound of a key in a lock, the sound of keys being dropped on the floor, and a deep grunt of annoyance.

"Oh *fuck*," Charlie whispered. "What the fuck is he doing back home?"

# 47

## Thump, thump, thump

"Get under the bed," Charlie said, very quietly.

"No," said Joe-Nathan.

"You have to." Charlie's neck was suddenly red and it was he who had the look of a five-year-old in his eyes, one who had perhaps heard strange noises in the middle of the night. "It's not safe. Go on, get under." Charlie pulled up the sheet that had been hanging down, obscuring the space between the bed and the floor, and gestured wildly and silently at the gap, encouraging Joe to get in there. Joe noticed that Charlie's eyebrows were drawn together so tightly they almost touched and that Charlie was trying not to breathe, or cry, or both.

Joe knew that even in very clean houses, the places that no one ever saw were usually neglected from a cleaning point of view; his mum had told him that. So what did that say about places where the things you *could* see were neglected? Would the underneath of Charlie's bed be better or worse than the top of it? Would it be any worse than anyone else's neglected underbed space?

Charlie put his hand on Joe's shoulder, pushing him down and shushing him. Joe flapped his hand away and contorted as he tried to do what he was being told *and* resist it simultaneously; the contortions increased as he tried to do the impossible: get onto the floor and under the bed without touching either the floor or the bed. Once he was under, facing out into the tiny bedroom, Charlie flung himself on top of the bed, so that it momentarily bowed and touched Joe's side. Joe shuddered and said "Ugh" from underneath.

"Shut up," said Charlie, in a barely audible hiss. "Not a word." And then it sounded like Charlie was turning the pages of a magazine.

Charlie and Joe were together in the bedroom in a strange silence. There were two types of silence, Joe had decided: the empty kind, like when he got home now that his mum wasn't there, and the full kind, which could hurt your ears as much as loud noises; this was the full kind, full to bursting. Joe and Charlie were each painfully aware of the other's presence above and below the bed as they listened to the weighty, grunting steps of Charlie's dad mounting the stairs with heft and slow purpose.

"Charlie?" came the gruff voice.

"Yeah," Charlie said.

The bedroom door opened and Joe looked at Charlie's dad's boots and ankles. Joe pulled gently on the sheet that hung down, to reassure himself that he couldn't be seen.

"You got money?" said Charlie's dad.

"Yes, thanks," Charlie replied.

"I need fifty, or they won't serve me at The Crown."

"Good luck with that, then."

"Little shit," said Charlie's dad, and he opened a drawer. It must have been a drawer in the bedside cabinet.

"Hey!" said Charlie. "What are you doing?"

"I know you got a stash in here."

"You can't have it."

"Call it a loan."

"Leave it out. Borrow money off your drinking buddies."

"Buddies? Hah! Here it is," said Charlie's dad. There was a soft sound of paper money being counted off, while Charlie protested half-heartedly. Then a sock was thrown down on the floor, and Joe realized that was where Charlie must keep his cash, in a sock. Joe kept his own cash in a porcelain money box in the shape of an owl, and the rest was in an account at Barclays bank. Joe smiled at the thought of the friendly owl and decided to make Charlie a wooden money box, because a sock was no good at all. Charlie would like that, and it would be useful as well as beautiful, which the best things always are; it would be a very nice thing to do for a friend. Joe smiled wider for a moment.

Charlie's dad's foot came so close that it jutted underneath the bed and Joe quickly retracted his right hand, clenching it into a fist so his fingers didn't touch the end of the boot, which looked crusted with cement. Joe held his breath and closed his eyes. He didn't listen to the words that were spoken between the two men, only heard their voices rise and fall in that way that means you can work out what is being said without words anyway. They were not arguing, but they were also not *not* arguing. Joe's palm felt hot and sweaty in a fist. He spread his fingers wide to let some air get to his hand, then he laid it flat on the carpet just in front of his face. *Ugh*, there were *bits* on his hand now, clinging to the dampness. In revulsion he turned his palm to his face and stared at the fluff there. His breath came quickly and he tried to slow it down; he didn't want Charlie's dad to hear him. All Joe's focus was on his hand, the voices above him just a backdrop. In the middle of his palm was a small, white square of paper; he shook his hand to try to get it off, but it was stuck. Slowly, Joe brought forward his other hand and used it to peel off the square of paper; the size and shape of it was familiar and oddly comforting. He turned it over and on the other side in faded black, red, and gold were the words "Imperial Leather."

Joe didn't blink. The soap stamp was almost white, as if it had been rubbed over like a used scratch card. Why was this under the bed? Had Charlie lost his mum too? This certainly felt like a house with no mum in it. Was she dead? If she was, how many soaps had been used since she died? Did Charlie peel off his Imperial Leather stamps and save them too? Joe twisted slightly left and right, trying to see if there were any more soap stamps around. But all he could see were a few tissues, a layer of dust, more lumps of fluff, and something like a bundled-up T-shirt.

"Stop being a whiny shit and do something useful, like get a job," Charlie's dad's voice said. His feet shuffled and the boots turned away. Joe watched as Charlie's dad walked out of the room, and listened as he descended the stairs, heard him stumble quickly about halfway, as though he might fall to the bottom, but he didn't. The front door opened and slammed shut, and Joe heard Charlie sigh loudly in a shudder; the bed rose as Charlie got off it. Charlie squatted down until Joe could see his face.

"You can come out now," Charlie said.

"Why did I have to hide?" Joe asked.

"I was a bit worried what my dad might say to you. He's not always very nice."

"Do you have friends that come here?"

"No friends like you," Charlie said, and laughed. "Come on, idiot, out you get." Charlie held out his hand and Joe slowly put out his own. "'S'alright," said Charlie, "I washed them earlier."

Joe held Charlie's hand and felt it slip a bit as Charlie pulled. Joe rearranged his grip and held tighter, pushed his other hand against the gritty carpet to get some purchase and help himself. Charlie put his other hand firmly around Joe's wrist and when Joe winced, Charlie said, "It's okay." But before Joe had a chance to move an inch from under the bed he heard a banging sound: *thump, thump, thump*, as if his heart were trying to get out of his chest.

"Oh no," said Charlie, and Joe realized that the banging sound wasn't coming from the inside of him, but from outside. The *thump, thump, thump* was coming up the stairs, and it was angry.

## 48
### Double negative

Charlie's dad was too big and moving too fast for the size of the room he was running into. There was no stopping time before he collided with something, but he wasn't looking for stopping time; he was clearly comfortable with collision. Charlie was still holding Joe's hand when Charlie's dad's boot collided with Charlie's back and Charlie held on to Joe when he was on his side, head inches away from Joe's, even though Joe had instinctively loosened his grip so that if Charlie let go, they would no longer be holding hands.

Charlie's dad was shouting. *"THINK YOU CAN HIDE SOMEONE IN HERE WITHOUT ME KNOWING?"*

But then he stopped shouting and crouched down to look at the stowaway under the bed, and said in a quiet voice that was even more frightening, "Is that a fucking bloke? Are you hiding a *bloke*? Are you *fucking* a bloke? Are you *fucking gay*?" These last two words he screamed as only men with deep voices can, and Charlie—still lying on the floor facing the underneath of the bed—dropped Joe's hand, clenched his fists to his chin, and squeezed his eyes tight shut as if he were bracing himself. There was a strange silence: hollow and full at the same time and Joe thought of the way the wind sounded noisy if you faced it, but suddenly went silent when you turned your head to one side. Then there was a thunderous *wallop* and Charlie's body lurched toward Joe. Charlie's eyes sprang open and he stared straight at Joe. Joe could see that the whites of Charlie's eyes were pink and full of tears and his mouth was twisted open as if to scream, but nothing came out.

"*AREN'T YOU GOING TO FIGHT BACK? YA POOF?*" Charlie's dad yelled.

"No," Charlie whispered, and it was a barely audible whisper that came from his throat, not his lips.

"I'll leave you to your boyfriend, then," he said, and Joe saw the boots turn away and almost immediately turn back again, pulling back in slow motion, bent at the knee, the heavy foot taking aim and striking Charlie somewhere between the shoulder blades. Charlie lurched forward again: breath and spit forced from his body so that Joe felt the spray on his face.

Joe had never had spit on his face before and the horror of it stopped every cell in his body from dividing, stopped his lungs working, pressed pause on every synapse and electrical impulse in his brain. He wanted to wipe his face but couldn't willingly get spit on his hands and there was no instinct to fight or flee, only the instinct to freeze.

"Sorry, Joe," Charlie whispered, and the whisper was so quiet that Joe might have imagined it. An unbroken stream of tears ran from the outer corner of Charlie's eye and down the side of his face.

The boys lay on the floor, unmoving for a minute or more after the front door slammed shut. All that could be heard was Charlie's breath. Neither of them thought that Charlie's dad was still in the house, but each was paralyzed in the position they were in when he left.

Charlie was the first to move. He rolled delicately away from the bed, groaning as he raised himself up on his hands and slowly got onto his knees and finally up onto his feet. Even then, he could not stand up straight.

"You're going to have to get yourself out from under there," Charlie said in an old man's voice, and Joe shuffled until he was almost out from under the bed, then he too went slowly from prostrate, to kneeling, to standing. Charlie's spit was dry on Joe's face and when he looked down, the fluff that was stuck to him was like white stars all over his dark hoodie. Joe was so uncomfortable with all the things that were different and unexpected and stuck to him that he felt dizzily trapped inside his own discomfort. But when he looked at Charlie and saw his pain, and the tears drying on *his* face, a door in that trap opened and Joe felt a rush of something that he did not know was called empathy. It was a hint of the way he felt sorry for the go-backs before they were returned to their rightful place, but it was more than that; stronger, deeper, fuller, as though it were happening to Joe himself and not to Charlie.

"Are you alright, Charlie?"

"Been better," Charlie said with a weak smile.

"Where is your mum?"

"Good question."

"How many soaps has she been gone?"

"Uh . . . *weird* question. I don't know how to answer that."

"What can I do to help you?"

"Nothing, mate. You can't do nothing."

Joe heard the word "mate" and could barely breathe; he also heard the double negative—*you can't do nothing*—and knew it meant that he could indeed do *something*; he could be useful and make Charlie something that he really needed. Something he needed much more than a money box.

## 49

### In many ways she hasn't

The next day was the day of Janet's funeral and Joe-Nathan set his alarm to the usual time; after all, it was still a Friday, even if he wasn't going into work; why would he want to sleep more on such a momentous day?

Everything that Joe did was tinged with extra clarity, as though every common, mundane thing in his world was aware that it was playing its usual role but on a day that was heavy with meaning. The pattern on his cereal bowl had blue geometric shapes on it and they contrasted more sharply than usual against the white of the rest of the bowl. The gleam where the sun hit his spoon was extra bright and hurt Joe's eyes. Each piece of cereal in his bowl seemed to sing out and be defined individually rather than as a collective, proudly knowing that it was fulfilling its destiny on a special day in Joe's life.

Joe sat at the kitchen table and stared at Janet's photograph until it was too blurry to see, then he blinked and round tears rolled down his cheeks; then he stared again until it was too blurry again and he did that repeatedly until it was time to get in the shower.

Hazel and Angus arrived at 10:04 a.m. Hazel made a pot of tea and set out a plate of biscuits in a nice pattern.

"I don't eat biscuits in the morning," said Joe.

"Funerals are like any other occasion," said Angus, "bombarded with the sort of food you would never normally eat, at times of the day and night you would never normally eat it." He had settled into a chair at the kitchen table, with a newspaper he'd brought with him. He held it open so it nearly covered his face and he spoke over the top of it, as if he lived there.

"Well, I call this elevenses," said Hazel.

Angus looked at his watch.

"An *early* elevenses," she said. And when Angus raised his eyebrows Hazel said, "For goodness' sake, it's just biscuits, you don't have to eat them."

But Joe watched as Angus quite methodically made his way through a caramel wafer, a wagon wheel, and three fig rolls.

As instructed by Hazel, Joe had washed but stayed in his dressing gown, so that he could be helped with the formalities of getting dressed. Angus himself wore a black suit and tie, with a white shirt. When he crossed his legs a pair of lime-green socks were exposed, and Joe noticed that a word was embroidered at the top of them, but he couldn't read what it said because it was partially obscured by the hem of Angus's trousers.

"What does it say on your socks?" Joe asked.

"What? Oh, it says 'Monday.' They're day-of-the-week socks," said Angus.

Joe's mouth went dry and Hazel stopped with the kettle halfway to the sink.

"Hah!" said Angus, and he slapped the table. "Just joking. They say 'Friday,' I wouldna do that to you, Joe. Look." Angus pulled his trouser leg up, revealing a pale, hairless, skinny leg and the word "Friday."

Joe exhaled and Hazel restarted her task of filling the kettle again.

"Ma underwear says 'Thursday,' though," he said quietly, grinning.

"Angus!" said Hazel.

Angus looked at Joe again and put his hand up to his mouth to hide his words from Hazel. "Not really. I'm going commando."

Chloe arrived just after eleven and hung her bag over the back of a chair. The kitchen was filling with people but Joe did not mind as much as normal. Chloe wore her usual black boots, but this was the first time Joe had seen her wearing a dress and thin black tights.

"Did your mum have any nail polish, Joe?" she asked, looking down at her hands and her chipped red polish.

"Janet wore it from time to time, so I'm sure we'll find some upstairs," Hazel said. "Shall we all go up now and get you dressed up smart?" she said to Joe.

Angus stayed where he was, eyes fixed to the newspaper, while the other three trooped up the stairs and into Joe's bedroom.

"Joe, you get your suit out and lay it on the bed," said Hazel. "Chloe and I will go and see what we can find in the way of manicure equipment in your mum's room."

Janet's room was peaceful and tidy and Chloe thought of an old-fashioned hotel room she had stayed in once when she went to an aunt's wedding. The bed was perfectly made, the eiderdown pulled tight and neat under the edge of the pillows. Janet's reading glasses sat on top of a copy of *The Shell Seekers* on the bedside table and those, along with her nightie (perfectly folded and neatly placed at the foot of the bed), made it feel as though Janet would be back to sleep here tonight.

"It's like she hasn't gone," said Chloe.

"Well, of course, in many ways she hasn't," said Hazel, who was over at Janet's dressing table. Chloe didn't ask what she meant, because it was obvious. "Here," said Hazel, turning back to Chloe. "Everything you need: nail polish remover, a file, and polish. Only two colors to choose from: clear or pink. What will you go for?"

Chloe shrugged. "Pink?"

"Do you want this?" Hazel squinted at a small tube she was holding at arm's length. "Cuticle cream?"

"Nope," said Chloe, taking all the things from Hazel. "I guess there'll be cotton wool in the bathroom."

Hazel brought her hands together in a soft clap. "Right, that's you sorted, then. Let's get the boy dressed, shall we?"

Joe was not 100 percent pleased that Chloe used his desk to paint her nails, but she moved his things carefully out of the way first and then laid toilet paper down to protect the surface before she started. Frankly, after his experience at Charlie's place, with the calendar, the milk, the furniture, and the lighting, the wallpaper, the carpet, the fluff, the spit, and the beating, he was able to accept the discomfort of Chloe's behavior a little more easily than usual.

Once he was dressed in the basics, he allowed Hazel to fix his cuff links and tie and then he sat on the bed because Hazel wanted to talk to him.

"How do you feel, Joe?" she asked.

"Okay," he said.

"Is anything worrying you about the funeral?"

"Where will I sit?"

"At the front with me and Angus, and Chloe too. We'll stay with you the whole time."

"When will I read my speech?"

"The vicar will tell you when. I'll come and stand next to you while you do it, and bring you back to your seat afterward."

"When will the song I chose be played?"

"Right at the end. The funeral director has that all in hand. Janet wanted your choice played last, then we'll all leave together."

Joe didn't say anything more.

"Do you have any other questions?" Hazel asked. "You can ask me *anything* at all."

There were many questions that Joe had wanted answered about Charlie and how he might be helped. But Joe had already worked out how best to help Charlie, all by himself. However, another question had been playing on his mind for a while now, and he needed to ask it.

"What is a blow job and how much should I pay for one?" Joe said.

Hazel didn't blink. Chloe snorted and then did a loud hoot of laughter.

And Hazel said, "Umm . . ."

## 50

## Hugo Boss

Chloe smiled and shook her head as she applied nail polish to the nails on her outstretched hand. She glanced at Hazel, who, with desperate eyes, seemed to be pleading with her to help with Joe-Nathan's question.

"Oh no," said Chloe, still smiling. "This one's all yours, Hazel. You got this."

"I think it's more of a young person's question," said Hazel. "The sort of thing young people do."

"Young people don't have a monopoly on blow jobs, Hazel. We didn't invent them and anyway, Joe asked *you*, not me, and you *did* say he could ask you *anything*." Chloe crossed her legs tightly, leaned forward to rest her elbows on them, blew on her fingers, and grinned.

Joe waited, looking from woman to woman, absorbing their banter with little comprehension.

Into the silence, Chloe sighed deeply. "It's a sex thing," she said. "That's why Hazel's getting her knickers in a twist."

"Huh?" said Joe.

Chloe sighed again hard and tapped something into her phone. "Here we go," she said. "The dictionary definition of a blow job." She held the phone in front of his face so he could read it for himself.

"Oh," he said, having read the blunt sentence.

"As for how much you should pay. Uh, well, you don't *have* to pay for it. Some people choose to." She looked at Joe's horrified expression, which was still glued to the definition on her phone. "Hey," she said, and then she said "*Hey*" again, more kindly, so that he looked at her. "You might not like the sound of a blow job, but one day, you might actually want someone to do it, and it's supposed to be a nice thing, so don't worry about it. It's one of the things people sometimes do when they're in a sexual relationship. How come you didn't just google it yourself?" she said.

"Mum said googling can be dangerous and misleading."

"Well, that certainly can be true."

Hazel mouthed an exaggerated *thank you* at Chloe, who shrugged like it was nothing, but said, "You owe me one."

Joe looked repeatedly at the kitchen clock, his watch, and the little upside-down timepiece that Hazel always wore on a fob clipped to her top like a nurse. He made a mental note of the exact time as the funeral crept closer to him from the future. There was something reassuring about the relentlessness of time, because it soothed Joe to know that there was no escape from the certainty of the funeral. If it were possible to escape it, then he would have to expend a terrible amount of energy trying to do just that. Knowing that he couldn't released him from the obligation of trying. He accepted this fate, as he accepted many fates, and it relieved him from a great deal of pointless thinking and worrying.

A hearse arrived at the house, with another big black car behind it. Joe sat in the back with Hazel, Angus, and Chloe, and looked out of the window at the people and the trees and the pavement. He knew this journey and the markers along the way, because this cemetery was the one he and his mum had visited the most. It was where Joe's dad was buried. It felt strange to be making this journey without her (although technically, she was *here* in the car in front of the one he was in). The others talked about Janet and what she would make of it all, but Joe didn't hear them; he only imagined that he was in the passenger seat of his mum's Fiesta while his mum drove, and when he saw the big oak tree near the graveyard that seemed to wave at him with five big branches, like five long fingers reaching majestically toward heaven, he held his hand outstretched against the cool glass of the window—as he always did—returning the waving gesture.

People loitered outside the crematorium. It was a boring-looking little building, and people often wondered why it wasn't made to look less boring, until they were there for the funeral of a loved one, at which point they realized it didn't matter. Hazel, Angus, and Chloe stood around Joe like bodyguards, shielding him from a rush of well-wishers, although no one moved quickly in the subdued gathering. Pip stepped uncertainly toward them. She wore old-fashioned black lace gloves and did a little wave at hip height, and a little smile, and her eyebrows came together in a sympathetic way.

"I just wanted to say hi, but we'll talk at the pub afterward, okay? Me and Hugo came here together." She looked over her shoulder at where Hugo was standing and when Joe looked his way, Hugo did one of the sad smiles he was so good at. People were not the same when they were not in their usual environment. Joe had already seen Pip at the pub, but seeing Hugo away from The Compass Store was unnerving. Joe realized that at work, he felt courage when Hugo was nearby, but here, away from the store, Hugo was just an ordinary man who looked slightly out of place, and Joe felt his own confidence slip.

Joe stared at Hugo and his breathing became audible to those nearest to him. Hugo looked different; he was dressed differently and didn't have a clipboard or any instructions to give out. He wasn't striding quickly by, calling out for someone to get a hazard sign, or asking how their day was going. Joe put his hand to his throat; it was hard to swallow.

"Hey, Joe," said Hugo, and Joe focused on the man. Hugo raised his hand, putting three fingers to his temple, and saluted him.

Joe saluted back and said, "Hugo Boss, sir," and Hugo Boss nodded firmly, like they do in the American movies.

## 51

## Nowhere to go back to

The coffin was at the front and Joe-Nathan stared at it, conflicted by the knowledge that his mum was inside. How could she not *be here* when she was literally here and also when she was so much a part of everything he did and said and thought? How could she not be *here* when she was *so here* that if only he hadn't been told that she'd died, he could easily imagine her alive somewhere in the world? How could she definitely be dead (which was such a final thing), when he was also easily able to forget—for long, solid seconds—that she had died, and start talking to her as though she were standing right next to him?

Sad, churchy music played and Joe looked at the picture of his mum on the folded card that was beside him on the pew. The vicar seemed happy and when she spoke about Janet it could have been mistaken for a speech at a birthday celebration. Again, this led Joe once or twice to smile and look to one side, as if his mum might be sitting there, smiling too. He didn't like the twang of electricity that fired his synapses when he remembered again that she was dead and in the box; so, he focused on the coffin, to stop himself forgetting, and let the vicar's words blur in his ears. Now and then his name was mentioned and his consciousness rose to the surface, but the box was sturdy enough to hold his attention, and for a while, everything else faded away.

Hazel nudged Joe's elbow and said it was time. She started to get up, and Joe felt inside his pocket for the eulogy. When he got to the reading stand, he smoothed the paper and looked out at those in front of him. He was neither surprised nor unsurprised by the number of people there, only bemused by the way he felt seeing these people from different places sitting in one room. There was Lucy, the social worker, and Iris from the pub; there was Angus and Chloe, and Hazel sitting right nearby. There were people from his mum's book club and people she used to work with, other neighbors and some people he didn't recognize but who were on the funeral invitation list she had left for him. They all looked out of place; they were like a room full of go-backs. At least they were all together, even if they were all out of place. Afterward, all these go-backs would be at the pub and then later they would take themselves back to where they belonged and maybe things could start to feel more normal again, as they had just begun to feel normal before today.

Joe was about to start reading when he noticed someone standing at the very back of the room. It was Charlie, leaning against the wall just inside the door, his face obscured in shadow; Joe recognized his T-shirt.

Joe felt uncomfortable: he knew that when Charlie left this place, anywhere he might go would not—in Joe's opinion—feel like the right place. He couldn't go to The Compass Store, and his home didn't seem like a good place for anyone. Surely there was nothing sadder than a go-back with nowhere to go back to?

Hazel cleared her throat and softly said, "Joe?"

Joe looked down at his piece of paper and read aloud the words he had constructed at the dining table under the watchful gaze of his mum and dad:

"My mum is dead. That is why we are here. My mum told me that when people die, the eulogy is the bit where all the lovely things get said about a person. After the eulogy the only words that last forever are the ones on the gravestone and it is my job to find the shortest number of words then, to say what she was like. So, this is the part where I say a bit more about her. This is what was good about her: My mum was good at looking after me, she kept me safe and taught me how to do things that I did not learn at school. She cooked for me and taught me how to cook so I could do it for myself. She cleaned and she taught me how to clean so I could do that for myself too. If I did not know what to do, I told her my problem and she would help me decide what to do. She is dead now but she still helps me decide what to do in the yellow book.

"It is hard to write the answers to all the questions a person might have in their life, but she tried because she did not like the idea of me being confused.

"My mum had very nice handwriting . . ." (Several people grunted in agreement when Joe said this, and he looked up to see that heads were nodding and some guests were holding tissues to their faces.) Joe hesitated while he found the place he had left off.

"My mum and me used to drink tea in the back garden after dinner and she would take me for walks in the cemetery on Saturdays because I like the words on the gravestones. She made an excellent packed lunch for me, and now I make an excellent packed lunch for me because she told me how to do it. So, it is almost the same as her doing it. I think." Joe paused here and again he heard some mumbling agreement and thought he heard Angus say, "Yes, I think it is."

"My mum was a very nice person. Not everybody is. Not everyone has a nice mum, or a nice dad . . ." Joe looked at Charlie at the back of the room and then back at his piece of paper. "But I did have a nice mum and dad, and a friend said to me once when I told them my mum had died, that I was the lucky one. And it is true, that I am. My mum liked home the best, but she cannot go back there now. Now she has to go to a place she has never been, but she will be alright, because my dad is there too."

Joe folded his piece of paper and put it back in his pocket. Hazel held out her arm and they walked back to the pew like an old couple. Soon after that, the theme tune from his favorite TV show started playing. It had all been very easy.

Afterward, Joe stood outside and people stood around and talked and he didn't know how long it would go on for, because there seemed no reason to it at all. He looked across the graveyard and saw Charlie in the distance, wandering away, his hands deep in his jeans pockets.

"I am going for a walk," said Joe.

"I'll come with you," said Chloe.

But Joe said, "No," and made his way alone, down a graveyard avenue, in the direction of Charlie.

## 52

### How he'd like to be remembered

Joe-Nathan made no noise at all as he approached Charlie but Charlie didn't seem surprised to find Joe beside him, staring down—just as he was—at a gravestone all curled round with ivy. Neither one looked at the other, but Joe said, "My dad is here."

"Here?" Charlie said.

"Buried here."

"Oh."

"Do you want to see?" Joe asked.

Charlie shrugged. "Sure."

They walked on, away from the people lingering outside the crematorium, under an arch of trees that threw down greenish light. Joe walked with his hands deep in his trouser pockets, like Charlie did, to see what it felt like. It felt soothing; he could understand why a person would do it.

When they got to Joe's dad's gravestone, they stopped and stared at it.

MIKE CLARKE

BELOVED HUSBAND AND FATHER

Charlie read the words out loud.

"Mum said it was how he would want to be remembered," said Joe.

They stood in silence for a while before Charlie said, "My dad was nice when I was little. I remember him doing all the nice things good dads are supposed to do." He hesitated. "Then Mum left—left us both—and he started drinking too much, getting angry, and hitting me. He'd hit me, and then he'd hug me and say sorry, sorry, sorry. And that's how it's been with him and me ever since. Except he doesn't say sorry anymore. I think even he knows there's no point in saying sorry for a thing you know you're just going to do again."

Joe didn't know what to say, so they stood in silence again long enough for shade to cover them, then sunlight, then shade again.

"How do you think he would like to be remembered?" Joe asked.

"How do you mean?"

"His epitaph. What would your dad want it to say?"

Charlie made a light scoffing sound, then he was quiet, but Joe didn't interrupt, just waited for Charlie to answer.

"I don't know how he'd like to be remembered. Not the way I see him, that's for sure. He wouldn't want to be remembered for the kind of man he's become. I suppose if you don't like the way you'd be remembered by others when you die, then you should change and be the kind of person you want to be known as. Too late for my dad though, I think."

There was silence once more.

"I know you call me Mean Charlie," said Charlie, and Joe pulled his hands from his pockets, crossed them tightly across his chest, and tucked his chin down into his collar.

"It's okay, I have been mean. But I wouldn't want to be remembered like that."

"Will you remember me as Joe-Nuthin?" said Joe.

"Huh? No." Charlie laughed and turned to face him. "You ain't nuthin', Joe, you're really somethin'. But don't tell anyone I said that. How do you want to be remembered?"

"I want to be remembered as A Man of No Mean Bones," said Joe. "My mum said I don't have a mean bone in my body."

"Think she was probably right," said Charlie. "You're certainly made of different stuff. Can't imagine you being mean to anyone on purpose."

"Are you mean on purpose?"

"I don't know. Yeah, I guess."

"Why?"

"Don't know."

Joe looked over at the crowd in the distance and saw Chloe waving at him, slowly, with her arm in a wide arc, beckoning him.

"Looks like you better go back," said Charlie.

"Where will you go?" asked Joe.

Charlie shrugged again, pressed his hands even deeper into his pockets, and looked at the ground. "Dunno."

It was just as Joe thought: there was nowhere for Charlie to go back to, no safe or good place to which he should return.

"Okay," said Joe, and he turned to leave.

"Hey, Joe," Charlie said, and Joe turned and waited for Charlie to speak. "I think you'll get your wish."

"What wish?"

"To be remembered the way you want to be," he said.

"Thank you," said Joe, and he returned his hands to his own pockets and smiled inside as he walked toward Chloe and the others.

"Who was that?" Chloe asked, when Joe arrived back at the crowd.

"Lovely service," said Hugo, coming up to stand beside them. "I thought your speech was excellent."

"Thank you," said Joe, nodding at the ground and avoiding Chloe's scrutiny.

"Your speech was lovely," said Pip, coming over.

"Thank you," said Joe, and he began to feel like he'd won the spelling competition at school again, the number of times he was congratulated by almost everyone there, the way the words *thank you* started to feel strange in his mouth because he'd said them so often.

Then Angus clapped his hands once, as though he were some sort of magician, and said it was time to go to the pub. Iris said, "Hear, hear!" and everyone made their way to their cars.

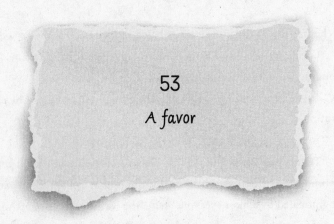

## 53
### A favor

"Who were you talking to at the cemetery?" Chloe asked again in the car on the way to the Ink and Feather.

Joe opened his mouth to speak but had no idea what would come out of his mouth. Chloe looked relaxed but there was something about her tone, a touch of something wrong, something impatient or cross. He didn't like to lie, but he didn't want to tell her it was Charlie.

"I'll be glad to sink a pint," said Angus. "Feeling sad makes me thirsty."

"Everything makes you thirsty," said Hazel.

"Nothing like feeling sad, though," said Angus.

Hazel nodded. "True."

Chloe was still looking at Joe, waiting for him to answer, but Hazel started talking to him about his speech and what a good job he'd done.

Chloe sat back hard in her seat, with a *huff* of annoyance, and kept her arms folded as she gazed out of the window, all the way to the pub.

As they went through the doors to the bar, Angus rubbed his hands together as though he were finally in an environment in which he knew what to do. He and Hazel chatted as they waited for their drinks and Chloe faced Joe and asked him again, "Joe, in the cemetery, who were you *talking* to?"

"Charlie," said Joe. "Mean Charlie," he added, quietly. He looked at his feet: the very shiny black toe of his shoe twisted against the ground, as he felt guilty for calling Charlie mean, and waited for Chloe to get angry.

But her voice did not rise in anger; rather, it lowered in some sort of defeated way. "Joe, *why*? Just explain to me, *please*, why you want anything to do with that completely horrible person."

"He is not completely horrible," said Joe.

"He says horrible things to you; he makes you feel bad; he did a horrible thing to you, shaving your head against your will. You are flogging a dead horse."

Joe frowned at Chloe and she waved a hand, explaining briefly, "It means you're wasting your time trying to make him like you."

"Everyone liked what he had said in my speech about how I was the lucky one, having nice parents. Only *you* did not like it when he said that."

"Because when he said it, he was trying to make you feel bad. Some things, Joe . . ." She practically growled in frustration. "Some things you just don't understand."

"Some things you do not understand," said Joe.

"Oh? Enlighten me," said Chloe, just as Angus handed her a vodka and tonic, and Joe a half-pint. Joe didn't understand what she meant by enlighten. He handed his glass back to Angus and held out his hand to shake it, then proceeded around the pub shaking everyone's hand, which took much, much longer than usual, because almost everyone held on to his hand for an uncomfortable amount of time, and talked with eyebrows all sympathetically angled together, until Joe moved on to the next handshake.

By the time he returned to his drink, the beer was warm. Chloe and Pip were huddled together at the table he had always sat at with his mum, and he slid nervously into a seat opposite them. Chloe's arm was slung across Pip's shoulders and Pip's was slung across Chloe's, like Tweedledum and Tweedledee, and their heads were touching.

"Joe!" said Pip, as if she hadn't seen him for years. She reached her hand across the table toward him, and he shook it.

"Formal," she said, slightly slurred, and giggled.

Joe held his hand out to shake Chloe's hand and she looked at it for a good seven seconds, then glanced up to look in his eyes, and held them for a further six. She slowly stuck out her own hand and shook his.

"Friend," she said, not resisting his grip. "*Real* friend," she added, before letting go of his hand.

"Am I your real friend?" Pip asked Chloe, leaning in to her, the sentence sounding more like one soft word: *amyereelfrend?*

"Course you are," said Chloe, looking at Joe.

Joe felt suddenly annoyed with Chloe, a feeling he had not experienced with her before, a feeling normally reserved for things like inefficiency in the postal system, or power cuts; anything that interfered with his routine.

"Charlie is my friend," he said. "A real friend."

"No, he fucking isn't!" said Chloe, and she pointed at Joe. "Stop it, just stop it. Back me up, Pip," she said, leaning away from her so that the woman was forced to sit more upright and pay attention.

"Back you up with what?" said Pip, as though she had just woken up but was determined to be competent.

"Okay, Joe keeps going on about wanting to be friends with Charlie, and how he's not all bad and how he wants Charlie to like him. But Charlie was fired the other day because his behavior toward Joe was so bad. And yet Joe won't give up and it's pissing me off. I mean if a person is *fired* for assaulting you, doesn't that tell you everything you need to know about whether or not you can be friends?"

Pip took a deep breath in, flaring her nostrils with importance and then tenting her fingers together. "Well . . . ," said Pip, "was shaving Joe's head the only thing that Charlie got fired for?"

"Christ, Pip, shaving his head is enough, isn't it? He did it against Joe's will. Even Joe admits that, right, Joe?"

"I do not like people touching my head," said Joe. "It was only okay when my mum did it."

"I didn't know it was just that one incident that Charlie got the sack for. I assumed he must've done something else. I mean, Hugo tells me nothing." Concentration creased the deep lines around Pip's eyes.

"What difference does it make?" Chloe was exasperated. "*Assault*." She repeated the word to emphasize the fact that it was sufficiently bad.

"Well, obviously assault and bullying are terrible, but I'm just thinking about mitigating circumstances."

"What are you? A lawyer?"

Pip ignored her and got her phone out. "I told you, Joe looked awful that day, that's why I messaged you."

"You messaged me because you said Charlie was being horrible to Joe and he was terrified."

Pip swiped at the screen, searching for her messages from the day of the haircutting incident. "I said, '*Just seen Charlie and Joe. Don't know what's happening but Joe looks really upset and Charlie looks furious. You should see Joe, he looks awful.'"*

"Yes," said Chloe. "And when I got in you said that Charlie was frog-marching Joe like he was a prisoner of war and Joe was terrified."

"Well, he *did* look terrified, but he didn't look like a prisoner of war because of *Charlie*; he looked like a prisoner of war because of what he'd done to himself. If you look at it from a different perspective—rightly or wrongly—maybe Charlie did him a favor."

## 54
### More like sawing

The Tuesday before Janet's funeral, Chloe had told Joe-Nathan very firmly that he was always more likely to be wrong than her, and that he had to cut his nails and get in touch with his hairdresser, because he needed a haircut.

As soon as Joe had got home after work that day, he cut his fingernails in the back garden like his mum used to do. It wasn't easy (it took ages to cut the nails on his right hand) and they were a bit sharp in places, so he went up to the workshop and filed them down on some fine-grade sandpaper. While he was there, he picked up Chloe's swear box and rotated it in his hands. Funny how everything felt different now his nails were short. He took it to the workbench and started to measure the top of the box. He stopped, set it down, and set an alarm for one hour. Chloe needed this box as soon as possible; to Joe, it felt like all her swears were being wasted and she could be saving money already if he could just get it finished. All that was needed was the lid—with a slot big enough for the largest coin (a two-pound piece)—and to sand it until it felt soft under the pads of his fingers.

When the timer went off, Joe had completed the swear box and he imagined handing it over to Chloe. She would probably curse when she received it, and she would have to put something inside straightaway, making it instantly useful. Joe suddenly wondered if paying money every time she swore would make Chloe stop swearing altogether, or at least slow her down. He didn't like the idea of that; it wouldn't be the same if Chloe didn't swear. As his mum had said, it suited her.

With his task finished, Joe had gone to the kitchen and looked inside the fridge. Right in the back were two bottles of beer. He had no idea how long they'd been there or if they went off, but he took one and opened it the way his dad had shown him, walked back up the garden with it, and sat on the steps of the workshop. It didn't taste as good as when he'd drunk it with his dad, but it felt right to have it after finishing a piece of work, just as a cup of tea on the bench after dinner still felt right, even if he couldn't drink it with his mum.

Joe placed the empty bottle in the glass recycling bin and went inside. He searched the blue and yellow books for "Haircuts" or "Hair" but there was nothing. Janet had inevitably forgotten to include some things. Chloe had told him to get in touch with his hairdresser, but that was impossible. He looked at the photo of his mum above the dining table, and said, "What do I do?"

There was nothing, not even an imagined answer. All went quiet in Joe's head, until one word popped in, humble and obvious: *Scissors.* He opened the kitchen drawer with all the utensils inside, took out a large pair of scissors, and went up to the bathroom with them. Chloe was right: his hair was long and getting in his eyes, covering his ears. He grabbed all the hair that flopped over his forehead, and held it up away from his face and snipped across it in one go. Like cutting his nails, it didn't happen as smoothly and cleanly as he expected it to, and the last part of the cut felt more like sawing through rope than the light snippety-snipping that his mum used to do. He picked up the hair over his ears and cut that away too; the result was much shorter and when Joe turned to the side to see his reflection in the bathroom cabinet, he could see the waxy whiteness of his scalp. He did the same with the other side, but his scalp wasn't visible this time, so he snipped away until it was, to try to get some symmetry. Next, he grabbed a handful of hair at the back and cut nice and close to his head, wincing as he did so, because he couldn't see what he was doing and didn't want to cut his skin. He breathed with relief when that cut too was painless. The hair on top was still quite long; he gave it a half-hearted cut so that a thick tuft stood straight up in the air and would no longer be able to fall onto his forehead. He stopped there, placing the scissors carefully into the sink and gathering up the chunks of dark brown hair from the floor and his shoulders. Joe thought that by far the worst part of his haircutting experience was the fact that it was so hard to clean up. It was like cleaning up after the Christmas tree, when the needles seemed impossible to get rid of; bits of hair seemed to materialize after he thought he'd cleaned it all away. In the end he wetted kitchen paper and tried to blot it from the linoleum floor. Eventually he was satisfied that the job was done.

He had showered, as his mum encouraged him to do after a haircut, and put his pajamas on. Everything was out of routine this evening: he was ready for bed and he hadn't eaten or watched an episode of *Friends* yet. His palms sweated slightly at the thought, but he closed his eyes and listened, focusing on the moment. It would be okay: he could heat up leftover curry in the microwave with some microwave rice. He could eat and be in front of the television within twelve minutes. Joe looked at the time; he could watch four episodes and be in bed at the usual hour and spend ten minutes looking at Pip's review list for quiz night.

And he wondered if anyone at work would notice his new haircut at work the following day. Chloe, at least, would be pleased.

## 55
## A compromise for comfort

As the state of Joe-Nathan's appearance on the day that Charlie had shaved his head became apparent, Chloe's face moved through a number of expressions as she first battled to be right about her assessment of Mean Charlie, and then started to struggle to keep that conviction alive.

"Oh, look, I can show you!" Pip picked up her phone again and started scrolling. "Owen forwarded a video on WhatsApp to a few people and I got sent it too. I guess no one showed it to you, Chloe, because, well, y'know."

"What? Because you mean I might have actually done something about it?" Chloe sounded defeated, but she took Pip's phone and shook her head as she watched the clip of Joe standing by his locker. The footage was a bit wobbly but there was the unmistakable sound of Owen sniggering. Joe stood pitifully beside his locker door, glancing sideways as though he thought Owen might be trying to film something other than himself. The video image turned to portrait as it got closer to Joe, so that he was more easily visible from head to foot: the pedal pushers; the shiny, black formal shoes; and then, ever nearer, a close-up of Joe's DIY haircut. Chloe's chin crumpled as she watched Joe smile nervously into Owen's camera, as if he were reluctantly posing for a family photo, rather than being humiliated for the way that he looked. And then the extreme close-up of Joe's hair: strands of it still long in places, short in others, painfully close to the scalp above his ears, as if it had been shaved with a wet razor (that part of his scalp was still visible even now). Just before the video ended, Chloe heard Owen say, "*Wait till Charlie sees this, oh man. He's gonna piss himself.*"

"But he didn't piss himself, did he?" said Pip as she took her phone back. "He got hold of Joe before anyone else could tease him, and shaved it all off."

Chloe stared at Joe, at how good his haircut actually looked, or, at least, how much better it looked than in the video she'd just witnessed.

"Oh fuck," she said, and closed her eyes.

"That reminds me," said Joe, and he opened his satchel, which was on the seat beside him. "I made this for you."

Chloe felt small. She felt as though she had read a book, missed an important chapter, and made her assumptions without that missing piece of information. She held out her hand and took the box from Joe without registering it. She turned it in her hands and ran her thumbs over the smooth surfaces of wood. She read the inscription without really seeing it, or comprehending it. She looked at the box, but all she could see was the view in her mind's eye: Joe in the storeroom, tears streaking his face, a discarded shaver on the floor, an image of herself, jumping on Charlie's back, calling him a bully.

*So* self-righteous, so *knowing*, and apparently so fucking wrong. And yet she had seen Charlie be mean to Joe with her own eyes; it hurt her to hear the way he spoke to him. What would motivate a person—even a person like Charlie—to forcibly and privately shave someone's head? If he had wanted to help, why hadn't he taken him to a barbershop, or given him a hat? Except that Joe would *not* have liked those options either. What could possibly be wrong with a person that they think that's an okay way to behave?

Charlie was mean, Chloe still did not doubt that. But what bothered her was the fact that in his own twisted way he did seem to have actually tried to help Joe, despite the fact that it was technically assault. She didn't think she was entirely wrong about Charlie, and yet . . . and yet right now, she was confused and she hated herself.

"Do you like it?" Joe's question seemed to come from so far away that Chloe had no notion that anyone was talking to her.

"Chloe?" said Pip, and again, to Chloe, the voice sounded far away, but it was her name, so awareness wriggled to the surface like bubbles released from under a rock and she found herself firmly at the table in the pub once more.

"Huh?" she said.

"Do you like it?" Joe said again.

Chloe looked down at the box as if for the first time. There was a slot in the top for money and—with his wood-burning pen—Joe had inscribed on the side:

**PAY HERE**

!*@#

**CHLOE'S SWEAR BOX**

The wood was pale and soft, and perfect. Everything was simple and in-line with no rough edges and no uneven joins.

"You made this for me?" she said.

"Yes," said Joe.

"I love it," she said. "But I don't deserve it."

"But it is useful," said Joe.

Chloe set the wooden box on the table and ran her finger over it. When she spoke, her gaze remained on the box, as if she were addressing it rather than Joe. "How is Charlie?" she said.

Joe didn't answer and Chloe raised her eyes to meet his.

"How is he?" she repeated.

"He is . . ." Joe didn't know how to answer the question, but Chloe waited and finally he said, "He is out of his place."

"What?"

"Out of place. Not where he is supposed to be. It makes me feel uncomfortable."

"But how does *he* feel about it?" Chloe persisted.

"I do not know," said Joe, because that was the truth. He only knew how *he* himself felt about it. How could he know how Charlie felt, if Charlie hadn't told him?

Chloe suddenly sat very upright and craned her neck to look round the pub. "Hugo!" she shouted, and Hugo looked over and waved. "Come here!" He made some sort of apology to the person he was standing with, placing his hand on their arm, before negotiating his way through the people talking in little groups.

He sat himself down heavily next to Joe and sighed as if he'd run here. He was drinking something clear in a short glass with a very thin short straw that he chased round the glass with his mouth until he found it and took a long sip.

"It's a long time since I had a Friday afternoon off." He raised his glass. "To Janet," he said, and they clinked their glasses. Joe was a little late with the gesture. Hugo found his straw again, a little easier this time, and took another long sip.

"Hugo?" Chloe said. "Is it possible for Charlie to get his job back?"

"What?" Hugo loosened his lips on his straw, and it momentarily stuck there before dropping back into the glass. "I thought you were the one keen to see him gone."

"I was, but I might have got my wires crossed." Chloe grimaced and held her hands together as if in prayer.

"Well, the short answer is no, I'm afraid. He's already been replaced. There are no hours for Charlie."

Joe turned his hand over and looked at his palms. His breathing became audible and the other three looked at him. "No hours for Charlie. No time. No place," he said.

"Charlie will be alright, Joe," said Pip. "He's strong."

"That's true," said Hugo, and he and Pip shared a look.

Joe closed his eyes and saw Charlie's body lurch toward him as he was kicked in the back. With his eyes still closed, Joe said, "If I give you some of my hours, will you give them to Charlie?" As the words left his lips, Joe's breathing became rapid. His routine would be changed if he gave away his hours, but then Charlie would be at work and that would make Joe feel better. It was a compromise for comfort.

"No," said Chloe. "Not you, Joe. I'll give up mine. Hugo. I'll go part-time and do a job share with Charlie."

"No can do," said Hugo. "It's not just that he's been replaced, but that he's got a complaint of assault and bullying against him. The Compass Store can't possibly employ him until the complaint has been reviewed, and only then if the accusation is revoked."

"We revoke it," said Chloe.

Hugo frowned and shook his head. "Okay, listen. I don't know what's going on here, but this is not the place to discuss this, and even if it were, things can't happen as quickly as you seem to think they can. For example, I can't simply ring HR and revoke the complaint. There's a process to go through, which will take time."

Chloe rested her head in her hands and Joe began lining up the coasters on the table.

"Would it be okay if Charlie joined our team for quiz night?" Pip said. "I mean, if he wants to."

Chloe glanced up at Hugo and Joe's hands hovered over the coasters. Hugo looked around at all of them, like children who had been denied what they really wanted and were now asking for something small, anything to feel like they'd won.

Hugo said, "If you want him there, then I don't see why not."

# 56
## The next best thing

At 6 p.m. in the Ink and Feather, Joe-Nathan—for the first time on the day of his mum's funeral—started to feel at ease, because it was only then that he was in the correct place at the right time. It was disconcerting to be surrounded by people who wanted to talk to him. But if he remained at the table the majority of the time, and walked very quickly—and stared at the carpet—when he wanted to use the toilet, then he didn't have to encounter conversation too often.

Just as the day of the funeral had rolled toward him when it hadn't yet happened, Joe now felt it rolling away behind him into the past. As it receded into the distance, Joe couldn't tell whether it was because he was moving forward, or because it was moving backward, a bit like when he had sat on a train next to another train at the station and didn't know which one was moving.

The new normality that had started to gather after his mum's death was something that Joe could now return to and build on. He hadn't got the chance to get used to the routines of his life without his mum around, but because the days leading up to her funeral—and the funeral itself—had been so out of his comfort zone (the experience with Charlie, the not-working on Friday, the burying of his mum), that now the rhythms of the days that preceded the funeral took on a relative familiarity he was keen to return to.

He had become accustomed, for instance, to not visiting cemeteries on a Saturday, because nobody had taken him to one since his mum died. So, the morning after the funeral, Joe programmed his alarm to its usual Saturday-morning setting, got up, and ate cereal in his pajamas, as he always had, since forever. Today the cereal looked quite normal in the bowl and the pattern on the crockery didn't stand out in any unusual way. He tidied away his bowl and spoon and wiped a cloth over the table. Then he dressed and made a list of jobs for himself. He set his alarm to go off six times during the day. When he had set it for twelve, he found that sometimes a task wouldn't be finished by the time the alarm went off and he was disappointed. With two hours allocated per task, if there was any spare time between tasks, then he would watch television and thus his day could be completely filled until he reached the time of day when the old Saturday routine of *Friends* and a takeaway could kick in, leaving him soothed and at peace, ready for bedtime.

As Janet had always said, when new things came into his life, eventually they would stop being new (if he gave them a chance) and join the gang of things he was used to. He just needed to be patient.

One of Joe's two-hour tasks that Saturday was to visit Charlie's house. This was Joe's third unannounced visit, and he was already starting to feel less intimidated by the change in scenery as he left his neighborhood and made his way toward the gasworks. He had felt more comfortable in his hoodie last time he came here, so he wore it again; the awkwardness of having his head covered was less bothersome than the vulnerability he felt when his head was exposed in new territory.

His step faltered slightly as he saw the same teenagers sitting on the same wall and he crossed the road on a diagonal, hoping that they wouldn't see him, when the usual question was shouted out at him.

"Hey, you again, you never answered that question about a blow job. You want one or not?"

Joe stopped in the middle of the street and turned to face the small group. "No. But thank you for the offer. I am going to wait until I am in a sexual relationship," he said, and then turned to finish crossing the road.

"Oh, poor Stacey, he doesn't fancy you," he heard a boy say.

"Shut up," said a girl, and then their voices and laughter faded until they were gone completely.

Charlie's house and the sad sofa with its collection of beer cans came into view and there was at least the comforting sense that he had found his way without worrying or thinking about it too much. The walk had seemed shorter than before, by virtue of the fact that he knew where he was going. The only thing that made his palms sweat slightly was the fact that he hadn't seen Charlie's dad come out of the Chinese takeaway this time, meaning there was the possibility that he would be at the house and might open the door. He had considered this with concern and, in caution, he knocked hard on Charlie's door and then took four large paces back, double the advised amount according to his mum (and even more if you considered that they were particularly *large* steps). This enabled him to get a good head start if Charlie's dad opened the door and was mean to him.

But it was Charlie who opened the door and he stepped outside, quickly and softly pulling the door behind him when he saw Joe.

"What are you doing here again?" he whispered, padding toward Joe in his socks, and touching Joe's elbow to encourage him out the gate. "My dad's here. He's asleep, but if he wakes up and finds you, he won't be happy."

Joe pulled his satchel around to the front and unfastened the buckle. He removed a big, sturdy, cream-colored envelope and handed it to Charlie.

"What's this?" Charlie asked. "You getting married or something?"

"Something," said Joe.

Charlie looked briefly over his shoulder at his front door and then slid his thumb into the envelope and removed the card; it was handmade, done with colored pens and glitter.

"You are invited to join our team, Pip's Players, for the annual Compass Store Quiz Night on Saturday, May 18. Be there or be square," he read aloud. "Did you make this?" Charlie said. Joe nodded.

"God, you're an idiot," said Charlie, shaking his head. He squinted hard at Joe. "*Pip's Players?*"

"The name was Pip's idea," said Joe.

"No shit," said Charlie. "Be there or be *square*?" he repeated. "Fuckin' hell."

"That bit was Chloe's idea."

"Seriously?"

Joe nodded. "She was drunk."

"That makes more sense."

"But she didn't throw up or sleep over," Joe added quickly.

"Chloe's okay with this?" Charlie asked.

"Yes," said Joe, and he looked up, trying to recall the order of reasoning. He counted each sentence on his fingers: "She wanted you to have your job back. Hugo said no. Quiz night is the next best thing."

Charlie scoffed. "*Chloe* wanted me to have my job back? Why?"

"She made a mistake. She decided that you were trying to help me when you cut my hair. She told Hugo to take her hours and give them to you. I told Hugo to take mine too, but he couldn't. He said it was The Rules."

Charlie stared at Joe, his gaze flicking back and forth between Joe's eyes, as if what he couldn't find in one, he might find in the other. He was silent.

Eventually, Joe said, "Will you come?"

Charlie looked down at the invitation and his chin creased. "I'm no good at quizzes," he said.

"Pip made a review sheet," said Joe, pulling one from his satchel.

Charlie took it and stared again at Joe. "I don't know."

"Please," said Joe. "It is the next best thing."

Charlie nodded upward. "Maybe. Okay. Yeah, why not?"

"Good," said Joe, and he looked at his watch. If he left now, there would be plenty of time to watch some TV before his next task started. He turned to walk away.

"Hey, Joe," said Charlie.

Joe turned to Charlie again. "Text me first, if you want to come over again. You know . . ." He tilted his head toward the house and Charlie's dad within. "Just in case."

## 57
### Dangerously numb

Charlie went back into his house, closing the door as softly as he could behind him and padding quietly into the kitchen. He reread the invitation and felt bad as he tore it in half and then in half again. A little cloud of glitter puffed at him and he pressed his foot on the pedal of the bin; it clanged as it sprang open and Charlie winced, pushing the card and envelope deep inside it.

"What are you doing?" Charlie's dad's voice was blurred with beer from the night before but clear enough to understand because of the dregs he'd just drained from a can on the coffee table when he woke up.

"Nothing," said Charlie, wiping his hands on his jeans and leaving glitter on them. "Just clearing up."

"Hah. Right," said Charlie's dad, and he pushed past Charlie, opened the bin, and started pulling out the torn-up pieces of paper.

"Dad . . . ," said Charlie.

"What?" said Charlie's dad, not looking up, rummaging in the bin and pulling out the pieces of card as he found them.

"Don't," said Charlie. But Charlie's dad ignored him and as he found the pieces of matching card and envelope, he laid them out on the kitchen counter. When he couldn't find any more, he put his hand deeper in the bin, and once satisfied that there were no more, he leaned over the bits he had found and started to rearrange them.

"Come here, and help me put this together. It's like a jigsaw. See, it's fun *and* I get to see what you're hiding from me."

Charlie didn't approach his dad. His eyes burned and he glanced over at the calendar—the chrome lorry outside the American diner—and realized that it was actually May now, not April anymore. He took the calendar from its nail on the wall and flipped it over to show the right month. The picture was of a woman in a pink-and-white uniform driving a pink Cadillac, she was smiling like mad, and as Charlie lined up the little hole with the nail on the wall, he felt a tear roll down his cheek, which he angrily wiped away.

"Quiz night!" Charlie's dad shouted. "Pip's Players!" He started laughing and the laugh turned into a cough and when the cough stopped, the laughing turned into something grim. "Glitter?" he said in a dark voice.

"It's just stupid," said Charlie. "It's nothing."

"Then why were you trying to hide it? Why did you tear it up? People don't hide 'nothing,' do they." Charlie's dad came and stood right in front of Charlie, his breath like a pub carpet. The invitation didn't really matter to him; it was just a prop, an anything, an excuse, a hook of any kind to hang his frustration on. Charlie knew that. He tried to step sideways, making a move to leave the kitchen, but Charlie's dad quickly grabbed his throat and pushed him against the wall. The pink lady smiled over Charlie's shoulder and the nail in the wall scraped his scalp behind his ear. Charlie didn't bother to reach back and touch the blood that rolled down his neck. He imagined smashing his forehead into his dad's nose (he could picture it) in an attempt to get him to loosen his grip. But he'd tried to fight back before and when he did, his dad was like a bulldog: relentless, powerful, and dangerously numb. Charlie had a week off work the last time he fought back. His best bet was to allow himself to be beaten; that way his dad would probably stop before Charlie was hospitalized.

"Glitter." Charlie's dad breathed the word foully into Charlie's face and Charlie imagined his dad's breath as a putrid, cloudy entity curling up like smoke into Charlie's nostrils and down into his lungs, so that what had once been inside his dad was now inside of him.

"I'll do you some breakfast if you like. We've got bacon and bread," said Charlie, his words a little strained against the stranglehold.

And Charlie's dad must have had the same idea as Charlie, because he responded by tipping his head back slightly and bringing it forward with sudden force against the bridge of Charlie's nose. Charlie cried out; pain flared like fire through the center of his face: fire in his nose, behind his eyes, and into his forehead. He felt as though he'd been shot in the head. Charlie's dad let go and Charlie slid to the floor, his face in his hands. His nose hurt so bad he willed time to pass so that it would diminish into afterpain. He had become accustomed to living with aches and twinges, the echoes of agony. But he couldn't get used to that sharp initial pain. And this was taking longer than normal to subside.

Charlie's dad walked away, scratching his bum cheek.

"Yeah, alright," said Charlie's dad, burping softly. "I will have that bacon sandwich."

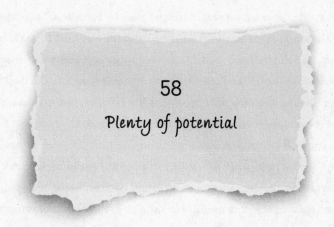

## 58
### Plenty of potential

Joe-Nathan's next task that Saturday—after he had returned from delivering the invitation to Charlie and watched some TV—was carpentry, and he was so eager to start on it that he watched the TV in an agitated state and looked repeatedly at the time, willing his alarm to go off sooner than it would.

As soon as the alarm sounded, he shot up from his armchair and stabbed at the remote control, grunting when the television wouldn't turn off instantly. Then he trotted to the workshop and assembled his materials.

When Joe cooked, he put all the ingredients on the kitchen counter before he started, and it was the same process with woodworking. He had drawn out the template for the piece he was making for Charlie and laid it out on the main workbench, along with a bottle of boiled linseed oil, a brush, wood glue, a piece of deer leather, a pair of strong scissors, a pull door handle, a selection of screws, a power drill, a sand-ing block, and his wood-burning pen. He checked that the bandsaw was plugged in and working (he hadn't used it since he last made a jigsaw for Hazel). Then he went to the back of the workshop where the woodstore was, and picked out the piece he had already allocated for the job. It was a largish piece, larger than he was used to working with. He had struggled to find something that wasn't too thin, which would make the finished article too fragile, and not too thick or dense, which would make the thing too heavy. But he had called Angus, who had come round with a good-sized piece of plywood.

With all the pieces laid out in front of him, Joe was satisfied that—once cut and assembled correctly—they would become more than the sum of their parts, something his dad had explained to him when they created one useful, beautiful object out of an assortment of pieces that had no specific purpose (but plenty of potential).

Knowing that his timer was set for two hours and the clock was ticking, Joe stuck the paper template to the plywood and set it against the bandsaw, carving out the shape on the paper, doing it slowly, getting it right the first time, cutting only wood and not his fingers (which had been the first rule of the workshop, according to Joe's dad). He was engrossed in the task and thought of nothing else while occupied with it.

Joe's life—before his mum died—had always been occupied from one moment to the next with a feeling of purpose and dedication, each moment as purposeful and dedicated as the next. But since her death, those moments took on a hierarchy in which some tasks were much more absorbing and enjoyable than others. There was a predictability in the fact that he did not enjoy the cleaning and tidying and laundry as much as some other jobs. Not only was he doing many more house-hold chores now, but he had not realized that Janet had protected him from the household tasks that he was less likely to enjoy. In addition, there was little satisfaction to be gained from cleaning and tidying an already clean and tidy house. He tried to envisage the process of cleaning and tidying Charlie's house, and while the thought of touch-ing some of the things revolted him (he could not get the image of the ashtray out of his mind), he *could* imagine the amount of satisfaction that would accompany completing the task of making it spotless. Thoughts of this kind invariably led Joe to picture the battered sofa in Charlie's front yard and Joe knew there was no hope for that at all. He didn't imagine cleaning or fixing it; he imagined setting light to it, waiting for the resulting pile of ashes to cool, then sweeping them up with a dustpan and brush, putting them in a paper bag and then into the black-lidded bin.

Two hours later, when his alarm sounded in the workshop, Joe felt there had been a mistake, as it seemed to him that very little time had passed. He looked at his watch and was confused that it too showed the passing of two full hours. But a lot had been achieved: the plywood had been cut into the correct shape; he had applied a coat of linseed oil to it, fixed the door handle to the back of it, and wrapped a piece of deer leather securely around the handle. He hadn't allocated another time slot to the job for today, which he regretted, as he would have liked to use the wood-burning pen for the inscription. However, he decided that tomorrow—Sunday—he would give himself a double (four-hour) slot to enable him to complete the job. He couldn't wait to give Charlie his gift. It was so much bigger, so much more useful, and far more beautiful than a money box.

## 59
### The sort who'll let you down

By Monday morning, knowing that Charlie's present was sitting finished on his workbench, and that this day represented the beginning of an entire week of work with potentially no surprises and nothing out of the norm, Joe-Nathan was feeling firmly at ease. His pace was slightly quicker and his feet hit the ground slightly harder than usual and his arm was strong at the elbow as he gave a wave, a rock-star gesture, and the peace sign to the trees on his way into The Compass Store. The compass mosaic was there for him as always, like a good friend, and when Joe's feet met it, he briskly turned northwest toward the staff-room. He deposited his satchel, collected his tabard, and put his lunch box in the fridge with a sense of belonging that brought him joy: the joy of knowing where he should be and simply being there.

"Hey, loser," Owen's voice fired at him from across the room, but even the insult fell within the realm of normality and therefore could not stop Joe from being relatively at ease. Joe looked over at Owen and tucked his neck into his shoulders. A man sitting next to Owen elbowed him and said, "Don't. You heard what Hugo said."

But Owen began slowly clapping and said, "Well done for what you done for Charlie."

Joe unwound his neck and smiled at Owen; he did this before realizing that Owen couldn't possibly know what he had done for Charlie, couldn't possibly know what was sitting on his workbench, and why.

Owen slapped his hands on the table in response to Joe's smile, and stood, but his companion whispered furtively at him until Owen sat back down again and Joe left the staff-room wondering what had just happened.

Thoughts of Owen and what he had meant were quickly soothed by the cool air of the warehouse and the full trolley of go-backs. Joe knew what he was doing and everything felt aligned in each moment. He was wearing the right shoes and the right top, his hair was not too long (it wouldn't be too long for a long time), and he had a nice work schedule lined up for the day.

"How's things, Joe?" Chloe said, leaning on the end of his trolley and snapping her gum.

"Good," said Joe.

"How you feeling since the funeral?"

"I think I have closure. Angus said I would."

Chloe snapped her gum and nodded. "I know what you mean." She hesitated, seemed to want to say something. Joe waited. "I was thinking," she said eventually. "The idea to invite Charlie onto our team for quiz night. I don't think it's such a good idea after all."

"But you said, '*Be there or be square.*'"

"Huh?"

"When I asked what I should put on the invitation."

"Christ, you mean an actual invitation, like a party invitation?"

"Yes."

"Well, I was drunk; so was Pip. Anyway, I'm just saying, I don't think it's a good idea. I agree he should have his job back. Probably. Maybe. But I don't want to do this pally 'sitting round the table like we're all friends with him' malarkey."

"Why?"

"I just think—you know—okay, I got it wrong about his motives behind the head-shaving incident, but that doesn't take away the fact he shouldn't have done it and that he was generally pretty mean and said some horrible things to you. I think quiz night feels a bit cozy."

"I made the invitation and invited him and he said yes," said Joe.

"You . . ." Chloe frowned. "You *made* an invitation?"

"Yes. With glitter."

"With gli—?" Chloe exhaled and shook her head sharply. "And he said he'd come?"

"Yes."

Chloe breathed out long and hard and pushed herself away from the trolley. "Well, that's that, then, you can't uninvite him."

"No. That would be rude." Joe knew this from his mum's yellow book: the section on invitations.

"But!" Chloe pointed a finger at Joe. "Don't expect him to turn up. He's the sort who will let you down."

"He will come," said Joe.

"He won't," said Chloe, and she walked away due west.

Neither Chloe's prediction nor Owen's confusing slow clap stayed with Joe for long. He stacked, he cleared, he cleaned a floor. He folded, he hung, he arranged fake flowers in a display of vases. He waved at Pip when she waved at him coming down aisle seven, and when she said (as she passed him), "Horizontal red, white, blue, white, red," Joe said, "Flag of Thailand," and she squealed and walked on.

Nothing could spoil the ordinariness of his day.

That evening (because Joe did not tend to think ahead) he didn't text Charlie until after dinner, to check that it was okay to bring his present over. He sent the message and was just about to go up to the workshop and bubble wrap the thing, when Charlie texted his reply:

Joe, don't come over tonight. Dad's here, in a bad mood. Another time.

Joe was disappointed. He knew how happy Charlie would be with the thing he had made. And if his dad was in a bad mood, maybe he could use it sooner rather than later. But no, Charlie had said *don't*, and there was no arguing with that. Joe didn't like the idea of seeing Charlie's dad in a bad mood. He would text him again tomorrow.

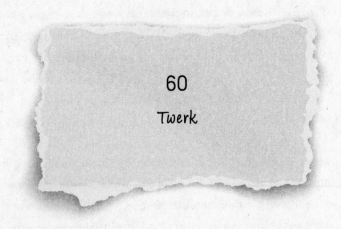

## 60
## Twerk

J oe-Nathan texted Charlie on Tuesday, Wednesday, and Thursday, and each time he got a similar response:

Not tonight, I'm not feeling great.

Not tonight, dad's home.

Don't come over, there won't be anyone in.

Every time Joe got a rejection text from Charlie he felt the weight of it pull his shoulders down. He sloped to the workshop and peeled back some of the Bubble Wrap, so he could see the thing inside and reassure himself of how pleased Charlie would be when he saw it.

Joe was doing what Charlie had asked: texting before he went over to his house; he was comfortable following rules, and so for four days, that's what he did. But on Friday night, after four half-pints of lager in the Ink and Feather, Joe decided that he was more comfortable *not* following the rule of texting first. He wanted to give Charlie his present, he didn't want to wait any longer, and he was nervous that if he texted, Charlie would say no again. The best way to avoid that, he reasoned, was to not text him at all.

Joe walked home quickly and went up to the spare bedroom. In the bottom of the wardrobe were some suitcases and bags; Joe selected a decent-sized case that had both wheels and straps, so that it could be rolled along the ground, carried by hand, or worn on his back like a big rucksack.

He took the bag to the workshop and carefully slid Charlie's present into it, making sure the Bubble Wrap didn't ruck up and expose a corner of the wood, not that any damage could be done that way, only that Joe would have felt out of sorts knowing it was not completely covered. He put his arms through the straps; they were too tight and needed some adjustment, but soon he was on his way to Charlie's house, hoping that Charlie would be in and not angry to see him, hoping that Charlie's dad would be out.

The weeds in the path on the way to Charlie's were becoming familiar markers. Joe noticed that they were going through changes: growing; some of them flowering; there was a bright yellow dandelion. There was nothing in the trees that looked anything like a hand signal, but Joe kept his thumbs in the bag straps, which was heartening, and a lady smiled at him while she cleaned bird poo off the windscreen of her car. No teenagers were on the wall, nobody called out or spoke to him, and Joe felt calm as he approached the battered green sofa, which today—auspiciously perhaps—had not one single beer can on the ground beside it.

Joe knocked on Charlie's door and took two large steps backward. Nothing.

He stepped forward and knocked again, more loudly this time. Two large steps back. Waited. Nothing.

The same sagging disappointment weighed heavy on Joe's shoulders—this time more literally—as he shifted uneasily under the weight of Charlie's gift.

He sighed and turned and lifted the latch on the crooked gate and closed it behind him. He was heading toward home when he sensed the slightest sound in the atmosphere that sounded like a door opening, and glanced over his shoulder to see that Charlie was in his doorway, looking out to see who had knocked.

"It's me," Joe shouted, and Charlie said nothing.

"Is your dad home?" Joe called out. Charlie shook his head, and Joe smiled to himself. He should have texted after all, he thought, because this would have been the time that Charlie would have said yes.

Charlie was far away when Joe started walking back toward him, and Joe couldn't work out why he appeared to be wearing an eye mask, the kind worn by bandits in old Saturday morning TV shows. Only as he got much closer (Charlie stayed in the doorway) did Joe notice that Charlie had two black eyes joined together by purplish bruising over the top of his nose. The dark coloring spread symmetrically from the inner corners of his eyes down toward his cheeks. The sight of Charlie's face slowed Joe's legs down until they came to a complete stop about three strides away, and his mouth didn't work for a while, so the boys just stared at each other for a minute. Eventually Charlie smiled at Joe as if to apologize for his face, a smile that was more like a shrug.

"What happened to your eyes?" said Joe.

"Don't worry about it. You should see the other guy!"

"Who is the other guy?"

Charlie's smile dropped and he looked at the ground. "You might as well come in, now you're here."

Joe followed Charlie into the house and shut the door behind him. Charlie was already in the kitchen. "I thought I told you to text before you came over."

"Every time I texted, you said no, so I decided not to. I want to give you something."

Charlie leaned in the same place as before, against the kitchen counter; his hand rested in a beam of sunlight. Joe glanced at the calendar; it was hanging straight and showed the month of May. He relaxed.

"Milk?" Charlie asked.

"No."

"Water? Beer? Um, tea?"

"No, thank you."

"Okay," said Charlie. They just looked at each other, Joe staring at Charlie's bruises, Charlie allowing them to be stared at, because, what could he do about it?

"What did you want to give me?" Charlie said.

"This." Joe turned and tried to shuffle off his rucksack, but it was tight to his back and the straps wouldn't slide down his arms. Charlie laughed as he watched Joe practically twerk. He laughed and he couldn't stop, and Joe continued to jiggle and bounce, with his feet firmly planted and his knees bent and his arms out straight behind him. Charlie laughed and eventually Joe stopped trying to get the bag off, and turned to watch as Charlie—bent at the waist and leaning on his own knees—struggled to breathe through his obvious amusement. Charlie waved a hand at Joe, but couldn't speak, and Joe was happy that he'd made his friend smile. And, when Charlie finally calmed (he said "Sorry" through his subsiding laughter), Joe turned around and did it again: jiggling and bouncing just to make Charlie laugh again, and Charlie did. He laughed until no noise came out and he waved frantically to get Joe to stop and, in the end, he sat on a kitchen stool and sighed the sigh of those worn out by laughter.

"I need help," said Joe.

"Join the club," said Charlie, wiping tears from his brownish, purple, yellowing skin, and Joe noticed that his eyes were bloodshot too. Everything on Charlie's face was not the color it was meant to be. Charlie stood and adjusted the clips on Joe's straps, letting the material run through them and loosening the rucksack so that it fell away from Joe's back. Charlie reached round to take the weight of the bag from underneath as Joe pulled first one, then the other strap down his arms and over his wrists.

"What the hell is in here?" Charlie asked, hefting the sack onto the counter.

Joe unzipped the bag carefully and slid it away from the piece of wood inside. Charlie got it out of the Bubble Wrap, picked it up, and said, "What's this?" Even though it was obvious what it was.

"This is something beautiful," said Joe, "but also useful, and my mum said the best presents are always at least one of those things, preferably both."

"How is this useful?" said Charlie, lifting it up and holding it against him.

"I do not understand," said Joe. "How is it not useful? It is for you to use in a fight; therefore, it is useful." Charlie turned it over in his arms and frowned so that Joe wondered if he really didn't know what it was.

So, just to make sure, he told him, "It's a shield."

# 61
## Happy soul

Charlie pushed his arm through the deer-skin strap that was attached to the back of the shield, then took a firm grip of the deer-skin-wrapped handle that was attached in just the right place so that the strap held firm just below his elbow, and it felt natural to hold the shield square in front of him.

"You made me a toy?" Charlie said.

"No!" said Joe-Nathan. "The shield was the most widespread defensive weapon in the world when hand-to-hand combat was more prevalent than remote technological warfare. It protects a warrior from enemy blows and can deflect thrown spears and other missiles. You could use a stick to ward off a blow, but a true shield always has some form of grip, and you, Charlie, need body protection."

"Why do you sound so dumb most of the time and then say something that makes you sound like a university professor?"

"I do not know," said Joe. "Why do you sometimes act mean and sometimes act nice?"

Charlie stared at Joe over the top of the shield but said nothing. Joe opened a smaller front zip pocket in the rucksack and extracted the yellow book of advice his mum had written. He opened it and read aloud:

*Rules of thumb: walk away from a fight, it takes courage. Avoid violence, that's wise. If you are attacked, try to shield yourself.*

*It takes courage to walk away when someone tries to fight you, because it makes them feel like they have won and they may say things to try and make you stay and fight back, especially if they think they can beat you or they want to hurt you. Do not listen to them, walk away, that is the wise thing to do. If you can't get away, then protect yourself: shield your face and eyes and shield your body.*

"And if that doesn't work?" Charlie said.

Joe looked back down at the book. "Call 999," he said.

Charlie grinned and suddenly adopted a pose: a lunge, feet wide apart and shield held up and out in front of him, as if he were defending himself against an enemy, as if Joe had just pulled out a toy sword and he was ready for a play-fight.

Joe smiled. "There is an inscription," he said, pointing at the front of the shield. Charlie took his arm out of the strap and turned the shield over.

"This is actually good, Joe, did you really make it yourself?"

Joe nodded and pointed again at the inscription.

Charlie ran his fingers over the cursive in the center of the shield as if it were braille. He read the words:

*A happy soul is the best shield for a cruel world.*

"Did you make that up?"

"No. Atticus said it. It was the quote I liked best out of the quotes for shields I looked at. There is another quote on the inside," said Joe. Charlie turned the shield over again and read the words:

*For the shield may be as important for victory,*
*as the sword or spear.*

"I wrote that on the inside because I think in your case, you need an actual shield for a good shield and not just a happy soul."

"Who said this one?" Charlie asked, his gaze glued to the words, his voice small.

"Charles Darwin."

"Do you think he's right?"

"About what?"

"That the shield is as important for victory as the sword?"

"If you are headed for a Pyrrhic victory, where you will lose as much by winning as the person you defeat, then yes, it is better to shield. If survival is the main aim, then yes, the shield."

"Christ," said Charlie. "Who *are* you?"

Joe looked past Charlie's head at a wonky kitchen cupboard door. "That broken hinge is making my hands sweat," he said.

"There he is! Stupid is back in the room!" said Charlie, clapping his hands.

"Will you use it?" Joe asked, focusing his eyes on the shield and trying not to look at the unsettling fixtures and fittings in the kitchen.

"I like it. But honestly? Probably not."

"Why not?"

"I just . . . well, what are you picturing? That someone goes to hit me and I just happen to have my shield nearby and I use it to block their punches?"

"Yes," said Joe.

"When you were here last time and I got kicked in the back, how would it have helped then?"

Joe conceded that it wouldn't have been much help.

"I *think*," said Charlie, "that I might be better off working on my happy soul."

Joe was home at just the right time to make boiled eggs and buttered soldiers, watch four episodes of *Friends*, and be in his pajamas and in bed on schedule. It was more soothing to think of Charlie now: he might not be in a good place, but at least he had protection; at least he had liked the thing that Joe had made him; at least he was even more likely to understand that Joe did not have a mean bone in his body.

Joe slept well and while he slept, he dreamed that his mum sat on a wall, swinging her legs, licking an ice cream, and smiling as she watched Joe play in the street with his friends. When he woke on Saturday morning, the echo of her was still there, and it didn't make him sad at all. He had been in touch with Hazel and asked if she would come with him to the cemetery that day.

She brought Angus along, even though he said, "I hate being among the dead."

"I like them," said Joe. "They are predictable."

As they walked through the cemetery avenues toward the place where his mum and dad were at rest, Joe found himself thinking about the following Saturday, which was not a thing he would normally do, but these were extraordinary times, and so perhaps it wasn't so unusual. Next Saturday would be the night of the quiz, and—remembering the poster that had advertised the event—he rubbed his palms on his legs; he still hadn't asked anyone what "BYOB" meant. He glanced at Hazel and thought about asking her, but it occurred to him that the last time he asked her a question he had discovered the meaning of blow jobs and that had been slightly unpleasant. Was a byob anything like a blow job? It sounded like it might be.

Nerves nudged the word out of his mouth: "Byob, byob, byob," he muttered, and once it started coming out, it wouldn't stop; it spilled out of him like something rolling down a hill at speed: "Byobyoby-obyobyobyob."

Hazel and Angus both stopped, and so did Joe, but the word would not. He twisted a finger on his scalp, where he might have once twisted it into his hair.

"Hey, buddy, what's up?" Angus said, reaching out to touch Joe's arm, and then pulling back before he made contact.

"Joe?" said Hazel. "Are you feeling nervous about visiting the grave?"

"Byobyobyobyob."

"I think we should sit down for a bit," said Angus. The three of them sat on a bench and eventually the byobs ran out and they all just kept quiet and listened to the breeze in the big trees and that was so much better.

Joe closed his eyes and tilted his head back.

"What is a byob?" he said after a while.

"Well, I was going to ask you the same thing," said Angus. "You're the one keeps talking about them." He snorted.

"You have not heard of them?" said Joe.

"Not me," said Angus. "Have you had much experience with byobs, Hazel?"

"Certainly not," said Hazel. "Not at my age." Hazel and Angus smiled at each other.

"It must be a spelling error," said Joe. "It was on a poster."

"How are you spelling it?" Angus asked.

"B-Y-O-B," said Joe.

"Oh! That means Bring Your Own Bottle. You sometimes get it on a party invite or to somewhere where there's no bar."

"What?" said Joe.

Hazel took up the answer. "It usually means a bottle of alcohol, but can be a bottle of anything you would like to drink, to take with you when you're going somewhere that might not have enough drinks for everyone coming. It helps a person throw a good party, even if they can't supply the booze."

"Oh," said Joe.

"Have you been worrying about that for a long time, Joe?" said Angus.

"A little while."

"Next time you want to know something, just ask straightaway, don't let things get on top of you."

Joe looked at Hazel. She closed her eyes briefly and smiled. "He's right," she said. "Ask absolutely anything, it doesn't matter what."

## 62

### In the book

The whole of the next working week was uneventful. It hadn't happened that way in ages, but Joe-Nathan floated through blissful predictable days that met all his simple expectations. Quiz night twinkled in the distance, as something *new*. But he was buoyed and drew reassurance about dealing with the *new thing* by the consistency of his normal life; it was a bedrock and a safety net, a reliable place that was there like the bass note in a song. The security of Joe's normality and the knowledge that Chloe and Pip would be there with him enabled Joe to feel a glimmer of excitement about the Saturday night quiz. It felt like a tiny spark of a fish within a sea of familiarity and was, therefore, more manageable.

"You been studying, Joe?" Chloe asked in the staff-room as he laid out his lunch in order of consumption, left to right. Joe knew that Chloe knew he didn't like to talk during lunch, so he gave a sharp nod and then touched each item as if to confirm its place in the eating order: cheese wrap, carrot sticks, caramel wafer, banana.

"I haven't," she said, and hunched over her pot of noodles. Nothing was said for some time but Chloe must have been in a talking mood, because she continued discussing quiz night as Joe continued to concentrate on making sure his lunch stayed perpendicular to the edge of the table, and chewed his food the correct number of times.

"What are you two talking about?" Pip asked, flopping into a chair beside Chloe and opening a bottle of water.

"What you mean is what am *I* talking about," Chloe said. "Joe isn't talking back. I was starting to wonder if I was invisible."

"He never talks during lunch, you know that."

"Yeah, I know," said Chloe. "Anyway, *I* was talking about quiz night and how I haven't reviewed. Joe has, though."

Pip clasped her hands primly in her lap and tilted her head at Chloe. "Why haven't you reviewed? What about my sheet?"

"I'm not worried about winning, I'm just looking forward to doing something different. Wholesome. Something that doesn't just involve going to a pub."

Pip huffed and pursed her lips. "I do understand, but it would be nice to win, and between the four of us, if one of us knows an answer that no one else does, then we might just do it!" Pip was leaning down close to the table, so that her whispers seemed to roll across it. "I've never won a quiz before, never won anything."

Joe paused before putting a carrot stick in his mouth. "Chloe says Charlie will not come to the quiz, so we might be a team of three."

Joe's voice during lunch was so unexpected that neither of the girls said anything, but simply stared. Joe continued to straighten his food and ate his carrot sticks as though the anomaly of talking was a genuine one-off, not to be repeated.

"Why won't he come?" Pip said to Chloe. "That's so disappointing."

"He hasn't actually said he won't come; I just know he won't."

"How do you know that?" Pip asked.

Chloe did a big sigh as if she were tired of explaining herself. "I've met a million Charlies before," she said. Joe looked up at her. "Not literally a million," Chloe clarified. "I mean there's a lot of people like Charlie out there: self-serving, overconfident, intolerant, and unreliable. They do stuff without thinking about the consequences and they don't really care about other people. Yes, I get it, maybe Charlie was trying to help Joe by shaving his head, but honestly, was that the best way to go about it? Anyway, it's not just about the hair incident; it's about what Charlie is. I don't know why he would have given Joe the impression he's going to come to the quiz. Why would he? What's in it for him? You start trusting a Charlie and it's gonna come back and bite you on the arse."

"Blimey," said Pip, and she tentatively changed the subject, leaving Joe to finish his lunch, and attempting to calm Chloe down.

When Joe was finished eating, he cleared his rubbish and his lunch box away and then he sat back down at the table. This had never happened before. Pip looked at him as if he might need medical attention.

"What are you doing?" Chloe said, just as surprised as Pip that he had sat back down with them.

Joe cleared his throat and laid his hands on his thighs. He looked at his hands and shifted them slightly, as if to align them with the table in the same way as his lunchtime things. He cleared his throat again.

"There is a section in the yellow book that you should read," said Joe. His gaze remained fixed on his lap.

"Who are you talking to?" Chloe asked.

"You," he said.

"Janet's advice book?" she said.

Joe nodded.

"That yellow book is your mum's guidance for you—not me—to help *you* navigate life and situations."

"You are mentioned in the section," Joe said.

"Oh," said Chloe, her eyebrows shooting up. "Really?"

"Yes, and I think you should read it."

"What's it about?" said Chloe.

"It is about the danger of making assumptions," said Joe, and he rose from the table and left to return to his shift, having looked neither woman in the eye since he sat down with them this time.

Pip folded her arms and grinned at Chloe. "You're in the book, you lucky cow."

Chloe checked Pip's face for sarcasm, but found none.

"I think he's trying to say you shouldn't make assumptions about Charlie," Pip clarified.

"Oh, you think?" said Chloe. Chloe reached into her bag for a cigarette and pushed herself back from the table.

"Charlie won't be there on Saturday," she said, talking around the unlit cigarette between her lips. "You'll see. He won't come."

# 63
## Quiz night

The quiz night attendees loitered around the entrance to The Compass Store. About forty people were there in various states of glamour ranging from jeans and T-shirts to dresses and suits and ties.

"Some of these people are better dressed for this quiz than I am when I go to a wedding," said Chloe, hooking her thumb through a hole in the cuff of her sweater.

"I am *smart casual*," said Joe-Nathan. "In my mum's yellow book, this kind of event calls for smart casual."

"You're actually more smart than casual," said Chloe, glancing down at his suit trousers and gleaming shoes. Her line of sight moved over Joe's shoulder as something behind him caught her attention. "Oh, dear god."

Joe turned to see Pip flouncing toward them in a way that made her midcalf, pale-pink hooped skirt swing from side to side like a pirate-ship ride at a theme park. She was wearing pink silky gloves that stopped just below her elbows and a pair of white high heels.

"Not smart casual," said Joe.

"Difficult to categorize that look," mumbled Chloe.

"Hi," said Pip breathlessly as she joined them. "I'm so excited about this. Aren't you?"

"When was the last time you went out?" Chloe asked, squinting as if Pip's outfit was hurting her eyes.

"Joe's mum's funeral," said Pip. "But I'm hoping that Hugo is going to ask me to go for a drink after tonight."

"A funeral is not 'going out,'" said Chloe, who now usually ignored any of Pip's sentences that included Hugo.

"Anyway," said Pip, "there's lots of people here. It should be fun! Has Charlie arrived?"

"Do you see him?" Chloe said.

Joe intervened in her cynicism by quickly saying, "Not yet."

"Well, it's still early." Pip looked at her watch and grimaced at Chloe.

The assembled Compass Store workers, clutching their various bags, bottles, and snacks, turned as one as the electric doors buzzed open.

"Welcome, one and all!" said Hugo, his arms outstretched. "Welcome to the Saturday night quiz!"

"Blimey, he looks like a fucking ringmaster," said Chloe. "Minus the whip, thank god."

"I don't mind the whip," said Pip, giggling hideously.

Hugo held the lapels of his red-and-gold blazer and bowed slightly before swinging one arm in an arc to usher everyone inside.

"What's with the top hat, Hugo?" Chloe said as she walked by him.

"Too much?" he said worriedly.

"You look lovely," said Pip. "I *love* the hat."

"Thank you," he said, and his confidence returned in a flash. "You look absolutely lovely, my dear."

"I am smart casual," said Joe.

"And very nice you look too," said Hugo.

As they walked through the store, not one person could help feeling the same way they did arriving for work at the start of a shift, no matter how they were dressed, but as they entered the Compass Store warehouse and witnessed its transformation, a buzz began to emerge in the crowd.

"Lovely," said Pip, and she twirled around. There were fairy lights—haphazard, but everywhere—which gave a magical effect. The high shelving had been pushed to the edges, leaving a large space that accommodated nine square tables, each laid with a tablecloth and artificial flickering candles. A long red carpet led from the edge of the seating area toward the open shutters (beside which lorries would park when they needed to be unloaded), and there, parked sideways, was a big white van, with an open hatch along one side that served as a counter, and it too was festooned with fairy lights.

"Ooh, I love it," said Pip. "Anything that makes me feel Christmassy is right up my street. And the lights do it every time. Of course, I had quite a hand in this. Hugo asked for my advice on decorations and—I'll have you know—the question topics. But that's very hush-hush." Joe and Pip stood side by side, looking up, turning slowly to take in the decorations, she with the touch of the frilly bridesmaid about her, he looking more like a groom.

"Jesus," said Chloe, setting her bag on a table and adjusting her black tights so that the run in them was hidden under the edge of her skirt. "You two look like Ken and bloody Barbie."

"Are you using your swear box?" Joe asked.

"Yeah, but it's not fucking big enough," Chloe said, and Pip laughed loudly.

"Sorry," said Pip. "I'm just so excited."

"Have you byobbed?" Joe asked.

"Ooh, never in public!" Pip said, grinning madly. When nobody found this funny, she cleared her throat and said, "I'm sorry, what?"

"Byob," Joe enunciated carefully. "It means to bring your own bottle of drink with you."

"You just say *bee-why-oh-bee*," said Pip.

"Oh, okay. Have you?"

Chloe opened a large brown leather bag and pulled out a bottle of vodka and a bottle of slimline tonic.

"Are these the tables from the staff-room?" Pip said, pulling up a corner of the tablecloth and looking underneath. "I think they are. Hugo has gone to so much trouble."

Chloe took three pint-size plastic cups from her bag and set them on the table, unscrewed the vodka bottle, and started to pour. "Do you want a vodka, Joe?" she asked.

"No, I brought my own drink," he said, and pulled a bottle of orange drink mix out of his satchel.

"Is that already mixed with water?" said Pip.

"No."

"Well, I just heard Hugo tell someone that the only place we're allowed to go inside the store is the toilets; will you get the water from there?"

"No!" Drinking water from the store toilets? Joe closed his eyes as the room momentarily spun.

"Well, you could mix it with tonic water," Pip suggested, nodding at the bottle on the table.

"Yeah, good idea," Chloe said.

Pip laid a silky pink-gloved hand over Chloe's and said, "Let's go to the ladies' before things get started."

"No, thanks, I don't need to go." Chloe frowned.

"It's not about needing to go; it's about being girly and going to the toilets together to *talk*."

Pip stood up, taking Chloe's hand with her, so that Chloe remained seated with one arm raised in the air. "Come *on*," said Pip, tugging on Chloe's hand. Chloe shook her head and whispered to Joe, "*Goody, now I get to talk about Hugo for ten minutes*." She laughed in spite of herself and told Joe not to get into trouble while they were gone.

As the girls walked away, Joe lined up the three cups so that they were neatly spaced and perpendicular to the table edge. He touched the base of each one and counted one, two, three, in his head. He didn't like that Chloe had only got three cups out. Where was Charlie's cup? Didn't she bring one for him? He touched the base of each cup again; two of them felt stable and one felt a bit wobbly because there was nothing in it—that was his cup—so he opened his bottle of squash and poured some in, to make it steady. Joe was thirsty, and he sniffed the cup with the neat cordial in it. How bad would it be if he didn't mix it with anything? He looked around at the other tables to see if anyone was watching, because if someone thought he was drinking undiluted cordial, then they might give him a funny look or say something that made him feel silly. People were only laughing and chatting among themselves; their collective noise was a pleasant buzz, and not one person appeared to be watching. So, he tipped the cup and took the tiniest sip.

"Ugh!" he said. It was not as bad as sherry, and he hadn't even tried the squash that Charlie had made him that day at his house; but this was too strong, and it gave him an instant sore throat, which made him want a drink even more.

Chloe and Pip had said he could mix his squash with tonic, which he'd never had before. But "tonic" was a nice word, with pleasant connotations, so he unscrewed the bottle and filled his cup halfway. He replaced the lid and then took a long sip (because he trusted Chloe and Pip).

"Agh!" Joe squealed, but the sound was lost in the general clatter of voices in the room. If anything, the cordial tasted worse—stronger—and just, just *horrible*. He pushed the cup away from him and lined up all three cups again, nice and neat, but a bit further away from him now, then waited for the girls to return—and Charlie to arrive—with his hands in his lap, trying to ignore the taste in his mouth.

Charlie would turn up, Joe told himself. He would. He had said he would.

Joe laid his satchel on his lap and took out his mobile phone, checked it for a message from Charlie, but there was none. So he sent one, just to be sure:

Hi Charlie, are you coming to the quiz?

And Charlie replied:

Why wouldn't I? What else would I do on a Saturday night?!

And for a moment Joe wondered if that meant yes or no. He decided it was a yes—definitely. He nodded his head firmly and put his phone back in his bag.

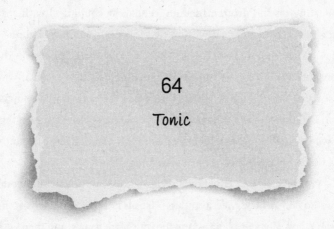

## 64
### Tonic

"I do not like tonic water," said Joe-Nathan when the girls returned to the table.

Chloe peered into Joe's cup. "Why not?" she asked.

"Too strong, tastes horrible."

"I think you might have too much squash in there and not enough tonic," said Chloe, and she poured more tonic in, until it reached the brim. "Try that."

Joe stared at the cup. It was hard to imagine how more—rather than less—of the stuff could taste better, but he was accustomed to doing as he was told so he took another sip and had to concede that, while it was still horrible, it was now—bizarrely—at least drinkable.

"Better?"

Joe nodded and decided that here was a new thing: this drink, this tonic, like all new things, was going to make him feel uncomfortable until he got used to it, so he took another tiny taste, and then another, and another, until gradually, but surprisingly quickly, he found that he wasn't scowling with every sip of it. And in that moment Joe felt that he was ready for till training and every sip he took of this faintly disgusting-tasting drink made him feel like he could deal with anything new that came his way. And that in itself was a new feeling.

A claxon sounded and jolted Joe from his reverie. All eyes in the room turned to Hugo. He stood behind a table next to Pamela, who was sitting with a laptop, a pile of papers, some pens, and an official look. Behind the two of them was a large, white projector screen that showed a grid with spaces for team names and scores; it swayed faintly in a warm breeze from the open warehouse doors.

"Welcome, folks," Hugo called out. "I hope you're enjoying yourselves so far." A little cheer went up. "This is how the evening is going to work. In a moment I'll be asking for your team names, and then we'll launch into round one of the quiz." A buzz of voices restarted in the room as people literally put their heads together to discuss and argue over team names. Hugo raised his voice and boomed, "Later, when we break, you can get your fish and chips from the van and when we've all had a chance to eat, we'll recommence with the second part of the evening." He spoke as if he were the referee in a boxing ring.

"He's quite masterful," said Pip.

"Get a grip, Pip," said Chloe, with the same expression Joe had pulled when he first tasted his drink.

"It is Hugo's hat that makes him masterful," said Joe. "A top hat is a symbol of prestige, wealth, and power. It is associated with the upper class."

"I associate it with fraudsters and con artists, magicians, and the little guy with the big mustache in Monopoly, or just a person who has made a questionable decision about how to dress," said Chloe.

Pip tutted and put her hand over Chloe's hand. "You mustn't be so quick to judge."

Chloe pulled her hand away sharply. "So, where's Charlie? He's going to miss the start."

"He *is* coming. He sent me a text," said Joe.

"Show me," said Chloe, and Joe gave her his phone, open at Charlie's message. Chloe's face softened sadly and she said, "He probably won't come, you know. Don't expect him to be here."

Hugo's voice raised higher just as Pip told Chloe to shush.

"So, let's hear those team names, then, and Pamela will type them into the system!"

There were some laughs as people called out their team names, clever things like *The Quizzard of Oz* and *I Am Smarticus*; Pip's face fell. "Do you think it's okay to call ourselves Pip's Players?" she said. "All these other names are really good, and ours is just, well . . . you know."

"A rose by any other name," said Chloe.

Joe squinted at Pip and Chloe in turn, partly because he was finding it hard to focus on them, but mainly because he didn't understand what they were talking about.

"What?" he said.

"It doesn't matter what we're called," Chloe said. "We're the best motherfucking team here, and we don't need to waste our time thinking of a good name. We'll use our brains where it matters, by correctly answering the fucking questions."

"Yes! Gosh, you're quite motivational," said Pip, and she poured herself another vodka and tonic.

Joe stared up at the fairy lights, and noticed how each light seemed to have a halo around it. He breathed in deeply and noticed how when he blinked it felt like his eyes were closing and opening in slow motion. He looked at Chloe and Pip and noticed that the edges of them were blurred and it was a very nice feeling to watch them talk and laugh, but that he didn't know what they were talking about and didn't really care. He thought of Charlie and wished he were here, but the feeling of disappointment was hazy rather than sharp, like a bruise instead of a cut (which was how disappointment usually felt to him). He lifted his cup and took a long drink of his orange squash with tonic and noticed that even though he didn't like it, he found he wanted more.

# 65
## Just a number

"Round one," Hugo said. "Flags of the world."

"Bollocks, I'm going to be shit at this," said Chloe, throwing her hands up.

"Oh my *god*," said Pip. "Flags! Joe and I know them, don't we, Joe? We truly are the best motherfucking team here!" She whispered this last bit.

"You're drunk," said Chloe.

"Drunk and ready for quizzing!" said Pip, and she giggled.

"Get a grip, Pip, get a grip, Pip," said Joe-Nathan, and he too giggled. At the sound of Joe's laughter, Pip and Chloe turned to stare at him as if he were a brand-new animal at the zoo. Chloe reached for his cup and sniffed at the tiny amount of liquid left in the bottom.

"Fuuuuck," she said, and held it under Pip's nose.

"Oh no, he's drunk too!" said Pip, and clamped a hand over her mouth.

"How . . . ?" said Chloe. "Joe, which bottle did you pour into your cup when we went to the toilets?"

"That one," said Joe, and he pointed to the tonic water. "No. This one." He pointed to the other. "Oh," he said, looking from one bottle to the other. "It was the clear one."

"They're both clear."

"Yes. I see that."

"How much did you have?"

"About there," said Joe, and he held a finger more than halfway up the plastic cup.

Chloe and Pip looked at each other. "That's half a pint of vodka," said Pip. "Do you feel alright, Joe?"

"I feel lovely. And soft," he said, and smiled very wide with his mouth shut, and swayed slightly in his seat.

"Not sick?"

Joe opened his eyes and looked at Chloe. "No. Why?"

"No wonder it tasted strong," said Chloe, half to herself. "Half a pint of vodka with orange squash. Yak!"

Hugo's voice boomed through the microphone. "Hope you've all got your answer sheets and pens at the ready. Question number one. How many stars are on the American flag?"

"Oh, I don't know that," said Pip, deflated. "I mean, I drew the American flag on the sheet, but I put a random number of stars on it."

"Fifty," said Joe.

"*Shuuuuuush*," said Chloe, leaning forward and interested now. "Are you sure?"

"One star for each state," he said firmly.

302

"Question number two! How many *stripes* are on the American flag?" A groan went up in the warehouse from those who had no idea about the stars and had no idea about the stripes either. Hugo looked a little deflated. "Come on, people, it's something you can guess at, even if you don't know."

"Joe—quietly now—do you know the answer?" Chloe whispered.

"To what?"

"How many stripes are on the American flag?"

"Thirteen," he whispered back.

"Really? That seems unlikely, why choose an unlucky number?" said Pip.

"They represent the thirteen colonies that rebelled against the British crown and became the first American states. Thirteen is not an unlucky number. It is just a number." Joe had always felt sorry for the number thirteen, passed over and avoided because of associations and assumptions that had nothing to do with the number itself and everything to do with people, undeserved fear, and misunderstanding.

To most people's relief, the following questions in the round mostly related to identifying flags and deciding what objects appeared on others: which flag has a bear, which has a dragon, and so on. Pip's tongue poked out of her mouth as she wrote down answers and she folded her arms in tight pleasure as she sat back and waited for each question. Knowing the answers—or having a decent shot at them—was distracting. But round two was sports, and while some tables hissed "*YES*" and punched their own hands, others moaned and replaced the lids on their pens in preparation for not using them.

"This is why I hate quizzes," said Chloe. "Just the sports round alone."

It was a poor round for Pip's Players and Joe found himself

thinking once more about Charlie. He looked at his phone, to see if he had messaged again. He even shook it—like a Magic 8 Ball—to see if another answer from Charlie would appear on the screen somehow.

"I've never seen you drunk," said Chloe.

"I have never been drunk," said Joe.

"You're drunk right now."

"Am I?"

"Yes. That's what that warm fuzzy feeling is."

"Oh," said Joe. "I am going to text Charlie."

"No," said Chloe. "First rule of being drunk: don't text anyone."

"Why not?"

"Just trust me, I know from experience, it's never a good idea. Wait till the morning."

"The morning will be too late. The quiz is now. I need to text now to find out where he is."

"Don't you understand that the reason he's not here is because he doesn't want to be? You've already messaged him. You can't make him want to come by messaging again."

"And it is a rule?"

"What is?"

"You said it is the first rule of being drunk."

"Oh yeah, it's a rule." Chloe winked at Pip.

Joe put his phone back in his satchel.

"What is the second rule of being drunk?"

"Stop now, or go for broke," said Chloe. She poured herself another and went to pour more into Joe's cup. Pip put her finger under the neck of the bottle, to stop the flow of vodka.

"I don't think that's a good idea," said Pip.

"Who died and made you mum?" Chloe said, wincing instantly at her insensitive choice of words.

Pip looked squarely at Joe. "As it's your first time drunk, I suggest you stop now, otherwise you're going to puke."

"Oh," said Joe. He nodded firmly and pushed his cup away.

"I would have loved to be a mum," said Pip, looking squarely at Chloe. "But it wasn't meant to be.

# 66
## Touching fish

So, this was drunk. Joe-Nathan recalled that there was a paragraph on being drunk under the pub section in his mum's yellow book, but he hadn't read it because he never had any intention of getting drunk. He had imagined that being drunk was only a horrible thing. A thing that made people unable to walk, see, or speak properly, all of which seemed like uncomfortable sensations. However, Joe quite liked the way he was seeing things now, and if he wasn't talking properly, then he hadn't noticed. He hadn't tried walking, but maybe he would in a moment. In fact, Joe felt good: relaxed, less concerned. He suddenly realized that although the cups were not lined up and there were sheets of paper that were not cleanly stacked, and the pen was half on and half off the table, he did not care. Okay, he cared a bit. That pen could easily fall. He moved it so that it was fully on the table with no part of it hanging over the edge. But it wasn't straight, and he didn't care at all, when he usually would. A lot.

Joe felt free from himself. And even though he loved himself, it was nice to be free.

Joe didn't feel purely a part of himself as separate to his surroundings, as he usually did. He could feel the atmosphere: the lights and the hum of people talking, the occasional burst of loud laughter, Hugo's big voice, and the way he could feel the table jiggle when Pip wrote down the answers. He felt as though his body and mind had slightly blended with these things, rather than having a force field around him, from which they—the sounds and the sights—were pushed away when they got too close.

"I like drunk," said Joe.

"Yeah? Well, don't get too used to it. Anyway, I'm starving. Hopefully we can get some food soon and that'll soak up some of the alcohol."

The thought of fish and chips in his stomach getting soggy as it soaked up alcohol actually made Joe feel queasy and his throat tightened. But by the time two more question rounds had passed, and people were invited to queue at the van for food, all he wanted to do was eat. It was more than an hour later than he would normally have his tea, and his stomach rumbled reliably as an indicator that he was out of sync with his routine.

While the quiz paused and people got their food, Hugo mingled and came to visit Pip's Players. He patted his top hat as he approached and sat down as if he were relieved to abandon his responsibilities as compère for a few moments.

"Are you enjoying yourselves?" Hugo looked at them all, and attempted to divide his attention among them equally as he made small talk, but his eyes were drawn repeatedly to Pip. He seemed only to realize he was dividing his time *un*equally when it was too late; then, he would pull his attention away from her and direct it at Chloe, or Joe; then his guard would slip again and he was back attending to Pip before his brain had calculated what his eyes were doing.

"What do you think of the decorations?" he said.

"I like them," said Joe.

"Thank you, Joe, that means a lot to me," said Hugo.

"It just goes to show," said Pip, looking up into the warehouse eaves, "you can make anywhere magical with enough fairy lights and the right company." When she said *right company* she met Hugo's eyes and he looked away after a couple of beats.

He made his apologies and said he couldn't spend all his time with them, said he needed to make sure everyone else was alright. But his eyes took one more lingering glance over his shoulder before he reached another table.

"Do you think he likes me?" said Pip.

Chloe shrugged. "Hard to tell with Hugo, he's so nice to everyone. He's really nice to Pamela, have you noticed?"

"No!" Pip twisted quickly to take a look at Pamela, who had her hair pinned up and was patting the underside of it, making sure it was all still in place.

"I'm messing with you," said Chloe. "Stop obsessing over the ringmaster."

Pip, Chloe, and Joe had queued for their food and were back at the table. Their yellowy polystyrene containers were open and little packets of salt, vinegar, and ketchup were efficiently opened, squeezed, and discarded. Chloe quickly wiped a smear of ketchup with a napkin and put it in her pocket before Joe had time to react to the red sauce.

"Are you sure you feel alright?" Pip asked as she scooped up some ketchup with a chip and put it in her mouth.

Joe didn't really want to talk. He concentrated on using the small and ineffectual wooden fork that had come with his meal, and wished that he had thought to bring his own cutlery.

"Can I go and get a knife and fork from the staff-room?" he asked.

"Just pick it up," said Chloe, eating her battered fish as if it were a slice of pizza.

Joe adopted a horrified expression, but was still looking at his food. *Pick it up!?* Holding actual food was a thing reserved only for lunchtime items: sandwiches, fruit, crisps, and chocolate. He tried to recall when he had touched his breakfast or an evening meal without a utensil, except when he had a sandwich for dinner.

"Yeah, pick it up," said Pip.

It was like when Joe had tried to get under Charlie's bed without touching the floor or the bed, like trying to *do* and *not do* something at the same time. He put down the wooden fork and tried to touch the fish but it was as though the fish and his hand were two magnets repelling each other.

"Pick. It. Up. Pick. It. Up," chanted Pip as if she were encouraging a rugby player to down a pint.

"What's the worst that could happen?" Chloe asked.

What *was* the worst that could happen? Joe wondered.

"The worst is . . ." He started the sentence without knowing how it would end, a thing that rarely, if ever, happened. Like an ordinary person—for once in his life—Joe just hoped that what he was trying to say would say itself, without him having to be certain (in advance) of his conviction for it.

". . . Just," he started again, trying to name the thing that might happen, ". . . something awful."

"I promise," said Pip, holding her hand roughly where her heart would be, "that nothing awful will happen if you pick up that fish with your hands and bite it. I *promise*."

Joe looked at Chloe, who nodded. "She's right. I promise too."

The girls ate slowly while they watched Joe attempt to touch his fish. He paused for a while and picked up his fork so he could eat some of the chips. Then he laid the fork down and went back to the fish: it was as though he were about to touch something that might electrocute him, but eventually his finger rested briefly on the batter and then he did it again and again, tapping it lightly. It was as though the fish itself needed to be acclimatized to his touch (like a frightened animal) rather than the other way round, and when he lifted the whole thing and took a bite, Pip could barely breathe.

"See!" she said, and she clapped her hands together quietly so as not to break the spell. "And nothing bad happened at all." She smiled at Chloe.

"Our baby boy is all grown up," said Chloe, tutting affectionately and resting her head on Pip's shoulder.

Nothing bad had happened, and that seemed obvious now, even to Joe. But he still approached a second (handheld) bite tentatively. He chewed and he looked at the girls as he did so; they were still smiling, and Pip was clutching Chloe's arm now. He nodded back as he ate, as if to say, *You were right. Nothing bad* had *happened*.

Yet.

And for a moment, it seemed like it was a very, very good thing.

Joe chewed and swallowed and bit again, and chewed and relaxed, and looked over to the fish-and-chip van and the people who were milling around it, eating chips, licking their fingers while they stood. Things were a little blurry still, and that was no doubt something to do with being drunk, but Joe saw someone he recognized, poking his head around the corner of the van, as if he wasn't sure if it was okay to make an appearance or not. Joe blinked hard to make sure he was seeing what he thought he had seen.

Yes. It was *him*.

He had disappeared again now, but there was no doubt about it. Donald Trump was hiding behind the chip van, right here, in the warehouse of The Compass Store. Joe stood, his hands out to the sides as if he were in a musical (because his hands were greasy and he didn't want to touch his own clothes). He stared straight ahead at the chip van.

"What's up?" Chloe said, turning to follow his gaze.

"Look who is here," said Joe.

"Is it Charlie?" said Pip, and she too quickly turned to see who Joe was looking at.

"No. Donald Trump," said Joe.

"Huh?" they both said, turning back just to look at Joe.

"Donald Trump. From America."

"I fucking hope not," said Chloe.

"I thought I saw Hugh Jackman when I was drunk once," said Pip.

"Who *are* you actually looking at?" said Chloe, trying to follow Joe's line of sight.

"Oh," said Joe. He couldn't see him now. "I really thought for a moment that I had seen his face."

"I even snogged him," said Pip, staring into the past.

"Who?" said Chloe.

"The guy I thought was Hugh Jackman."

## 67

### All linked

"You can't always trust your senses when you're drunk," said Chloe.

"Why?" said Joe.

"I dunno, really. Alcohol sort of makes everything numb and not work properly. When you've had too much, that is. A little bit won't have much effect."

Joe sat down again and stared at his greasy fingers.

"You did good, Joe, eating your fish and chips like that. Here . . ." Pip pulled a packet of wet wipes from her handbag and tugged one free for him. He wiped between each finger like a fastidious mechanic getting oil off a bike chain.

"Don't wipe your fingerprints off," said Chloe.

"I need soap," he said, beginning to rise from his seat.

"No time," said Pip, twitching at the sound of feedback on the mic. "Time for the next round, and I have a sneaky feeling we're going to need you for this one." Pip pursed her lips in a failed attempt to keep a smile inside and winked hard at Chloe.

Hugo tapped the microphone, and next to him, Pamela bustled her bosom and Pip breathed the word *tart* under her breath. Chloe laughed and squeezed Pip's hand and Joe watched these tiny actions and wondered whether or not they were all linked.

"Did you all enjoy your fish and chips?" Hugo cried out, like a talk show host. His audience were all oiled up now and responded with noise and banter.

"Back to the serious business of quizzing now," said Hugo. "Round four: *Friends*—the popular American TV show of the nineteen nineties."

There was a mixed reaction; at least one or two people at every table seemed very happy about the topic, and at least one or two people at every table looked completely blank. But Pip's Players were quietly ecstatic. Pip planted her elbows on the table and lowered her head between them.

"See what a little bit of influence can get you," she whispered.

"You are a fucking genius," said Chloe. "Way to use your sexual power, girlfriend."

"Wow," said Joe. "What a coincidence. *Friends* is probably my best topic ever."

Pip smiled at Chloe as Joe started to roll his shirtsleeves up.

"As always, there will be ten questions, and if you think this will be your best round, then you can play your joker now and whatever you score, it will be doubled up for this round only."

"Ooh, ooh," said Joe, and he shot his hand up, lifting out of his seat as he did so.

Pamela looked around the room and assigned the jokers on her laptop, checking to make sure they had transferred to the spreadsheet hanging behind Hugo. Currently Pip's Players were in third place.

"First question," Hugo bellowed. "Phoebe thinks she has kissed Ralph Lauren at Rachel's workplace. But *who*, in fact, did Phoebe kiss?"

"Ooh! Do you think Hugo's asking a kissing question because he wants to kiss *me*?" Pip asked Chloe.

"No!" said Chloe, adopting the same furtive intensity with which Pip had asked the question.

Pip slumped in her chair.

"I know it," said Joe, and he quietly relayed the answer to his teammates.

"Question two. What does Monica start making large quantities of in an attempt to get over her boyfriend Richard?"

"Ooh," said Chloe, looking feverishly at Pip. "Do you think Hugo is asking a question about getting over someone because he thinks you should get over *him*?"

"I know it," said Joe, and he cupped his hands around his face and mouthed the answer carefully at Pip.

"Question three," boomed Hugo. "With whom does Barry go on his and Rachel's honeymoon?"

"Ooh, do you think . . . ," Chloe started to say, holding her hands to her heart with mocking passion.

"Fuck off," said Pip. But then she softened and laughed and Chloe poked her and said, "Course he wants to kiss you; you're irresistible, mate. The question is, do you really want to kiss *him*?"

"I know it," said Joe, but when he went to tell them the answer to the quiz question, they weren't listening. "What are you talking about?" he asked.

"Pip's in *lurve* with Hugo," said Chloe. She spoke the sentence with great clarity during one of those moments when a noisy place suddenly becomes quiet just long enough for a sentence to slip into its silence.

"Shut uuuup!" whispered Pip, and the two women giggled onto their knuckles on the table.

"I really need to wash my hands," said Joe.

"Not yet," said Pip. "Seven more questions and then you're free to go do it."

Joe squeezed his hands into fists and then unfurled them again and again, identifying and reliving the greasy and sticky places and the different textures that were there as the result of picking up his fish and chips. There was salt under his fingernails. His entire focus was on his hands; it was as though, for now, they were his whole and only universe.

"Joe," said Chloe. "It doesn't matter as much as you think it does. I promise. Just stay till the end of the round, and then I'll get you to the toilets."

Joe sat on his hands, hating the grease and the salt that was on them. The plastic chair pressed against his skin and relieved his discomfort in the same way that pressing against a paper cut can stop the pain. He thought of Charlie's house and all the things that made him uncomfortable there. He tried to use his thoughts of Charlie's house as a comparison, so that the matter of his unclean hands might seem insignificant. He had endured at Charlie's, he had got under the bed, even had Charlie's spit on his face. Joe closed his eyes but the thought of Charlie not being at the quiz, as he had hoped, made tears well up and fill the space behind his eyelids, so that he had to open them to let them out.

"What's wrong?" said Pip.

"Charlie," said Joe, and the tears were free to roll down his face. Joe looked up at the fairy lights: they looked too big now, swimming and magnified beyond his tears. He looked around at the white tables, at the people he worked with wearing clothes that they didn't work in. Joe searched for something—anything—that was as it should be, any right thing in the right place; but there was nothing here.

"Joe?" said Chloe. "Joe?" Her voice was low, slow, kind, and—like an anchor—it pulled him slightly steadier.

"You," said Joe, as he attempted to focus on her solidly blurry presence. "Chloe. You always seem exactly where you should be. Even when you are clearly not. Why?"

"I don't know what you're talking about." She held up a hand. "But if it's not a quiz question, ask me again later. You feel sick?"

"A bit."

"Shit. Let's get through these questions, and we'll get you out of here. We'd still like to win, and we need you in order to do that, right?"

"Right," said Joe, and sniffed.

# 68
## Terminally separate

t was true—in Joe-Nathan's opinion—what Pip had said about enough fairy lights and the right company making anything magical. It was certainly true in *Friends* when Phoebe got married in the street, in the snow. But it wasn't quite the right company without Charlie. Joe looked into the depths of the warehouse ceiling and tried to feel the magic, but he missed his mum and needed the toilet and the fairy lights were losing their power to make everything okay. People were concentrating and whispering possible answers to each other; there was intermittent laughter and Chloe and Pip were smiling and nudging each other. Where Joe had started to feel at one with the crowd and his surroundings, he gradually slipped away from that into his more familiar state: one where he was more acutely aware of residing inside his own skin than other people were, more aware than they were of how terminally separate we all are from all other people.

Joe missed his mum.

"Question four," Hugo boomed over the microphone. "What does Phoebe want to be written on her gravestone?"

Chloe's face widened—her eyebrows shot up and her mouth opened in a big O. Joe suddenly felt like the parent, and wanted to let Chloe answer before he did. She leaned close to the table and took the pen from Pip, not wanting to risk anyone else overhearing her answer.

Focusing on *Friends* comforted Joe but he couldn't let the sorrow of Charlie's absence go. From his satchel he retrieved his mobile phone and glanced up at Chloe, who shook her head maternally. Nevertheless, Joe typed the words Where are you? and pressed send. He stared at the small screen and watched the little dots moving like three fingers drumming on a table: Charlie was typing. The lift that Joe felt when he saw those three dots dropped as they disappeared and became nothing and he returned his phone to his bag. Chloe was right: Charlie had let him down, just as she'd predicted he would.

The *Friends* round came to an end and while Pamela took charge of the scores and the jokers, Hugo trotted over to Pip's Players and sat in what should have been Charlie's chair, or Janet's chair, but which was now just a chair that reminded Joe of the current disappointments in his life.

"What do you think?" Hugo breathed. "Is it going okay?"

"I think you're the best question master ever," said Pip.

"Really?"

Pip nodded quickly and smiled hard.

"Question eleven," said Hugo quietly. "Would you like to have dinner with me?"

"Pardon?" said Pip, clutching the hem of her dress.

"Oh god," said Chloe.

"I am going to the toilet," said Joe, standing carefully.

"I'll come," said Chloe.

"The next round starts in a second," said Hugo, looking up at them both with concern.

Pip was too flushed with sudden joy to look concerned, but said, "Don't be long," to Chloe.

"I'll just get Joe to the mosaic and then I'll come back," she said, and held out a crooked arm for Joe, who just touched her elbow for the merest guidance, like a blind man about to be led across a road.

# 69
## The apology

"Mosaic, mosaic," Joe-Nathan said. Walking after drinking a lot of vodka didn't feel like walking usually did. He squeezed his eyes shut so that things did not swim in his vision so strangely, and held tighter to Chloe's arm.

"I think I ought to get you all the way to the bathrooms," said Chloe.

"Mosaic first," Joe said. "I need to be at the center."

Chloe firmly led the way to the mosaic. "We're here," she said. But Joe already knew, because he could feel the rough difference in the texture of the floor beneath his shoes.

"West," said Joe.

"No, southeast," said Chloe, and she took him to the shower room. "People probably won't think to come in here; they'll use the other toilets instead."

Joe—eyes still shut—felt for the taps. "I need to wash my hands first." He washed his hands for a long, long time, still enjoying the relative peace and darkness behind his eyelids, but not enjoying the feeling that he was on a gently rocking ship. He forgot for a while where he was and that Chloe was in the room with him.

"Are they clean?" he asked, looking blindly in her direction and holding his hands up.

"Of course they're fucking clean, you've been washing them for five minutes."

Joe opened his eyes to see Chloe looking at her phone. She put it in her back pocket and pulled some paper towels out of the dispenser.

"Will you be alright to get back on your own, if I go?"

"Where are you going?"

"Back to the warehouse. Pip says it's a geography round and she doesn't want to be alone with it. You okay on your own?" Joe nodded and Chloe let the door swing shut behind her; he heard her footsteps fade.

Joe stared at his reflection. There was a spot of ketchup on his collar. He watched himself point at it in the mirror. "Japan," he said.

So, this is what he looked like drunk: not much different, just a bit untucked. And yet, he could see something out of the ordinary about himself, something he couldn't quite decipher. Something around the eyes that looked like indifference, as though nothing was as important to him as it usually was. He went to the toilet and even that was a different experience when drunk, like the difference between real life and life on TV. He pushed the shower room door open slowly and stepped into the store. It was so quiet, like a vacuum, and Joe was shocked by its imposing empty presence. It was funny to think these full shelves were here all the time, even when no one was around to see them or stack them, in the same way that it was strange to see people he worked with outside of work.

Joe had always felt the air was cleaner inside The Compass Store than anywhere else, something to do with the shiny white walls and floors and the lighting. He tipped his head back and breathed in deeply, as if he were filling his lungs with mountain air.

With his head tilted back, he heard a sound. He looked at the ceiling and focused everything on what he could hear, trying to interpret the rhythmic *pad-pad-pad*.

*Oh*, he suddenly realized, *it's footsteps*. Why hadn't he known that straightaway? It was Chloe returning to him no doubt, or maybe someone else who had thought to use the shower room instead of the usual toilets. He squinted in the direction of the footsteps and brought aisle nine into focus. Through slitted eyes he saw, once again, Donald Trump. This time he was headed straight toward Joe with a slow, determined kind of walk, a far cry from the shy way that he had peered briefly around the side of the fish-and-chip van earlier. It only took one blink for Joe to realize that Donald's face was simply a mask: a horrible mask of a horrible person, which was not—in all honesty—much worse than a mask of a nice person. Joe hated all masks, not least because they made the difficult task of interpreting an expression completely impossible.

Donald lifted his mask so that it sat on top of his head. Underneath the mask was Owen's face and he was smiling. Joe managed a small smile in return, because, awful as Owen could make Joe feel, he did not make Joe feel worse than Donald Trump did. And after all, Owen *was* smiling, although it was not the nicest smile in the world.

Owen was half an aisle away and he raised his arm in a way that made Joe raise his own in return: they were going to wave at each other, like trees, and that was definitely a positive and friendly action. Joe felt his smile get wider and he slowly moved his arm back and forth.

"This is for losing Charlie his job," Owen shouted.

"Charlie?" said Joe. His ears heard Charlie's name and the other words, but they didn't reach his brain in the correct order fast enough to decode their meaning before it was too late to comprehend what everything meant when it was all put together.

Owen pulled his own arm back in the air, twisting away slightly as he did so, like a cricketer, and Joe noticed he was gripping something in his hand, a ball perhaps? Owen swung forward and, once more, the speed of things slowed down so that the forward thrust—the release of the object from Owen's hand—happened as if a brake had been applied to time and every detail was visible in the decelerated trajectory, and as it came toward him through the atmosphere Joe saw that it was a tin of tomatoes, which seemed to reveal its curves and text and colors with plenty of time to examine them.

"Oh dear," said Joe, as the tin rotated lazily through the air toward him. In a flash—in his mind's eye—he imagined stacking an entire shelf of such items, so that they were neat and tidy and all facing the right way, and then—in another flash—the heavy can hit Joe in the forehead with a leaden thud.

The bright, white Compass Store went black and he hit the floor in silence.

# 70

## When my heart beats

He would never know how long he had lain there unconscious, because he hadn't looked at the clock before he passed out. But when Joe-Nathan came to, he felt as though a heavy weight were pressing his head into the floor and he struggled to raise himself off the ground. He gently touched the front of his head, and gently touched the back of it; the front had been hit by a full metal can and the back had met the floor with gusto. His head throbbed.

"You alright?" said an indistinct, slurred voice.

Joe flinched as he turned toward the question, because pain shot through his skull when he moved. There, sitting on the floor with his back against the wall outside the shower room, was Charlie, and Joe could see that he had that same indifferent look in his eyes that he had seen in his own eyes in the mirror earlier. Charlie must be drunk too. Joe just stared at him.

"Are you *alright*?" Charlie repeated, and he was—definitely—very slurred.

Joe wasn't sure if he was alright or not. He was certainly in no ordinary state, but was he alright? Impossible to say without seeing a doctor.

"It hurts when my heart beats," said Joe.

Charlie laughed weakly as though there was something funny about that. He managed to raise an eyebrow and whisper, "Me too." But Joe did not understand.

"Did you see Donald Trump?" said Joe.

Charlie stared at Joe for a long, long time before answering. "I don't really understand the question," he said. "But then again, I'm not feeling very well."

"Neither am I," said Joe, and he crawled toward Charlie and sat next to him, with his own back against the wall. He crossed his arms like Charlie did: two deadbeats too smashed to be of use to anyone.

"What happened to you?" said Charlie.

"Owen threw tomatoes at me," said Joe.

Charlie looked at the lump and laceration between Joe's eyebrows.

"Tomatoes did that?" Charlie said.

"They were in a tin," said Joe.

"Oh right, explains a lot," said Charlie.

"I think Owen is bullying me," Joe said.

"That's GBH, wounding with intent," Charlie whispered.

"I don't know what that means," Joe whispered back.

"Doesn't matter," said Charlie.

The boys sat in silence for a while. To an outsider, they might have looked like they were sleeping in a doorway after a wild night out. Joe opened his mouth with a little gasp as he remembered that he wanted to ask Charlie something.

325

"Why did you not come to the quiz tonight?"

"I'm here, aren't I?" Charlie said, but he didn't open his eyes.

"You are late, and you did not come to the quiz. You are just here, in the store."

"I tried, though," said Charlie, and he tilted his head toward Joe, opened his eyes briefly, smiled the smallest of smiles.

Joe looked more closely at Charlie: his top was stained red under his hands.

"Did you get hit with tomatoes?"

"No. Fight."

"Did you shield yourself?"

"Yes."

"Why did you not walk away?"

"Couldn't."

"It would not have happened if you had come to the quiz."

They sat in silence for a while longer and Joe heard Charlie's breathing change, as if he'd fallen asleep. Joe tapped him on the shoulder, and tapped him harder when he didn't respond.

"What?" said Charlie, like he was drunk.

"I am glad you came, even if you *are* late. Chloe said you wouldn't."

"Sometimes you have to try new things," said Charlie.

Joe nodded; this was a concept very familiar to him, something his mum had told him over and over, something he struggled with every day.

"When you do *new things* often enough, they become *old things*," Joe said.

"True," said Charlie, but Joe could hardly hear him. "Just don't sit still, Joe, keep challenging yourself."

Joe squinted at Charlie. "Why do you sound like people do in films, when they are dying?" he said.

"Maybe it's because I am," said Charlie, and he lifted his hands away from his stomach. Joe was repelled by all the red and tried to shuffle away. Nevertheless, he was fascinated by the fact that Charlie's stomach had a piece of wood sticking out of it.

"What is that?" he said.

"It's a piece of that shield you made me," said Charlie. Then his eyes closed again and he didn't say anything else.

# 71

## The one where Charlie dies

Charlie was not well. That was for certain. And there was a lot of blood. And perhaps worst of all, it was Joe-Nathan's fault. He had made Charlie a shield for protection, *not* so that he would end up being impaled by it. Joe had thought that he and Charlie were in the same position: 1. both drunk (but now Joe thought Charlie probably wasn't drunk); and 2. both sitting against a wall with their arms folded because it looked cool (but now Joe realized that Charlie was just trying to keep his blood inside of himself). Charlie had told Joe to not sit still and to challenge himself, and Joe realized that if he didn't challenge himself right now, then Charlie's last words would be about the shield that Joe had made, which would have killed him.

Joe needed help in order to help Charlie. He took out his phone and texted "help" to Chloe, then stared at his phone for exactly one minute and one second. She didn't reply. Joe stood, then staggered in the direction of the mosaic. His thoughts would not line up: he had an idea, but it slipped away like something oily in his hands. His head pounded and his ears rushed. First, he thought *Chloe*, then he thought *Pip*, then *Hugo Boss*. But all this meant going to the warehouse and suddenly it seemed too far away. He turned back to Charlie, then changed his mind and headed for the mosaic again, but he stumbled into a shelf and a plant pot fell to the floor and smashed.

Joe looked down at the broken pieces and remembered his mum cracking eggs into a bowl before whisking them up for breakfast. "Look, Joe," she'd said. "It's so easy to break something and so difficult to put it back together." The shards on the floor swam in Joe's vision but it was impossible to tell if this was because he was drunk, concussed, or overwhelmed with the desire to tidy them up. But he looked at Charlie and knew he would be of no use to him at all if he passed out. He didn't trust himself to stay conscious before he had a chance to tell anyone that Charlie was in trouble.

As he wavered on the edge of decision, Joe saw a go-back trolley and smiled briefly to himself as—momentarily—he was transported to one of his happy places. Then he was abruptly brought back to the present. He heard the echo of Charlie's words: *challenge yourself*, and he started to empty the trolley, carefully removing towels, a hair dryer, a set of spanners, and some candlesticks. He laid them neatly on the floor and took hold of the trolley bar as if he were gripping the handles of a motorbike and wheeled it over to Charlie.

Charlie was slumped to one side and blood had started to seep onto the floor. The sight of all that red coming out of his friend made the edges of Joe's vision go black. He looked away and breathed hard through his nose. It was wrong, just *wrong* of the universe to allow people to faint at the sight of blood. If blood was around, then bleeding people needed other people to *help*, not pass out.

Joe remembered what Angus had said about putting his body in a wheelie bin and he tipped the trolley on to its side. It might be easier and less messy to push or roll Charlie into it rather than lift him in.

Joe reached out to touch Charlie, and it was like trying to make himself touch an electric fence. He watched as his fingers nearly touched Charlie's shoulder but he couldn't quite get them to make actual contact. *Challenge yourself*, he heard Charlie say again, and he looked at Charlie's face: the way it showed pain even though he was asleep. Reluctantly, but with grit, Joe reset the trolley to standing and rolled it closer to Charlie, before crouching down beside him (averting his eyes from the worst of the mess). He whimpered as he pushed his arms underneath Charlie; he could feel the wetness of blood smearing about, and then the initial weight of Charlie's body forced him to kneel down in it. His funeral trousers would be ruined, and if he didn't get help quick, he was going to need them.

Joe cried out and felt tears on his face as he lifted Charlie in his arms, with his right arm under Charlie's knees and his left under his back and arms, holding him tight and careful, like a baby. Something slick was on his hands and he tried to think of other things, but nothing else was strong enough to outnumber the horrible thoughts that accompanied the knowledge that the wet warmth on his hands and arms was blood. The only thing that drove Joe on was the thought that Charlie might die if Joe didn't get covered in his blood; and out of those two excruciating notions, the one where Charlie dies was the most unbearable.

For thirty-two seconds Joe felt completely at ease; it was when Charlie was in the go-back trolley, and Joe was pushing him through the store toward the exit, his gaze fixed to the ceiling, knowing that he was heading in the direction of people who could help: people at the hospital. After thirty-two seconds, Joe found himself outside in an alien world, one that continually assaulted his physical and mental sensitivities. It was hard to push a heavy trolley over pavement, and the one just outside The Compass Store was uneven. The trolley jolted against the cracked paving and Charlie's head flopped backward so that his face pointed skyward (mouth open, eyes closed). The trolley wouldn't move, no matter how hard Joe pushed, so he went to the front of the trolley, put his fingers between the metal gaps, and lifted the end of it over the lip of the stone. Then he started pushing again and made it to the road. Thankfully it was not busy this time of night, and the hospital was close enough that Joe could see a part of it from here. He had to get there quickly, but he was frightened of the curb; if a small piece of cracked pavement could cause him such difficulty, then getting the trolley down on one side of the road and up again on the other side was going to be seriously challenging.

Joe glanced over his shoulder and looked for the thing that might anchor him. There it was: the peace tree. He stretched his arm to the sky and gave the peace sign back. It was a moment, that was all, just enough to reassure him that the things in his life that made him feel secure were still there, if only in the background, even if they were only just visible in the fading light.

Joe looked down at himself. He was covered in blood. Charlie was gap-mouthed and listless, neither obviously dead nor obviously alive. There was nothing in this scenario that was within Joe's comfort zone. Everything about everything that was happening was *new*, except for the fact that he was pushing a go-back trolley. And there was nothing Joe could think of to relieve his discomfort, except to keep going until he got to the hospital.

Joe remembered the time that his mum had read an article about phobias and had been very interested and told lots of people about it. He remembered what she told him about a method for curing a phobia, called *flooding*, which basically involved making a person do the thing they were most scared of until they didn't have the energy to be scared of it anymore. Fear takes force; it doesn't feel weak, although it can appear as weakness. Fear is tiring, especially when you keep it up for a long time, and the fact is that after a while you can become so tired you don't even have the strength to feel frightened anymore. Janet had wondered if this method might be useful in helping Joe deal with some things in his life. But Joe had more energy than most people did for the things he didn't like, and Janet was reluctant to take Joe's comfort away. Why would you take a child's comfort away, even if they were a grown-up?

Joe had never tried flooding. This was the closest he had ever come to it.

## 72
## Next of kin

The receptionist at A&E didn't know who was in a worse state:
the rather neat and tidy unconscious young man slumped in the
supermarket trolley, or the wild-eyed, panting, moaning young
man, covered in blood with a lump like a boiled egg on his forehead,
who was pushing the trolley. In her experience, unconsciousness was
better evidence of urgency. She stood up and called for help. Immediately people appeared and got Charlie out of the trolley, talking about
recovery position and quickly assessing the sight of the stab wound.
Within moments it was as if they had been expecting exactly Charlie
and Joe-Nathan to be here.

They took Charlie on a gurney through some double doors and
Joe trotted to keep up.

"Is this your friend?" a man in a white coat asked.

"Yes," said Joe. "He is my friend."

"What happened to him?"

"He got a piece of wood in him."

"Yes. How? Did someone stab him?"

"I . . . I do not know. He was in a fight."

"Who with? What time?"

"I do not know."

"Did you find him?" the doctor asked. The doctor asked Joe questions and simultaneously gave instructions to other people in white coats, who buzzed around Charlie. He was like one man finding it easy to be two or three people at the same time. It was impressive; Joe could only just handle being himself.

"We're preparing him for the OR right now," said the doctor.

"The OR?" said Joe.

"Yes. And anything you can tell us might be useful. Especially time-wise."

Joe's chin crumpled. Knowing what time it was—or what time something happened—was something he was usually very, very good at. It hurt him to not know *now*, when someone was truly interested. He put his hands up to his face to cover his eyes, but when he saw the crimson palms of his hands, the way the lines were crusted maroon, he squealed, and then howled. He wiped at his face with his jacket sleeve but it was stiff with dried blood, which made him howl again and cry harder. He wanted to get away—from himself—which was impossible, so he shifted his weight from foot to foot.

"Are you hurt?" asked the doctor, eyeing Joe with concern. "Were you in the fight?"

"Yes. Donald Trump threw a tin of tomatoes at me. But it was Owen."

The doctor squinted at Joe's forehead. "Okay," he said, his voice suddenly much softer than before. "And you don't know what time your friend got stabbed?"

Joe shook his head.

"Or who was responsible?"

"It was me."

"You stabbed him?" asked the doctor, his eyes wide.

"No!"

"Then . . . ? I don't understand."

"I am responsible. I made the weapon, but it was not a weapon when I made it. It was a shield. But if you break a shield up, I see now that it becomes a weapon."

"A lot of things can be used for stabbing," said the doctor, "if they're pointy enough." He smiled.

Joe looked at the doctor, and felt his shoulders drop, and a large breath slowly left him. "I cannot look at myself. I am very dirty."

"Just hold on a minute, I'll get someone to help you." The doctor nodded at Joe and held a hand up as if to say *stay there*, and went to talk to a nurse out of earshot.

Joe found himself in a very sterile room, on a sterile chair, staring at a floor that gleamed with sterile reflections. It was lovely. The trick was not to look at himself.

Beside him sat a nurse, who had called Chloe. She hadn't spoken since, and that was lovely too.

There was a knock at the door, and the nurse opened it, said something about the police coming for questioning, and writing names and telephone numbers on a form. Joe closed his eyes; he couldn't take any more surprises, couldn't take anything else that was new. Not today. He had challenged himself enough and couldn't face looking at a policeman who might be standing there with handcuffs. Any questions would have to be answered from the inside of his eyelids; they were the only parts of his body that were clean.

He heard people enter the room and knew they were standing in front of him.

"Christ, you look like shit," said Chloe.

Joe opened his eyes: there before him was Chloe, Pip, and Hugo Boss in his top hat. Pip had a very sad expression on her face; she let go of Hugo's arm, to which she had been clinging, and stepped forward as if to touch Joe on the shoulder.

"You're covered in . . . ," she said.

But he managed to yelp "*Don't*" and clamp his eyes shut to block all three of them out before she made contact.

"What the fuck happened?" said Chloe. "How'd you get that fuckin' great lump on your head?"

"Charlie came to the quiz," said Joe.

"Yeah, we heard. He's in a bad way," said Hugo.

"He said he did not start the fight," said Joe. "And he did not throw anything at me." Joe touched the lump on his forehead very gently. "This was Owen," he said.

"Why?" said Pip.

"He said it was because I got Charlie fired. But it was *you* that fired him." Joe briefly opened his eyes to look at Hugo. "I cannot fire anyone," said Joe. "I do not have that sort of power." He closed his eyes again.

"Well, Owen could have killed you. He'll need to be reported to the police. I'll help you do that, Joe," Hugo added. "Plus I'll definitely be firing him, and happily," said Hugo. "I'm getting quite used to firing people now," he said as an aside to Pip, and she leaned into him.

"I think Charlie got hurt before he got to The Compass Store. But we don't know what happened." That was Chloe's voice. "Did he say anything to you about who did it?" she asked.

Joe didn't reply. He could guess who had hurt Charlie, but that wasn't the question he'd been asked; Charlie had not *said* who had done it, and *that* was Chloe's question.

"Joe? Do you know who hurt Charlie?" Chloe repeated.

"He did not say who had done it," Joe said. There, that was the question answered, and that was normally enough for Joe. But not tonight. Tonight, he felt that he should tell them who he *guessed* had hurt Charlie, which was not something he would normally do, especially when it felt like a secret thing that only he and Charlie knew about. After all, that was his mum's advice in the yellow book:

*I believe there are some circumstances when a friend's secret is dangerous and requires you to find help for them and you might have to tell someone in order to get that help. I'm afraid you will just have to work out for yourself when that is the case.*

"Charlie's dad," Joe said, interrupting the chat that was buzzing around him.

"He's been called, apparently," said Hugo. "He's next of kin after all."

Joe didn't know what that meant: *next of kin*.

"Nextovkin nextovkin nextovkin," he said, and rocked gently. It was a lovely word, *nextovkin*; it sounded like something you'd find in a medicine cabinet. "Nextovkin, nextovkin, nextovkin."

"Hang on a minute, Joe," said Chloe. "Stop. Please. Why did you say '*Charlie's dad*'?"

Joe paused his *nextovkins* to answer her. "Because of my guess," he said, tipping his head—and his closed eyes—toward her voice.

"What's your guess?"

"I guess that Charlie's dad stabbed him."

"What? Why would you think that?"

"Because I have seen him beat Charlie up. I think I heard him push him down the stairs. I have seen Charlie's dad kick him in the back, and another time—when I was not there—he made his face very bruised. His eyes went purple." Joe paused and opened his eyes. Hugo, Pip, and Chloe were silent and stared at him as though they hadn't heard him, so just in case, he repeated and clarified. "His eyes went purple, but *not* in a good way."

# 73
## The wrong option

Before the evening had really begun that Saturday night, Charlie's dad was already drunk. It was a shame that he'd been out in the afternoon and come back home before his later drinking session. If Charlie's dad had worked that day, as he often did, he would have come home, slept in the bath until it got cold, got out, got dressed, and left the house. Maybe there would have been words, but then again, it was possible that he and Charlie would have wished each other a pleasant night out and been done with it; it wasn't unheard-of.

Instead, Charlie's dad staggered into the house at five o'clock and started scratching for a fight.

Charlie knew how to play this game. If his dad was afternoon-drunk, he could weave around his father's provocations like a wiry young boxer ducking blows from a very large, very slow competitor. He ran his dad a bath and made him a potato-chip sandwich. He buttered the bread, put in some brown sauce, and shook a whole packet of Frazzles into it. He pressed the bread down to make everything stick and took it to his dad in the living room.

"Poor man's bacon sandwich," said Charlie, handing his dad the plate. He couldn't help remembering—every time he did this—the way his dad had laughed the first time Charlie had made him a Frazzle sandwich, when he was about nine years old. It was a happy memory that had stuck with him, like lots of happy little memories that fought the brave fight to outweigh the unhappy ones.

But his dad didn't laugh tonight.

"Fuck off," he grumbled, barely audible, as he took a bite and ineffectively tried to roll a cigarette.

"Want me to do that?" Charlie said, nodding at the papers and tobacco, which were dropping onto the carpet.

Charlie's dad made a sound that could have been a yes or a no, and Charlie crouched down and picked a lump of threaded tobacco off the floor, then took the green-and-gold packet from his dad's hand. His dad's other hand shot out surprisingly fast and gripped Charlie's neck.

Charlie smiled, and his dad barked a laugh and let go. "Good boy," he grumbled, as if a hand round his son's throat and a pat on the back were the same thing.

Charlie sat cross-legged on the carpet and made a couple of tidy roll-ups while Charlie's dad ate the sandwich. Drinking blocked up Charlie's dad's nose, so he ate with his mouth open.

Once rolled, Charlie laid the thin cigarettes on the coffee table next to the ashtray and got up off the floor.

"Out tonight?" his dad asked. Charlie stopped as he was on the threshold of the room, but didn't turn around. He could feel his dad's eyes staring at the back of his head.

When two people are close, they understand what is being said, but more importantly they understand what is not being said. Charlie's dad was no less astute or intelligent when he was drunk, but slightly less particular about hiding what he was really trying to say. And the biggest problem with *this* was that it was slightly harder to pretend that you hadn't heard the intent, the *real* question.

And the real question that Charlie heard in his father's words was: *Are you going to that fucking quiz tonight, you poof?*

Charlie had choices now: 1. He could pretend that he hadn't heard the real question, but his dad would know that he probably had, and then there would be the tension that arose from each of them knowing what the other was thinking, but not saying; 2. Charlie could answer the unasked question and admit that he *was* going to the quiz; or 3. Charlie could lie and say that he was doing something else. If he lied well enough, his dad might let it drop and once his dad had gone out himself, Charlie would be free. But there were risks that went with each of these choices. Charlie needed to choose the option that was least likely to lead to a fight.

Charlie would choose the wrong option tonight.

With his back still to his dad he said, "I think I might stay in, crack a few cans, and watch TV."

Charlie's dad gave a cough like a casual knowing laugh. "Good idea, son," he said. "Think I'll join you. Boys' night in."

Charlie closed his eyes and his head dropped almost imperceptibly. "I'll run you a bath," he said, and climbed the stairs with heavy legs.

Charlie sat on the closed toilet while the bath ran. He held an empty bottle of Matey in his hands and stared at the face of the sailor boy, who just kept smiling and smiling and never gave up.

"What are you smiling at, you idiot?" Charlie asked the bottle of bubble bath.

He sniffed the empty bottle. Disappointing. In the old days Matey smelled so clean, but now it smelled like fake fruit. He looked at the sailor boy again. "Want to swap lives?" he said. And the sailor boy just smiled. "Yeah, didn't think so," Charlie said, and threw the bottle in the bin.

Charlie wanted to go to the quiz. He wasn't even sure why. He wanted to go so much that he felt the same as he did when a girl he really liked agreed to go on a date with him. Quiz night was lame, but it was an escape. He felt like he was in prison and a bunch of nerds had come up with a plan to break him out. Yeah, it was just one night, but somehow, it seemed important.

When the bath was full, Charlie swirled his hands through the water to make sure it was the right temperature.

His dad knew. His dad would remember that the quiz was tonight. He would have stored it in his memory, not because he was organized and liked to keep up to date with Charlie's social life. No. He would have remembered the date of the quiz so that he could use it like a weapon against Charlie, like a bullet for his gun. Charlie stood with his wet hands on his hips and stared, unblinking, at the water that was still moving from where he had stirred it. He could, of course, just leave the house while his dad soaked in here, but the repercussions of that were predictable. Was quiz night worth the beating he would get for sneaking out when he'd said he was staying in? Charlie checked the time; it was still early. He could get his dad even drunker, *really* drunk; if he did that after a hot bath, his dad would almost certainly fall asleep and then Charlie could leave the house, creep back in later: his dad would no doubt still be in the armchair, mouth open, face lit up by the flickering light of the television, none the wiser. It was risky, but it was a plan.

# 74

## Unspoken communication

Charlie brought his dad a beer in the bath. Charlie's dad rested it on his stomach and shut his eyes. It wasn't that Charlie wished he would slip under the water and drown, but if it happened, then there was nothing Charlie could do about it. It was never *going* to happen, so there was no point in feeling guilty about such thoughts. Charlie's dad was a big man who had been dozing in the bath for years; his meaty feet were like two hams wedged at the end of the tub, his stomach like the back of a pink hippo; he had to hunker down in order to get his shoulders anywhere near the water. It would be harder for Charlie's dad to get his head under than to keep it above, so he was perfectly safe.

Thirty minutes after Charlie took his dad the beer, he heard the pipes groaning as the plug was pulled and water drained down, finding its way out. Charlie handed his dad another can when he got to the bottom of the stairs and asked if he wanted to shotgun it, just for a laugh. His dad agreed and they stood in the backyard, each holding a can horizontally. They looked at each other and pierced a hole in the side and while Charlie let most of it get all over him, his dad expertly drained his without spilling a drop.

"Idiot," said his dad, looking at the wet stain on Charlie's front. They went into the house and smoked and watched TV. Charlie asked what his dad wanted to eat later and they commented on the television show, made the odd remark about people at Charlie's dad's work, and Charlie tried not to look when he sensed that his dad's eyes were closing. If his dad caught him looking as he fell asleep, it could make him dangerously alert.

When his dad's breathing became measured with sleep, Charlie put both hands on the arms of his chair and pushed himself silently to standing. He pointed the remote control at the TV and increased the volume so it would become like white noise, obscure other noises, and keep his father asleep. He left the living room, moved like air through the door. Not one part of his body touched anything it didn't need to. His feet were the only thing in physical contact with the house as he stepped carefully and expertly up the stairs, avoiding all the parts that made a sound. Charlie had experience of returning home late at night and the effect a creaking floorboard could have on the way the night ended. Halfway up the stairs, his phone chimed with an incoming message. He peered through the bars of the balustrade to see if his dad had stirred.

Hi Charlie, are you coming to the quiz?

It was Joe. He glanced again at his sleeping father. He typed, and then crept to the top of the staircase.

Why wouldn't I? What else would I do on a Saturday night?!

Charlie peeled off his clothes—damp with lager—and put them in a pile on his bedroom floor. He opened drawers softly and put on his other pair of jeans, a clean T-shirt, and sprayed some deodorant over his clothes and down the waistband of his trousers for luck. He took a couple of notes from his money sock and stuffed them in his back pocket. There was hardly any left; he really needed to get a job.

He looked around his room on his way out; there was nothing *in* the room to look at. He stood on the landing at the top of the stairs and got his phone out of his back pocket. He checked the time of Joe's message and realized he was going to be late for the quiz. He would just quickly send a message saying he was on his way. But suddenly there was a shadow in his vision at the bottom of the staircase; where there had been space, there was now the wide bulk of his dad. Everything about him looked out-of-control drunk, except his eyes, which could penetrate a skull.

"What are you doing?" said his dad. His words were welded together with alcohol and came out more like *wharrayadoon?* Charlie understood him perfectly.

"Nothing."

"Who are you talking to?" *Whoraryatalkintoo?* Charlie's dad waved his hand—as if it were made of very soft rubber—in the vague direction of Charlie's phone.

"Nobody."

Charlie knew—now that his dad was awake and interrogating him—that he had no choice but to confess he was going out. Either that, or stay in. And he *could* have stayed in. But he kept seeing Joe's face smiling stupidly, and Chloe's face chewing something, scowling at him, and Pip's too-nice-to-be-true expression, her hand patting his in a way that made him feel better about himself. And for some reason, Charlie just wanted that. He knew that something as wholesome as a quiz night with friendly workmates wasn't for him, like a big present under a Christmas tree that you know is for someone else. But Charlie couldn't help wondering what it would be like, if those people that were outside of his life could be a real part of his own life, just for a few hours.

"I'm, er, going out after all," said Charlie, holding his phone in the air by way of explanation. "Owen and the lads are off to The Kings; I'm going to join them."

"Boys' night in, I thought."

"You were asleep when they messaged, so I thought . . . y'know . . . might as well."

"What about quiz night?"

Charlie frowned. "What?"

"It's quiz night. That's where you're going."

"No, don't be stupid. Fucking quiz night?"

"Stupid?" said Charlie's dad, and he tilted his head to one side.

Charlie started walking down the stairs. He hated to be trapped at the top when his dad was angry; it was such a long way to the front door from up there, and his dad was difficult to get round.

"Not you, just the idea that I would go to a quiz night." Charlie squinted again, which only served to imply that it was crazy to think he would go to a quiz night.

"I think you're going there."

"Nah, just The Kings," said Charlie, casually as he could manage.

Charlie's feet were level with his dad's hands, which hung heavy by his sides. Charlie paused and he and his dad made the kind of eye contact that holds all the awful honesty of unspoken communication.

A hand shot out quickly, grabbed Charlie around the ankle, and pulled. Charlie's phone flew into the air, and his backside slammed onto the edge of a step, the back of his head hit another, but he pulled his foot away and managed to clamber up a couple of stairs awkwardly, like a spider walking backward. They made eye contact again and Charlie waited two beats, then realized he could have used the extra seconds to turn and get away. He wouldn't waste the next two. Charlie quickly spun onto his front and scrambled forward. He felt his dad grab the toe of his shoe, but he pulled away. Charlie's dad mounted the stairs like a troll: slow but confident that there was nowhere for his quarry to hide when he reached the top. Charlie, like a hunted animal, looked at his surroundings—his tiny bedroom—and knew he was in for a beating.

He turned and looked one way, then the other, then the other again. There was nothing here to help. It was the visual equivalent of pacing when there was nowhere to go.

Charlie saw the edge of something pale poking out from under his bed, and he squatted down, pulling Joe's shield out, and—as his dad thundered through the door—Charlie turned and held it in front of himself.

Like lightning, Charlie felt a heavy blow to his nuts; all his breath left him and he fell to the floor. His dad yanked the shield from Charlie's weakened grip and said casually, "What the fuck is this?" before he swung it round and smashed it against the wall. It broke and splintered and Charlie's dad swore and looked at the palm of his hand, where a sliver of wood was stuck in his meaty fist. He frowned hard and looked like a huge ugly baby about to cry. Charlie saw a crack in his dad's concentration that he might just be able to slip through, and he moved—like the flick at the end of a whip—around the side of his father. But Charlie's dad grabbed him and flung him like a doll against the wall, just as he had with the shield, and Charlie landed on the broken pieces.

# 75
## The go-back

Charlie's dad left his son there on the floor and wandered out of the room, trying to pick the splinter out of his hand. By the time he reached the bottom of the stairs he couldn't remember what the fight was about. By the time he slumped into his armchair he'd forgotten the fight altogether, didn't once look through his mind's eye at his boy lying face down on his bedroom floor. And the "next of kin" never came to the hospital that night, because he was drunk and asleep in front of the television and the police would have to remind him of what he had done, when they visited him the following morning.

Charlie didn't remember making it down the stairs or out of the front door. Didn't recall looking at his phone and thinking about replying to Joe-Nathan's message and asking for help. The first thing he was conscious of after being thrown against his bedroom wall was the sight of Joe lying on the bright, white floor of The Compass Store with his arms and legs spread out like a starfish. The last thing he remembered was telling Joe that he thought he might be dying. He knew nothing about getting to the hospital in a trolley.

Joe loved the hospital, but hated being the filthiest thing in it. On quiz night, Chloe made a phone call from the hospital on Joe's phone, and Hazel and Angus came to collect him and take him home. When he was clean and washed, he had watched four episodes of *Friends*, went to bed in freshly ironed pajamas, got up at the correct time for a Sunday, had his breakfast, and finished his chores. Hazel and Angus had taken him back to the hospital on Sunday, and he was happy to be back in the gleaming white building with the sound of shoes squeaking on polished floors. At visiting time there was a little crowd of them; Chloe, Pip, and Hugo were back to see Charlie too.

As well as feeling generally at ease in the hospital, Joe was also very happy to see Charlie in the hospital bed, because while it was not a place he had ever seen him before and even though it could hardly be thought of as the place where Charlie belonged long-term, Joe was able to breathe more easily knowing that Charlie was here.

Charlie was not your usual go-back item, because it was not obvious where he should be returned to when he was out of place. Chloe was also not the typical go-back item, because she just belonged anywhere, as if she herself were the place she should always be.

In contrast, Joe belonged exactly in certain places at certain times. He was The Go-Back, the easiest kind of go-back. But Charlie? No, Charlie didn't seem to belong anywhere and so there was never anywhere he should be going back to.

So, until Joe could work out Charlie's place in the world, he felt at ease that he was—for the moment—safely inside clean, crisp white sheets, fed, and safe. That was about as good as it could get, for now.

"What time will Charlie wake up?" Joe asked.

"No one's set an alarm, Joe, we just have to wait," Chloe said.

"And there's more important questions than when he'll wake up," said Hugo.

"What questions?" said Joe, and everyone looked at the floor.

Pip elbowed Hugo and he looked at her and shrugged, then looked at Joe. "Like whether Charlie will press charges against his dad. If what you said about him is true," he said.

"Sometimes people don't want to get their parents in trouble," said Pip.

"I know that," said Joe. "Plus, I could be wrong."

"About what?" said Hugo. "You mean you're not sure if Charlie's dad is beating him?"

"Well," said Joe, looking at Chloe. "Chloe did point out to me that I am always more likely to be wrong than right about interpreting someone like Charlie."

"Sorry, Joe. That was a shitty thing to say," said Chloe. She even wore an *I'm sorry* smile on her face. Pip's smile said *everything is going to be okay*, and Hugo's said *we can't do anything but wait*.

Joe wondered how many kinds of smiles actually existed, because it was a lot. You could basically think anything and smile at the same time, so the possibilities were only limited by the number of thoughts that a person could have.

## 76
## To be in the book

The plastic chairs outside Charlie's room were too close together and Joe-Nathan's eyes widened when anyone approached and looked like they might sit next to him. His frightened expression was enough to make people walk away.

"Here," said Hazel, putting her handbag on the chair to the right of him and a bottle of water on the chair to the left. "This will stop anyone sitting there."

Joe briefly eyed the handbag to make sure the strap was nowhere near his leg.

Chloe looked at her watch. "I can't stay long," she said.

"Why not?" said Joe.

"I have stuff to do," she said vaguely. Everyone looked at her. "And I hate hospitals." Angus nodded. "Okay, I'm *bored*," she admitted, throwing her hands up as if the silence of her companions had forced her to confess her real motive.

"I hate waiting about too," said Angus. "That's what the vending machine is for, to give you something to do while you wait."

Chloe and Angus went to get drinks for everybody except Joe, who could not be persuaded to eat or drink something from such a contraption.

"Have the police spoken to Charlie yet?" Hazel asked.

"They showed up last night, asking questions, but Charlie was in no state to answer," said Pip.

"He was unconscious," Hugo clarified.

"Exactly."

"They spoke to Joe and asked him what he knew about what had happened to Charlie. But the trouble is, no one knows exactly."

"Oh really," said Hazel. "And yet, I think we kind of know exactly what has happened here."

"We shouldn't make assumptions," said Pip. "They can be dangerous."

"My mum has a section on assumptions in the yellow book," said Joe.

"Oh yes!" said Pip. "I remember you saying that."

Joe unclipped his satchel, which was lying in his lap.

"You carry that book about with you now, do you?" said Hazel.

"I carry my mobile phone and my wallet with me, because they are important for everyday life and emergencies. My mum's advice is also important for everyday life and emergencies. So, it makes sense for me to carry that around, too."

"Oh, Joe," said Hazel, and her chin crumpled, so that Joe touched his own and recalled how he had felt when his own chin had crumpled at times. He laid the book on top of his satchel and opened it, smoothing the page down with his hand.

"Assumptions," he said, and then he read aloud from the yellow book:

*Assumptions are things that people think are true even when there is no proof.*

*It is very hard not to make assumptions about people and situations, so it is perhaps best that you allow yourself to make them but be sure to understand that you might be wrong. Ask questions if you think your assumptions might be affecting your relationship with someone in a negative way. Assumptions are lazy, but we use them because they can be useful, and in some cases, they may even save your life. It's sometimes difficult to tell the difference between an assumption and a gut reaction, because they can feel the same. In these cases, I recommend following your gut reaction, even at the risk of upsetting someone. There will be time later to find out if you were right or wrong. By which I mean if your gut tells you to get yourself out of a situation, then get out of the situation.*

*People will make assumptions about you all your life. They may think they know an awful lot about you, based on just a little bit of information. But how can they know you, Joe, if they haven't talked to you or seen the way you live? They think they know you based on the way that you look, but how can they? You are so much more than the way that you look. How you look is a small percentage of who you are. So, please don't make assumptions based on appearances alone. People make assumptions based on the words that you use, the things you say. But you must be careful, because sometimes it is more important to understand the way in which something is said, rather than what is actually said. Smiles are not always good and straight faces can be sarcastic rather than sincere. You—more than most—must be wary of this, and trust your gut instinct.*

Joe paused at this, and remembered the first time he had gone to Charlie's house and Charlie's dad had said nice things in a mean way, and Charlie had said mean things, but Joe's gut reaction was that he was being nice. He focused again on the page, and continued to read aloud.

*Use assumptions—like many things—as a rule of thumb, but know that they can mislead you.*

*If you ever assume that someone or something is dangerous, always err on the side of caution, that is simply sensible.*

*PS. I write this a long time after my original advice because I wanted to give you a concrete example. Your friend Chloe is the type of person that people make assumptions about. They look at the way she presents herself and they listen to her words, but if they're not careful, they will miss the important things: her strong values, her fierce loyalty, and her raw honesty, which will all—no doubt—get her into trouble now and then, but are about the best things you can ask for in a friend. Assumptions are based on the first and the most shallow things we know about a person. And anyone with any sense knows that is simply not enough.*

Joe closed the book and folded his hands over it. "In this situation, according to my mum's advice, it would be dangerous to *not* assume that Charlie's dad is beating him up."

No one replied and Joe—checking their faces—saw that they

were all focused on someone else. He followed their gaze and found himself looking at Chloe.

"I always liked your mum," said Chloe.

"I wish she'd lived long enough to put *me* in the book," said Pip. Joe turned back to stare at her. "I mean, not just for that. I wish she was still alive full stop. But to be in the book . . ." Pip sighed.

"I might write my own advice book, and if I do, you can be in it," said Joe.

"Really?" said Pip. "What section?"

"I will write a section on kindness. And you can be in that."

Pip swallowed hard, and Hugo squeezed her hand.

"And maybe I will have a section on preparing for a quiz, and you can be in that part too."

# 77

## Nobody knows where he goes

When the police appeared, their uniforms and excellent posture contrasted sharply with those of the people seated outside Charlie's room, who had all (except Joe) begun to slump and look disheveled.

Before the police arrived, a nurse told Joe and the others to go home, that they would call with any news, and Chloe had sat up in her seat and started to pull her coat on, until Pip said, "We'll wait, that's what friends do." She turned to Chloe. "Fierce, loyal friends in particular."

"Charlie and me are not that close, I don't know if you noticed," said Chloe pointedly.

"You're here for him, not *him*," said Pip, tilting her head first at Joe and then at the door behind which Charlie was in bed.

Hazel had left earlier with Angus, who was "bored off his tits," and also said, "People only wait for people to wake up in hospital in films, not real life," and Chloe couldn't see the point of hanging around either. Even Hugo was making noises. The police were a welcome distraction.

"Is there a Joe Nathan here?" said one of them.

"I am Joe-Nathan." Joe raised his hand.

"Would you mind joining us for a chat, Mr. Nathan, with one of your friends?"

Chloe stood up. "Joe-Nathan is his first name," she said. "I'll come with him. Moral support."

"That okay with you, Mr. Nathan?" said the taller of the two.

"Joe-Nathan," said Joe. "Not *Mr.* Nathan."

"You can call me Tom," said the policeman, and he held his hand out for Joe to shake. Joe-Nathan shook his hand (then everyone else's) and then he and Chloe were led to a room where they sat at a table. The two officers sat opposite them, smiling; one held a clipboard and pen.

Joe wondered what was written on the paper on the clipboard; he imagined a single line of text that read, "Should Joe-Nathan go to prison?" and then underneath that question two little tick boxes, one with the word "yes" next to it, the other with the word "no." The pen would be used for the tick, depending on Joe-Nathan's answers.

Joe's palms began to sweat and he felt a tingling in his armpits and heat in the center of his back that rose up to his neck. He imagined himself in prison: he would not have his own television; he would not be able to watch *Friends*; he would share a cell with an angry tattooed man; he would not be able to prepare his own packed lunch; he would not be able to go to The Compass Store or stand on the mosaic; there would be no trees to wave at; and his parents' photos would not be there at mealtimes. Unless—would he be able to take those with him, once he was arrested?

Joe rocked gently. He closed his eyes and pictured the peace tree near work. He held his fingers in the air, gave the peace sign, wondering if he could imagine all the trees and wave at them even when he was locked away in jail.

"You alright, son?" said Tom.

"If I go to prison, can I take my mum and dad's photos with me?" Joe asked.

Tom looked at Chloe, and squinted ever so slightly before turning back to Joe.

"You're not going to prison. That's not what this is about."

"Oh." Joe breathed in so deeply that he worried there would not be enough air in the room if a window wasn't opened.

"We just want to get a better idea about what has happened here, with Charlie Parker."

Joe felt a little rush in his blood. He hadn't known Charlie's last name before this moment. He looked at Chloe and grinned.

"What are you grinning at?" she said, smiling back.

"Two things: one, because I am not going to prison, and two, Charlie's last name. I like it. Charlie Parker was an American jazz musician. He played the saxophone."

Chloe smiled at the police. "Perhaps you should ask those questions? And perhaps, please, try to understand, even if it's difficult."

"Okay, I don't want you to worry, Joe, you're not in any trouble. We're just trying to get as clear a picture as possible about Charlie's situation and we think you might have some information. You haven't got anything to worry about. You seem like the kind of person who tells the truth and wants to be helpful, and that's all we want."

Chloe crossed her arms and leaned back in her chair. For the first time in her life, she was finding a police officer mildly attractive. It was unnerving, but not unpleasant.

"So, Joe, you had a bit of a rough night last night . . ." The policeman pointed at his own head and Joe mirrored him by gently touching the little square of gauze that had been taped on; there had been a thin cut over his bump. "But you still managed to help your friend out. You probably saved Charlie's life."

Joe froze and stared at Tom.

"Did I?"

"Well, there *were* more efficient ways to save his life, if I'm honest, but your way got him here in time, so, yes, you did."

Joe smiled.

"I know you've been asked this before, but do you know what time you found Charlie?"

Joe shook his head. This question again, the one that he desperately wanted to answer.

"Well," said Chloe, "I brought Joe to the shower room about eight o'clock and when I came to look for him again and found him gone, it was about eight thirty. So, between those two times, Joe must have found Charlie. Oh, and I can show you when he texted me for help." She got her phone out and scrolled through her messages, then turned the screen to show him.

"Thanks, that helps," said Tom, and the other officer wrote something down. Tom faced Joe again. "Do you know how Charlie came to be stabbed?"

"I do not know exactly what happened," said Joe, staring at his hands in his lap.

The policeman's voice went soft and low. "Can you tell me what you *think* happened?"

Joe searched the policeman's face and felt relief at being asked this question, because *this* was the question that he wanted to answer.

"I think Charlie Parker's dad stabbed him."

"And why do you think that?"

Joe swallowed and he felt his Adam's apple move slowly in his throat, as if it were suddenly too big.

"Take your time," said the officer.

"Because I have seen him being beaten up by his dad before, and I saw him another time with black eyes and nose, and another time I saw bruises on him, here"—Joe twisted in his seat and put his hand near his kidneys and then on his ribs—"and here," he said, patting himself in all the right places. "I took him some arnica cream to help him."

The policeman nodded and jotted something down. Joe was pleased; if people understood that Joe had tried to help, then he definitely wouldn't have to go to prison. The officer glanced up at Joe and squinted his eyes kindly. "The time that you actually saw Charlie being beaten up, what happened then?"

"Charlie hid me under his bed." Joe recalled the fluff on the carpet and closed his eyes against the memory. "And then I watched his face while his dad kicked him in the back."

There was a moment's silence in the room and Chloe crossed and uncrossed her legs and crossed them again and folded her arms tighter under her arms. She didn't stop moving until her fidgeting caught Joe's attention and when he looked at her he noticed how upset she was.

"What is wrong, Chloe?" he asked. But Chloe just screwed up her nose and shook her head.

"That sounds horrible," said the policeman, drawing Joe's attention back to him.

"It was!" said Joe, and his eyes got very wide. "Charlie spat in my face when it happened. He did not mean to, but it was awful." Joe waved his open palm in front of his face. "All over me." He shuddered at the memory and wondered why Tom smiled.

"Does Charlie have any relatives that you know of?"

"Yes," said Joe.

"Who?"

"His dad," said Joe.

"No, sorry." Tom's eyes flicked to Chloe momentarily. "I mean, do you know if Charlie has any relatives *other* than his dad?"

"Oh. No. Nobody. I asked him where his mum was and he said that was a good question. But he did not answer it."

"And you don't know of anywhere safe that Charlie could go?" Now Tom looked at both Joe and Chloe. "Although, we will ask Charlie himself, when he wakes up."

"No," said Joe. "There is no place for Charlie. He is a go-back with nowhere to go back to. Nobody knows where he goes. No place to go back."

# 78
## The place we belong

J oe-Nathan glitched. "Go-back-go-back-go-back-go-back-go-back," he repeated, and Chloe heard Tom quietly say to his colleague, "I think that will do. The CPS will make a decision on this; it's GBH at least. When Charlie's ready to talk, we'll know more about whether his dad intended to stab him."

The policeman turned his attention back to Joe.

"Thank you for the information. You were very useful."

Joe-Nathan stopped saying "go-back."

"Well done, Joe. You really helped Charlie. And it's not easy to get a person into a trolley, takes a lot of grit, so I applaud you for that."

"Charlie is a go-back, but he does not belong anywhere," said Joe.

"Some people take longer than others to work out where they belong," said Tom, nodding.

"True," said Chloe, starting to nod in time with Tom.

"He has nowhere to go," said Joe.

"He does still have his home," said the other officer.

"But he cannot go back there. It is not safe. And it is not *nice*," said Joe, seeing images click into his mind's eye as if through a View-Master: loose hinges, wonky calendar, peeled wallpaper, full ashtray, moldering sofa, crushed beer cans. "Nothing is good there. Can he stay here?"

"In the hospital?" said the officer. "No. There are charities that can help someone in Charlie's position."

Chloe gave a little snort of air. "I can't see Charlie going for that," she said.

The policeman shrugged. "Some people don't," he said. "It all depends."

Joe and Chloe walked slowly down a hospital corridor. One of the lovely things about a hospital corridor, Joe realized, was that it was so wide, he didn't feel nervous about anyone brushing past him. He also liked the fact that there were no anomalies in the flooring, not like paving stones, which had their cracks and weeds. And it wasn't even that Joe didn't like cracks and weeds, but that they were distracting, and it was nice not to be thinking about every little detail all the time. A hospital corridor was a blank canvas for his thoughts.

Chloe walked beside Joe and their feet hit the floor in unison; her hands were plunged deep in her pockets and she looked down as she walked. She was silent. It was lovely.

"What do you think will happen to Charlie?" she said eventually.

"I do not know."

"I think you're right," she added. "About Charlie not belonging anywhere."

"A go-back," said Joe.

"With nowhere to go back to." Chloe completed the sentence.

They got to the end of the corridor and looked at the long list of directions and arrows printed on a big board.

"Let's go that way," said Chloe, and pointed right.

"But Charlie's that way," said Joe, looking at the signs and pointing left.

"Nice to walk, though, isn't it? And sometimes, even if you know where you need to end up, it's good to take a diversion, don't you think?"

"No."

Joe looked at the list of hospital destinations: trauma, cardiac, theater direct admissions, ambulatory monitoring, phlebotomy, coronary care unit, intensive care unit, maternity unit, cafeteria, exit.

"It should be alphabetical," said Joe. "Or have some order at least, like the mosaic does."

Chloe stared at the list. "Yeah, I agree."

"It is like life," said Joe, still reading the list of places to go in the hospital. "It is all here." He pointed at the board. "You get born and after that, stuff happens."

"Yeah," said Chloe again, and she snorted. "Maybe that's why it's not in alphabetical order—after all, life isn't alphabetical. They have put 'Exit' at the end, so they got that bit right."

Joe frowned; he wasn't quite sure what she meant.

"Diversion, then? Or straight back to the waiting room?" Chloe asked.

But Joe had a question. "Do you think that it is possible for a person to not know where they belong, and so it is difficult for them to know where to go when they want to return to the place they fit in?"

"I think," said Chloe, "that *most* people are trying to find out where they belong. I think *you're* different because you *do* know where you want to be, and where you should be at all times. For you, that works. Other people don't want their life to be like that and then again a lot of people get no choice."

"Like Charlie."

"Only Charlie can answer that." Chloe looked at her nails and picked at the nail polish. "I think you think of the place that a person belongs as being a place they have already found. Your home, your mum and dad, they were always something you could go back to. Not everyone has that. The place a person belongs might be in their future; they might not have found it yet. Might not ever find it."

"Might not ever find a place they belong?" Joe leaned on one foot, then the other, wiped his palms on his trousers.

"Yeah, maybe not. Sometimes the place we belong is just about the people in our lives, not the actual place. Sometimes the *place* we belong is just the place where the people who love us hang out." Chloe shrugged. "And if it feels like no one loves you, then you just got to keep looking."

"I think I know where Charlie can go," said Joe.

"Me too," said Chloe, and she reached out to put her hand on Joe's shoulder, but he swerved and she pulled her hand away before she touched him, remembering he would hate that.

# 79
## The best kind of nuthin

Joe-Nathan licked some icing off a spoon and put the spoon in the sink. He opened his mum's yellow book and found the page with the heading *Birthdays*.

## BIRTHDAYS

*Write your friends' birthdays on the calendar and make sure you give them a card on the right day. If you forget, then give them a card late. Better late than never with birthday cards.*

*Joe, it makes me sad to think that if you are reading this book, then I'll never get to spend your birthday with you again. I felt the same when I wrote the section on Christmas. I love celebrating with you. You're a traditionalist and you love cards, cake, and a present. Remember that other people might like those things too. And maybe one day you will even care about someone enough to make them a cake.*

*I am not there to organize your special day, so here is a suggestion: two weeks beforehand think about inviting some friends over to spend time with you on your birthday. I know that you enjoy the things you do on a normal day, and that you get a lot of pleasure from your routine. But it would make me happy to think you were with people who care about you on your birthday, even if it does take you out of your comfort zone. You don't have to do too much, but you need to provide food and some drinks. If you want to do more, you could have music and games. If a friend wants to help you organize something, then think about letting them. It might be fun. Just tell them what you like.*

*Happy birthday, Joe-Nathan, my lovely boy. I wish I was there.*

Joe carried the cake into the garden.

"Don't bring it out yet. It's too hot; the icing will melt," said Pip.

"Oh," said Joe, and he took it back into the house.

Joe returned to the garden, shielding his eyes against the sun to watch Pip hold the chair that Hugo was standing on. Hugo wobbled slightly, but managed to tie one end of bunting to the tree in the corner of the first third of the garden; then they moved the chair and Hugo tied the other end of the bunting to the house. Then they all stood in the center of the lawn and looked up at the crisscrossed bunting, which moved in the barely there breeze, casting triangular shadows that were anchored by thin lines of shadow on the newly mown grass.

Joe faced the sun and turned 360 degrees. "I wish Charlie was here," he said.

"Me too," said Hugo, folding up the chair and leaning it against the house.

Pip looked at her watch. "This is a lovely way to spend the evening, Joe," she said. "What time are Angus and Hazel arriving?"

"I expect it will be 6:02. Hazel is punctual, but Angus makes her late."

"Well, two minutes is hardly late," said Hugo.

Joe stared at him. "In what way is it not late?"

Angus appeared around the side of the house in a Hawaiian shirt. "Just in case you only provided softies, I brought this." He held a bottle of whiskey in the air.

"Not exactly a summer drink!" Hazel said, appearing behind him. She held up a plastic carrier bag. "I brought everything we need to make a jug of Pimm's, including the jug! I'm just going to . . ." She wafted an arm in the direction of the kitchen, bottles clinking, and disappeared into the house.

"I think it's arrived," said Hugo, poised as if listening to thunder in the very far distance.

"Really?" said Pip, straining to identify a new sound in the air. "Oh yes. You have such good hearing, Hugo," she said, and gazed at him as though this were his superpower.

Joe heard it too; it sounded like the purr of an engine. "My birthday present?" he said. He breathed in deeply and closed his eyes. His heart thumped in his chest and he prayed that they had not bought him a car. The thought of driving was terrifying.

Chloe had read the yellow book. At first, she had skipped to the part where she was mentioned, and then returned to the parts she felt were relevant to her own life. Then she realized that somehow Janet's advice was relevant to pretty much *every* part of her own life, and so, she read the book cover to cover. When she came to the section on birthdays, she talked to Joe about a party and asked what he would like for a present.

Joe had asked for the same thing every year since he was old enough to answer the question: "A toy, some chocolate, and a surprise." But in the last few months, he had started to become an independent man, and so this year he also asked for socks, as that seemed like a boring but grown-up thing to do. Chloe had said she would think of something, as if his ideas weren't good enough.

The sound of a van backing up the driveway rumbled clearly into earshot.

"I think you ought to go inside and wait," said Hugo. "Don't want to spoil the surprise."

Joe nodded and trotted into the house, up the stairs, and into the bathroom.

The Imperial Leather soap was a new one, several washes away from being ready for de-stickering. Joe felt no inclination to hurry the soap along; he would have more help with that now anyway. He washed his hands and looked at the friendly man reflected back at him in the bathroom mirror.

"How do you do?" he said.

"Very well, thank you."

"Happy birthday," he said.

"Happy birthday to you too."

Joe bowed slightly, smiled at his reflection, and saw a gentle kind of happiness in his eyes. He tried to think where he had seen eyes just like that recently, but couldn't bring the answer to mind. He dried his hands. Today he had put extra towels in the bathroom, for his visitors, and he looked proudly at them now, patting each in turn.

"Everyday use," he said, touching the first towel. "Fancy, guest, fancy-guest," he said, touching the other towels. He smiled to himself again and went to his bedroom. His stamp album with the Imperial Leather stickers inside was open on his desk. He smoothed a hand over the page, and closed it up, returning it to its place on the shelf.

"*Joe? Joe!*" He heard his name called from the bottom of the stairs and scurried to the landing. Whoever had called his name was no longer there, so he went down and into the garden.

There before him, in the center of the back lawn, was his birthday present. It must have been a struggle to get it here.

It was the perfect size, would seat four people quite easily. It looked comfortable, and while Joe had been nervous about his present, now that it was here in front of him, he realized that Chloe truly did sometimes know better than him.

The color was perfect: a soft, antique orange, in velvety velour—with a longish fringe that brushed the edges of the grass. It was better than a car, much better than anything else that it was possible to buy in a shop.

It was a large sofa, just like the one in the coffee shop in *Friends*, just like the one in the opening credits that they dance around and sit upon. Joe could hardly breathe. Next to the sofa was a standard lamp with a Tiffany-style lampshade, and although the sun was still too bright to really allow the effect of it, Joe could see that the lamp was actually working.

Joe had wondered many, many times what it would feel like to sit on a sofa like this, how it would feel to let himself sink slightly into it, touching the fabric with the lightest touch of his fingertips. What he had always wanted—but never dreamed possible—was having a sofa like this with friends perched all over it, friends that were his in the real world and not just on television. And that was the most important thing; he realized that now, because here they were: his friends, lounging on the perfect outdoor couch; it was enough. Joe didn't believe it could possibly feel better to sit on the thing himself.

Angus and Hazel each sat sidesaddle on an arm, Pip and Hugo sat on the sofa seats themselves at the outer edges, and, in the middle—between them—sat Chloe and Charlie. All grinning so hard it probably hurt.

Joe stood frozen, with a hand over his mouth. If he didn't breathe soon, he would probably faint.

"Come on," said Chloe, and she and Charlie moved apart to make room for Joe in between them. It didn't take a professor to see that there wasn't enough room for Joe to sit without being in extremely close contact with other people's bodies pressed against him. He took a tentative step forward, hoping that the space would seem bigger when he got closer to it.

But it didn't.

*Challenge yourself*, he said inwardly. *Try something new on your birthday.*

Joe turned his back to the sofa and stuck his bum out a little bit as he walked backward toward it. He squeezed his eyes shut and let himself drop into the too-tight space, with all the inner tranquility of a person about to bungee jump. When Charlie had moved into the house, and taken Janet's bedroom, Joe had needed to redefine what he considered "too close." Living with a person who wasn't his mum or dad was a difficult adjustment, one he was still getting used to. But some things were relative, and closeness was one of them.

Joe felt Charlie's thigh brush against his left leg, and Chloe's pressed against his right. He opened his eyes and looked down: there were just too many legs. Joe was happy, but terrified. Heat rose up his neck and the heat became a sound like a quiet groan when it reached his throat and when it reached his mouth he loudly announced "No!" and jumped up from the sofa.

Joe surveyed the scene in front of him, let the laughter soak into him through his pores. He was a happy man. A man who had the best kind of nuthin, and the best kind of everything: no mean bones, and six good friends.

# Epilogue

t made sense for Joe-Nathan and Charlie to live together and Joe hoped that Charlie would feel like he belonged. He got his job back at The Compass Store, but Hugo said it was just while Charlie found his feet. Charlie had other ambitions, but right now, what he needed were safe places and kind friends, and plenty of time to decide what to make of his future.

Joe had been frightened that Charlie would take over too much of his life and Charlie had worried about the same thing. But it didn't happen, because neither of them wanted it. It didn't mean that Joe didn't drive Charlie mad with his habits and rules and it didn't mean that Joe didn't ever rock in his chair with frustration when Charlie left his things lying about. And it didn't mean they didn't do anything together, because they did. They worked together in the workshop some weekends and some evenings, and Charlie even made Joe an epitaph plaque that read, "Joe-Nuthin, a man of no mean bones." And it only said "Nuthin" because Joe had requested it that way.

Every other Saturday, Joe and Charlie went to a cemetery. Almost always the one where Janet and Mike were buried, but sometimes other places. Eventually Janet's headstone was finished. It had taken a long time to think of just the right words to have carved into the stone. And one sunny Saturday afternoon, Joe and Charlie went to see it in place. It wasn't easy to sum up a life in just a few words. But Joe-Nathan had done his best for his mum:

HERE LIES JANET CLARKE

WHO LOVED WELL WHEN HER HEART BEAT,

AND ALSO WHEN IT DIDN'T.

# Acknowledgments

I was at rock bottom when I started writing *Joe Nuthin's Guide to Life*. I was on the verge of giving up writing forever and was refusing to take calls or read emails that had anything to do with it. It felt like my life was going wrong in every direction, including the writing, and—although I usually like to talk about *everything*—I no longer wanted to talk about anything.

For getting me to talk, and for the pivotal conversation that resulted, I would like to thank Clare Hey, my UK editor at Simon & Schuster. At the beginning of our meeting, which I reluctantly attended, I believe I felt and behaved something like a sociopathic stray cat. But Clare talked me down with all the finesse and tenderness of a bomb-disposal expert and managed to defuse me. By the end of that meeting, I was calmer and a little bit hopeful about writing for the first time in a long time. In a conversational moment that I will always treasure, Clare told me about her wonderful uncle David. David

Hey was a man who shook everyone's hand, every time he went to the pub. He reminded me of a character called Joe Nuthin, who I'd thought of a couple of years previously. I told Clare about him and saw her eyes light up. This was a book that she wanted to read. So, thank you to Clare for that, and for the encouragement to keep going once I'd started.

I'm very lucky to have Judith Murray, at Greene & Heaton, as my agent. As well as being a brilliant agent, she's just a lovely human being, and when we meet, I always hope a little bit of her will rub off on me so I can be just a little more like her. I want to thank her for her honesty—it hurts sometimes, but I value it above all character traits, and it means I can trust her and that when she says she loves it, she means it. Thanks for your encouragement, friendship, support, and professionalism. And most authors with an agent will know how very lucky I am when I say thank you, Judith, for always replying to messages swiftly, for always being there.

Also at Greene & Heaton, I'd like to thank Kate Rizzo, not just for having the greatest surname on Earth, but also for her work on foreign rights. And to Sally Oliver—at first for being so responsive and helpful from an administrative point of view, but then for writing *The Weight of Loss*, which I read and loved, and for becoming such a good friend.

At Simon & Schuster UK, I would like to thank Richard Vlietstra, deputy head of marketing, who helped keep me sane, who—over months of remote experimentation—helped me find the perfect cooking method for a soft-boiled egg and had me crying with laughter at his emails. Your hard work, friendship, and sense of fun are deeply appreciated. Thank you to Judith Long, who is an excellent editor with an eye for detail that I very much admire, and who is also warm and recommends just the right books. Thank you to Laura Gerrard, for copyediting and Victoria Godden for proofreading. For marketing, thank you to Justine Gold and in production, thanks to Francesca Sironi and Karin Seifried. Pip Watkins did the cover for *Joe Nuthin's Guide to Life*; the moment I saw the artwork, I fell in love with it, so thank you, Pip. Finally, but not least, thank you to the S&S sales team, a large group of wonderful individuals who have worked hard for my book.

At Simon & Schuster USA, for the early drafts I would like to thank Jackie Cantor, such a warmhearted senior editor, who I greatly miss. Thank you, Jackie, for saying yes to the first draft of *Joe Nuthin*. And thanks also to Andrew Nguyen, assistant editor, who had such a lovely reaction on first reading *Joe Nuthin*, and for saying that Joe stayed with him long after reading the book. Thank you to Abby Zidle, executive editor, and Frankie Yackel, assistant editor, for all your advice and support. Also at Simon & Schuster US, thanks to Jen Bergstrom, publisher; Aimee Bell, editor-in-chief; Sally Marvin, director of publicity & marketing; Bianca Salvant, senior marketing manager; Lisa Litwack, art director; and Caroline Pallotta, senior managing editor.

*Joe Nuthin* was written during a very difficult emotional time in my life. I'm not sure what kind of a state I would have been in if I didn't have such good friends holding me together, counseling me, advising me, listening to me, making me laugh. I think *Joe Nuthin* would be a different kind of book if I didn't have these people in my life. Thank you to Amy and Adam Schiller, who are like family to me, in all the good ways. Thank you to Amy Tubay, in Portland, for all our online chats that you get up so early for because of the time difference; you look beautiful when you've just fallen out of bed and switched the camera on. I love that we're both inspired to write like demons after our chats. To my Sarahs: Sarah Cole, Sarah Fisher, and Sarah McCarter, for your friendship, wisdom, and walks. Thank you to Kenton O'Hara, who told me that one of the good things to come out of lockdown was that we rekindled our friendship over Zoom; I couldn't agree more. All of these friends are such different characters, but they are all inspiring, wise, and funny. An extra thank-you to Sarah Fisher and Amy Tubay, for being such brilliant beta readers of *Joe Nuthin*. And thank you to my mum, Patricia, who listened to a few excerpts of the first draft and cried in the right places.

Without going into details, I want to mention that I had trouble with depression while writing *Joe Nuthin*; I think it's helpful to speak up when that's been the case. One day, when I just couldn't get out of bed anymore, I rang my GP and was amazed at the service I got. I was called back quickly by Dr. Dan James and we talked for forty-five minutes. He continued to hand-hold me over the phone through the following weeks. I was particularly fortunate that he had experience of dealing with authors and he was sensitive to the fact that while I needed space away from my thoughts, this might interfere with writing a novel. I'm so grateful to him and want to thank him for helping me get back on my feet.

I want to thank my children, Cleo and Dylan. You are such good company, good conversationalists, and very funny. If I can take credit for any of that, then I'll take it, but you are your own people and maybe I just got lucky. So many of the things that Joe says and does in the novel have come from things that my children (and myself) have said or done, even though we're all neurotypical and Joe is neurodivergent (though undiagnosed in the book). Some of my favorite quotes from Joe are direct quotes from my children, and many of his quirks—like mirroring the trees with hand signals—are ours too. I feel that he is a character all of his own, but the reason I care for him so much is because he is built out of the people I love.

To Rob, thank you for many things, but mainly for being in my life.

Lastly, I would like to thank Joe-Nathan, the protagonist of the book. I remember very clearly that when I came to my desk to write, I took sanctuary in Joe. It sounds dramatic, but sometimes it felt like he was saving me. And when I came to read the manuscript back, I couldn't understand—and still don't fully understand—how someone as pure and lovely as Joe came out of me during those dark times. I hope I have done him justice and that you see him as I do.

# Joe Nuthin's Guide to Life

### Helen Fisher

*This reading group guide* for Joe Nuthin's Guide to Life
includes an introduction, discussion questions, and ideas for
enhancing your book club. The questions are intended to help
your reading group find new and interesting angles and topics for your discussion. We hope that these ideas will enrich
your conversation and increase your enjoyment of the book.

## Introduction

Joe-Nathan likes the two parts of his name separate, just like dinner and dessert. Mean Charlie at work sometimes calls him Joe-Nuthin. But Joe is far from nothing. Joe is a good friend, good at his job, good at making things and at following rules, and he is learning how to do lots of things by himself.

Joe's mother knows there are a million things he isn't yet prepared for. While she helps to guide him every day, she is also writing notebooks of advice for Joe, of all the things she hasn't yet told him about life and things he might forget.

By following her advice, Joe's life is about to be more of a surprise than he expects. Because he's about to learn that remarkable things can happen when you leave your comfort zone, and that you can do even the hardest things with a little help from your friends.

## Topics and Questions for Discussion

1. The novel opens with Janet's entry about fear, from the yellow book of advice, before we are introduced to Joe-Nathan and the other characters. How does this set up the story thematically? How does it set up Joe's character?

2. Time is a guiding force in Joe's life. Joe depends on routine, and he likes how time moves at the same pace and pushes things along. How does time operate in this novel? Does the novel move at a steady pace? At what points does the pace of the novel slow down? What is the purpose of those slow-motion moments, and how do they make you feel?

3. Between Janet, the blue book, the yellow book, and *Friends*, Joe has guides and references to make sense of life and the world around him. Do you have a "Janet" in your life? Or do you have a book or piece of media you use as a guide and reference point in your life?

4. Epitaphs fascinate Joe. Considering Joe's appreciation of structure and direction in his life (for example, the Compass Store being laid out like an actual compass so he can always find his way around the store), how do you think the epitaphs play into that? Do epitaphs help Joe find structure in other parts of his life? What do you see as the purpose of the epitaphs in this novel?

5. Joe is a neurodivergent character with OCD. How does the author make Joe a relatable character even when the reader may not be familiar with neurodivergent thought processes? Are there specific passages, descriptions, or scenes in which you felt you could really understand Joe's thought process and how he sees the world? How does the author put you in Joe's shoes?

6. Following the previous question, there are subplots in the novel that Joe does not pick up on at first, but we as readers may see. Consider Pip's crush on Hugo, or moments when people are mean to Joe and he does not realize. How does the author convey these things to the reader while maintaining Joe's perspective and without spelling them out?

7. This novel deals a lot with death and grief. How do the characters represent different ways of handling grief? Consider thinking about other characters in addition to Joe, like Angus and Hazel.

8. In literature, a foil is a character that contrasts with another character in order to highlight the other's qualities. They're not so much opposites as they are sides of the same coin. How is Charlie a foil of Joe? How can Chloe and Charlie be considered foils of each other? What character traits are accentuated when you look at these pairings? Are there any other characters that you think may be a foil of another?

9. Reflect on the friendships present in the novel. Consider what Janet writes about friends, how Chloe is a good friend but can be wrong at times, and how Charlie appears mean but does try to be a friend to Joe. What does the novel teach you about friendship? How does friendship relate to family?

10. Assumptions play a large role in this story. People make assumptions about Joe nearly every day of his life, and in the yellow book of advice, Janet warns Joe to be careful before he assumes anything. What assumptions did you have about the story or certain characters when you started reading? Were you proven wrong?

11. Joe sees and understands the world differently than neurotypical people. When Pip tries to explain why he does not need to be nice to bullies with a story about her cat, Joe asks questions until Pip has to reconsider her own perspective. Chloe says that

"He does this . . . He makes you think" (pg. 141). Was there a moment in the book when Joe made you think or reconsider a view you had?

12. In the epilogue, Charlie makes Joe an epitaph plaque, and Joe requests that he write "Joe-Nuthin" instead of "Joe-Nathan." Why do you think Joe chooses to keep this nickname?

13. Return to the prologue and the first question in this guide. What did this novel teach you about fear? What did Joe learn about fear?

## Enhance Your Book Club

1. We see snippets from the blue and yellow books Janet made for Joe throughout the novel. Discuss in a group what you would like to have seen Janet write. Try writing your own entries for the yellow book of advice and share with the group. What can you all learn from each other?

2. Host a *Friends* viewing party. Watch the episodes Joe references in the novel and whichever other episodes are your favorites.

3. If you were to write an epitaph for yourself, what would it say? Individually, everyone should write an epitaph for themselves and then share with the group. See if the group would highlight the same qualities that you would about yourself. This is not a game and there is no winner, but bonus points go to whoever can come up with the funniest epitaph!